Praise for
TAKEN

"Jacka's excellent third urban fantasy thriller starring British freelance diviner Alex Verus features magical dueling with prestige and lives at stake . . . The action is fast and smart, playing with thriller conventions so that while readers get excitement, they also are encouraged to think about what magic might mean in human terms. A superb book in an outstanding, provocative series."   —*Publishers Weekly* (starred review)

"Tons of fun and lots of excitement in this fast-paced thriller . . . On top of putting together top-notch plots, Benedict Jacka also writes well, often with the ability to bring places to life as much as his characters, especially the city of London."   —*SF Site*

"*Taken* is the third book in the Alex Verus series, which is fast becoming a 'must read' for me. All of the books are evenly paced with action [and] witty dialogue . . . I am really enjoying the Alex Verus series, with its solid writing, [its] ever-expanding universe, and its uniquely powerful hero."
          —*All Things Urban Fantasy*

"Each book in this engrossing series outshines the one preceding it, and readers will find themselves easily and completely drawn into Alex's world of mystery, magic, and menace . . . Jacka skillfully balances action and suspense with a smooth flow that results in rapid page-turning. Urban fantasy readers who have not yet made Alex's acquaintance are advised to do so immediately."   —*Bitten by Books*

continued . . .

CURSED

"Benedict Jacka started off his Alex Verus series with a bang with *Fated* and doesn't lose pace with *Cursed*." —*SF Site*

"Jacka follows his urban fantasy debut, *Fated*, with an even more impressive tale of gunplay and spellcraft in present-day London . . . Readers will savor this tasty blend of magic, explosions, and moral complexity."
—*Publishers Weekly* (starred review)

"A wonderfully fun, action-packed story with witty dialogue, making it another great installment for the Alex Verus series." —*All Things Urban Fantasy*

"*Cursed* ups the ante in almost every department of the book, and it will fetch the author more fans as they strive to find satisfaction from books other than the Dresden Files. Be sure to check out this wonderful series." —*Fantasy Book Critic*

"Benedict Jacka is a master storyteller. He has a wonderful way of taking familiar ideas and polishing them until they glow, then intertwining them with something new . . . A brilliant urban fantasy that is so professionally polished and paced that you barely remember to come up for air. *Cursed* takes everything that was great about *Fated* and then puts it on a diet of steroids. It is fun and action-packed but now bigger, angrier, and absolutely nuts. I loved it." —*Fantasy Faction*

"If you like an action-packed, magic-fueled story, then this is the series for you. It has a fast-paced story which captivated me from start till finish and had a complex mystery that you could really get into." —*Under the Covers Book Blog*

"*Cursed* is fun and exciting, exactly what I wanted out of it. Jacka lays another strong foundation for this fledgling series that has the potential to become something huge."
—*Whatchamacallit Reviews*

FATED

"Harry Dresden would like Alex Verus tremendously—and be a little nervous around him. I just added Benedict Jacka to my must-read list. *Fated* is an excellent novel, a gorgeously realized world with a uniquely powerful, vulnerable protagonist. Books this good remind me why I got into the storytelling business in the first place."

—Jim Butcher, #1 *New York Times* bestselling author

"Benedict Jacka writes a deft thrill ride of an urban fantasy—a stay-up-all-night read. Alex Verus is a very smart man surviving in a very dangerous world."

—Patricia Briggs, #1 *New York Times* bestselling author

"[An] extremely promising urban fantasy series starter . . . Jacka deftly invents the rules of magic as he goes along, creating an emotionally satisfying story arc and a protagonist who will keep readers coming back."

—*Publishers Weekly* (starred review)

"Benedict Jacka joins the top ranks of urban fantasy writers with *Fated* . . . [He] will become a favorite for fans of Jim Butcher, Simon Green, and/or John Levitt. His recipe for success combines believable and well-developed characters, lots of action, enough suspense to keep one up all night, and a new twist on magic . . . *Fated* is one of the strongest first books in a series I've read in a long time, and a series I will definitely follow to its conclusion. Few writers have mastered the ability to bring so many different types of characters to life so vividly."

—*SF Site*

"An excellent example of not just great urban fantasy but also of brilliant storytelling. There is a near-perfect mix of everything, and it has been masterfully crafted with a meticulous eye for those pieces of humanity that make a great protagonist and a fantastic story."

—*Fantasy Faction*

Ace Books by Benedict Jacka

FATED
CURSED
TAKEN
CHOSEN

chosen

BENEDICT JACKA

ACE BOOKS, NEW YORK

THE BERKLEY PUBLISHING GROUP
Published by the Penguin Group
Penguin Group (USA) Inc.
375 Hudson Street, New York, New York 10014, USA

USA I Canada I UK I Ireland I Australia I New Zealand I India I South Africa I China

Penguin Books Ltd., Registered Offices: 80 Strand, London WC2R 0RL, England
For more information about the Penguin Group, visit penguin.com.

CHOSEN

An Ace Book / published by arrangement with the author

Ace Books are published by The Berkley Publishing Group.
ACE and the "A" design are trademarks of Penguin Group (USA) Inc.

For information, address: The Berkley Publishing Group,
a division of Penguin Group (USA) Inc.,
375 Hudson Street, New York, New York 10014.

ISBN: 978-0-425-26492-8

PUBLISHING HISTORY
Ace mass-market edition / September 2013

PRINTED IN THE UNITED STATES OF AMERICA

10 9 8 7 6 5 4 3 2 1

Cover photographs: River Thames © Michael Trevillion / Trevillion Images; abstract
waves © Uka/Shutterstock; abstract wavy lines © Tarchyshnik Andrei / Shutterstock.
Cover design by Judith Lagerman.

This is a work of fiction. Names, characters, places, and incidents either are the product
of the author's imagination or are used fictitiously, and any resemblance to actual persons,
living or dead, business establishments, events, or locales is entirely coincidental.
The publisher does not have any control over and does not assume any responsibility for
author or third-party websites or their content.

ALWAYS LEARNING   **PEARSON**

chosen

chapter 1

The night was warm and still. Through the open windows of my flat a gentle breeze blew, faint scents carrying on the air: tarmac, burnt rubber, the distant smell of a barbecue. The street outside was filled with the steady whisper of traffic, voices rising briefly above the background noise before fading into it again, and from two blocks over came the rhythmic thump of club music. A helicopter was prowling the skies above, tracking the wail of police sirens, and from time to time it would pass overhead in a clatter of rotors.

Inside, my flat was peaceful. Flies moved in lazy arcs under the light, and birds and animals looked quietly down from the pictures on the walls. The coffee table had been moved to the centre of the room; it was covered with cardboard hexes and wooden playing pieces, and four out of the five of us were sitting around it. Sonder and I were on chairs, Luna was sitting cross-legged on a beanbag, and Variam was at one end of the sofa, scowling down at his cards. At the other end of the sofa and a little way from the game was Anne, curled up with her legs tucked under her.

"Uh, Variam?" Sonder said. Sonder has messy black hair and glasses, and always seems to have a permanent air of scruffiness about him, as though he's just slept in his clothes. "Your turn."

Variam picked up the dice and threw them without looking. "Seven."

Luna stretched to see. "That's an *eight*, you idiot."

Sonder perked up. "Awesome! Five ore, two grain."

Variam ignored them both. "We should be practising," he told me.

"You've been practising for weeks," I said, waiting for Sonder to finish scooping cards before taking my own.

"It's better than just sitting here."

"Are you done?" Sonder asked Variam.

Variam nodded, and Sonder picked up the dice. "We could do more combat drills," Variam said as Sonder made his roll.

"You don't *need* more combat drills."

"She does," Variam said, pointing at Anne.

Luna looked at Variam in annoyance. "Your appointment tomorrow's for a consultation, not a battle," I said before Luna could start an argument. "She just wants to find out a bit about you. I'll be surprised if she even asks you to cast a spell."

Sonder hesitated, looking between us. "We might need to show her what we can do," Variam said.

"Variam, she's a little old lady," I said. "She lives in a terraced house in Brondesbury. She is not going to want you to show her how well you can incinerate things."

Variam sat back with an aggravated look. "Um," Sonder said. "I'll get a city and a development card." He pushed the dice over to Luna. "Your turn."

Luna waited for Sonder to withdraw his hand before picking up the dice and rolling them. To my mage's sight Luna's curse appeared as a silvery aura, twining around her limbs and body like living mist. Silver tendrils played over the dice as they bounced, and disappeared once the dice came to rest. "Seven," Luna said with satisfaction. "Let's see, I think the robber can go"—she picked up the black piece and traced a circle with it over the board—"there." She set it down in the middle of Variam's settlements and held out a hand, fingers extended. "Gimme."

Variam woke up. "What?"

"Card, please."

"Why are you going for me? *They're* going to win!"

"Annoying you is more fun. Card, please."

Variam scowled and held his cards out with poor grace. Luna took her time over picking one, making Variam's scowl deepen before she plucked one out. The silver mist of her curse pulled in close to her fingers as she did. Luna's curse brings bad luck, and it's quite lethal; even a strand of that mist is dangerous, and skin-to-skin contact is deadly. Once upon a time Luna would never have been able to get so close to another person without putting them at risk, but she's been training to control her curse for nearly a year and a half now and it's paid off. The silver mist was layered in near to her skin, bright and dense, and only a few faint traces had spread to the playing pieces, leaving them bathed in tiny silver auras. The auras around the items weren't a problem; her curse doesn't do much to objects. Living creatures are another story.

The dice came around to me, and after the resources had been counted out I looked at my hand. The first to ten points would win, and I had eight. Glancing into the future in which I turned over the top development card, I saw that it was a victory point. "Settlement," I said, placing the wooden playing piece down on the map, then rose to my feet. "I'm getting a drink; you guys want something?"

"Could I have some water?" Sonder asked.

"I kind of want a drink, but I'm not sure what," Luna said.

"I think there's some of the cordial left that I made

yesterday," Anne said in her soft voice. "The elderflower and lime?"

Luna perked up. "Oh, that was nice."

I walked into the kitchen, took the bottle out of the fridge, and was just filling a glass when I felt the presence behind me. I held out the drink without looking, and it was taken from my hand after a moment's pause. "Thank you," Anne said.

Anne is tall and slim, only an inch or so shorter than me, with black hair that brushes her shoulders and reddish-brown eyes. She looks striking, but she's got a quiet, unobtrusive manner that tends not to draw attention. "What's up?" I asked, filling another glass.

"You could have won that game, couldn't you?" Anne said.

I turned with a smile. "Guess I need a better poker face."

Back in the living room I could hear raised voices: Variam and Luna had started arguing again. "Were you letting them win?" Anne asked curiously.

"To win I'd have needed Luna or Vari to trade me their cards," I said. "Probably could have convinced them, but I'd have had to lie."

"You don't think it's worth it?"

"I've done enough shady stuff," I said. "I'd rather stay friends unless I've got a really good reason not to."

Anne gave a smile, but it faded quickly. She glanced back over her shoulder, up at the cupboards. "Something wrong?" I said.

"There's someone outside."

I straightened, suddenly alert. "Where?"

Anne is a life mage, and a powerful one. Most people think "life mage" means "healer," and they're half right, but life magic is far more than that—it gives control over every aspect of a living creature, healing or harming with a touch. Life mages can sense life, "seeing" living creatures, and Anne's particularly good at it. Her accuracy is amazing; she can learn more in a minute just by looking at you than a doctor could work out in twenty-four hours with a full hospital's worth of equipment. I've never been able to figure out exactly how she does it, though she's tried to explain it a couple of times. She just seems to read a person's body in the same way that you or I can read the expression on someone's face.

On a practical note, this makes Anne really, really good at spotting people—she can notice them through walls, floors, and even solid rock if she feels like it, and if she's ever met them she can recognise them with perfect accuracy. "He was down on the street," Anne said. "I didn't pay any attention at first, but . . . he moved away and came up to the rooftop. It looked like he was trying to watch us."

"Who is he?"

"I've never met him before," Anne said. "He's about eighteen years old, not very big or strong but he's healthy, and he's on his own." She pointed up through the wall at a slight angle. "About seventy feet that way."

"No one's after you or Vari at the moment, are they?"

"Not that I know about," Anne said simply.

There was a reason I was asking. Anne and Variam are what you might call very advanced apprentices; they aren't mages but they're experienced enough that they probably should be. Four years ago they got involved with a Dark mage called Sagash. The official story (at least, the story the Council believes) is that Anne and Variam entered Sagash's service as apprentices before leaving nine months later. What actually happened was that Sagash kidnapped Anne and tortured her until she did what she was told. Variam went looking for her, and when he tracked her down there was an almighty battle. Their next stop was a rakshasa named Jagadev, who arranged for their entry into the Light apprentice program and took them into his household right up until last winter, when Anne got arrested by the Council on suspicion of being an accessory to murder. In the aftermath Jagadev kicked them out and I let them move into my flat. When you have a history like that you attract a lot of attention, and in the time I'd known Anne and Variam they'd been hunted by assassins, constructs, a pair of Council Keepers, and two different Dark mages, just for starters. It's not that they look for trouble but it does seem to follow them around.

Of course, Anne and Variam aren't the only ones with a bad reputation. The Council thinks I was trained as a Dark apprentice too—the difference is, in my case they're *right*, and if our mystery guest wasn't after Anne or Variam there was a good chance he was after me. But while we'd been talking I'd had the time to confirm he was there and I'd gathered enough information to decide that he wasn't any immediate threat. My abilities aren't as good as Anne's at analysing living creatures but they're much better for sensing danger, and I'd already decided I could handle this on my own. "I'll go have a chat," I told Anne.

Anne hesitated, glancing back at the living room. "I'll be okay," I said. "When Vari and Luna finish arguing and Sonder wins on his next turn, tell them I'll be back in five minutes."

Anne looked concerned, but nodded. "Be careful."

· · · · · · · · · ·

The roof of my flat has a great view. It's not especially high, but it's right in the middle of the densest part of Camden. Brickwork and bridges and parapets and aerials and chimneys reach up all around, surrounding you in a sea of buildings, as though you're looking out over a horizon made from the cityscape. It was a clear night and a few fuzzy stars shone down from above, struggling against the light pollution, while to the left a crescent moon was rising. The scent of food drifted on the warm air: Indian from the restaurants at the end of the street, Italian from the one a block over, barbecue from the gardens near the canal. I moved into a chimney's shadow and let the darkness cover me.

The guy trying to spy on us was three rooftops over, and as I got a closer look I mentally changed his designation from "guy" to "kid." I could have sneaked up on him without too much trouble, but as I looked into the future I saw that he was going to come my way before long. I settled down to wait.

A few minutes passed. The helicopter that had been buzzing around the council estate to the south passed overhead again, the discordant clatter of the rotors drowning out everything else until it lost interest and flew away north, its lights blinking white-green-red in the night. A pack of teenagers in hoodies swaggered down the street below us, shouting drunkenly; there was the tinkling crash of a bottle breaking, followed by a scuffle and a yell. Once the street was quiet again the kid left the cover of his rooftop and crept towards my hiding place.

Divination magic works by sensing probabilities. To me, potential futures appear as lines of light against the darkness; the brighter and more vivid, the more likely. By glancing over the futures in which I stepped out into the kid's line of sight I could watch him despite the objects between us, and as I did I kept an eye on the futures of the kid's actions. Most of them showed a sudden flurry of movement as he saw me, while in a few he continued to move steadily, unaware. I saw that the futures in which he stayed unaware of me were the ones in which I moved left around the chimney and I did just that, matching my actions to the futures in which I was undetected. I hardly had to pay attention to do it; I've had so much practice at using my divination for stealth that it's become automatic. The kid passed by, oblivious, and walked onto the roof of my flat.

I'd had time to do a fairly thorough scan of the rooftops around us, flicking through the futures in which I went searching in different directions, and I was pretty sure the kid was alone. As I watched, he moved to the ladder leading down to my balcony and crouched, peering over the edge.

I rose silently from behind the chimney and walked quietly up behind, stopping ten feet away. "Looking for someone?" I said to his back.

The kid jumped, trying to leap up, spin around, and look in every direction all at once. He nearly fell over the edge, and as he saw me he scrambled to reach into his jacket, fumbling out a weapon. It was a short combat knife, about the length of his hand, and he promptly dropped it with a clatter. He bent down to grab it, nearly fell off the roof again, and finally got it pointing in my direction, breathing fast.

I watched the whole thing with an expression of mild interest. "Finished?"

The kid didn't answer, staring at me with wide eyes. "So I'm guessing you're looking for me?" I said.

Silence. The kid was Chinese, though looking through the futures I could tell he spoke with a London accent; I pegged him as British-born. He was small and wiry, and looked quick. "You know," I said, "if you're just going to stand there staring, this is going to be a really one-sided conversation."

Yet more silence. I opened my mouth to make a snarky comment and stopped as I suddenly recognised the emotion in the kid's eyes. He was terrified—not just jumpy, but scared out of his wits. And the person he was terrified of was me.

I'm really not used to people being afraid of me. Don't get me wrong, a lot of mages get uneasy around diviners, but it's because they think you might dig out their secrets— they know a diviner's no physical threat. And while secrets can be as deadly as any other weapon in the magical world, fear is an instinctual thing. When you know you can beat someone up it's a lot harder to be scared of them.

Obviously this kid hadn't gotten that particular memo. He was practically paralysed, to the point where it looked like he could barely move. I wasn't worried about the knife—from what I could see he looked more likely to stab himself than anyone else. "Who sent you?" I said, my voice sharp and commanding. I didn't ask who he was—this guy was a pawn, not a king.

The tone of voice worked, and the kid mumbled an answer before he could stop himself. "Will."

"You his apprentice?" I asked. The kid stared at me in obvious confusion and I cocked my head. He wasn't acting like a mage. "Adept, then?"

He started, and I nodded to myself. "Okay, what do you want to know?"

"Huh?"

I shrugged. "You came here to find something out, right? Let's hear it."

The kid continued to stare at me. Apparently this hadn't been in the script. "Okay, look," I said. "Could we speed this up? I've got company over, and don't take this personally, but you're not turning out to be the most fascinating conversation partner."

"Are—" The kid's voice wavered and he swallowed. "You're Verus, aren't you?"

"Yes. I'm the big bad scary Verus."

"What were you doing?" the kid said.

I stared at him for a second before answering slowly and carefully. "I was playing a board game."

The kid hesitated. "So you've discovered my secret," I said. "Congrats." I nodded to the knife. "Now put that away. You obviously don't have a clue how to use it."

By the way, just in case any of you are thinking about trying this at home, this is *not* how you're supposed to handle a nervous guy with a knife. If someone pulls a weapon on you, the correct response is to run—or if you can't manage that, to deck them before they get the chance to draw it. But I'd been looking into the futures in which I engaged the kid and it was woefully obvious that he had absolutely no idea how to use the thing. If I went for him it was three to one that he'd fall off the roof and probably stab himself in the process.

The kid started and looked down at the blade—he'd obviously forgotten he was holding it—but didn't lower the weapon. I sighed, suddenly running out of patience. *Oh, screw this.* I walked to one side. "Get out of here."

The kid stared at me again. "Beat it," I said, gesturing. I'd left the kid a clear path back where he came. "If your boss wants to spy on me, tell him to come do it himself."

The kid looked from me to the empty darkness and began slowly moving away, trying to retreat and watch me at the same time. I took another look into the futures and saw how easy it would be to take him down. Lunge, grab, twist, and he'd be on the ground. The knife would be out of his hand and into mine, and then we could have a nice long chat about exactly who'd sent him here.

I didn't do it. I would have, once. A spy usually just means someone's being nosy, but it can also mean they're thinking about making a move on you, which means that it's fairly common for mages who realise they're being spied on to shoot first and ask questions later. On top of that, the kind of people I used to hang out with tended to assume that *not* reacting to a potential threat with immediate violence was a sign of weakness. It might be nothing, but why take the chance?

But here's the thing about living like a paranoid hermit: it sucks. It's impossible to explain just how *tired* you can get of violence—that weary feeling where you see someone who's looking for trouble and want to ask, *Do we really have to do this?* The more time I spent with Luna and Sonder and Variam and Anne, the more I realised that I liked not treating everyone I met as a potential threat. Going after the kid and interrogating him felt like stepping away from that, and I didn't want to do it. So I stood and watched as he edged around me. Once he had a clear line of retreat he turned and ran into the darkness. The sound of racing footsteps faded and I was alone.

Now that I look back, I wonder what would have happened if I'd done things differently. If I'd spoken or acted another way, could I have avoided the whole ugly mess? Or would it just have made things worse? Maybe someone else could have managed it. I don't know.

But at the time I had no idea what was coming. I just waited to make sure the kid was gone, then headed back down to my flat to tell Anne and the others the story.

I woke the next morning to the pleasant feeling of light and warmth. From long habit, the first thing I did was scan the future for danger, looking for the telltale flashes of threats and violence. Absolutely nothing came up and I stayed relaxed, turning to get my head out of the light before opening my eyes. The sun was streaming into my bedroom, the rays lighting up my bed and carpet in brilliant colour, and glancing up through the window I could see a bright blue sky. It was going to be a clear summer's day.

My bedroom's a comfortable size, with two tall windows that let in the morning sun and give a view out onto the rooftops of Camden. The walls are white and bare except for a couple of pictures I inherited from the previous owner, and there's a long desk that's usually cluttered with whatever magic items I'm working on at the moment. A door leads into the living room. From under the door I could smell something tasty coming from the kitchen and I didn't even need to look to know that Anne was there.

I wasn't in a hurry so I just lay there in my bed, enjoying the sun and quiet while lazily looking through the futures ahead of me. Once I was completely awake I got up and took a few steps on the carpet in my bare feet, stretching my legs before dressing and opening the door.

The living room was neat and clean except for the corner

with Variam's camp bed, which looked as though it had been converted into a nest for a medium-sized tornado. Variam has a ridiculous amount of energy and only sleeps about six hours a night, which usually means that by the time I'm up he's already left the house. I washed, shaved, and wandered into the kitchen, where Anne was making breakfast.

Since Anne and Variam had moved in last winter, my home had gone from a fairly lonely place to something more like a shared house. It had been eight months since Anne and Variam had arrived, and between seeing them and taking lessons from me Luna was spending so much time here that she might as well be living here too. We'd all had plenty of time to learn each other's quirks, and one of the first things we'd found out was everyone else's cooking styles. My cooking can be best described as functional. I'm one of those people who doesn't care much about food—I like it enough to appreciate it when it's done well but not enough to learn to get really good. The end result is edible, but I don't think there's much chance anyone's ever going to get excited about eating it.

Anne's a superb cook. She told us that she grew up doing the cooking for her house, and it shows—she can make a meal out of literally anything and it'll taste good. Luna isn't bad, but she's accident prone. The bad luck from her curse may not affect her, but it works just fine on everything else, and putting her in an environment filled with lit fires, sharp knives, and potentially poisonous substances is just a *really* bad idea. Her last attempt at oil frying is the reason I've got a CO_2 extinguisher mounted on the wall. Variam is terrible. His dishes come in three flavours: scorched, charred, and burnt to a crisp. I have the suspicion that he makes it awful on purpose just so he doesn't get asked to do it again, but I can't prove it.

Anne met me with a smile and a plate of delicious fried stuff. "Anne, I love you," I said as I took it from her.

Anne laughed. "You probably say that to any woman who feeds you."

"I didn't say it to the last woman who used this kitchen before you and Luna." I sat down at the table and started eating. It tasted as good as it smelt.

"Really?"

"Yeah," I said between mouthfuls. "Turned out she was working for a guy who wanted to kill us. She helped catch me and Luna so he could have a try at murdering us both. Was one of my more spectacularly dysfunctional breakups."

Anne paused and looked at me. "You're not joking, are you?"

"I'll tell you the story sometime," I said. "Vari gone out?"

"He went for a run." Anne took the remainder of the sausages, hash browns, and bacon from the pan and divided them in two. Half went on her plate and the other half in another pan, which she closed carefully.

I nodded at the pan. "For Vari?"

"Mm-hm." Anne took her plate over and sat opposite me. She had just as much food as I did. Anne may be thin, but she eats a lot.

"It really annoys Luna that you're always so nice to him."

"I know," Anne said with a rueful look. "I keep telling her I don't mind."

I laughed. "You never mind being nice to people."

"Well . . . maybe sometimes," Anne said with a quick smile. "Vari can be bad-tempered, but he's not a bully. He never tries to control anyone. And . . . he's a little nervous at the moment."

I looked at Anne in surprise. "Why now?"

"He's worried we've been looking for a master for too long," Anne said. "We're not really supposed to be in the apprentice program, are we? Vari thinks that the longer this goes on, the more chance someone will start paying attention to us."

Well, that spoiled the fun a bit. I didn't answer, but Anne was watching me and I knew she could already tell from my reaction that Vari was right.

One of the reasons I'd invited Anne and Variam to stay with me last winter had been for their protection. They're not recognised members of magical society, but I am (just about), and the idea had been that I'd try to find them a master. Unfortunately that had proven a lot harder than I'd expected. It turns out that if you add up the number of novice mages in Britain looking for a master, and the number of qualified and respected Light or independent master mages looking for an apprentice, there are way more applicants than places. And Anne and Variam's record only made things worse—to most Light and independent mages, being associated with a Dark mage, a rakshasa, and a murder investigation is sort of the equivalent of being a illegal immigrant, a terrorist, and a registered sex offender all at once. By this point I'd been at it for more than half a year and it was starting to feel depressingly like job hunting, right down to the *we regret to inform you* rejection letters and the creeping sense of futility.

The one bit of good news was that Anne and Variam were still enrolled in the Light apprentice program, a kind of university structure where apprentices are taught in small classes, meaning that even if they don't have a master they still have opportunities for study. Problem is, you're not supposed to be allowed into the program unless you're sponsored. Jagadev had arranged for Anne and Variam's entry, and when the two of them had moved into my flat people had assumed I'd taken over their sponsorship, even though officially I hadn't. If I petitioned I *might* be able to manage it . . . but then again I might not, and whether or not it worked it would draw all the wrong kinds of attention. "Do you want to push harder?" I asked Anne.

"How?"

"You know why you've been turned down so much," I said. "It's the whole history with Sagash and Jagadev." I hesitated, choosing my words carefully. "There are mages who'd be less concerned by that."

"Dark mages?" Anne said quietly.

"Not all of them," I said. "It's just . . . Look, so far I've been pretty picky about the mages I've approached. If anything's made me even a little bit twitchy, I've steered clear. I could change that. It's not something I want to do, but . . . as things stand right now, you and Vari have absolutely no rights under mage law. Living with me gives you a little protection but not much, and it's not like I'm exactly short on enemies. I don't like the idea of you guys signing up with a mage I don't trust, but in the long run it might actually make you both safer."

Anne had listened quietly as I spoke, watching me closely. As I finished my food, she thought for a second and shook her head. "No."

"Not all of them are going to be bad. They're just ones I'm not sure about."

"Then I don't want to go near them. I don't want to be apprenticed to a mage I don't trust. I'd rather have no master than a bad one."

"It might take a while—"

"Then I'll wait," Anne said. "I don't care how long it takes. I was Sagash's apprentice once and I'm not doing that again, not *ever*." Her eyes were set and there was an anger there that brought me up short. "As long as there's any chance they could be like that, I'm never going with them."

I leant back in surprise. "Okay. I guess we'll cross off that plan."

Anne stared right through me, and for just a moment I wondered where I'd seen that expression of hers before. A memory flickered through my head: green light flashing off bones, a body falling . . .

Then Anne seemed to realise what she was doing and the moment was gone. "Um . . ." She brushed her hair back, turning her face away, suddenly embarrassed. "Sorry, I didn't mean . . . Is it okay us still staying here? I don't want to . . ."

"Oh, it's fine," I said, though inwardly I was curious. What had triggered *that*? "Look, you guys have been here long enough to see how active a social life I usually have. It's nice having people to talk to."

"You don't mind being so crowded?" Anne asked. "I mean, this flat's not that big."

I shrugged. "I'm kind of the self-contained type. As long as you guys don't start sleeping in my bedroom I'm fine." Though come to think of it, I always used to have trouble sleeping if anyone else was in the flat. For some reason Anne and Variam didn't trigger that reflex.

Anne smiled, but it faded quickly. She looked like she was working her way up to asking something. "What is it?" I said.

"Um . . ." Anne said. "It's just . . . You don't get uncomfortable when I'm near you, do you?"

I looked at her in surprise. "That's a weird question. No, why?"

Anne looked away. "Mages . . . usually don't like it if I'm close to them."

"Why not?"

"You know . . ." Anne stopped and started again. "People show their feelings in their bodies. The tension, the way they move . . . If they're afraid or uncomfortable I can see it."

I looked at Anne, puzzled. "Okay." I had the feeling she was trying to tell me something, but I wasn't sure what.

I heard the sound of the back door from below. "Vari's back," Anne said before I could check. She got up, taking the plates to the sink. I thought about asking more, but I could already hear Variam running up the stairs and decided to leave it for another time. A second later Variam came in, and by the time we'd sorted out who would get to use the shower first I'd forgotten about it.

chapter 2

Anne and Variam's appointment was for eleven o'clock; they were seeing a mage who'd been recommended to me as someone who might be able to help out with their finding-a-master problem. After they were gone I went to wash up, found that Anne had done it already, and went downstairs to open the shop.

My day job when I don't have anything life-threatening to deal with is running a business called the Arcana Emporium, the name of which is a long-winded way of saying "magic shop." I don't publicise that I'm a mage, but I don't exactly hide it either, and one of the odd things I've learnt over the years is just how much you can get away with if you're blatant enough. Hide something behind smoke and mirrors and make people work to find it, and they'll tear the place down looking for what's there. Put up a sign up saying *magic shop*, and no one believes you.

I still don't know where most of my customers come from. I don't advertise and I'm off the main street, so most of it has to be word of mouth. Every now and again I'll

Google my shop to see what people are saying about me and I swear I get the *weirdest* results. There are people out there who think I'm everything from a reincarnated angel from the pharaoh dynasties of Egypt to a thousand-year-old half dragon who's secretly sponsoring a quest across time and space in an attempt to kill himself. (No, I don't know why.) I suppose I should be grateful there isn't any slash fiction. On second thought, I'm not going to look too closely just in case there is.

Anyway, the result of all this is that I get a pretty bizarre mix of customers. The biggest group are the tourists and curiosity-shoppers, and they're pretty easy to deal with. They take for granted that magic isn't real, and so for them it's a simple business transaction. I get money, and they get something weird to take home, where they'll tell stories about the funny guy who pretends to sell magic items. Mixed in with the normals are the clued-in—sensitives, adepts, apprentices, and even the odd mage. They're the ones my stock is actually *for*, and they're definitely the only ones who have any idea how to use it. I like talking to these guys.

The problem customers are the ones in between. They know that magic's real, but they expect it to behave like . . . well, like what they mean when they say "like magic." Now don't get me wrong, magic can do some pretty impressive stuff, but it has limits and it has rules. If you try to mess with it without knowing what you're doing, it's far more likely to complicate your life than it is to help. It's not a universal solution to whatever issues you might currently have.

None of which stops people from coming in here expecting me to fix their problems for them.

|||||||||

The man stepped forward and slapped something down on the counter with a *thump*. Then he glared at me. "Well?"

"Um," I said.

He pointed. "Do you know what that is?"

I looked at the thing on my counter. It was covered with silver scales, and it smelt. "It's a fish."

"Do you know where it came from?"

"I'd guess the sea."

"It was on my chair. That's where it came from."

"Okay," I said. "Does this happen often?"

"This is the third time!"

"So . . . you've attracted the attention of a compulsively generous fishmonger?"

"What?" The man stared at me. "What are you talking about?"

"Sorry. What seems to be the problem?"

"The *problem*," the man said, speaking slowly and clearly, "is that it's a curse."

"Ah," I said. "And you know this because . . . ?"

"My cat told me."

"Your cat," I said. "Right. It's all starting to make sense now."

The man rolled his eyes. "You know what, forget it, I'll do it myself. Where are your spell components?"

I pointed. "Second rack in the corner."

The man turned and walked off. "Hey," I called. "Could you take your fish with you, please?"

The next three customers wanted a knife, a selection of herbs, and a crystal ball, respectively. The fourth harangued me at length about why the shop had been closed yesterday even though the sign said that it didn't close until five and did I know how much travelling time I'd cost her? By the time she'd finished threatening to report me to the Office of Fair Trading and stormed off, a queue had grown up behind her.

Luna came in just as I was dealing with customer number . . . something or other, a bearded guy in a worn leather jacket. He smelt of beer and was taking much, much longer than he should to get the message that I was not going to sell him a love potion. "Hi, Alex!" Luna called over the sound of the bell.

"I already told you, there isn't a formula," I told the man. "If there were, Chanel would be selling it already . . . Where have you been?"

"Duelling class ran late," Luna said, weaving between the customers. As she moved I saw the invisible silver mist mould itself to her body, clinging in a tight, dense layer on top of her exercise clothes instead of reaching out to the people in the shop. Once upon a time Luna could never have gotten that close to a crowd—she would have stopped at the edge and hesitated—but she's been my apprentice for more than a year and she's done a lot of growing. Not just in magical skill, but in confidence too. "I can use the shower, right?"

"Huh? Yeah, sure." Luna disappeared into the corridor leading to the stairs up to my flat, and I turned back to the man at the counter. "Look, man, you got to help me," the man began again.

"Look," I said. "Even if I could make you a love potion—which, by the way, I can't—have you any idea how unethical this is? You're screwing around with someone's emotions. It's not something you do without a *really* good reason."

Luna stuck her head back into the shop. "Hey, Alex? Is there supposed to be a fish out here?"

I covered my eyes. "No. There's not."

"What should I do with it?"

"Look," the man started again. "You got to help me."

"No, I don't," I told him, and turned to Luna. "I don't care. Put it in the freezer or something."

"Are you sure?"

"Why?"

"Isn't that supposed to spoil the taste?"

"Look, man, I really need this," the man said.

"I don't care," I said to both of them, then looked at Luna. "Put it wherever you're supposed to put it."

"Where's that?"

"How should I know?"

"Well," Luna said logically, "are we having this for dinner, or is it for something else?"

"I don't care! Just get rid of it!"

Luna disappeared with the fish. "Um, excuse me," a boy in his twenties said. He'd been waiting behind Love Potion Guy for five minutes, tapping his foot. "Do you have—"

"No," I said, and turned back to Love Potion Guy. "I can't help you, and I guarantee that if you try to go through with this plan it'll make things worse. Just sort things out the normal way."

Love Potion Guy stared at me hopelessly. "I can't."

Mr. Impatient started up again. "Excuse me, I need—"

"I don't have them," I said.

Luna stuck her head back in. "Hey, Alex?"

"*Now* what?"

"There's about a dozen more fish in your bedroom."

I closed my eyes. "Please tell me you're making this up."

"Yup."

I opened my eyes and stared at her. Luna was grinning. "Couldn't resist, sorry. First fish was real, though. I put it in the fridge."

I took a deep breath, mentally calculating throwing angles between the items within reach and Luna's head, but she beat a quick retreat. "Listen," Love Potion Guy began again.

"No," I said. "You've told me that story twice and a third time's not going to help."

"I need—" Mr. Impatient began.

"I already told you, I don't have them."

"You haven't—"

"Doesn't change the fact that this isn't that kind of shop."

"But—"

"They're real, not fake, and just because I sell knives doesn't mean I sell cards."

"Look—" Love Potion Guy said.

I looked back and forth between Love Potion Guy and Mr. Impatient, answering the questions without waiting for them to ask them. "No, no, yes, no, it wouldn't help, yes every day, it doesn't matter because I still wouldn't do it, I've already tried that, just try talking to her, first because they're not profitable enough and second because I don't care, if you do it's because they're trying to con you, the Magic Box on the other side of Camden and here's one of their cards." I dropped a business card into Mr. Impatient's hand and looked between them. They were staring at me. "Are we done here? Because there's a guy behind you who wants to find out how much money he's been left in a will and *he's* not going to take no for an answer either."

We weren't done. Getting rid of the whole crowd took the best part of an hour, but at least the crazies all left at more or less the same time, possibly because of some weird kind of magnetic principle. By the time Luna came back, the shop was empty. I was slumped in the chair and gave her a glower. "Sorry," Luna said in an I'm-not-sorry-at-all tone.

"Funny how you always time your jokes for when I'm too busy to go after you."

"Oh, come on," Luna said with a grin. "Your face was hilarious."

"I'm getting a vision," I said. "It's my mystical diviner's powers. I foresee myself suddenly assigning you many more shifts at the shop."

"No, you won't," Luna said with perfect confidence.

"Oh, really?"

"You're not going to make me do it on my own," Luna said. "The only reason you keep the shop is so you can run the counter yourself."

I blinked and looked at her. "How do you figure that?"

When I first met Luna she was twenty-one. She's twenty-three now, a blue-eyed, fair-skinned, wavy-haired half-English-half-Italian girl whose life's been trending steadily

upwards over the past two years despite occasional inter-
ludes of danger and violence. Luna's always been fit, but
lately she's turned into quite an athlete—she was introduced
to azimuth duelling last winter and took to it like a duck to
water, and she's been practising hard ever since. "Well, it's
not like you do it for the money," Luna said. Her hair was
damp, the water darkening it from its usual light brown, and
as she spoke she started untangling it with the aid of a
hairbrush.

"It makes a profit."

"Not much."

"How do you know?"

"Because I used to get your stock, remember?" Luna
said. Before Luna had been my apprentice she'd worked for
me part time, searching for magical items. I'd bought them
from her and divided them up; the weaker ones I put up for
sale in the restricted section, and the dangerous ones I kept
for myself. "You hardly ever sell the expensive stuff."

"Have you been going through my records?"

"You don't have any proper ones; I checked. Anyway, if
you cared that much about it you'd keep regular hours."

"I have regular hours."

"Unless something comes up."

"Stuff *does* keep coming up."

"But you could hire an assistant," Luna said. "If you
really wanted to dump the work on someone else you could
have done it by now."

"Well, yeah." For years I've had vague plans for getting
someone to help run the place, but I've always put it off. For
one thing there aren't many people I'd trust with the job, but
even if I *could* find someone I'm not sure I'd do it. The
people in the magical community whom I feel closest to
aren't the established mages but the have-nots—apprentices,
adepts, lesser talents, and all the other small-time practitio-
ners out there—and those are the people that my shop lets
me meet.

Luna finished brushing her hair and started tying it back in a ponytail. "So who are Anne and Vari seeing this time?"

"Her name's Dr. Shirland," I said. "Mind mage. She's an independent."

"If she's a mind mage, how's she going to teach Anne and Vari?"

"She's not, but she might know someone who will. From what I've heard she's supposed to be some kind of consultant. I'm hoping she can get Anne and Vari an interview with a life or fire mage who could teach them."

"Oh, like that guy they met in the spring?"

I rolled my eyes. "Let's hope it goes a bit better than that. Last thing we need is another . . ." A future ahead of us caught my attention and I stopped, concentrating.

Luna tilted her head. "What is it?"

"Someone's coming," I said. The pattern was different from a regular customer; as I focused on the future in which she walked through the door I saw the flicker of auras. "A mage."

Luna had been sitting on the counter; now she hopped off, suddenly alert. "Trouble?"

"Don't think so." I was already looking for the flash and chaos of combat and couldn't see it. "Get your focus just in case."

Luna vanished. I walked forward and flipped the sign in the window from *OPEN* to *CLOSED* before returning to my desk to quickly check the weapons underneath. As Luna reappeared I stood behind the counter and waited. A few seconds later the bell rang and the door swung open.

I'd been watching the woman as she'd walked down the street, and by the time she stepped in I'd had the chance to take a good look at her. She was big and hefty-looking, with brown hair and a round, pleasant face, and she wore a wide-cut suit. "Hi," she said, looking from Luna to me. "Verus, right?"

"That's me," I said. *And you're Keeper Caldera.*

"Keeper Caldera. Good to meet you." Caldera walked forward to shake my hand. "Mind if we have a word?"

Keepers are the enforcement arm of the Light Council, a mixture of soldiers, police, and internal investigators. Most mages are wary of them, and for good reason; if a Keeper wants to talk to you, it's usually bad news. "Depends on the word."

"You're not under investigation," Caldera said. "I'd just like to ask a few questions about something I'm working on."

I hesitated. I wasn't keen on talking to a Keeper, but if I brushed Caldera off she'd probably just come back again. "All right," I said reluctantly. "Not here though." I'm still wary about having other mages around my shop and I didn't really want customers looking through the window and seeing us.

"Fine by me," Caldera said. "Tell you what, there's a really nice pub just around the corner. I'll buy you a pint."

"Uh . . ." Okay, that wasn't standard Keeper procedure as far as I knew. "I guess that works. Let me close up and I'll meet you outside."

⁜⁜⁜⁜⁜⁜⁜⁜⁜⁜

Caldera's definition of "around the corner" turned out to be on the optimistic side, and it took us twenty minutes to make our way through the busy Camden streets. Luna kept pace with me, staying half a step behind to keep me out of the radius of her curse; Caldera hadn't specifically invited her but I'd signalled for her to come, and apart from a glance Caldera hadn't objected. I kept an eye out the whole way, scanning for danger; it wasn't that Caldera had done anything particularly suspicious, but my past experiences with Keepers have generally been less than positive. Nothing pinged; if I was in danger, it wasn't the immediate kind.

The pub Caldera had picked for us looked like it had been built some time around the Iron Age: an old, crooked building with irregular floors and low ceilings, filled with nooks and crannies. It obviously hadn't been designed for tall people, and I had to duck as I followed Caldera down the stairs into the stone cellar. "Right," Caldera said as she led us past the patrons and to a secluded corner. "What are you having?"

"Just a Coke, please," Luna said.

"Seriously?"

"I don't drink."

"Fair enough. You?"

"Whatever they've got on tap," I said.

Caldera winced. "Okay, look. I'll get you something good." She headed to the bar.

"Is she really a Keeper?" Luna asked once Caldera was gone.

"Oh yeah," I said, looking around the drawings and photos on the grubby paint-on-brick walls. I'd already looked into the future in which I asked Caldera, and I'd seen her show me her Keeper's signet with its distinctive magical fingerprint. "Though it's the first time I've had one ask me out to the pub."

"Here we go," Caldera announced, returning with a drink in either hand. She set them down in front of us and dropped into a corner seat with a contented sigh.

I took a dubious look at the contents of the pint glass she'd pushed in front of me. "What is it?"

"Porter," Caldera said. "Try it."

I checked to make sure it wasn't going to poison me or anything, then took a sip. I raised my eyebrows. "Huh."

"Like it?"

"Tastes . . . interesting." I took another drink. It had a fruity flavour, with an odd aftertaste.

"Pretty good, right?" Caldera said. "Notice how it turns into a roasted coffee flavour after the raisin start? Not many pubs in London sell this stuff. They only brew it in London, bottle-conditioned—have to pour it out carefully to leave the yeast sediment in the bottom."

"Hm. I'll have to try it again next time."

"There we go. Done some good today."

I gave Caldera an amused look. "Not that I'm questioning your expertise on beer, but wasn't there something you wanted to ask?"

"Right." Caldera glanced at Luna. "You're okay with her sitting in on this, right?"

"Luna's my apprentice," I said. "You can tell her anything you'd tell me."

Luna gave me a quick, warm look. "All right," Caldera said, looking straight at me. "It's to do with your old master, Richard Drakh."

I felt my muscles tense. My past with Richard was the one thing I did *not* want to talk about with Luna, or anyone else for that matter. "What's happened?"

"There are rumours going around," Caldera said, watching me carefully. "That he's coming back."

The old half-healed, never-healed memories flashed through my mind, fear and helplessness and pain. I shut them out with an effort of will, keeping my voice steady. "There are always rumours."

"It's been ten years."

"So?"

"So they didn't start from nowhere, did they?" Caldera said. "The powers-that-be want to know what's going on."

"Because they don't have any hard evidence?"

"Can't say."

Caldera's poker face wasn't bad, but I'm pretty good at reading people and I knew the answer to my question was yes. The Council didn't have any proof that Richard was back—this was just a fishing expedition. A bit of the tension went out of my muscles. Luna watched the two of us from over her Coke, her eyes filled with curiosity. "You're hoping I might know something," I said. "Because I used to be Richard's apprentice. Right?"

"Pretty much."

"I haven't seen him in more than ten years." I met Caldera's eyes. "I'm guessing you looked up my background before coming here?"

Caldera's expression didn't change. "Heard the story."

"Then you know why I stayed away," I said. "I haven't heard anything about him. Not when I left, and not after I left. And you know what? I'm fine with that."

Caldera held my gaze for a second. "All right," she said after a pause. "What about his Chosen, then? Deleo. Does she know something?"

I looked away. "Deleo and I aren't exactly friends."

"You were in contact with her last year, right?"

"Briefly."

"Learn anything?"

"Yeah." I turned back to Caldera. "I learnt that Deleo's crazier than a sack of rabid weasels. You want to interview her, go right ahead, but I'm not going to be standing next to you when you do it."

Caldera made a pacifying gesture. "All right. Look, we don't have many people to ask, okay? Not like Dark mages are going to cooperate with a Keeper."

"They don't cooperate with *anyone*. And I'm a rogue, remember? You think they're going to trust me?" I shook my head. "What are you expecting to turn up?"

"Okay," Caldera said. "Here's how it is. I wasn't around back when Richard was active, but from what I heard he had a lot of people running scared. Some of the Guardian types thought he had a plan, was working on something big with the Dark mages, I don't know. Then all of a sudden, right when he was at the top of his game, he disappeared. Rumour was he'd gone somewhere, but he never showed up and neither did those two apprentices of his. After a few years the guys on the case filed all three of them as missing-presumed-dead and forgot about it."

"Those two apprentices" had been Tobruk and Shireen.

Deleo and I had been numbers three and four. "If they'd known Richard they wouldn't have filed him as 'presumed' anything."

"So where do you think he went?"

I shrugged.

"I thought diviners knew everything."

"Richard disappeared in the summer ten years ago," I said. Come to think of it, it was ten years almost to the day. It had been August then, and it was August now. "By the time he vanished . . . Well, let's just say he and I weren't on the best of terms."

"You have to have some clue," Caldera said. She was leaning forward, hands clasped, frank and persuasive. "Come on. You're not seriously telling me you didn't know *anything*."

"You don't know what Richard was like," I said quietly. I held Caldera's eyes, allowing a little of the memories to show through, letting her see I was telling the truth. "Those mages were right to be scared of him. You think he told me his plans? I lived in his mansion for two years, and by the end of it the biggest thing I'd learnt about him was how much I *didn't* know. Anything you saw of him, it was because he wanted you to see it."

"You're a diviner, right? You never took a look to see?"

"That's not how it works," I said, and shook my head. "I'm sorry, Caldera. I don't have what you're looking for. I don't know what Richard's plans were. As far as I know, no one did."

A silence fell over the table. Caldera drew back and I could tell she was disappointed. My phone chimed and I glanced at it. "I'd better go."

Caldera held out a card. "If you think of anything or if anything happens, give me a call, okay?"

I hesitated, then slipped it into my pocket. "Thanks for the drink."

ı ı ı ı ı ı ı ı ı

"Who was that message from?" Luna asked once we were
back out on the streets.

"Anne," I said. "She says they've finished, but she's not
going to be back until late." I frowned. Something about the
message had sounded a little off. I glanced through the
futures in which I called Anne and Variam, just to make
sure they were all right. Well, they were answering their
phones . . .

I snapped back to the present to realise Luna had asked
me something about Caldera. "Not sure," I said. "Listen, I
think I'm going to go pay a visit to our mind mage consultant. You go back to the shop and meet up with Vari."

"Can't I come?"

"Next time. Anyway, I'm taking you out tonight, remember? Go get ready."

Luna had been about to keep on pushing, but that diverted
her. "Where are we going?"

"It's a surprise."

"What kind of surprise?"

"An educational surprise."

Luna gave me a suspicious look. "It'll be fun," I said.
"Wear something nice."

"Like what, battle armour?"

"I'll leave that up to your judgement. Remember, seven
o'clock. Don't be late."

ı ı ı ı ı ı ı ı ı

The quickest route from Camden to Brondesbury is the
overground line, which was once called the Silverlink
Metro but now goes by the unimaginative name of the London Overground. I watched the rooftops and gardens of
north-central London go by, then got off and walked to
where Anne and Variam had met Dr. Ruth Shirland.

Dr. Shirland lived in a terraced house in a small closed-in

street. It was a residential area and solidly middle class, the kind of place where you're paying a lot more for the location than for the building. It's not the kind of place you'd expect a mage to live, but I've seen stranger choices. I rang the bell and waited.

Dr. Shirland opened the door. She was about sixty years old, short and delicate looking, with grey curly hair, small round glasses, and the kind of wrinkles you get from smiling a lot. "Oh, hello," she said. "Alex Verus, isn't it? Come right in."

"Thanks."

I was escorted into a small and cosy sitting room with a modest number of chairs and a lot of bookshelves. I accepted tea, refused biscuits, and was inspected by a fat black-and-white tomcat who sniffed my hand, permitted himself to be stroked, then curled up on an armchair clearly reserved for his exclusive use. "Thanks for seeing me," I said.

"It's no trouble," Dr. Shirland said. "Though I do have a patient in an hour."

"A patient?"

"I'm a consulting psychologist," Dr. Shirland said. "I see mages, but I have a regular practice as well."

"Yeah, I imagine being able to read thoughts *would* make psychology easier. Are you reading mine now?"

Dr. Shirland raised an eyebrow. "Would you believe me if I told you I wasn't?"

"Probably not."

"Why not?"

"Call it a precaution," I said. "Besides, in my experience most mages can never resist using their powers."

"Would you include yourself in that category?"

"I can't read thoughts."

"But you can see what someone's going to say."

"But you can look inside someone's head even if it's something they're *not* going to say."

"It's actually more complicated than that," Dr. Shirland

said, "but most people aren't concerned with technical details. I imagine they don't draw much distinction between your being able to predict some of the things they do and all of the things they do?"

"Not generally."

"Being psychically naked before another is quite a frightening concept," Dr. Shirland said. "Once that line is crossed, it makes very little difference how far one goes. The breach of privacy is just as extreme either way."

I thought about it and gave a slight smile. "I suppose that's a fair point."

Dr. Shirland sipped her tea. I sat back in the armchair. From the other chair, the cat opened an eye to take a look at me and then went to sleep.

"I understand you've taken on the role of sponsor for Anne and Variam?" Dr. Shirland said.

"It's not officially registered, but yes."

Dr. Shirland gave a nod. "Before we go any further, please understand that I will not repeat to you anything that either of them has told me in confidence. The only information I will give is that which I believe is appropriate for you to receive as a sponsor."

"Understood."

"Good," Dr. Shirland said briskly. "I understand you've been trying to find Anne and Variam an apprenticeship with a Light mage or a Light-leaning independent?"

"Yes."

"In my judgement the chances of your succeeding in doing so are very low, with one exception."

I was silent. "Well, I'd hoped for better," I said after a moment, "but I guess I'll take what I can get. What's the exception?"

"I think Variam might have a future as a Council Keeper."

I stared at her. "You're kidding."

"Not at all."

"Vari hates Keepers!"

"So he told me. I understand he and Anne came under investigation last year."

"If by 'came under investigation' you mean 'were arrested,' then yes. And Vari had issues with them before that. He thinks the Council abandoned them both and he's . . . pretty much right. He's got a giant chip on his shoulder about mages in general and Light mages in particular, and if there's one group you're to blame for what Light mages do, it's the Keepers."

"I understand, but all the same I think that's where his abilities would be best appreciated. He's a fighter and he's determined, and he's an essentially active personality who needs work to do. He'll always have some difficulty with discipline, but the Council have employed fire mages before, you know. The Keeper orders are where they traditionally put them."

"And the fact that he's associated with a Dark mage?"

"In my opinion, that's the strongest reason to recommend it. The Keepers are the only arm of the Council who deal with Dark mages on a regular basis. Firsthand knowledge of Dark culture without being a Dark mage would be a selling point to them. If Variam can convince them he's what he says he is, there's a good chance they'll give him the chance to prove himself."

I thought for a minute. "Did you have someone in mind?"

"I gave Variam the contact details of a Keeper who I think might be a good match. The decision has to be his, of course."

I turned it over in my mind and shrugged. "Well, I still think it still sounds weird, but I guess it could work. What about Anne?"

"Anne is going to be more difficult."

"Why?"

"Well for one thing, she's a life mage."

I frowned. "Why's that a problem?"

"Because life mages can do more than heal."

"They can do the opposite, I know." I'd seen Anne do it, though only twice. "I don't see how it matters. Pretty much every mage can kill you one way or another."

"From your point of view, perhaps," Dr. Shirland said. "But most mages are rarely threatened, and when they are it's usually in a way they can understand and deal with. And if they're an elemental mage, then of course they have their shields. A powerful protection, at least against most things."

"Life magic goes through shields?"

"As if they weren't there. I've never seen it myself but I've spoken to people who have. Just imagine how frightening that would be. Always to have been in a privileged position, safe and powerful, and to have that suddenly taken away. A life mage who can touch another person can do literally anything they want to them."

"But if you're looking for an apprentice—" I began, then stopped.

Dr. Shirland nodded. "Typically in a master-apprentice relationship, all the power lies with the master. But with a life apprentice, every time the master comes within arm's reach he places his life in her hands."

I thought about it, then shook my head in frustration. "It still doesn't make sense. Okay, I can see why that would make some mages jumpy, especially the paranoid ones. But they can't be like that all the time. I mean, mages get life magic treatments, don't they? They have to let life mages get close *sometimes*."

"Ones they trust."

"And they wouldn't trust her," I said with a sigh. Now I saw what she was getting at. "Because of Sagash and Jagadev and the murders last year."

"Yes," Dr. Shirland said. "They'd consider her— potentially, at least—touched by darkness."

I brooded over that for a moment. "Could you change their minds?" I said.

"No."

"Why not?"

"Because I think they may be right."

I looked up in surprise. Dr. Shirland was looking steadily at me. "What do you mean?"

"Anne was held by Sagash for a period of nine months," Dr. Shirland said, "beginning almost four years ago and ending a little over three years ago. Has she spoken to you about what happened over that period?"

"She doesn't talk about it."

Dr. Shirland nodded. "During our conversation, Anne spoke freely about her life since she and Variam moved in with you. However, the closer we moved to that time, the more reticent she became. I could feel it casting a shadow over everything she said."

"Yeah, but . . ." I raked my fingers through my hair. "The whole reason Anne got involved in all this was because Sagash kidnapped her. And the reason Vari got involved was because he went to try to rescue her. They're the *victims* in all this. It's not fair to blame them."

"It's not a matter of blame. If I approached anyone to refer Anne as an apprentice, the first question they'd ask would be whether she was potentially dangerous. And I wouldn't honestly be able to answer no."

"That's ridiculous," I said. "Anne's probably the nicest person I know. She won't even kill flies. She might be *powerful*, but she's not dangerous. She's . . . I don't know. Innocent."

Dr. Shirland gave me a look. "I don't think she's quite so innocent as you believe."

I started to answer and then stopped.

Last winter I was called in on a missing-persons case. A contact of mine from the Council had noticed that apprentices were going missing but didn't know who was doing it or how, and he sent me to find out. I found out. It led to me and Anne being trapped in a room stacked with dead bodies, being hunted down by a once-human creature called Vitus Aubuchon. I'd distracted Vitus and Anne had killed him. Don't get me wrong, it had been more than justified—not only had Vitus been the one *responsible* for all those dead bodies, he'd just cut Anne's throat and had been in the process of trying to kill me too.

But looking back on it, I had a disturbing thought. Getting good with spells takes time and effort. When apprentices try something new they usually spend ages fumbling around before they can make it work, and even then they're clumsy. Anne hadn't been clumsy. She'd ripped Vitus's life out of his body in a single action. It had been very quick and very efficient.

I looked up to see that Dr. Shirland was watching me. "What happened to her when she was with Sagash?" I said.

"Anne did not volunteer details."

"Did you find some out anyway?"

"You mean by entering her mind?"

I gave a nod.

Dr. Shirland looked at me with raised eyebrows. "You're asking me if I entered her mind to search her memories and feelings without her consent—an action that not only would be a breach of trust but which would also add further psychic damage to what was clearly already an intensely traumatic experience?"

"Pretty much."

"No." Dr. Shirland's tone made it clear the subject was closed.

"Sorry," I said. "Just checking."

There was a pause. "So is there anything you can do?" I said.

"With finding her a master?" Dr. Shirland shook her head. "I don't think there's anyone I could recommend in good conscience until this is resolved. I invited her to come back and talk further, but she gave me a very polite refusal."

I sat in silence for a little while. "Well," I said at last, "thanks for the help. I appreciate the effort."

"You're welcome. Call me if you'd like to talk again."

⌁⌁⌁⌁⌁⌁⌁⌁⌁⌁

I spent the journey home thinking, and was still thinking as I walked through the shop and started up the stairs to my flat. As I climbed I heard a *thud* from above, followed by another *thud* five seconds later.

Variam was slumped on the sofa in the living room. Vari is short and wiry, with Indian-dark skin and thin arms and legs. He wears a Sikh turban and dresses in clothes that always seem to have just been thrown together but still manage to look good. Despite how small he is, Vari's got presence; he draws attention wherever he goes, and seems to make friends and enemies equally fast. Right now he was sprawled with his legs out, glowering. As I walked in he threw a tennis ball to bounce off the wall with the *thud* I'd heard earlier before catching it again. He flicked me a glance and went back to glaring at the wall.

I stepped over Variam and went into the kitchen to fetch myself a drink. Once I'd filled the glass I came back in and leant against the doorjamb, watching Variam chuck the ball against the wall with a *thud* each time. "Want a drink?" I said.

Variam gave a negative sort of grunt.

"So I'm guessing you didn't like what she had to tell you."

Variam shot me a look.

I walked over and dropped into an armchair with a sigh. "The Keeper idea might not be a bad one, you know. I thought it was crazy at first, too, but it does kind of make sense."

"I don't care about the Keepers."

"What is it, then?"

Variam bounced the ball off the wall with another *thud*, and took a while to answer. "It's just me."

"What is?"

"All the time, she was talking like me and Anne were going to be somewhere different. If I signed up with some Keeper we'd be split up, right?"

"Well, there might be some way . . ."

Vari looked at me.

I raised a hand. "Okay, okay. Yeah, you probably would be. You'd still be able to see her, but apprentice training is pretty focused. You wouldn't be able to do everything together anymore."

Vari went back to throwing the ball. "Would that be so bad?" I said.

"We're supposed to stick together," Variam said.

"Hard to fit in with getting a master."

"What if I get one and Anne doesn't?"

"It's not like I'm going to kick her out. She can still stay here."

Variam threw the ball to go *thud* again. "Supposed to be my job."

"Why does it matter to you so badly?" I said curiously. Since I've known Variam he's always watched over Anne, but I've never asked him why.

Variam was silent and I knew he was thinking about answering, but when he finally spoke all that he said was, "I don't want to talk about it."

I glanced at my watch. It was ten to seven, and looking through the futures ahead I could tell that Luna would arrive in five minutes. "Luna and I are going to be out till late," I said, getting up. "If you get hungry there's a fish in the fridge."

chapter 3

It was a summer evening in Leicester Square. The sun was dipping behind the buildings to the west, shafts of golden light slipping down the streets to light up the shop fronts and windows. The square was packed with people, Londoners and out-of-towners and tourists all crowding together into one noisy boisterous mass. Along the north side sketch artists had set up shop, selling caricatures and celebrity portraits to the curious, while the square of grass itself was scattered with sitting people. The smells of cooking food drifted from the restaurants all around the edge, pizza and noodles and steak.

Luna and I sat at a table at the edge of one of the outdoor restaurants, right by the rope barrier that marked off the seating area. "How much do you know about probability?" I asked her.

"A little," Luna said with a shrug. "We did it in school."

I took out a deck of cards and sorted quickly through it, taking out the four aces. "An event's probability is a measurement of how certain we are that it'll occur. If we're sure it won't happen, the probability is zero. If we're sure it will happen, the probability is one. Otherwise it's somewhere in between." I showed the aces to Luna, then put the rest of the deck away and shuffled the four aces together. "If I keep shuffling these four cards, what's the probability that the ace of spades will be on top when I finish?"

"Uh . . . a quarter?"

I nodded. "A shuffle isn't random, but if it's being done properly it might as well be. Too many variables." I finished shuffling and dealt the four cards facedown. "If I tell you to pick a card, what's the probability you'll pick the ace of spades?"

"A quarter again?"

"Pretty much. You could probably do better if you paid attention to my patterns, but if you just guess then that's right." I pointed at one of the cards. "What's the probability *that* card's the ace of spades?"

"Still a quarter."

I shook my head. "Wrong. It's zero." I pointed at another card. "Zero." Another card. "Zero." The last card. "One." I flipped it to show the black-on-white of the ace of spades.

Luna frowned for a second, then her frown cleared. "Oh, I get it."

"While the cards are being shuffled, they're random," I said. "Once they're dealt they're not random anymore—you just don't know what they are. That's the difference between your magic and mine. I can't change how the cards are dealt, but I can see them. But you *can* change how the cards are dealt. Your magic works on all those little chaotic unpredictable things—reflexes, bounces, how something falls or slips. I think if you practise enough you should be able to start controlling it."

Luna gave me a suspicious look. "Why did you take me out here to tell me this?"

I gave Luna a grin. "Because tonight we're going there." I pointed across the square to the bright lights of the casino.

The Empire Casino is on the north side of Leicester Square, dwarfed by the cinemas towering around it. It's not the nicest casino in London and it's not the most high-class, but it does have one big thing in its favour: it's anonymous. Its position right in the heart of the West End means that it gets a near-constant stream of tourists and travellers and businessmen, which is handy when you don't want to attract attention.

Luna got carded at the door. "Oh look, he thinks you look under twenty-one," I said once she was done.

"Yeah, yeah," Luna said as we walked down the steps into the entrance tunnel. "I still don't think this is going to work."

The tunnel opened up into a lobby with two stairways leading farther down: one to the slots and the poker room, the other to the main casino floor. I gave the receptionist a nod and headed towards one of the flights of stairs. "Look, my curse hurts things," Luna said, keeping her voice down. "It doesn't do helpful."

"It protects you."

"It protects me from *accidents*. There's a difference."

We came out onto the casino floor and into a hubbub of noise. The casino was laid out in two storeys, the main floor taken up with gaming tables and the bar while the balcony running around the room above held restaurants and a lounge. Although there were no windows, the room was filled with light: from the ceiling a yellow-white glow shone from flashy-looking chandeliers, and on the walls big projection screens displayed sports matches. The air smelt of fabric and sweat. "You remember last year?" I said. "When Deleo and Khazad tracked you down in that parking garage?"

"Yeah . . ."

"They were using a tracer. Your curse burned it out from thirty feet away."

"I guess."

"So that was more than just protecting you from accidents," I said. "The tracer was dangerous only because it
could have showed them where you were, but the curse fried
it anyway. That means one of two things. Either the curse
picks up on what you subconsciously *know* is dangerous, or
it's got enough awareness to be able to recognise indirect
threats and neutralise them on its own initiative. Which
means it ought to be able to help you in other ways too." I
gestured to the floor around us. "This is your element. Pure
chance is exactly what your magic has power over. I think
you can do this."

"All right," Luna said with a sigh. "I'll give it a shot."

I pulled a pack of notes from my pocket. "You buy chips
on the tables. If you lose this, come back and I'll get you
some more."

Luna counted it, eyebrows raised. "Five hundred
pounds?"

"Yep."

"Isn't that kind of a lot to throw away?"

"Wait till you see how much the other players lose," I
said. "Have fun."

⁘⁘⁘⁘⁘⁘

Once Luna was gone I took a walk through the casino,
letting the sights and sounds wash around me. It had been
a while since I'd been in one, and being here again felt like
coming back to an old home.

I used to spend a lot of time in casinos, back in my early
twenties. By the end of the summer of ten years ago I'd
broken away from Richard and his remaining apprentices
for good, but I was in bad shape. The extended nightmare of
my last year in Richard's mansion and that horrible final
battle with Tobruk had left me seriously screwed up mentally
and I wasn't in any condition to start putting my life back

together. On top of that I had no home, no money, and no prospects. All I had was myself and my magic.

So I turned to gambling and got my first nice surprise in a long while when I discovered how easy it was. Okay, there were a few hiccups (it turns out casinos are quite happy to decide that you must be cheating *somehow* even if they can't prove how), but once I learnt to be careful it was a low-effort, risk-free source of income. There was a real rush to it too, at least to begin with. I'd just spent the best part of two years being the runt among the apprentices, always having to watch my back in case a more powerful mage decided to squash me. Now all of a sudden, instead of being below everyone else, I was above them. I could take everyone else's money and there was nothing they could do about it. It was exciting.

But over the years the excitement faded. I learnt the same thing that everyone learns sooner or later: *nothing's* any fun if you can have as much of it as you like. When you're poor money's desperately important, but the wealthier you get the less it matters. I like money for the freedom and the independence that it gives me, and that works only up to a point—once you're over a certain limit then getting any richer doesn't help.

I also started to feel sorry for the people I was taking money from. The men (and it's mostly men, though you do get the odd woman) that you meet in a casino aren't the most attractive guys in the world, but they're still people and often they're gambling with money they really can't afford to lose. I started to go less and less often, and finally I just stopped. I have enough money in my bank accounts—I don't need to keep stealing.

So as I went around the tables I didn't make much of an effort. I played blackjack, and although the table maximum was a thousand pounds I kept my bets small, winning just enough that I'd be able to resupply Luna if needed. As I did

I kept an eye on her, watching through the crowd. She'd gravitated to the roulette tables and occasionally I'd see the silver mist of her curse drift outwards to touch the wheel. I could tell she was doing something, though I wasn't sure what. When the table she was playing at broke up I went to join her at the bar. "How's it going?" I asked as she ordered.

"Badly."

"How much did you lose?"

"I don't want to know," Luna said gloomily. "About half."

"Get anywhere?"

"Well, every time I sit down at a table, everyone seems to start losing," Luna said. "The wheel on that last one just came up zero three times in a row. Does that count?"

The bartender came back with Luna's drink and she took a sip, turning to look out over the casino floor. I gave her a glance as she did. She was wearing a yellow-gold dress that set off her pale skin, and she had her hair loose around her shoulders instead of in the bunches that she'd used when I'd first known her. It made her look older, more like an adult. She was annoyed, but it was a positive sort of annoyance, the kind where you're trying to solve a problem. Luna's come a long way since the day she first walked into my shop. "You look good," I said. "The dress Arachne's?"

"Oh, thanks," Luna said, looking pleased. "It's the outfit she was showing me in the spring. She did some alterations for me."

"What kind?"

"The shoes are flat, see?" Luna said, lifting a foot to demonstrate. "And the way the skirt is cut lets me run in it. The purse has got a pouch for my whip, and it's roomy enough for that pocket kit you gave me."

I blinked at Luna. "Well, points for being prepared, but what exactly did you think we'd be doing tonight?"

"I have no idea. I'm just going to be ready for when the fight starts this time."

"There's not going to be a fight. We're just here to play."

Luna gave me an extremely sceptical look. "I'm serious," I said.

"Uh-huh," Luna said. "How many magic items are you carrying again?"

"Nothing much."

"Like?"

"Just a few condensers," I said. "And a feather ring and a decoy. Oh, and some glitterdust. And my gate stones, but I always carry those. I guess one or two others. Maybe three or four."

Luna just looked at me. "What?" I said. "Most of them aren't even for combat."

"And you wonder where I'm getting this from."

I shook my head. "Whatever makes you happy. I'll be in the poker room."

⁞ ⁞ ⁞ ⁞ ⁞

To reach the poker room I had to go through a tunnel of slot machines, their lights blinking blue-yellow-white, but the poker room itself was quieter. A steady murmur of conversation blended with the rustle of cards and the clink of chips, and cheesy eighties music played at a low volume over the speakers. I found a seat at a table and joined in.

Poker's a mixture of probability and psychology, and it's probably my favourite of the card games. Although there are rules on what hand beats what, poker isn't actually a game of who's got the best hand—it's a game of wagering based on incomplete information. If you have complete information (such as by oh, say, divination), then there's no challenge. So as I started playing I deliberately *didn't* look into the future to see what hands everyone else had. It spoils the fun, and it's harder for me to justify to my conscience. In games like blackjack and roulette you're playing against the house, but in poker you're playing against the other customers of the casino.

An hour or so passed and I settled into the game, slipping

into that particular mental zone of focus. New players came; old players left. Luna didn't call, which I took as a good sign.

The player opposite me at the table, a balding business-man with a round face, went all in against the scruffy-looking guy to my right. His two pair met a straight. The businessman banged the table, swore in Cantonese, and left. A few minutes later he was replaced by a kid.

I was the blind on the next hand. The kid raised high, and I folded. Next hand I was dealer. The kid checked, I raised, he reraised, and I folded again. I folded the next few hands, and the kid did the same. Next round I was dealt a pair of queens. I raised, the kid reraised, and I matched him. He called my raises all the way to the river and showed a middle pair. I got back what I'd lost from the earlier fold and some more besides.

Next round the same thing happened again. The kid kept on raising at me, ignoring everyone else. Sometimes it worked, but he lost more than he won. "Very aggressive," I said as his single ace fell to my top pair. The kid didn't answer.

Two hands later we ended up head-to-head again. "Two players," the dealer said, laying out the flop.

"You know, I'm starting to think you're following me," I said, glancing at the face-up cards. There was a two, a five, and a nine. My ace-five gave me a pair, and I had position.

"So this is how you make your money," the kid said with a faint American accent. He knocked on the table to check.

I gave the kid a sharp glance. "Depends who I'm playing against." He was twenty or so, with messy black hair, and he looked athletic and fit. I threw in a chip.

"Raise of five pounds," the dealer said. He was Austra-lian, with ginger hair and a beard, and his name tag said *BRUCE*. He turned to the kid, who matched the bet without looking. The dealer put out another card. It was another two. The kid checked again.

"Been in the country long?" I said, tossing in more chips. The kid's accent and body language were close to British, but slightly off.

"I've got unfinished business," the kid said. He didn't take his eyes off mine.

"Raise of fifteen pounds," the dealer said to the kid. He matched the bet and the dealer dealt out a final card, a seven.

The kid threw in some chips. "Raise of twenty-seven pounds," the dealer said to me. I thought briefly, then shrugged and matched the bet. The kid flipped over his cards to show an off-suit six and eight.

A ripple of laughter went up around the table. The dealer slid out the five, seven, and nine from the face-up cards. "Straight." He looked at me.

I shook my head and tossed my cards into the discard. "Nice hand."

The dealer pushed the pile of chips to the kid, replenishing his stack. "Tough beat," the guy on my right said.

The Romanian man at the end of the table shook his head. "You were lucky," he told the kid. "The odds were—"

"I don't care about the odds," the kid said, without looking at the man.

The Romanian looked at me and raised his hands in a *what can you do?* gesture. "You don't know who I am, do you?" the kid told me.

"Sorry," I said. "Have we met?"

The kid's eyes flashed with utter fury. It was there for only a moment, but I've seen that look before and it brought me up short. The kid hated me—not just dislike, but bone-deep hatred. He wasn't here to play. He was here for me.

I held quite still, looking around me with my diviner's senses, and felt a chill go down my spine. The room was full of people, but scattered through the crowd were a handful of boys and girls who looked about the same age as the kid in front of me, and they were all watching me. A black girl with a shock of curly dyed-gold hair was glaring at me from the right side of the room, while a boy who looked like he should be on a recruiting poster for the U.S. Army was by the door, watching with folded arms. There was another kid with South American looks standing at my back. He was in position to get me from behind, and as I focused I could feel a faint trace of magic in him, ready to strike.

"You haven't even figured it out, have you?" the kid said. His eyes hadn't left me since he'd sat down.

"Who are you?" I said.

"The name's Will," the kid said.

The dealer had been looking between the two of us. "Hey," he said. "There a problem here?"

The kid—Will—ignored him, keeping his eyes fixed on me. His name sounded familiar, but I had bigger problems to worry about—I was flicking through the futures and I could see that the window for talking was narrowing fast. Will and his friends were about to try to force me to go with them, and if I refused they were going to attack.

"What'll it be, Verus?" Will said.

It didn't surprise me that Will knew my name. "What do you want?"

"I think we should take this outside," Will said, his dark eyes staring into mine.

"Hey," another player said in annoyance. He obviously hadn't figured out what was going on, though from the glances some of the other players were giving they were starting to. "You folding or what?"

"Sir," the dealer said politely. "Let's leave it for after the game, okay?"

I calculated quickly. The boy behind me was a life-drinker, and he was ready to put his lethal touch into my back. I could probably dodge his first strike, but my position was bad. Packed into the middle of the crowd I had little room to move, and anything that missed me would hit the other customers. On top of that, the poker room was a dead end with only one way out. "You know, I think I'm going to take a break," I said.

I tossed a chip to the dealer. "Fold my hands till I get back, okay, Bruce?"

"Thank you, sir," Bruce said, but his eyes were wary. I rose to my feet, keeping my movements slow and easy. Will got up as I started to move, and he and the life-drinker followed me closely out.

Gold-hair girl and Captain America fell in behind them, giving me looks as they did. The girl looked the more aggressive, but I knew both would hesitate before striking. The life-drinker wouldn't. I could sense the spell waiting in his hands, cold and hungry, and I knew he was eager to use it. I mentally moved him above Will on the priority list. I've been life-drained before, and I know exactly how deadly it is.

The slot machine tunnel was wide enough for only one person, and as I walked into it the group behind me were forced into single file. That was better; now the life-drinker was between me and the rest of them. As we approached the stairs to the reception area, the doors to the main casino floor swung open and two boys stepped out. One of them was a skinny Indian kid with square glasses. The other I recognised from last night: it was the one who'd been spying on us. He stopped as he saw me, his eyes going wide.

I halted as well, making the line behind me bunch up. "Will?" the Indian boy said, trying to peer past me. "I wiped the—"

"Dhruv!" the Chinese kid whispered. "That's him!"

The Indian boy froze. "So," I said to the Chinese kid. "I guess this answers the question of who you're working for, huh?"

The life-drinker had been about to push me forward, but now he stopped and gave the Chinese kid a suspicious look. "You talked to him?"

The Chinese kid looked back and forth between me and the life-drinker. "No, uh—"

"Hey," gold-hair girl called from the back. "What's going—"

For just a second the group of them were distracted, and as the girl started to say *on* I whipped my heel up and back, kicking the life-drinker hard and accurately in the crotch. In the same instant I lunged forward off the other leg, sprinting for the two boys ahead of me. Dhruv and the Chinese kid flinched away and I ran between them, slamming through the doors and onto the casino floor.

Shouts came from the corridor behind, but I had a couple of seconds' lead and in combat that's a long time. I had absolutely no intention of fighting if I could avoid it—Will and his friends wanted this fight, and as far as I was concerned that was a good reason to get out of here. I curved around the bar and was just starting to turn towards the stairs when I heard a flurry of footsteps behind me and someone hit me at waist level. We both went tumbling to the carpet, and as I tried to pull myself up I heard a snarl and felt Will hurling himself on top of me with inhuman speed.

I twisted onto my side and got my leg back just in time. I had one glimpse of Will falling towards me, his eyes filled with insane fury, then I kicked up off the floor, my foot catching him in the stomach hard enough to send him flying. He did a funny sort of flip in midair and came down on hands and toes. Gold-hair girl was coming in after him and she was about to throw a fire spell, but before either could line up on me I pulled a crystal from my pocket and crushed it.

Mist surged from between my fingers, a dull grey cloud blanketing the area in an instant. I couldn't see but I heard running steps and I rolled left just in time for Will to miss me, charging blindly through the space in which I'd been. I came to my feet and listened.

Calls and chatter were going up from all around as the casino's inhabitants started to notice what was going on. From outside I knew the mist from the condenser would look like a grey cloud about forty feet wide, spread out over the floor and half of the bar. Will had stumbled back out of the cloud and he and his friends were spreading out to surround it. I could sense magic being channelled: time, space, life, fire. Apprentices or adepts? I guessed adepts.

Will and the others were arguing and seemed reluctant to enter, but even so my position wasn't great. The mist cloud wouldn't last forever and if I made a break for it now I'd be run down in the open. I needed to whittle down the odds. Two steps brought me to the bar and I grabbed a bottle of white rum, lifting it by the neck.

I heard Will's voice raised above the others. "Bev, burn it!" Fire magic surged and the mist flashed orange-red. The chatter of the casino turned into shouts and screams.

The flames had run along the ground, a three-foot wall of fire springing up in a line from the caster. A second wall of fire followed and this one came straight at me. I leapt blindly, warned by my divination magic, and felt heat sting my right side as the fire licked against the bar. Glancing through the futures I saw that it was gold-hair girl. She was trying to burn me out, fill the mist with flames, but neither she nor the life-drinker was facing me and I knew they'd lost my position. Definitely adepts. I started running at gold-hair girl, and as she sent a third blast of ground fire I burst out of the mist into the lights of the casino.

The girl was facing the wrong way and the fire went far to my right; I was already swinging and as she turned, her mouth making a little O of surprise, I smashed the bottle over her head. She stumbled and went to her knees. The life-drinker was next to her, green-black light flickering at his palm, and he had just enough time to take a step towards me before I snapped my other arm out to fling a handful of glittering dust into his face.

One of the reasons I like glitterdust is that no one takes it seriously—people see the pretty sparkles and think it's a joke. They change their mind fast when they get hit by the stuff, but by then it's too late. Glitterdust sticks to whatever it hits and if that dust gets in your eyes you're blind until you can wash it out. The life-drinker yelled and fell backwards, clawing at his eyes, his spell fizzling out as he staggered blindly into a chair and went over.

My precognition shrilled a warning and I jumped forward, hearing a hiss as something cut the air behind me. I caught my balance and spun, glimpsing in that moment that a space was opening up as the casino players scrambled hurriedly away. Captain America was facing me with his eyes set and he was holding a sword, a long-handled katana which he was just bringing back after missing with the first slash. I grabbed a chair and as he swung again I blocked it, closing on his outside, but as I did I saw Will come racing around holding a sword of his own and I changed direction to dive back into the cloud.

The temperature inside the mist was higher now, and I could see a fuzzy glow from the bar; the fire was spreading. With my magic I knew the adepts had congregated again. The life-drinker was still blind, but the fire girl had gotten up and I bit back a curse. She was about to send that ground fire into my hiding place again. The fire was already starting to burn away the mist and I didn't want to be around when it reached the spirits in the bar. *Where the hell did they get those swords?*

The casino was in chaos, men pushing and shoving to get away as the crowd began to panic, the dealers and arriving security trying to maintain order and get out the fire extinguishers. The adepts were between me and the exit, and as the next burst of fire came racing into the mist I vaulted the bar and ran out the other side of the cloud, heading for the stairs up to the balcony.

I was almost at the stairs when I heard the shout and knew that the adepts were chasing me again. I should have been able to outpace them, but as I reached the top I heard a hiss from behind me and had to throw myself into a roll to dodge another slash. I came to my feet to face Will.

He was moving fast, much too fast, and as I focused on him I could sense the aura of time magic accelerating his movements. He was wielding a battered-looking shortsword and he came at me hard, slashing and stabbing. If he'd been moving at normal speed I might have managed a disarm but he was so quick that all I could do was keep backing away. I caught up a drink from a table and threw it at Will's face, glass and all. He ducked under it and I took the moment's breather to put the table between us. "What the hell is your problem?" I snapped at him.

Will slashed at me and I shoved the table into him, making his stroke fall short. "Who are you?" I said. "What do you even want?"

"Shut up," Will said. He was breathing fast; spots of colour rode in his cheeks and his eyes were burning.

"I've never seen you before!" I shouted. Inwardly I was trying to figure out how the hell to throw off this band of crazies. I didn't have anything fast enough to hit this guy, but the fire downstairs was spreading, casino security was rushing around, and someone must have called the police by now. The longer I could keep him talking, the more pressure there'd be for his team to pull out.

Will snarled. "You don't even *remember*?"

"Remember *what*?"

"No!" Will shouted back. "I won't let you forget! I want you to know why before I kill you!"

"You're out of your mind," I said in disbelief. Another one of them was working his way around behind me, and I put my back against the glass balustrade, my hand on the railing. The drop to the casino floor was fifteen feet and there was a table beneath.

"Sedona, Arizona!" Will shouted over the chaos of the casino. "Eleven years ago! I was there and so were you!"

"I don't—" I started to say, then froze, meeting Will's gaze. His eyes were dark and wide, filled with rage . . . and familiar. A horrible fear shot through me. *Oh no. It can't be. Please tell me it's not—*

"My name is Will Traviss," Will said through clenched

teeth. "You." He drew his sword back. "Killed." His other hand came down on the table. "My." His head went down and he tensed. *"Sister!"* He came over the table in a rush.

My thoughts were frozen but instinct sent me backwards over the railing, the sword stroke going over my head. I caught the edge of the balcony and then swung and dropped, hitting the table and rolling to land in a crouch on the casino floor. Will was right behind, splintering the table as he came after me.

I fought on reflex, still half stunned, trying to get away. From around me I caught fleeting glimpses of the chaos: fire licking across the bar, security men abandoning their extinguishers and running, two players scrabbling for chips at an overturned table. One security man grabbed Captain America as he came charging into the fight again and the American kid snapped an elbow into the man's face, sending him staggering back with blood spurting from his nose. Gold-hair girl sent ground fire roaring out and Captain America tried to flank me, but it was Will who was the most dangerous, his sword a flickering blur. I couldn't spare the half second to grab a weapon or stun them, and all I could do was keep dodging and backing away.

The futures were lines of light in my vision, the paths in which I was safe glowing against the dull background of the futures in which I fell. There was no time for thought, only reflex. Slip the thrust, dodge right so that the ground fire would block Captain America, come up to face Will again. The futures in which I was safe shifted, twisted, and with a sudden chill I saw that they were growing fewer. Only a dozen now, and attacks were starting to get through. Will's sword opened a gash along my forearm, and as I jumped away from the next slash ground fire scorched my leg. Only five safe futures. I tried to break past Captain America but metal projectiles cut the air, forcing me back.

Four safe futures. I got Captain America between me and Will, but before I could exploit it the girl sent another burst of ground fire that pushed me out of position. Two safe futures. I ducked under Will's slash and hit him shoulder first, coming up to take another cut on the arm, sliding back just far enough to avoid a fatal blow. One safe future and there were no choices at all now, just a single razor-thin path through the whirl of flame and blades. Feint at the girl, jump back. One safe future. Dodge the spray, duck the sword. Fire all over the casino. Still one safe future. Deflect, stabbing pain as metal cut skin. Twist and weave. One safe future.

One safe future—

One safe future—

No safe futures.

I had just time to think *Oh*, then Will's sword rammed through my gut.

It felt like a murderously hard punch. The impact came first and I lost my breath in a gasp, then an instant later agony ripped through my lower body. I tried to scream but my lungs were empty. Another blow hit me from behind and I was driven downwards, the sword grating on bone as the impact pushed me off the blade, and the second wave of pain was so horrendous that my vision greyed out.

When I came to I was on the floor. My lower body hurt with a hideous pain, every movement sending waves of agony spidering outwards. I could hear the crackle of flames and smell smoke on the air. "—cameras are still blind," someone was saying.

"Lee," Will said. "Lee!"

"Huh?" It was the Chinese kid's voice, somewhere close.

"Get him out of here."

"What about him?" another voice said. It was the Indian boy.

My vision cleared enough to make out people standing above me: Will, gold-hair girl, Captain America. They turned to look down at me. "He's still alive," the girl said, sounding surprised.

Will gave me a glance and looked away. The Indian boy

appeared in my line of sight, pushing his glasses up to peer down at me. An expression of nausea crossed his face as he saw my lower body. "We could take him—" he began.

"No," Will said without looking.

"He's the only lead we've got to Rachel."

"No," Will said again. He flicked the sword and I saw drops of liquid—my blood—fly away. "We finish it." He turned back towards me, meeting my eyes. His face was set and cold, and in a sudden flash of insight I knew it was the same expression I'd worn in the past, when I made the decision to kill. Will took a step forward.

Running footsteps sounded from my left and a strand of silver mist wrapped around Will, soaking into his body. Will jumped back in surprise, his sword coming up into a defensive guard. An instant later a girl skidded to a halt in front of me, putting herself between me and him.

The girl was Luna. The gold dress hung lightly off her, not hindering her movements, and the silver mist of her curse spread out around her, tendrils lashing outwards and curving away from me. In her right hand she held a tapered wand, fifteen inches long and ivory-coloured with a sphere set at the base. From the tip a strand of silver mist emerged, growing from the wand to form an invisible whip, and as I watched in a daze she levelled it at Will. Her voice shook a little, but her hand was steady. "Get away from him, you bastard."

Gold-hair girl and Captain America looked at each other in confusion, then at their leader. "Will?" Captain America said.

"Who's she?" gold-hair girl said.

Will hesitated, then shook his head. "It doesn't matter." But he didn't seem as certain anymore. "Move," he told Luna.

"Make me," Luna said.

Will pointed his sword at Luna. "I don't want to hurt you."

Luna laughed. Tension vibrated through her voice but

her stance didn't waver. "Trust me, you *really* don't want to get close enough to stick me with that."

Will hesitated again, and I could see the silver glow of Luna's curse clinging to him. My heart was in my throat: half hope, half fear. "Bev," Will said, gesturing at me. "Fry him and let's go."

The gold-haired girl hesitated, looking from Luna to me, then shook her head. She threw out an arm and ground fire roared out, racing towards me.

Luna stepped between us and her whip lashed out to meet the attack head-on. Silver mist tore into the fire, eradicated it, and the ground fire sputtered to a halt in a flash of light. Gold-hair girl stared at Luna in confusion, trying to understand where her spell had gone.

Luna pivoted smoothly and brought her whip around for the backswing, the strand leaping out eagerly to wrap around the other girl. Luna's curse is invisible to anyone who doesn't know exactly what to look for; to Will and the others, she would just look like a girl waving a wand. "What are you doing?" Will demanded. "Finish him!"

Gold-hair girl tried again, and this time she put more power into the spell. Luna's whip was already moving and the fire didn't make it even halfway before the strand hit it. The silver mist simply erased the spell, destroying the magic before it could reach her. Again Luna's backswing hit the girl, the silver aura around her growing.

Fire was spreading all around the room, and the heat and smoke was making it hard to breathe. We were the only ones left on the casino floor; everyone else had fled. I desperately wanted to help but it was all I could do to stay conscious.

"Screw this," Will said angrily, striding forward towards Luna, sword ready. He tried to grab Luna and throw her aside, but she twisted and shoved him back, the silver mist surging gleefully into Will as he entered the lethal danger zone of Luna's curse. The gold-haired girl aimed at me again, and she looked pissed off. Fire ignited as she cast her spell.

I felt the snap as Luna's curse took hold. The ground fire twisted, missing badly. Instead of burning me it homed in on Will, the wall of flame engulfing his legs.

Will screamed and jumped back, shoes and trousers alight. He hit the floor, flailing desperately to put the fire out. The Indian boy rushed to help, and gold-hair girl stared from him to Luna in horror. For an instant she was frozen, and so she was standing still when half the bar exploded with a roar and a *thump* that sent a heavy bottle flying with laser-guided precision into the side of her head. There was a thud of glass on bone and she dropped like a rock.

Captain America darted to the girl's side. Luna stood on the balls of her feet, whip poised, ready to strike again. Will came up, legs charred and smoking, eyes crazed with pain. From outside I could hear the wail of sirens, growing louder. "Will!" Captain America shouted, hoisting the girl; he staggered as he did. "Time to go!"

"No!" Will shouted. "He's right there!" He started towards us but stopped almost instantly; the fire was still burning, forming a wall of flame between him and us.

"Will, it's *time to go!*" the Indian boy shouted. He grabbed the taller boy, dragging him away. Captain America was already on his way out, sprinting with the girl in his arms without giving us a backwards glance. Will fought the Indian boy for a second, then snarled at me from across the flames and turned and ran.

Luna's eyes tracked them all the way out, then as they disappeared from sight she sagged in relief, stumbling and then coughing from the smoke. She looked at me and flinched as her eyes reached my stomach. "Oh crap. Alex? Alex, can you hear me?"

The sirens were right outside the casino. Luna fumbled a handkerchief from her bag and held it over her nose and mouth, looking from side to side. The whole far end of the room was in flames and the fire was getting closer. "Shit, shit, shit," Luna said to herself. "Look, you're going to be okay, all right? I just need to move you . . . but I can't . . . oh crap. Uh—"

Don't need to move, I thought dizzily. *Sixty seconds and the firemen'll be here. Call and it'll be forty-five,* I wanted to tell her but couldn't manage speaking. The pain was getting worse, and I was vaguely aware I was going into shock.

"Help!" Luna shouted. She crouched down near me, eyes searching through the flame and smoke. "Is anybody there? We're in here!"

First the crackle of flames, then I heard thudding footsteps. "Help!" Luna shouted. "Over here!"

Men appeared out of the smoke, thick helmets with lowered visors making them look like stormtroopers. They wore the yellow-and-blue of the London fire brigade. "He's been hurt!" Luna said, coughing and backing away as they closed on us. "You need to—"

The fireman at the front said something that was too muffled through his helmet to hear. Luna shook her head, watching helplessly. Two of the firemen positioned themselves on either side of me. I knew they were about to lift me up and I knew that the pain would be unbelievable. I tried to tell them, but I don't think they heard me. I heard the firemen counting and felt gloved hands on me, then they lifted me in a well-rehearsed surge.

My magic was as accurate as ever and the pain was exactly as horrendous as I'd predicted. The only mercy was that I was aware of it for only a few seconds before everything went black.

chapter 4

I drifted, and I dreamed.

Old memories flitted through my mind, familiar faces and ones half forgotten: Rachel, Shireen, Arachne, Helikaon, Richard. From time to time I heard voices that weren't my own, distant murmurs fading in and out of hearing, but I couldn't make out the words. Eventually the voices went away and I fell into a deeper dream, one that was less a dream than a memory. I knew that it wasn't real, that I was seeing the past and not the present, but somehow it didn't seem to matter and I watched quietly without trying to wake. The colours were vibrant, the sounds crisp and clear, as if I were experiencing it for the first time.

The scene was a desert, islands of red rock rising into bumpy hills. The hills were barren but greenery covered the lower levels, bushes and stubby trees growing in defiance of the heat. The sun was setting, casting long shadows across the empty land, and the sky above was a fantastic glow of red and yellow and blue. A vehicle bounced across the rocky ground in a plume of dust, the only sign of human life for miles. As it drew near one of the hills it slowed and stopped. Four people got out.

They were young, no more than nineteen or twenty, and wore the clothes of city dwellers. The first out was a girl, small and slight, with short dark-red hair and impatient movements. She looked from side to side at the emptiness all around and turned back to the car. "Well?"

The boy she was talking to was her age, taller than her but without her quick confidence. His hair was black and untidy, messed with the dust of travel. He looked familiar, and so he should: he was me from eleven years ago. He didn't answer the girl, looking towards the hill and frowning.

"Alex!" the girl demanded. Her name was Shireen. "Today?"

"All right! Give me a minute."

Another girl—Rachel—had left the car, moving to stand next to Shireen. She was pretty, with deep blue eyes that gave her a thoughtful look, and she grimaced at the dust, waving a hand to try to get it away from her clothes and hair. "Is this the right place?"

Shireen shrugged. "That's what I want to know." She glanced at the other boy, then folded her arms with poor grace and waited.

The dust thrown up by the car settled. The desert throbbed with heat, the air burning hot from the long day, but neither Shireen nor the other boy seemed to notice. "Why would anyone live out here?" Rachel asked, looking around at the barren landscape with revulsion.

"Hiding from us," Shireen said.

Rachel frowned. "Why does Richard want this girl, anyway?"

Shireen shrugged again. Rachel fell silent.

Minutes passed, then my younger self stirred. "They're there."

Everyone turned to look. "You're sure?" Shireen said.

"Of course I'm sure," my younger self said. He pointed

at the hill of red sandstone ahead. "That hill's got a canyon through it, with an opening at the centre. That's where they are. They've got a camp in the middle."

"Finally," Shireen said, and walked back to the car.

My younger self frowned at her. "What are you doing? We can't drive, they'll hear us."

"How many are there?" Rachel said.

"Just two. A boy and a girl."

"Wasn't there supposed to be a third one? A little kid?"

My younger self shrugged. "Might be. It's hard to see from this distance."

There was a laugh from the fourth member of the party. "Only here for one thing and you can't even do that."

My younger self turned, scowling, to look at the boy who'd been leaning against the car. Tobruk was tall and good-looking, with muscles that showed through his T-shirt. His origin was hard to place; he could have passed for West Indian, African, Middle Eastern, or a mix of all three. He grinned a lot, and he was grinning now. "What's your problem?" my younger self said.

Tobruk's grin didn't slip. "Don't fucking talk back to me, Alex."

"Hey," Shireen said, her voice sharp. "Quit it."

"You're not in charge," Rachel told Tobruk. "Stop acting like it."

Tobruk gave Rachel a lazy look. He didn't move but there was something considering in his gaze, and Rachel shied away. Shireen shook her head in disgust. "Boys," she muttered, then looked at my younger self. "Which way to the other entrance?"

My younger self took his eyes from Tobruk with a start and pointed. Shireen gave a nod. "We'll go round the other side. You stay here and make sure they don't get out this way." She gave the two of them a pitying look. "Try not to screw it up." She left, and Rachel followed.

Tobruk watched them go. My younger self did too, then

looked at Tobruk. Tobruk showed his teeth in a grin. My younger self looked away. Rachel and Shireen disappeared into the trees. Tobruk leant back against the car and appeared to go to sleep.

Ten minutes passed. The sun dipped towards the horizon and the shadows lengthened. Tobruk opened his eyes, stretched, and began ambling towards the canyon entrance. "Where are you going?" my younger self said.

"Coming?" Tobruk said over his shoulder.

"Shireen said . . ."

"You always do as you're told?" Tobruk said, sounding bored.

My younger self hesitated, looking after Shireen and Rachel, and then hurried after Tobruk. The entrance was visible in the sunset, the western edge casting a tall shadow against the rock. "Aren't they expecting us to stay back there?" my younger self said.

Tobruk shook his head. "You are such a pussy."

My younger self looked away angrily, and Tobruk gave him a pitying look. "You don't have a clue why Richard sent us, do you?"

"He wants the girl."

"So why doesn't he do it himself?"

My younger self shrugged. "We're apprentices. They get us to do their work."

Tobruk gave a wave as if acknowledging the point. "He wants us to prove ourselves, see? Show what we can do."

My younger self gave Tobruk a puzzled look and Tobruk laughed, slinging an arm around his shoulders. "You're so cute. Stick with me, huh? I'll take care of you." His grip tightened. "Till Richard doesn't want you."

My younger self struggled to get out of Tobruk's grip. Tobruk held on for a few seconds, just to prove he could, then let go. My younger self backed off, rubbing his neck and glaring at Tobruk. Tobruk didn't look back but instead walked into the canyon, passing out of the light and into the shadow as he picked his way between the rocks. After a few seconds my younger self followed.

"So what?" my younger self said after a minute. The canyon entrance was narrowing behind them as they went deeper. "You want to be the one to bring her in?"

Tobruk shrugged. "Why do you want to be there?" my younger self asked.

"'Cause I'm fucking tired of driving you round the desert," Tobruk said. "Those bitches are going to screw it up. They don't have the balls to finish it and the girl's going to go running off and I'll have to find her again."

"They . . ." My younger self paused. "Wait, what do you mean, 'finish it'?"

"He just wants the girl, right?"

My younger self stared at him. Tobruk shot a grin over his shoulder. "Losing your nerve?"

My younger self stopped. Tobruk didn't, and my younger self had to hurry to catch up. "It's not that . . ." he began. "Look, I don't think we—"

"Out in the desert where no one'll see," Tobruk said. He sounded bored again. "That's what you said, right? This was your idea."

"But . . ." My younger self's face was uncertain. "We don't have to do this."

"So?"

"I mean, we don't have to do it *this* way. We could—I don't know. Knock him out or something."

Tobruk turned to look at my younger self, eyebrows raised. "So?"

My younger self hesitated.

Tobruk shook his head. "Just shut up and stay out of the way."

The two of them kept going, and the canyon began to widen. Above, the sky was darkening from blue to purple, the strands of cloud glowing yellow-red. "I think—" my younger self started to say, and as he did the *crack* of a gunshot came from up ahead, the sound echoing around the canyon walls. Tobruk broke into a sprint and after a moment my younger self followed. The canyon twisted left and right, then opened out.

The centre of the hill was hollow and open to the sky, creating a sheltered bowl of enclosed ground hidden from outside eyes. The trees and bushes were denser here and there was even a little grass marking some kind of water source. An old beat-up car was parked in the shade, and two tents had been pitched under the trees, one taller and sized for two, the other only big enough for a child. Birds had been roosting in the trees but now were fleeing from the sound of the shot, flying up over the edge of the rocks and disappearing from sight.

Shireen and Rachel were near the tents, blue-red light flickering in front of them. They were shoulder to shoulder and Rachel was holding a water shield in a hemisphere angled to protect them both, the blue glow weak but holding steady. Shireen's hand was wreathed in orange-red and she was pointing it at the boy ahead of them.

The boy was maybe sixteen or seventeen; he was pointing a gun at Shireen, and he was obviously way out of his depth. He was shouting at Shireen and she was shouting back, their voices overlapping. A girl was a little way behind the boy, standing at the edge of the tents; she had long brown hair and looked afraid. Tobruk and my younger self were behind them but still some distance away and Tobruk kept running, moving with a long, loping stride that made surprisingly little noise.

"Drop it!" Shireen was shouting at the boy.

"Don't move!" the boy shouted back. He half-turned his head, trying to watch Shireen and the girl at the same time. "Cath, run!"

"What about you?" the girl shouted.

"I said drop it!" Shireen shouted again.

"Don't come any closer!" the boy shouted. "Cath, get out, please!"

"You too! Come on!"

Rachel saw Tobruk and my younger self coming up behind the boy and flicked her eyes quickly back, keeping the shield steady. Shireen made a frustrated sound. The spell hovering at her hand was an incineration burst but she didn't strike. "We just want her!" Shireen said. "Put the gun—"

Tobruk hadn't stopped or slowed. As Shireen started to say *down*, Tobruk sent a blast of red fire into the boy's back.

The boy screamed, twisting, his body and arm alight. Tobruk hit him again, the jet of flame engulfing the boy's body, and he hit the ground, flailing desperately, trying to put out the fire. The girl's eyes went wide in horror and she ran forward. "Matt!"

Tobruk closed his fingers into a fist and the fire that was licking at the boy's body flared up, turning an ugly dark-red. It intensified, burning hotter and fiercer, clinging to him and eating into his flesh. The boy's shrieks became ear-piercing, horrible, an animal sound. The girl had been trying to beat out the flames but they scorched her, driving her back as the shape within the fire writhed and blackened.

The shrieks cut off abruptly. The flames crackled a moment longer, then Tobruk relaxed his hand and they guttered and died. Where the boy had been was a charred, shapeless mass, glowing with heat. The smell was hideous, thick and putrid and sweet. Smoke rose into the air.

"Matt!" the girl screamed. She fell to her knees by the smoking corpse, shaking her head, tears starting to leak from her eyes. "Matt, oh God, no. No, no, no—"

Shireen and Rachel were staring at the corpse and so was my younger self, all three of them frozen. Tobruk walked forward and grabbed the girl by the hair, dragging her away. She screamed and wept and fought, trying to get back to the body, as Tobruk shoved her to the ground. "Little help?" Tobruk called.

No one else moved. Tobruk got an arm around the girl's neck and began choking her. She fought desperately, trying to break free.

"Tobruk?" Shireen said. She'd recovered first and stared between him and the body. "What the hell?"

"You going to give me a hand?" Tobruk said.

"You—" Shireen drew in a breath. "You fucking psycho! What the *hell*?"

"This really the time?" Tobruk said. The girl's face was going red, her eyes bulging as Tobruk squeezed tighter.

"You're killing her!" Rachel said.

The girl gave a final spasm and went limp, slumping. "Chill," Tobruk said. He flipped her over onto her front and pulled a length of cord from his pocket, tying her hands.

"You didn't have to kill him!" Shireen shouted. "We didn't have to do this!"

"You all going to say that?"

"We just wanted the girl! We didn't have to—"

Tobruk looked up at Shireen and she flinched, stepping back. "No loose ends," Tobruk said. "Remember?"

Shireen hesitated. "That's not what—"

"How'd you think this was going to go?" Tobruk said. He finished binding the girl and stood, getting a grip and lifting her in a fireman's carry, then started walking back towards the canyon. "I'm done here," he said without looking back. "You want to stick around, you can walk."

Shireen gave a final look at the corpse, then hurried after Tobruk. She caught up to him near the mouth of the canyon and began arguing as she paced him, her voice fading into echoes as they both disappeared behind the rocks. Rachel and my younger self didn't move, staring at the remains. My younger self turned to look at her and eventually she met his gaze. For a long moment they stared at each other, some kind of strange communication passing between them, then Rachel looked away and followed Shireen.

My younger self was left alone. He stared at the remains for a long time until a sound made him look around. The campsite was silent. He turned, stumbling, and broke into a run towards the canyon. Above, the sky was darkening and the first birds were beginning to circle, drawn to the carrion below.

⁙⁙⁙⁙⁙

I swam up to consciousness slowly. As my senses returned one at a time, I became gradually aware of my surroundings: warm air, echoes in the distance, the presence of magic. I felt the touch of soft hands on my body, running from my stomach to my chest, and heard the rustle of movement. It was all very peaceful and I lay back, enjoying the sensations. Only after a few minutes did I open my eyes.

I was lying on a raised bed in a small cave. Soft light glowed from orbs set into the walls, casting a dim glow over the room. The cave had been stacked with rolls of fabric and bolts of cloth, but they'd been pushed to the far side to leave a clear space around the bed. The air was warm and dry.

Anne was sitting next to me. Her clothes were rumpled and her grey blouse was marked with dark stains that looked like dried blood, but her posture was alert and her hand was resting on my arm. Her face was more drawn than I remembered, and her red-brown eyes were watching me. "Alex?" she said in her soft voice.

I just looked at her. Somehow, I'd never noticed before just how beautiful Anne was. After the pain and violence of the battle in the casino, and the death and ugliness of the dream, she was something gentle and beautiful, and I lay quietly, taking in the sight.

"Alex?" Anne said again. Her hand tightened on my arm, just slightly. "Can you hear me?"

"I'm—" My voice came out as a rasp, and I had to stop and swallow. "Yeah."

Anne's eyes filled with tears and she turned away. I looked at her, puzzled. "Why are you crying?"

Anne's voice was muffled. "Why do you *think*?" She paused a second then turned back, eyes still red but set in concentration. She touched her hand to my forehead, chest, stomach, and I felt the stir of magic against my bare skin as she spoke under her breath. "Brain activity is okay, respiration is okay, blood pressure . . ." She chewed her lip. "Still low . . . Do you think you can manage drinking?"

Now that I thought about it, I was really thirsty. "Yeah."

"Just a little," Anne warned me as she held a straw to my lips. I sucked it down greedily and was disappointed when she pulled it away.

"Hey," I said weakly.

"I don't want to test the mend to your stomach," Anne said. "I wouldn't give you anything at all unless I had to . . . You can have some more in an hour."

I lay quietly for a little while. I wasn't wearing anything except my underwear and the bedclothes had been drawn back to expose my chest, but that didn't really feel all that important right now. "We're in Arachne's cave, right?"

Anne nodded.

"Who else is here?"

"Luna's sleeping through there." Anne nodded at a solid wall. She smiled slightly, wiping away the last traces of tears. "She's going to be angry she wasn't here to see you wake up. She stayed up all night while I was working."

"All night?" I glanced at the cave. "How long was I out?"

"Sixteen hours," Anne said. "I could have woken you earlier, but you needed the rest." She looked out into the cavern. "Arachne's in the cavern, and Variam and Sonder are getting supplies. I asked for some stuff from the flat and the market."

"You've been up all night?" I asked. Casting spells for

that long takes it out of you, especially on top of lack of sleep.

Anne shook her head. "There are biochemical processes that keep you awake. I can go a lot longer than this."

I glanced at her clothes. "Uh, how did you get those bloodstains?"

Anne looked at me with eyebrows raised. "They're yours."

"Oh."

I was quiet for a little while as Anne continued to check over me. "How close was I . . ." I said. I didn't add *to dying*, but the words hung in the air.

Anne didn't meet my eyes, but her hand tightened on my wrist for an instant before moving to the side of my neck. "You don't want to know."

"So remember when you told me that it felt like you didn't need to worry about me so much? I guess I kind of screwed that up, didn't I?"

Anne gave something between a laugh and a sob and dropped her head, her hair brushing my chest. "Don't . . ." She drew a breath and looked up at me. "Don't do anything like this again. Please."

I smiled. "I'll work on that."

Footsteps sounded from the tunnel, and Anne straightened as Luna walked in. She'd changed clothes at some point during the night and was wearing something less eye-catching. "Hey!" she said cheerfully as she saw me. "You're up!"

"You don't sound too surprised."

"Well, yeah," Luna said. "You had Anne with you." She pulled up a chair, keeping her distance. The silver mist of her curse curled around her at the edge of my vision, marking the boundary beyond which she couldn't safely approach. "So how's it feel to be back from the dead?"

"A lot better than the alternative," I said. I felt tired and fragile, but there was no pain and I could talk. Anne's good at what she does. I glanced between the two of them. "What did I miss?"

Anne looked at Luna. "Well," Luna said, settling back into her chair. "You remember the firemen picking you up?"

"Not much else, but yeah."

"They got you out the front door. They were bringing the hoses in and there was smoke everywhere. It was packed outside and I was worried those guys might still be around, so I stuck next to you and called Anne and Vari and told them to get moving. Then the police started setting up barriers and the ambulance showed up and the medics got to you. I was on the phone to Anne and she was giving me advice on what to do and she told me to let them treat you until she got there. They put you in the ambulance and I got them to take me too and they took us to the hospital." Luna stopped.

I thought for a second, trying to figure it out. "The hospital?"

"Yeah."

"Did they . . . discharge me or something?"

"Ah . . ." Luna said. "Not exactly."

I looked around at the walls of Arachne's cave, puzzled. "Then how did I end up here?"

"Anne said not to tell you about that until 'you're better."

I looked from Luna to Anne, eyebrows raised. "Let's just say we're lucky that Vari looks good in a uniform," Luna added.

"Luna!" Anne said.

"Sorry."

I sighed and laid my head back. "You know what, I don't want to know."

"So did you see me against those guys?" Luna said. "Did you catch the bit where I blocked that fire wall with my whip?"

"From my angle it was kind of hard to miss."

"Good! I was worried you were too far gone to see it."

"I'm glad you've got your priorities straight," I said dryly.

"So I saved your life back there," Luna said, ignoring my comment. "Didn't I?"

"Yes."

"I mean, really saved your life. You would have died if I hadn't been there, right?"

"Yes."

"You looked really helpless when you were on the floor like that. You were just lying there sprawled out and—"

"Is there somewhere you're going with this?"

"So now do I get to be the master and you have to do what I say?"

I glared at her. "No!"

"Well, you know, maybe you're slowing down with age. Do you think I should start being your bodyguard?"

"You're going to have to work on your coverage if you're planning to take that up," I said. "Where were you while I was fighting anyway?"

"I was in the bathroom."

"Right. If I ever get killed when you're supposed to be protecting me, that'll make a great explanation."

"So do you think any of the security cameras got the fight?" Luna said. "Because if they did I could show it to Vari and the others at duelling class."

I couldn't help laughing, and Luna grinned too. "So," she said, becoming serious, "who were they?"

My smile faded. "That's . . . a long story." Talking with Anne and Luna had let me briefly forget everything from last night, but now it suddenly came back again.

The silence stretched out, and Anne and Luna looked at each other. "Well, I guess it can wait," Luna suggested.

"I'll tell you," I said. "Just . . . I don't really want to tell this story more than once."

"We'll wait until Vari and Sonder are back," Anne said. "In the meantime, you should rest." She gave Luna a glance.

Luna nodded and rose. "I'll tell them." She paused at the tunnel leading out, one hand on the rock wall. "Alex? Glad you're okay." She disappeared.

ı ı ı ı ı ı ı ı ı

"You've gotten careless," Arachne told me.

"I know," I said with a sigh. "Things have been quiet lately."

"Not that quiet."

"Okay, not that quiet. But the last few months it's been the subtle sort of trouble, you know? It's been politics I've been worried about, not assassins going after me right in the middle of a bloody casino."

Arachne is about the size of a rhino and much taller, eight hairy legs running up to a black arachnid body highlighted in cobalt blue. Eight black eyes are clustered above a set of fangs that wouldn't look out of place on a sabre-toothed tiger, and she can scuttle at lightning speed. One glance at her would make most people would run screaming, but I have exactly the opposite reaction and I prefer Arachne's company to pretty much anyone else's. I was glad Luna and Anne and Variam had brought me here; it was probably the safest place they could have picked.

Arachne's lair is under Hampstead Heath. The entrance tunnel is hidden beneath an old tree and leads down into a huge circular cavern hung with a dazzling rainbow of clothes and fabrics. The walls, floor, and ceiling are stone, worn smooth from centuries of use except for a jagged patch around one of the side caves that marks the spot where someone was inconsiderate enough to set off some explosives last year. Anne had helped me into a robe and escorted me into the main chamber, and I was resting on a sofa, talking to Arachne as she sewed on her workbench. Anne was sitting quietly by the main entrance, and Luna had gone out to make a call.

"I still can't believe they attacked me out in the open like that," I said. "It seems crazy."

"From the sound of it this boy doesn't seem to care very much about risks."

"I guess that's it, isn't it?" I said. "I've gotten used to dealing with professionals. They wouldn't take a risk like that; they're predictable. It's the bloody amateurs you have to watch out for."

"Well, just in case you run into any more amateurs, I think you ought to wear something a little more protective," Arachne said. Arachne's voice has a clicking rustle to it, not quite loud enough to be obtrusive but enough to remind you it's there. "I've been telling you that for months."

"Yeah, yeah. You were right, I was wrong."

"I hope this'll teach you a little more humility at least."

"Look, I've already got Luna giving me grief me over this. I don't need it from you too."

"It's good to be reminded of one's mortality from time to time." Arachne can't smile, but her voice sounded amused. "Though perhaps in future you could find a slightly less extreme way of doing it."

Voices echoed down the tunnel and Variam and Sonder arrived, walking down with Luna in the lead. As soon as Variam and Sonder saw me they wanted to know if I was all right, and it took me a while to convince them that I was, which led in turn to Luna giving Variam and Sonder another retelling of her version of the fight in the casino.

By the time it was done we were sitting in a rough circle on Arachne's sofas, while Arachne worked quietly off to one side. "So," Variam said. "Who are these guys and how do we get rid of them?"

"I might have found out something about that," Sonder said unexpectedly. "I was asking around and there's this new group showing up among the adepts."

Adepts are the next step down from mages on the power scale; they can use magic but only in one very specific way. A time mage like Sonder can speed time up, slow it down, look into the past, and even do really weird stuff like kicking something out of the timeline entirely, at least in theory. A time adept can only do one of those things—they have one spell they can use, and that's it. They don't get the best treatment from mages and a lot of them carry a fair bit of resentment as a result. "They're supposed to be some kind of vigilantes?" Sonder said. "Or they've been getting into fights, anyway. I don't know if they're the same people, though—the ones I heard about are supposed to only have a problem with Dark mages."

"What makes you think they're not the same ones?" I said dryly.

"But you're not . . ." Sonder began, then trailed off. "Oh."

"What sort of fights?" Luna asked.

"I think they're supposed to be pro-adept?" Sonder said. "They attacked some Dark mage in Bristol a while back."

Variam shot Luna a glance, frowning. "If they're so pro-adept, how come they were after you?"

Luna shrugged. "They weren't, they were after Alex. I just got in the way."

"Okay . . ." Variam said doubtfully, looking at me.

I hesitated, on the edge of speaking. It would be so easy to change the subject, and for a moment I grabbed at the idea. Tell them an edited version, skate over the worst bits, and move on. For all the time that I'd spent with Anne and Variam and Sonder and Luna over the past year I'd never told them much about myself, not even Luna. And they trusted me—if I told them I didn't want to talk about it, they'd accept it.

Except . . .

Except that they *did* trust me. When I'd been hurt, they'd come without hesitation. Sonder and Luna had been at my side all the way through the search for the fateweaver and the attack on Arachne last year, and Anne and Variam had joined them after the events of last winter. Hadn't they earned the right to know what was really going on? And if they were willing to put themselves at risk, shouldn't I at least tell them why?

The silence stretched out, the four of them glancing at me and waiting for me to speak. From the other side of the room, I could hear the soft *whisk-whisk* of Arachne's needle. "The adept who stabbed me is called Will Traviss," I said at last. It was an effort to get the words out. "He thinks I killed his sister."

The four of them looked at each other. "Why does he think that?" Variam said.

"Because I did," I said. "Or as good as." It was hard to say it, but an odd sort of relief, too. At least I wouldn't have to hide it anymore.

I wanted to look away but forced myself to meet their eyes. All of them looked taken aback, and Sonder looked outright shocked. "What I'm about to tell you happened ten to twelve years ago," I said. "There's no way to make this short, so you're going to have to be patient. And . . . just so you know, this story doesn't have a happy ending." I took a breath and began.

chapter 5

"In my last year of school," I began, "I was recruited by a Dark mage named Richard Drakh." Even after all these years, saying his name still brought back a touch of the old fear. "My magic had started to come in a couple of years before, but I didn't understand what I was doing. I didn't know anything about the magical world, or Dark and Light mages, or anything like that. Richard offered me a position as his apprentice, and I said yes. I left home and moved into Richard's mansion.

"There were three other apprentices that he'd recruited around the same time, and they were about the same age as me. Two of them were girls—a fire mage named Shireen, and a water mage named Rachel. They'd known each other from before and they were pretty much best friends. The last apprentice was a boy, Tobruk, and he was a fire mage too. Tobruk was the strongest, Shireen was close behind, both of them were stronger than Rachel, and all of them were stronger than me. Richard trained us and when we were ready he introduced us into magical society, Dark and

Light. We met other mages, we took part in contests and tournaments, and all the time we competed with each other. I treated it like a game, back then.

"Richard started giving us assignments. We'd be sent to do an investigation, or get hold of something and bring it back. As the months went by the assignments got more dangerous. For us, and for everyone else. Sometimes the people we were sent after didn't cooperate; sometimes there were others after the same thing we were. There were fights. Rachel got shot on one mission and would have died if Shireen hadn't pulled her out. We got more ruthless after that. Richard didn't give us any explanation for why we were being sent out, and he didn't answer questions. We got into the habit of following orders.

"In September of that year, Richard sent us out to find a girl. Her name was Catherine Traviss, and Richard wanted her brought back to the mansion, alive—he was very clear on that part. Somehow or other she'd found out Richard was after her, and she'd fled to the United States with her younger brother. I guess she was hoping that would be far enough. It wasn't. We followed her to the U.S. and tracked her down in Arizona. She'd travelled with her boyfriend, a guy called Matthew Stewart, and the two of them were camped out in the desert. I found them, and Shireen and Rachel and Tobruk went in to get her. Her boyfriend tried to fight them off . . ." I trailed off, remembering what had come after. The way in which fire magic kills is horrible beyond description. I tried to think of some way to make them understand just how awful the sight and sound and smell had been, and couldn't. I wasn't sure I wanted to.

"Tobruk killed him," I said at last. "It . . . wasn't pretty. We got Catherine. Alive, just like Richard said. And we brought her back.

"I guess that was the point at which I started having doubts. Don't get me wrong, we'd done some shady stuff already, but there'd always been some way to justify it. Most of the time the people we were going up against weren't any nicer than we were—either they were Dark apprentices too, or as good as. But Catherine and her boyfriend hadn't been part of that world. They hadn't done anything at all.

"Richard hadn't told us why he wanted Catherine. I'd had some idea he just wanted to talk to her, which was pretty stupid of me now that I think about it. Richard had her locked in the cells beneath the mansion and told us to make sure she stayed there. Shireen and Rachel didn't go near her. Tobruk did.

"Tobruk was . . . None of us were especially nice people back then, but Tobruk was the worst. I think out of all the Dark apprentices I met in that time, he was the cruellest. He started making regular visits down to Catherine and he'd . . . amuse himself with her." I stopped. I didn't want to go into the details; just remembering it was nauseating. I took a quick glance around the four faces watching me. Sonder looked uncomprehending, but something flickered in Anne's eyes and I had the sudden unpleasant feeling that she knew exactly what I was leaving out.

"It took me longer than it should have, but I decided to help Catherine escape. I scouted out the guard shifts, then one night I crept down and got her out of her cell." I fell silent briefly. "It didn't work. Richard was waiting for me and Rachel and Shireen and Tobruk were with him. He gave me one chance to put Catherine back. I didn't take it. Tobruk put me down. When I woke up I was in a cell of my own.

"I'd taken it for granted, being under Richard's protection. When Richard took that protection away . . . then suddenly I was in the same position Catherine was. And Tobruk made sure I got the same experience. Not exactly the same— his tastes didn't run that way—but he was pretty creative at coming up with substitutes.

"It went on for a long time. I didn't see anyone except Tobruk, and the rest of the time I was left alone. But even if I wasn't Richard's apprentice I was still a diviner, and every now and again Tobruk and Rachel and Shireen would run up against something that they couldn't handle but I could. The trips were short and I was always watched, but I was patient. Eventually I found a way out.

"I was more careful this time. I'd learnt Richard had a new enemy, a Light mage, and I waited until he was busy with her before I made my escape. This time it worked. I made it away, but I knew Richard would send the other three after me. The only question was which one would catch me first.

"I went to the Light mages for help. They didn't want to know—as far as they were concerned it was one Dark mage against another. I went to every mage that I'd gotten to know during my time as Richard's apprentice, and they all turned me away. They didn't want to get involved—they were all just waiting for Richard to finish me off. And finally I went to the last place I could think of. Here. To Arachne." I glanced over at Arachne, still sewing quietly. I knew she could hear me, but she didn't react. "She could have turned me away like the others. She didn't. She took me in. Arachne hid me and let me heal and rest, but she couldn't keep me hidden forever. When I was ready I took the help she gave me and went out to face the people chasing me. The first one to find me was Shireen, and she was . . . different. She was under orders to bring me back, but for the first time she wasn't sure. I'd spoken to her a few times towards the end, and maybe something I said made her change her mind. Or maybe she changed it herself. She went back to the mansion empty-handed and I never saw her again.

"And then Tobruk came. He was stronger and tougher and better trained than me, but I'd had time to prepare and I knew what he'd do. He could have killed me if he'd gone all-out, but he couldn't resist playing cat and mouse one last time. And even at the end, he never really believed that someone as weak as me could threaten him. I set a trap for him in an old building, and I killed him and turned the building into his funeral pyre. And then I kept running and getting ready for whoever would come next.

"Nobody came. Days went by, then weeks, then months. Nobody else came after me. And I never saw Richard again."

I stopped talking. The cavern fell silent but for the *whisk* of Arachne's needle. Seconds dragged by.

Luna was the first to speak. "So do we go after this Will guy or wait for him to come back?"

Everyone turned to stare at her. "What?" Luna said.

Sonder looked disbelieving. "Didn't you hear that story?"

"Yes," Luna said.

"This guy, Will . . . He's not just some monster. He's got a reason for doing this."

"Everybody who's tried to kill us has had a reason," Luna pointed out. "That doesn't mean I'm going to let them."

"You said that Catherine girl had a little brother," Variam said. "You think it's the same guy?"

I nodded. "When we attacked Catherine's camp we only saw her and her boyfriend, but there were tents for three people. She was supposed to have taken her brother with her when she ran . . . Will would be about the right age."

"And now he wants revenge for what happened to his sister," Variam said.

"You didn't hurt her, though," Luna said.

"No, I just showed the people who *did* hurt her where to find her. Somehow I don't think that argument's going to impress him very much."

Silence fell again, and it stretched until it became uncomfortable. Suddenly I couldn't bear to sit there any longer; I didn't want to look at their faces for fear of what I'd find there. "I need a rest," I said, rising to my feet. I felt Anne look up at me but raised a hand, not meeting her eyes. "I'm just tired. I'll talk to you later." I walked back towards the cave in which I'd woken up. As I left the cavern I heard the murmurs start up behind me.

∎∎∎∎∎∎∎∎∎∎

Back in the smaller room, I lay on my back on the bed and let my breath out in a sigh. I was more tired than I should have been and I knew that even with Anne's healing, I hadn't yet recovered from last night's injuries.

Well, I've told them. Now that I'd done it I felt drained. I'd known I couldn't keep it hidden forever, but I'd always put it off. I stared up at the rock ceiling and wondered how they'd treat me now. In the years since I'd known Luna and Sonder and Anne and Variam, I'd played the role of a . . . what? Protector? Teacher? Friend? Something I wasn't, anyway. They hadn't known about my past, and so when I'd been with them I'd been able to escape it.

Was that why I'd worked so hard to help the four of them? When I'd joined Richard I'd been too self-centred to ever really care about helping anyone. When had that changed? Over the last year and a half I'd put myself in danger to help Luna and Sonder and then Variam and Anne, not just once but over and over again, and as I thought about it I realised that I didn't regret it at all. I'd do it again without a second thought.

Maybe while I was with the four of them, I'd been able to pretend to be a different person. And at some point I'd noticed that I liked being that person a lot more than I liked who I used to be.

But the person I'd been pretending to be wouldn't have gotten two innocent kids killed . . .

Lost in my own thoughts, I didn't notice Luna's approach until I heard her footsteps echoing down the corridor. "Hey," she said as she walked in, then pulled out a chair and dropped into it. "They're still arguing."

"Yeah, that figures." I pulled myself upright and looked at Luna. "Still want to be my apprentice?"

Luna looked at me in surprise. "Why wouldn't I?"

"Because of what I told you out there."

"Oh." Luna shrugged. "I'd guessed most of that already."

I stared at her.

"Okay, I didn't know the details," Luna said. "But I knew you used to be a Dark mage. There was going to be *something*."

"What about Catherine?"

Luna shrugged again. "You've kind of got a thing about people coming to you for help. Especially if they're young. I figured it had to be something like that."

I looked at Luna's face, frank and straightforward, and had to laugh. All this time I'd been trying to keep it hidden and she'd known all along. I spend so much time finding out other people's secrets, and somehow it had never occurred to me that someone else could do the same to me. "It doesn't bother you?" I said once I'd caught my breath. "Having a master who was trained as a Dark mage?"

"I don't care," Luna said. I stopped laughing to see that she was looking at me steadily. "I go to classes and matches and I hear everyone talking about Dark and Light, and they all seem to think that the faction you're part of is the most important thing in the world. Well, I don't like either of them. Neither of them are ever going to want me, because I'm not a mage. They don't care about me. Why should I care about them?"

I fell silent. "It's not that simple," I said at last. "I know you've got reason not to like either faction. But they *are* different, and I shouldn't have joined up with Richard the way I did."

Luna gave me a puzzled look. "If you don't like Dark mages, why did you join Richard in the first place?"

I sighed. "Short answer? Because I hated pretty much everyone. I felt like the world had treated me like crap, and this was my chance to turn it around. No one had ever cared about me, so why should I care about anyone else? When you spend all your time lonely and miserable, it's really easy to start hating everyone who has what you don't." I glanced at Luna. "You understand that, don't you?"

Luna's eyes went distant, and she nodded. We sat in silence for a little while. "Why did you change your mind?" Luna said quietly.

"Because of Catherine and that boy," I said. "I guess . . . The way I'd always justified it to myself was that the rest of the world had started it. But those two hadn't done anything to me. So I tried to fix it. And I failed."

Luna sat without speaking and I wondered what she was thinking about. It was a relief when I heard footsteps and Anne and Variam arrived. I looked between them, then down the tunnel. "Sonder?" I said.

"He had to leave," Anne said. There was a slight distance in her manner, but at least she didn't flinch when I looked at her.

"He's still choking on the whole ex–Dark mage thing," Variam said. "He said he'd call."

It wasn't really a surprise. Sonder had always been the idealistic one, and I had the feeling it was going to take a while for him to get used to this . . . if he ever did. I glanced at Variam. "How about you?"

"I figure we owe you," Variam said.

"I don't want you to get involved in this because you feel you have to."

"Yeah, well, that's my call, right?" Variam shrugged. "You're about the only mage who's ever stuck around to help us out. I'm not leaving because of some old grudge."

I didn't say anything but I gave Variam a nod, and he gave me one back. I looked at Anne, who answered in her soft voice. "I'm not blaming Sonder for leaving," she said, and again there was that trace of remoteness that hadn't been there before. "But . . . what's done is done. I don't want anyone else to die." Her eyes held mine and there was a question there.

"Neither do I," I said, and I felt Anne relax slightly.

"Okay," Luna said, raising a hand. "Not to point out the obvious, but *they* seem just fine with someone dying, as long as it's you."

"Is there any way to talk to them?" Anne asked.

"Yeah, I got a close look at these guys," Luna said. "They really didn't seem in a talking mood."

"How many of 'em are there, and what can they do?" Variam said.

"Six that I saw," I said. "At least three are magic-users, probably adepts. Will can accelerate himself, the girl throws ground fire, and the tall one's a life-drinker. I caught a whiff of space magic too."

"Only four of them were fighting though," Luna said.

"That we saw," I said. "If they can put together an attack team of six, they've probably got others."

"If their group's that big, they're going to have trouble hiding," Variam said with a frown. "There should be some way to track them down."

"But if you go following them it'll just lead to another fight," Anne said.

"You got any better ideas?"

"There has to be some way to get them to listen," Anne said. "Otherwise it'll turn into a battle, and the longer that goes on the harder it'll be to stop."

"Can you think of anything?" I said. "Because Luna's right—they *really* didn't seem interested in talking things out."

Anne bit her lip, thinking. "Could we try the Council?" Luna asked. "What about Talisid?"

"He's still in Russia from that business last month, and I can't think of any other Council mages I'd trust with this."

"What about Caldera?"

"What do you mean?"

"Well, Caldera was asking about Richard," Luna said. "Then the same day, these guys go after you. It's probably not a coincidence, right?"

I thought about it. "Caldera was looking into rumours of Richard coming back," I said. "Maybe those same rumours are the reason Will's group made their move now."

"If she's a Keeper, she'd know more about these guys, wouldn't she?" Luna said.

"More bloody Keepers," Variam muttered.

"What happened to Catherine?" Anne asked.

Luna and Variam looked at Anne in surprise. "You mean back then?" I said. "She was alive when I escaped. Beyond that . . . I don't know."

"Maybe she's still alive," Anne said.

"Didn't Will tell Alex she was dead?" Luna asked.

"But he also thought Alex killed her," Anne said. "If he was wrong about that, maybe he's wrong about her being dead too."

I sighed. "I'd like to believe it, but . . . I don't know. Odds aren't good."

"It's possible though, isn't it?" Anne said. "And if she is alive, you could find her."

"I guess," I said reluctantly. "But Anne, it was ten *years* ago. It's one hell of a cold trail."

"But think about what would happen if you did," Anne said. "It would take away this boy's reason to go after you, wouldn't it?" She looked at me. "You said you wanted a way to deal with these adepts without having to fight them. Even if you can't find Catherine, you might turn up something that helps."

Variam and Luna looked at each other, then at me. "I guess it's worth a try," Variam said unwillingly.

"Where would you look, though?" Luna asked.

"It's not where." My heart sank as I said it. "It's who. There's only one person who'd know."

⁝⁝⁝⁝⁝⁝⁝

We spoke for another hour before breaking up for the evening. I wanted to go home, but Anne flatly refused to let me out of Arachne's lair until I'd had a full day's rest, and I gave in. Anne stayed to keep an eye on me, Luna stayed to keep Anne company, and in the end we all spent the night there. Before going to sleep I made two calls and left two messages: one to the number Caldera had left me, and one to an unnamed number that cut in to a voice mail service. "It's Alex," I said into the phone. "We need to meet. Call me back." I hung up and walked back down the tunnel. The day had tired me more than I'd realised, and as soon as I lay down I fell into a dreamless sleep.

ıı ı ı ı ı ı ıı

The next day dawned hot and dry, the heat reaching down into the earth to raise the temperature of Arachne's cave. Anne checked on me several times, and by the afternoon finally decided I was fit for action. "Now, do try not to get stabbed again," Arachne said as I got ready to leave. "At least not until next week."

"Would you lay off already? It's not like I do this regularly."

"Well, whether you do or don't, come back in a couple of days. I'll have something for you."

I nodded. "Okay."

"I think you're doing the right thing."

I looked at Arachne in surprise. "Trying to find Catherine?"

"Your friend Anne came to the right answer, even if she might not know why," Arachne said. "Whatever you find at the end of this, you've needed to do it for a long time."

"Let's hope you're right," I said. Anne and Variam and Luna emerged from one of the side caves and I waved to them. "I'll see you soon."

ıı ı ı ı ı ı ıı

It was a beautiful day and Hampstead Heath was packed, people soaking up the warmth of the sun and resting in the shade. Students threw Frisbees on the greens while families walked at a leisurely pace down the wooded paths, children and dogs racing around their ankles. The four of us left the Heath and crossed Kentish Town, taking the bridge over the canal.

Coming back to my shop felt less like coming home and more like making camp in enemy territory. I scanned my shop and flat thoroughly from a distance, then we entered on foot and searched the building from top to bottom. Once we were done Anne and Variam left to make a circuit of the block.

"Anything?" I asked once Anne was back.

"I don't think so," Anne said. "The streets are crowded but I can't see anyone watching."

I nodded. "I can't find anything either."

"That's kind of weird," Luna said curiously. "Shouldn't they be staking the place out or something?"

"Who cares?" Variam said. "They'll show up sooner or later."

"No, Luna's right," I said with a frown. "If I were them and I'd lost the trail at the casino, I'd try to pick us up again here."

"Luna said their leader was injured in the fight," Anne said. "They might be waiting for him to recover."

"Well," I said, "for now, we wait."

⁓⁓⁓⁓⁓⁓⁓⁓⁓

Anne, Variam, and Luna all had afternoon classes, but they skipped them and the four of us stayed inside for the day. I ran the three of them through the building's defences, making sure they knew how to activate them if they were needed and to stay out of the way once they were. If Will and his friends decided they wanted a rematch I was going to be ready for them.

At four o'clock the phone rang. Not my mobile but the landline, which I hardly ever use. I picked it up and spoke. "It's Alex. We need to meet."

A woman's voice spoke from the other end of the line, familiar and cold. "What do you want?"

"I've got questions."

"I don't care."

"I have something to trade. Information."

"And?"

"Have I ever called you before?" I asked. "You think I'd be coming to you if this wasn't important?"

Silence. "Tonight at ten o'clock," the voice said at last. "The market at the Old Truman Brewery. Try anything and I'll kill you." She hung up before I could answer.

I put the phone down and turned to the others. "Well, it's a start."

"Was that Rachel?" Luna said. She and Variam were looking at me, while Anne was looking out the window.

"Call her Deleo," I said. "For some reason her old name really pisses her off."

"She's going to help?" Variam said.

"She's going to talk."

"Alex?" Anne said, a warning note in her voice. "We've got a problem."

We all turned to look. "That boy from two nights ago is back," Anne said. "And he's not alone."

Variam and Luna rose, and I started scanning futures. "How many?" Variam said.

"Two that I can see," Anne said. "Him and another the same age."

"It's them," I said. Looking into the futures in which I left the shop and turned right, I could see myself running straight into them. "Four . . . no, five. Probably more."

Luna had drawn her whip and was standing by the door. "What's the plan?"

I thought quickly. Will's group were down the street and they were coming closer. But there were other people out there too . . . An odd idea occurred to me. "I'm going to open the shop."

Anne, Variam, and Luna all turned to stare at me.

ı ı ı ı ı ı ı ı ı

"Alex?" Luna said quietly from my left. "What exactly is the plan here?"

The sign on my shop's front door said *OPEN*, and a steady stream of customers was trickling in. It was a sunny day in tourist season, the busiest time of the year, and already the shop was starting to fill up. An American couple chatted loudly over the sword and knife table, while a girl with a satchel and long skirts was going through the herb and powder rack. Luna had taken up a position in the back left corner, Variam was behind the counter with me, and Anne had slipped into the roped-off area holding the magical items to the right, partly hidden from view. "I'm playing a hunch," I said.

"*What* hunch?"

The girl in the skirts approached the counter. "Do you have any aconite?"

"Sorry," I said. "That stuff's too dangerous to sell over the counter."

She nodded. "Could I order some? I can show you some ID if you'd like."

We sorted it out, I agreed to get some for her by next week, and she bought some other herbs. From the selection and her pentacle necklace I pegged her as a Wiccan. I rang up the sale and she left.

"This is stupid," Variam said through his teeth once she was gone.

"Mr. Diplomacy's got a point," Luna said. She kept her voice down, her eyes tracking the customers. "This is way more crowded than the casino. If a fight starts here I don't think I can miss all these guys."

"That's the idea," I said.

"They're coming," Anne said quietly.

Through the shop window, on the other side of the street, I saw the Chinese kid. I met his eyes through the glass; he flinched visibly and ducked back behind a van. "That's right," I murmured. "Now go tell Will we know you're here."

"Why are we waiting?" Variam said.

"It's their move," I said.

"Yeah, how about we take that move and shove it—"

Another customer came to the counter and Variam fell silent, glowering. As I finished serving them, my phone rang and I glanced at it. It was a new number, and I answered. "Caldera," I said. "Hi."

"Hey, Verus," Caldera said. I could hear traffic in the background; it sounded like she was near a main road. "Got your message."

"Mind coming to my shop for a chat?"

"Thought you didn't know anything?"

"I had what you might call a motivational experience." Across the street, three figures had appeared. It was Will, the gold-haired girl, and the Indian kid.

"All right, I'll head over. Should be with you in an hour or two."

Will and the other two began walking towards us, crossing the street. They were heading straight for the shop. "Uh, Caldera?" I said, not taking my eyes off them. "You might want to hurry."

"What's the rush?"

"Let's just say you're not the only one with an interest in Richard's old apprentices."

The bell rang as Will strode through the door. His two companions followed him in to flank him, eyes flicking from side to side, gold-hair girl on his left and the Indian boy on his right. Anne caught my attention with a movement of her head and as I glanced at her she held up two fingers and gestured outside the shop to either side. I made a small motion to show I'd understood and kept my eyes on Will.

Will and the other two approached the counter. I'd dropped the phone as soon as they entered and my hand was under the counter, resting on the concealed shelf. They came to a halt ten feet away, staring at me.

There was a long silence. The shop was still filled with the buzz of conversation, but around the counter all was quiet. I could feel the potential for violence but couldn't see it in the futures . . . yet. "Looking for something?" I said at last.

Will's gaze slid off me and scanned the others. He dismissed Anne with a glance and studied Variam briefly before settling on Luna. "Who are you?"

"The one who kicked your ass," Luna said. The handle of her whip was hidden behind her forearm, and the silver mist of her curse coiled around her, quick and eager. She looked casual but I could tell she was ready to spring.

Will's eyes narrowed, and he looked back at me. "Getting reinforcements?"

"Pretty much," I said. "Mind if I ask you something?"

Will ignored me and addressed the others. "Why are you helping this piece of shit?"

"None of your business," Variam said.

"Because we're his friends," Luna said. "You have a problem with him, you have a problem with us."

"Friends?" the gold-hair girl said in a London accent, and laughed.

"Do you know what he did?" the Indian boy said, addressing Luna and Variam.

"Yeah, actually, we do," Luna said. "He told us."

"And you're on his side?" Will said incredulously.

"So you're Dark mages too?" the Indian boy said.

"It's not about sides," Anne said, speaking for the first time in her soft voice. All three of them turned to her, and she met their eyes. "We *are* his friends. And if you try to kill him we won't stand aside."

I felt an odd choking sensation and blinked before shaking it away quickly. But Will and the other two looked off-balance, and in a sudden flash of insight I realised that they hadn't come in here prepared to confront anyone but me. Friends hadn't been in the script.

A customer approached, a middle-aged man with a balding head. "Um, excuse me," he said. "Could I get—?"

Will and the girl turned to stare at him. The man trailed off. ". . . I'll come back," he finished, and backed away.

"Is that what this is about?" the Indian boy asked me, gesturing around the shop. "Human shields?"

"Call it that if you like," I said. "The question is, do you want to start a fight in the middle of them?"

Will gave me a look of utter contempt. "You really are a piece of work, aren't you?"

"Yeah, given that you tried to murder me I can't say I care much about your good opinion," I said. "Now let's do a head count. You're outnumbered, outgunned, and in the middle of a crowd full of civilian witnesses. So again—do you *really* want to start a fight here?"

Will tensed. My precognition lit up and I closed my hand on the gun beneath the counter. He was about to—

The Indian boy grabbed Will. "Will! *No.*"

Will's lips curled but he didn't move. The customers seemed to be belatedly noticing that something was going on and a few of them had backed away, giving us some space. "I'm gonna fuck you up," gold-hair girl told me and Luna.

"Try to send that ground fire at me or Alex," Luna told the girl clearly, "and I will stuff it down your throat."

"Bev!" The Indian boy caught the girl's arm, his voice urgent. "Don't! Remember the plan!"

Will shook the Indian boy off, but his face was controlled again and the moment was gone. "Big man, hiding behind kids," he said, staring at me. "Why don't you come out on your own?"

"Because I'd lose," I said. "Last time we tried that you beat me, remember?"

Will's lip curled. "Scared?"

"Actually, yes," I said. "I'd rather not get killed if it's all the same to you. Oh, and while we're at it, what makes you so sure your sister's dead?"

Will had been about to snap something back at me, but that made him stop. "Is that some kind of joke?"

"The last time I saw Catherine, she was still alive," I said. "How about this? You stop trying to kill me, and I'll do all I can to find her."

Will stared at me. "That's bullshit!" the girl said angrily. "We know she's dead, we got told—"

"Bev!" the Indian boy snapped.

I held Will's gaze. "Well?" I said when he didn't move. "How about it?"

For just an instant I thought I saw a flicker of doubt in Will's eyes, then he took a step back. "Come on," he said to the other two and backed away, not taking his eyes off me. Gold-hair girl and the Indian boy gave us suspicious looks but followed. The three of them retreated to the door and pulled it shut behind them. The bell went *ding-ding* as they withdrew into the street, and they were gone.

chapter 6

The four of us stood silently, looking with our different senses to figure out what would come next. "Well," Luna said at last. "I guess that could have gone worse."

"They're going," Anne said, looking at the wall.

"Looks like," I said. I raised my voice, addressing the customers still scattered around the shop. "Sorry, everyone, we're closing. Going to have to leave."

There was some grumbling, but the more perceptive of the customers had caught the tail end of the confrontation and had figured out that staying might not be the best plan. Once I'd finished herding them out, I locked the door and flipped the sign to *CLOSED*.

"They out of range?" Variam asked Anne.

Anne nodded. "They didn't slow down."

"How did you know they wouldn't start a fight?" Luna said curiously.

"Remember when you jumped in front of me at the casino?" I said. "They could have swarmed you but they didn't. They just tried to get you out of the way."

Luna frowned. "So?"

"Will's lot think they're the good guys," I said with a sigh. "They weren't planning on hurting anyone except me. I think the way they were expecting this to go was that they'd show up, I'd fight them, and they'd defeat the evil Dark mage with their bravery and teamwork. Me having friends wasn't in the script." *I'm still getting used to it myself.*

"Do you think they'll listen?" Anne asked. "To what you said?"

"I don't know," I said. "Meeting you guys threw them off, I think. They'll probably pull back and try to figure out what to do next." I tapped my fingers on the counter, thinking. "I can see this going two ways. If they stop thinking of me as the enemy and start thinking of me as a person, they'll come back to negotiate. See what they can get."

"He won't," Variam said.

Anne frowned at Variam. "They might."

"*They* might," Variam said. "*He* won't."

I didn't answer, feeling a twinge of unease. There'd been a moment where Will had hesitated. Wasn't there a chance he might listen? Logic said yes, but . . .

Something flickered in the futures ahead, and I took a glance. "Caldera's coming," I said, and that made me relax slightly. I didn't really think that Will and his friends would come back so soon, but if they did, having another mage around would help.

"Keepers," Variam said. "Always show up after it's too late."

· · · · · · · · · ·

"Hey, Verus," Caldera said as I let her in. "So what's the rush?"

"We had some visitors," I told her. "I'd like you to meet Anne and Variam."

We did introductions. Variam gave Caldera a barely civil nod. Anne was polite as usual. "So what's up?" Caldera said.

"I'm looking for information on a group," I said. "They're young, eighteen to early twenties, mostly adepts I think. New on the scene and aggressive, leader is a guy called Will."

"Whoa, whoa, whoa," Caldera said with a frown. "I thought you wanted to talk about Richard."

"I think this *is* connected to Richard."

"Yeah? Why?"

"That's"—I hesitated—"not something I want to go into."

Caldera turned away with an expression of disgust. "It's personal," I said.

"What do you think I am, directory enquiries?" Caldera said. She shook her head and turned to walk away. "You're having a laugh."

"Wait," I said. "This is important."

Caldera paused, looking back with her hand on the door. "I've got a job to do, all right? You've got something to tell me, spit it out."

"Let's trade," I said. "I need to know about this group. Tell me, and I'll help you out with your investigation."

"So you're going to tell me what's going on with Richard?"

"No. I told you, I don't know where he is."

"Then what have you got?"

"I can help you some other way."

"How?"

"Come on," I said. "You're seriously telling me you can't think of anything a diviner would be able to help you out with? Try me."

Caldera measured me with her eyes, and I knew what she was thinking: she was weighing up whether to trust me. Luna, Anne, and Variam stayed quiet, for which I was grateful. "All right," Caldera said at last, and took her hand off the door. She walked up and gave me a challenging look. "I want you to get me into Richard's mansion."

I stared at her. "Are you serious?" When Caldera only

raised her eyebrows, I went on. "You want to break into a Dark mage's house? Do you have any idea just how many things could go wrong with that?"

"No, but you can make a list if it'll make you feel better."

"If you're looking for interesting ways to commit suicide, why don't you just go interview Deleo? It'd be faster."

"Can't find her."

I hesitated, belatedly remembering that I *was* going to go interview Deleo that same night. I hoped Luna and the others were keeping a straight face. If I offered to bring Caldera along, would she accept that instead? No, bad idea, very bad idea. As soon as Deleo spotted Caldera she'd vanish, and that was if we were *lucky*. Given the choice between breaking into Richard's mansion and pissing off Deleo, I'd rather break into the mansion.

"So are you in or out?" Caldera said, mistaking my hesitation. "Look, all the information I've got says the place is deserted. And you're a diviner, aren't you? Aren't you supposed to be good at sniffing out traps?"

I really didn't like the idea. Diviners *are* good at sniffing out traps, and I'm good even by diviner standards, but it's the kind of thing you don't want to do unless you have to—there are a lot of things that can go wrong. On the other hand it's something I know how to do, and looking into the future I could see that Caldera wasn't going to be bargained down. "All right," I said at last, not trying to hide my reluctance. "My help on a trip into Richard's mansion, in exchange for the information on the adepts."

"I can get that to you in a couple of days."

"Or you could give it to me right now."

Caldera raised her eyebrows. "How do you figure?"

"Here's the thing," I said. "I think you know how to do your job. And since these adepts are obviously connected to the rumours about Richard, I think you *already* looked them up." I'd also looked into the future and seen fragments of her telling me about them, but I left out that part. "So how about it?"

"So what's stopping you from doing a vanishing act as soon as I tell you what you want to hear?"

"At some point we're going to have to trust each other," I said. "And if you *don't* trust me, then you really shouldn't be relying on me to break you into a Dark mage's mansion."

Caldera studied me for a moment, then shrugged. "Fine. Then we're hitting the mansion tomorrow morning."

"Are you in some sort of hurry?"

"Aren't you?" Caldera stuck out her hand. "Deal?"

I took it. "Deal."

We shook hands, and I felt the tension in the shop go away. "How do you know about these guys?" Luna asked.

"Ways and means," Caldera said. She leant back against the wall and glanced at me. "Ready?"

I got a notebook and a pencil. "The guys you're talking about are an adept vigilante group," Caldera said. "They got going about a month ago and they're calling themselves the Nightstalkers."

I looked up from the page, eyebrows raised. "The Nightstalkers?"

"You listening or not?"

I started writing and Caldera went on. "The leader is named William Traviss and he's eighteen years old," she said. "Time adept who can use haste. British-born, moved to the States when he was nine following the death of his parents. Only other family was an older sister, and she disappeared soon after. He grew up in the United States and picked up a police record to go with it, juvie stuff mostly. At some point—we don't know when—he started recruiting other adepts. His line was that adepts needed to stand up and protect themselves—we're being oppressed by the evil magocracy, band together and throw off your shackles, that kind of thing. Once he'd gotten a core group together, he moved back here and they started operations."

"What kind of operations?"

"Small stuff to start. Recruitment, throwing their weight around. Then they started messing with Dark mages, targeting their operations, mostly with a view to rescuing people. Their big splash was Bristol. A Dark mage named Locus was running a major slaving nexus out of the inner city, buying and selling sensitives and adepts. The Nightstalkers took him on and actually won. Didn't kill him, but they messed him up pretty badly, and when he ran they broke all the slaves loose. They got a lot of converts from that."

I closed my eyes briefly and looked away. *And the lessons they'll have taken away from that are that all Dark mages are evil, and that violence works. Great.* "And since then?"

"Word is they're looking for Richard."

"You guys planning to do anything about all this?" Variam said.

"Like what?" Caldera said. "Get between Dark mages and a bunch of militant adepts?"

"Thought you were supposed to keep the peace?"

"In case you haven't noticed, Dark mages aren't exactly popular," Caldera said. "Doesn't matter if there's a truce; no one's that motivated to get in the way."

Variam looked away in disgust. "Look, I'm not saying I like it," Caldera said. "But the Keepers do what the Council says. And as long as these adepts stick to going after Dark mages the Council couldn't give a shit. Some of them are probably cheering them on."

"Yeah, that sounds about right," I said. "Come on, Vari. It's not like this is anything new."

"Who are the others?" Luna asked.

"Second-in-command to William is Dhruv Chaudhury," Caldera said. "He and William go back a way. He's supposed to be the brains of the group, comes up with the ideas.

Magnetism adept, can create magnetic monopoles. Next up is Kyle Summers. Supposed to be a space magic user—not a gater—but other than that we don't have much on him. Seems to have some military background, though he's not much older than the others."

"I guess that's Captain America," I said to myself. "What about a life-drinker? Same age as Will, South American looks?"

"Oh yes," Caldera said. "Jaime Cordeiro, otherwise known as Ja-Ja. We're very interested in Mr. Cordeiro. The Brazilian police were investigating him for murder, but he got out of the country before any charges were laid. Met William in the U.S. and followed him here. Suspected of life-draining, though nothing's been proven. I'd keep your distance from him if I were you."

"What about the fire girl?" Luna said.

Caldera shook her head. "That's all I got. We know there are at least three others in the group, but we haven't got details. Our guess is they're new recruits that William picked up since arriving in the U.K. and they haven't been around long enough to pick up a reputation. Sorry."

I took my pencil off the page and studied what I'd written. It read, *Will: Time/acceleration. Dhruv: Magnetism/monopole. Gold-hair: Fire/ground fire. Life-drinker: Life/drain. Cap. America: Space/? Chinese kid: ?/?.* "It's a start," I said. I pushed the notebook over to Luna for her to read. "What's your take on these guys?"

"Short version?" Caldera said. "They're out of their league. They've been lucky so far but sooner or later they're going to piss off the wrong guy." She looked at me with slightly raised eyebrows as if implying that I might know something about that.

"Call me if anything else comes up?"

"I'll tell you face to face," Caldera said. "Tomorrow morning, remember? Don't be late." She gave the others a nod and left.

|||||||||

Both Variam and Luna wanted to come with me to the meeting with Deleo, but in the end I took only Luna. It was dark by the time we left, and we took the Tube to our destination, the trains busy with people heading out for a night on the town.

The Old Truman Brewery is a complex of buildings near Brick Lane, spread over two blocks and surrounded by a strange mixture of trendy shops and decaying buildings. The brewery closed in the 1980s and was promptly converted into an arts and events centre, and nowadays it's a dense, confusing sprawl of brick and concrete, wide indoor spaces mixing with art galleries, bars, and fashion stalls. On Sundays it turns into a hipster magnet, thousands of twenty- and thirtysomethings in odd outfits swarming the place in search of food, clothes, posters, jewellery, and just about everything else. How busy it is on other days varies, depending on whether there's an event running or not. Tonight there wasn't one and the building was dark.

It was an odd choice of place for a meeting. At night the brewery's as deserted as any other event hall, and entry would be easy enough—the brewery's not much more than a giant concrete shed and so has pretty basic security since it doesn't have anything worth stealing. On the other hand, if you're looking for privacy in Central London there are better places to go and the closely packed buildings are perfect for an ambush. Ambushes aren't much threat to a diviner, but Cinder and Deleo aren't diviners. As we watched the building I explained all that to Luna.

"So why did they pick it?" Luna asked.

"Maybe they didn't have time to set up somewhere better," I said with a frown.

"So does that mean they're busy with something?"

I shrugged. "Or they just don't think I'm important enough to be worth the trouble. I want you to stay out here."

I pointed over the courtyard to a crumpled car on top of a storage container. "That should do—you'll be able to drop behind the wall if something goes wrong. Watch the entrance and call me if anyone goes in."

Luna nodded. Once upon a time she would have pushed to come in with me but she's had enough experience with Cinder and Deleo to know that they are not people you want to mess with. "Do you think they'll try anything?"

"I wish I knew," I said. "If they do, run like hell and we'll meet back at the shop."

ɪ ɪ ɪ ɪ ɪ ɪ ɪ ɪ ɪ

The inside of the brewery was wide and dark, brick walls painted white and square pillars running from the ceiling down to the concrete floor. The ground floor was empty, but glass fronting along the far side gave a view out onto a shopping street dotted with people. Cinder and Deleo wouldn't be here: too conspicuous. I took the fire stairs up.

The second floor was made up of a main hall twice the size of a basketball court, double doors along the sides opening onto ramps which led down into other areas. The pillars were still here, surrounded with wood and metal display stands, currently empty. The roof rose and fell in peaks, corrugated metal framing frosted glass windows looking up into the black sky, and fluorescent lights hung dark and still. The building was empty and I settled down to wait.

Rachel kept me waiting almost forty-five minutes. It was on purpose; Rachel knows what I can do and she knew that as long as I could see they were coming I wouldn't give up and leave. It was just a way of annoying me, and I rested my back against one of the pillars and made myself relax. The old brewery had the vaguely eerie feeling that all large public places have after dark, echoing and silent and empty.

When Rachel and Cinder finally showed up it was at the other end of the brewery, opening a gate into a sealed area out of my sight. I'd already picked my location—the open double doors connecting the main hall and a side hall—and as they arrived I took two gold discs from my pocket, laying them to the right and left of the doorway. The discs were a one-shot item that would create a wall of force, blocking the doorway with a near-impenetrable barrier. When you're dealing with mages it's a good idea to take precautions. I stood two steps back from the doorway inside the smaller hall and waited. After a few minutes I heard footsteps echoing around the big hall ahead, boots ringing on concrete. Green-red light began to flicker around the pillars; it brightened as the footsteps grew louder, and Cinder and Rachel came striding around the corner.

Cinder and Rachel work together and they're both scary as hell, though in very different ways. Cinder is big, as tall as me and much more muscular, with the build of a boxer or a wrestler. His eyes flicked from side to side, passing over me quickly and watching for threats. Rachel was looking straight at me before she even came around the corner, her eyes locked onto mine. She'd grown her hair out since the last time I'd seen her and she moved smoothly, with no trace of injury from her old battles. Rachel's quite beautiful, but she hides the top half of her face behind a mask, black silk showing only her blue eyes. Both she and Cinder had light spells active; Cinder's was a flame-red orb flickering at his hands, while Rachel's wavered between blue and sea-green and hovered at her shoulder. They came to a stop thirty feet away.

The first rule of dealing with Dark mages is that you don't show fear. Both Cinder and Rachel are terrifyingly powerful, far more powerful than I am, and I know my chances of taking either of them in a straight-up fight are just about zero. My instinct on seeing them was to turn and run. Instead I stood with arms folded and told them, "You're late."

"Deal with it," Cinder said in his rumbling voice.

"You can use gate spells," I pointed out. "You can

literally cross the world in under a minute. How is it possible for you to be late?"

"Why are you here?" Rachel said. She hadn't stopped staring at me.

Rachel scares me. It's not just that she's willing and able to disintegrate me into a pile of dust; it's that she's insane. Back when I knew her as an apprentice she was pretty and thoughtful, always sticking close to Shireen, but something happened to her after I left and when I saw her again last year she was very different from the girl I'd once known. As I looked into the future Rachel's actions were jagged; shifting and unpredictable. Cinder's stance was watchful, but I couldn't see any futures in which he attacked me; he wasn't going to start a fight without a reason. Rachel might. Futures in which we stood and talked mixed with flickers of chaos and violence, and the hell of it was I had no idea what would set her off. "I'm looking for someone," I said. "I think you might be able to help."

"Don't waste my time," Rachel said. There was an edge to her voice; Rachel and I never really got on but ever since I met her again last year she's hated me and I don't know why. "What do you know?"

"There's a . . . potential threat," I said. "Right now it's not an active danger to either of you, but before long it's going to be. Tell me where to find the person I'm looking for, and I'll give you warning."

"A warning," Rachel said with contempt. "That's all you have?"

"It's something that matters to you."

Rachel stepped forward. The light at her shoulder deepened to a dark sea-green, and I felt the futures of violence fork and multiply. "You sold me to Belthas," she said in a low, dangerous voice.

I wanted to back away but forced myself to stand still. "You got me captured by Morden," I said, keeping my voice level. "Your construct nearly strangled me, you tried to abduct my apprentice, and you've threatened to kill me more times than I can count. Don't give me the self-righteous act."

Rachel stared at me and inwardly I tensed. If she struck I'd have to move very fast. Then Rachel's eyes cleared and the futures were suddenly peaceful again. "Try it again," she said, "and I'll kill you."

"Again with the threatening to kill me," I said. "Look, will you just listen for thirty seconds? If you can't help me, you can say so and we can both stop wasting each other's time."

Cinder's lips twitched as though he wanted to grin. Rachel's eyes bored into me for a long moment, then she looked to her left. "Get on with it."

"I want to find out what happened to that girl Richard was holding," I said. "Catherine Traviss."

Rachel's head snapped around to stare at me and she went utterly still. "You were still free to move around back then," I said. "What happened to her after I—?"

"She sent you, didn't she?" Rachel whispered.

"What? Who?"

"Get out."

I opened my mouth to answer . . . and my precognition screamed a warning. Rachel was standing tense, frozen, but if I spoke a single word she was going to come at me with all her power and do her absolute best to kill me. "Get out," Rachel whispered again.

I began to back away. "Del," Cinder rumbled, looking suddenly uneasy.

"Get out." Rachel's voice rose suddenly to a scream, echoing in the empty building. "Get out. GET OUT! GET OUT! GET—"

I didn't quite run but I got as close as I could to it without turning my back. I could feel the futures of violence spreading, getting closer, and the only way out was away. I had one last glimpse of Rachel, fists clenched and her face white with rage, then I put a wall between us and turned and ran.

Rachel and Cinder didn't follow. Searching back with my

magic I could catch murmurs of conversation, Cinder's deep voice mixing with fragments from Rachel. Footsteps sounded, and I knew they were leaving. I kept my distance until I felt the flicker of gate magic from the other side of the building and I knew Rachel was gone.

Once my heart had stopped pounding I retraced my steps to the doorway where I'd met the two of them. The gold discs of the forcewall were untouched and I picked them up, slipping them into my trouser pocket. What the hell had *that* been about?

Something flickered on my precognition and I knew Cinder was coming back. I thought of withdrawing but my line of retreat was clear, and looking into the future I saw that the futures of combat were gone. I stood in the doorway and waited until Cinder appeared in the gloom, the red light still flickering at his hand. "So," I said. "I'm guessing Deleo doesn't want another chat."

I haven't known Cinder as long as I've known Rachel, but I get on a lot better with him than I do with her. We teamed up a couple of times last year, and while we're not exactly friends we do have a kind of working relationship. Cinder shook his head, his brow furrowed. "What the hell set her off?" I asked.

"Del's . . . got stuff," Cinder said. His voice wasn't friendly but it wasn't hostile either, and I knew that was the closest he was going to get to an apology.

"No kidding. I'm not going to be ringing her up any time soon if that's what you're asking."

Cinder hesitated. "Who was she?"

I looked at him in surprise. "Catherine?"

Cinder gave a nod. "Someone Deleo and I . . . treated badly," I said. "I lost track of her when I left. Deleo never mentioned her?"

"She doesn't talk about back then," Cinder said.

I looked away. "Yeah," I said. "I guess I can understand that."

We stood in silence for a little while. "Del's got something to do," Cinder said at last. "You want to stay away till she's done."

I looked at Cinder, then nodded. Cinder withdrew, keeping an eye on me, and his light faded away around the corner and disappeared. I stood in the darkness for a while then left.

i i i i i i i i i

t was after midnight when Luna and I got back. Anne and Variam reported that all had been quiet, and once we were assembled in the living room I told them the story.

"Do you think there's any way to persuade her?" Anne asked once I was finished.

"No," Luna said, shaking her head very definitely. "You've never met this woman. She does *not* do compromises."

"So now what?" Variam asked.

"I don't know," I said. "I guess I could try digging around but I think it'd just end up the same way. The only answers to what happened back then are inside Rachel's head."

"What about Sonder?" Anne asked.

I grimaced. "Right now I'm not sure Sonder wants to be around me. And ten years is a hell of a gap, even for someone as good as he is."

"You're going to the mansion tomorrow, right?" Variam said.

"That's about the only angle I can see that's left. And honestly, I'm not expecting much. What's there going to be after all this time?"

We sat in silence for a little while. "Do you think it's time to give up on this whole finding-Catherine thing?" Luna asked.

"But then what else is there to try?" Anne asked. "It's the best chance of settling this peacefully."

Variam rolled his eyes. "Yeah, good luck with that."

"No, Anne's right," I said. "I want to do this. I just can't see how."

Luna had been looking down at the coffee table, but now she shrugged and raised her eyes to look at me. "Well, I can think of *one* way."

I looked at her and then flinched. "Oh, you're kidding."

"You said it," Luna pointed out. "The only answers are inside Rachel's head."

Variam looked between us. "What are you talking about?"

⁙⁙⁙⁙⁙

"So let me get this straight," Variam said twenty minutes later. "You're going to some kind of freaky dream-place to get the information out of Rachel while she's asleep?"

"More or less," I said, taking off my shoes.

"You can see people's memories in Elsewhere," Luna said. She didn't mention how she knew.

"So just out of curiosity," Variam said, "how's Miss Psycho Bitch going to react if she catches you going through her head?"

"I'm going to guess 'badly,'" I said as I slid my shoes under my bed. "Let's hope she doesn't notice."

"Should I come?" Luna asked.

I shook my head. "One can hide better than two. Besides, I need someone to keep watch. Will's lot know where I live, and I still don't trust them not to try some sort of night raid."

"I'll do it," Anne volunteered. "I can stay awake."

"Is it good for you to keep doing that?"

"I slept last night," Anne pointed out. "Besides, I can spot them before anyone else."

"Wake me up at dawn," Variam said. "I'll take watch and you can get a few hours."

Luna yawned. "Fair enough. Night."

Luna and Variam squabbled briefly over the bathroom before going to bed, Luna withdrawing to the spare room while Variam set up the camp bed in the corner of the living room and fell asleep almost instantly. Anne curled up on the living room sofa with a book, the faint light of the lamp making her bare arms and neck glow softly in the darkness. I pulled the connecting door most of the way shut and hung up my coat before lying down on my bed with a sigh. It was too hot to sleep fully clothed but I was too tired to undress, so I pulled off my socks and left it at that. The clock by my bed read 12:48 and I watched it for a while as I listened to the sounds fade away. With Anne and Luna and Variam all here my flat felt lived-in and cosy, alert and alive. The day's work on top of the last traces of fatigue from my injury had tired me more than I realised, and in only minutes my eyes drifted closed. As I did I reached out with my mind, searching for a place I'd been to before, a place to which I'd return again. Sleep came.

chapter 7

opened my eyes.

I was standing in my bedroom, and I was alone. White light streamed through the windows, mixing with the ambient glow of the walls and ceiling and floor. There were no shadows; everything was bright and clear. Through the windows I could see the buildings and towers of a great empty city. There were hints of London in the architecture but it was different, vaster, the streets wider and the buildings huge and open. Beyond the buildings was empty sky.

I walked through my flat, down the stairs, and out of the shop. My front door opened out into a long avenue stretching off into the distance, torches mounted along either side burning with yellow flames, and I began walking forward. Without looking I knew the route back to my flat would have disappeared. It didn't matter; here in Elsewhere, one place was as good as another.

I turned off the avenue and into one of the buildings, passing through the hallway and out onto a narrower street. Elsewhere felt different from the last time I'd been here. In the past the city had always been silent, empty of movement and growth. This time as I walked I kept noticing life: trees planted in rows and growing in gardens, birds gliding overhead. As I turned one corner I saw a fox trotting quickly across the road ahead of me. It stopped and looked at me, then kept going, disappearing into an alleyway. I could hear a very faint murmur of sound at the edge of my hearing, not the hum of a real city, but what might have been an echo of one. The street I was on ended in a medium-sized square, buildings on three sides and an arcade on the fourth marking the boundary with a wide plaza. I found a stone bench under a tree and sat down.

I've never really understood how Elsewhere works. In my early visits I tried to figure out the rules, and every time I ended up making things worse. Intuition seems to work better than reason here; the more times I've come the more I've learnt to trust my instincts. Right now my instincts told me that if I stayed here long enough, the person I needed would find me. So I sat, and waited.

I heard her before I saw her: footsteps echoing off the stone from the direction of the plaza. Looking up I saw her walking through the columns of the arcade, small and athletic, short dark-red hair and a quick smile. "Hey, Alex," Shireen said. "Wondered when you'd come."

Shireen looked different from how I'd seen her in the dream. Physically she was almost the same, but her manner was easier—back when we'd both been apprentices Shireen had always been full of energy but there'd been a tension there, a temper. Now she seemed relaxed. "Hey," I said.

"So." Shireen dropped down on the bench next to me. "How's things?"

"Don't take this the wrong way," I said. "But before we get started on this, there's something I'd like to know. What exactly are you?"

Shireen didn't look insulted—more like amused. "What do you think I am?"

"You look like Shireen and you sound like Shireen," I said. "But Shireen died ten years ago. It's like you're a picture of how she was the last time I saw her. How are you still here?"

Shireen's smile faded, and she studied me for a moment. "I'm an afterimage," she said at last. "A picture when the original is gone. But I can see and I can feel and I can remember. I know what you're looking for."

"Catherine," I said.

Shireen nodded. "I can show you what happened to her."

"Any chance you can skip ahead and give me the short version?"

"No." Shireen sounded quite definite. "I've helped you before and I'll help you now, but this time I want something back. I'll show you what happened to Catherine and where she is, but only if you see the whole story."

"Which story?"

"Rachel's," Shireen said. "What happened to Catherine, how Richard disappeared, why I'm talking to you now. It all comes back to her and it's time you understood why. Don't forget— if it wasn't for me you would have been lost last year. You owe me."

I looked at Shireen for a moment. "That's all you want?" I said at last. "For me to know the story?"

"That's part of it," Shireen said. "There's one more thing, but I won't ask until you've seen what really happened ten years ago. The parts you *weren't* there for."

"I can't promise I'll say yes to that. Not without knowing what it is."

"I understand."

I stood in silence for a little while. "How are you going to show me this?"

"Rachel's memories," Shireen said. "You'll see what she saw."

I frowned at that. I've walked through my own memories in Elsewhere, watching the events unfold as if they were happening all over again, but never someone else's. No one knows much about Elsewhere, but if there's one thing they agree on, it's that you shape it yourself. "How can you do that?"

"You'll know once you've seen it," Shireen said. "I know I keep saying that, but it's true." She grinned suddenly. "Come on. Aren't you curious?"

I gave Shireen a narrow look, then looked away, out through the arcade to the white stone of the plaza. Around us the city was quiet, waiting. I turned back. "Let's do it."

Shireen nodded and held out her hand, palm up. "Hold on tight."

I took her hand, and—

＊＊＊＊＊＊＊＊＊

was standing on a grassy slope, green trees scattered around and rhododendrons flowering to either side. I was in what was either quite a small park or a very large garden, and it looked well kept and tended. I could see glimpses of a wall surrounding the greenery, and just visible over the trees behind was a big white-painted house. The sky was overcast but light, the sun glowing through the clouds. It looked almost natural, but something about it was just slightly off.

At the bottom of the slope was a pond. There was a willow tree leaning over it, and under the willow was a girl, fifteen or sixteen years old and dressed neatly in blue and white. She was sitting cross-legged by the pond, looking down at the water with her face set in concentration. I was standing in plain view, but she didn't seem to notice me. Hesitantly I moved, then when she didn't react I came closer.

The girl was Rachel, but it took me a moment before I was sure that it was really her; she looked very different from the woman she would grow into. In Richard's mansion Rachel had been pretty but elusive, rarely showing what she was thinking. When I'd met her again last year, that ambivalence had hardened into a diamond mask that showed nothing of what might be behind it. But here, as she stared down at the water, there was an openness which I'd only seen hints of when we'd first met, something soft and unformed.

Rachel's eyes were still fixed on the pond, and as she stared at it the surface rippled. She extended a hand, soft blue light starting to flicker at her palm, and as she did a droplet of water rose from the pond's surface to hover at her fingertips. The light brightened and another droplet rose, then another, a thin stream of water flowing upwards to gather in a floating orb. Carefully Rachel raised her hand and the orb rose with it, wobbling as it did, droplets breaking off to hover for a few moments before melding together again. Rachel's movements were slow and careful, and there was a strange dreamlike look to her eyes, as though she were seeing something wonderful and far away.

There was a rustle of leaves. Rachel started, the light winked out, and the orb of water fell back into the pond with a splash. She scrambled to to her feet.

The girl who'd just brushed her way through the willow fronds was a younger version of Shireen. She was wearing a T-shirt and jeans, scuffed and dirty, and she was looking at Rachel with satisfaction. "So it *was* you," she said.

Rachel took a step back. "How did you get in here?"

"Climbed over the wall," Shireen said. "Come on, I just want to talk."

"How long were you watching?"

"Long enough." Rachel drew back and Shireen raised a hand. "It's okay, it's okay. Hey, you want to see something?"

Orange light flared at Shireen's hand and a flame caught in the air above her fingers, clearer and brighter than Rachel's spell. Rachel had been backing away, but as she saw the magic she halted, staring. "Cool, huh?" Shireen said.

Slowly Rachel came closer, until the two of them stood

face to face under the willow tree. "How do you . . . ?" she asked, gazing at the light as if fascinated.

"Do it?" Shireen said. "Same as you."

"How do you make it so strong?" Rachel said. She hadn't taken her eyes away.

Shireen shrugged. "I don't know, it's always been like that." She closed her hand and the spell winked out. "Do your parents know?"

Rachel hesitated, then shook her head. "I'm keeping it secret from mine," Shireen said.

"What is this?" Rachel asked. "How can we use it? What *are* we?"

"Don't know," Shireen said again. She grinned. "But it'll be fun finding out, right?"

Rachel looked back at Shireen, then gave a little smile. "I'm Shireen," Shireen said. "You?"

"Rachel."

The scene blurred and shifted. I had a last glimpse of the two of them standing together by the water's edge, then—

⁙⁙⁙⁙⁙

We were indoors, in a roomy bedroom with a high ceiling. The furnishings were new and well kept but anonymous, the sort you'd get at a good boarding school or hotel. Tall windows let in lots of light, giving a view out onto a row of houses. In the distance the hum of cars rose and fell.

Rachel was lying on the bed reading. She was wearing what looked like a uniform—white blouse with a dark green skirt—and there was a green pullover slung over the back of a chair. She was older now, close to the age she'd been when we'd first met, and she looked more sure of herself, her movements more confident. Muffled footsteps sounded on the carpet outside and the door swung open. Rachel spoke in annoyance, not raising her eyes. "You're supposed to knock."

Shireen shut the door behind her. "Nice to see you too."

Rachel looked in surprise and her face lit up. "You're here! Wait, how did—?"

"Caught an early train." Shireen wasn't wearing a uniform and compared to Rachel she looked scruffy, but she moved with the same energy she'd always had. She dropped into a chair, glancing around. "Wow, you get nice rooms."

"This is the best one," Rachel said. "Haven't you got school?"

"Forget about that—this is important. You remember what we were talking about back in the summer?"

Rachel sat up, alert. "You've found a teacher?"

"He found me," Shireen said. "His name's Richard Drakh and he's looking for apprentices. I wasn't sure at first but I did some asking around and this guy's the real deal. He's *really* powerful. People are careful around him."

"So what does he want?"

"Heh," Shireen said. "He asked me something like that. He's offering me an apprenticeship. And he's got more than one place." Shireen raised her eyebrows. "Interested?"

"He's offering me one too?"

"Well, kind of."

Rachel sat back with a frown. "I just said that I knew someone else who'd be interested and asked whether he had other places," Shireen said. "He said yes. I think he wants you."

"If he wants me, why didn't he ask me?"

"Maybe he doesn't know about you yet. Come on, Rach, who cares who was first?"

I'd been looking between the two girls as they talked. As Shireen spoke I turned back to Rachel—and jerked back, throat constricting as I tried to scream. *Something* was standing behind her: a spindly shape, tall and slender and utterly inhuman, its features a blur of shadow. Its head reached nearly to the ceiling and it was holding still.

And just as suddenly it was gone. I stood in the centre of the room, looking wildly from side to side, heart hammering. The room was empty except for me and the two girls.

". . . going to be a full-time gig," Shireen was saying. Neither she nor Rachel had shown any reaction; they were talking as though nothing had happened. "He's going to show me his place on Saturday. If I say yes—if *we* say yes—we're going to move in. It's going to be magic lessons, introductions, the whole thing. Everything we need."

"What about school?"

"Who cares about school?"

"The university applications—"

"Forget that. This is like getting an offer from Oxford and Cambridge and Harvard all at once. It's our big chance."

Rachel got up and walked to the window, the book still hanging from one hand, and I followed her to peer out. Nothing. There was no trace of whatever that thing had been, but my heart was still pounding. I knew I'd seen it. "What's wrong?" Shireen asked.

Rachel turned back with a frown. "I don't want to leave."

Shireen looked at her in surprise. "Why not?"

"Because things are good here," Rachel said. "The other girls do what I want."

Shireen rolled her eyes. "That's because they're scared of you. You're a big fish in a small pond."

"Well, what's wrong with that?"

"Look, what you're doing here is kid stuff," Shireen said. "Okay, so you're queen of your dorm—"

"House."

Shireen waved a hand. "Whatever. It doesn't *get* you anything. And next year you're going to uni and things are going to change. It's not going to be so easy to push people around."

Rachel shrugged. "What are they going to do about it?"

"It's not what they'll do," Shireen said. "It's who might notice."

"What do you mean?"

Shireen glanced at the window. "Look, the more I learn about this stuff, the more I get the feeling we're not that safe. If Richard Drakh could find us, someone else could too."

An uneasy expression flickered across Rachel's face. "Like who?"

"I don't know," Shireen said. "But I've heard stories. Sometimes magic-users around our age just . . . go missing. And no one seems that keen on talking about where."

Shireen and Rachel stayed silent for a moment. The sun had gone behind a cloud, and the light on the houses outside was muted. "Look," Shireen said. "You've been wanting your magic to be stronger, right? This guy can teach us."

Rachel sighed. "Fine, I'll listen to him. But he's going to have to be *really* convincing."

· · · · · · · · ·

The shift was quicker this time, and in only an instant I was in another bedroom, this one expensive-looking and cluttered with clothes. I recognised it as being like my room in Richard's mansion but the layout was different, and it took me a moment to realise that it was one of the girls' rooms, either Shireen's or Rachel's.

The door slammed open and Shireen stormed through in midsentence. "—self-righteous *assholes*!" The door banged off the wall and Shireen kicked it before turning on Rachel, who'd been following behind. "Can you believe this? What century do these guys think they're in?"

Rachel shrugged and shut the door. "They act like we're pretty little dolls on a shelf," Shireen said, pacing up and down. "And they expect us to be *grateful*. 'Oh yes, sir, I'm a good little girl.' Never any respect. We just don't matter."

"I told you," Rachel said. "Back home we were special. Now we're just two more apprentices."

Shireen flung herself into a chair, brooding. "I bet they'd act different if we were boys. They pay attention to Tobruk."

"Do you think—" Rachel began.

There was a tentative knock on the door. "What?" Shireen shouted.

The door cracked open and a nervous-looking face appeared in the gap. "Get us something to eat," Shireen said.

The face hesitated. I vaguely remembered him: Zander, one of the easily forgotten, often-changing servant population of Richard's mansion. "Uh—" Zander said.

"Did I stutter?" Shireen said. "You want me to tell Richard you're not doing your job?"

Zander paled and vanished. The door clicked shut and the sound of his hurrying footsteps faded away. Shireen shook her head. "Even the servants are taking the piss now."

Rachel hadn't paid attention to Zander; she was looking thoughtful. "Do you think this was what Richard meant?"

"The whole power thing?" Shireen said. She drummed her fingers. "Maybe he's right. It's the only way we're ever going to change anything, isn't it?"

"It's the only way they're ever going to respect us."

"Fine," Shireen said. "Let's teach them some respect."

As she spoke the words Shireen faded, and so did Rachel. The clothes vanished and the windows darkened, layers of dust covering the furniture and bed. I was alone in an empty room.

A hand tapped me on the shoulder and I spun with a yelp. Shireen gave me a quizzical look. "What's wrong?"

"Don't scare me like that," I muttered. The room around us looked decayed and abandoned, as though it had been deserted for years.

"Who did you think I was?"

"A minute ago," I said. "I thought I saw . . ."

"Saw what?"

"Never mind." I looked at Shireen. "So that was the way it happened? Richard came to you and you went to Rachel?"

"I could always talk Rachel into things." Shireen walked

over to inspect the chair where her younger self had been sitting. It was worn and faded now, with holes in the fabric. "She'd argue but she'd go along with it in the end."

"You were stupid."

"We were teenagers," Shireen said. "Anyway, it's not like you can talk."

"Oh, I haven't got anything to be proud of either," I said with a sigh. "My reasons for signing up were much dumber than yours . . . What were you talking about at the end?"

"When?"

"About respect. Changing things."

"We always figured we were going to do something special with our magic," Shireen said. "Like in the movies, when the heroine gets her powers, you know? She always ends up fighting a bunch of bad guys and saving the world."

"Saving the world?"

"I'm not saying we went out to do charity work," Shireen said. "But we saw a lot of mage society while we were with Richard and we didn't much like the way it treated women. Too many apprentice girls getting stepped on and *way* too many female slaves."

I looked at Shireen for a moment. "If you had a problem with slaves," I said at last, "maybe you should have tried doing something about the ones in your basement."

Shireen didn't meet my eyes and there was an awkward silence. "Sorry," she said at last.

I kept gazing at Shireen. For a moment I felt the old rage starting to rise, then with an effort of will I shook it off. "Forget it."

"You said something like that to me back then," Shireen said at last. "That time I came to your cell. Remember?"

I looked at her curiously. "So you *were* listening? I was never sure . . ."

"I didn't want to," Shireen said. "I went upstairs and tried to forget about it. But it was like . . . a seed, I guess. All the next few weeks I'd be in the middle of doing something and I'd start thinking about you and Catherine. It wouldn't stop bugging me."

"Well, I'm sorry if thinking about what was happening to the two of us was making your life less convenient."

"You can really be a dick sometimes," Shireen said. "But you know what? That was kind of why it worked. I didn't like you and you didn't like me, and so you were the one person who told me the truth."

I looked at the empty space where Rachel had stood. "Do you think this is how it works for all Dark mages? Just drifting, going a little further each day? Then one day you look around and realise what you're turning into . . ."

"It was for me," Shireen said simply.

"What happened when you want back to the mansion, Shireen?"

Shireen went still.

"The last I saw you, it was at the abandoned block," I said. "You said you were going back to find Rachel and Catherine, and I watched you walk away and I never saw you again. What happened after that?"

Shireen was silent for a moment. "When I left the mansion I was looking for you," she said at last. "But I didn't know what I was going to do when I found you. I didn't know if I wanted to fight you or talk to you or bring you back or . . . The one thing I was sure of was that we were out of time. Either it was going to be Tobruk, or . . ." She stopped, frowning.

"Or what?"

"You have to go." Shireen turned on me. "Now!"

I looked around in confusion. The room was empty. "Go where?"

"Out of Elsewhere. You're in danger. You have to wake up." The lines of the room around us began to blur and dissolve, the colours fading into each other. Shireen advanced until she was right in front of me, staring up at me. "Wake up!" The colours blurred into grey and we were falling, my stomach lurching as we dropped. I couldn't see Shireen or anything else but I could hear her voice shouting at me. "Wake up! Wake—!"

ı ı ı ı ı ı ı ı ı

"—up! Alex, *wake up*!"

I came awake with a start. My room was dark and a slim figure was leaning over me, shaking me. "Huh?" I sat up, shaking my head. "What?"

"Will's friends, the adepts, they're back." Anne's voice was low and urgent. "They're here."

My precognition was nagging at me, warning of danger. The clock by my bed said 3:17 and the city outside was quiet. From the direction of the living room I could hear movement; Luna and Variam were up. I was still disoriented from waking and couldn't process it all. "Where?"

"I don't know—" Anne looked back over her shoulder. "They've gone."

"Gone where?" The warning of danger was getting louder and louder. Something was coming for us but I couldn't see what. Nobody was going to come through the door, but . . .

"I can't see, they're out of my range. They came onto the roof and they were doing something, then they started running."

"On the—?" Suddenly the visions of the future ahead snapped into focus and my eyes went wide. "Oh *shit*." I lunged off the bed, grabbing Anne. She made a startled noise as I dived for the side of the room, shoving her under the desk before rolling in myself.

There was a roar and what felt like a blow to every part of my body at once. The floor bucked and settled, and a vibration went through the building as what felt like a landslide hit all around us with a thundering crash. Dust filled the air.

I tried to roll back out from under the desk and scraped against something jagged; there was rubble piled across the floor. I scrambled out on my hands and knees and felt a breeze: looking up, I saw sky. Half the roof of my flat was gone.

It had been some kind of explosive, and from the mess it must have gone off right above my bed. Where my bed and table had been was a pile of rubble, forming a slope up to the hole in the roof. The wall onto the street had survived but half the interior wall was gone, including the door through to the living room. Anne struggled out from underneath the desk, coughing, and I helped her up. "Can you move?"

Anne shook her head; she hadn't had the second's warning I had and she looked dazed. "I'm okay."

I looked around to see that the doorway to my living room was a pile of shattered bricks and plaster. We were sitting ducks in here, and the only way out was up. I started climbing. "Come on."

The rubble was unstable and the jagged edges hurt my skin, but at least barefoot I could climb well. "Can you spot Luna and Vari?" I called down to Anne as I reached up for a handhold. I was about to grab a piece of the ceiling but saw that it would start a landslide and reached for a broken beam instead.

"They're okay but there's someone coming!" Anne called up. "Ahead and to your left."

I took one look into the futures, saw the flicker of combat, and put on a burst of speed, scraping my elbow as I scrambled up onto the half-destroyed roof. Where the front of my roof had been was now a pit, dust still swirling in the night air. I could hear shouts and noise from the buildings around.

A figure came jogging out of the shadows ahead. He was only a silhouette in the darkness, but I knew who it was—Jaime Cordeiro, aka Ja-Ja, aka the life-drinker, the one Caldera had warned me about and the last person on Will's team

I wanted to get close to. He swerved towards me, his palm coming up.

I reached into my pocket for a weapon and my fingers closed on nothing: my items were buried under the rubble ten feet below. Ja-Ja lunged and I dived, rolling and coming back to my feet to turn and face him. Ja-Ja managed to brake before going over the edge and started back towards me. I danced back, the roof cool under my bare feet, not taking my eyes off Ja-Ja's hands. One touch and I'd be dead or crippled. Ja-Ja lunged again and I dodged behind a chimney. He moved left, then right; I matched him, keeping the brick-work between us.

Ja-Ja crouched, tensed. From the faint glow of the city lights I could see he was wearing clear plastic goggles; Will's lot were learning from experience. Bad sign. I heard a crash from the direction of my flat, followed by a surge of fire magic, and I knew that more were coming in from below but I couldn't take my eyes off Ja-Ja. I had to take him down, but I didn't have a weapon and I couldn't risk coming within reach—

A hand touched Ja-Ja from behind, and he spun to face Anne. She was standing close, her arm extended and the fingers of her left hand resting lightly against his chest. Ja-Ja looked at her face to face and his expression was ugly. "Back off or I hurt you, bitch."

Anne met Ja-Ja's gaze, her eyes steady. "Don't."

Ja-Ja didn't ask twice. His right hand came up fast and he slapped it into Anne between her breasts. Green-black light flickered around his arm and I had an instant to see the attack in my mage's sight: focused and lethal, designed to rip the life from Anne's body. One hit from that spell would kill most people. Two hits would kill anyone. Before I could move the spell flashed through Ja-Ja's palm and into Anne.

Nothing happened. The green-black light vanished. Anne looked at Ja-Ja.

Ja-Ja looked taken aback. He looked down at his palm, then up at Anne, then tried again. Again the lethal green-black light flickered from his hand and into Anne's body. Again nothing happened.

"Please stop doing that," Anne said.

"That should have worked," Ja-Ja muttered. He was still standing with his hand against Anne. All of a sudden instead of looking threatening he looked faintly ridiculous.

"It's okay," I said brightly. "It happens to a lot of guys."

"Shut up," Ja-Ja snapped.

"I'm sure it doesn't happen to you usually. Maybe you can take a rest and try again in a few minutes."

Ja-Ja snarled. "I said *shut up!*" He drew back for a punch.

Anne's fingers hadn't left Ja-Ja, and as he started to swing, leaf-green light flickered from her hand into his body. He crumpled instantly, unconscious before he hit the floor. Anne glanced at me. "Maybe you should stop taunting them."

No one else had come; we were alone on the roof. Ja-Ja was out but I could still sense fire magic and there was danger ahead. "What's going on down there?" I said. "Are Vari and Luna okay?"

"They're not hurt," Anne said, looking down through the roof. "They're at the top of the stairs; Will and the others didn't—" She cut off, frowning. "That's strange. They're pulling back."

The futures of danger suddenly multiplied, branching, and as I looked at them my heart sank. "Oh crap." I started running the way Ja-Ja had come, across the rooftops. "Come on!"

Anne looked from me to my flat, startled. "Luna and Vari—"

"They're not coming for Luna and Vari!" I called back. "They're coming for us!"

I heard a sharp breath and then Anne was running after me. "How?" she called.

"Gater!" I'd already looked into the future and seen the

oval portal appearing above my flat and Will's group pouring through it. Given the trend I was guessing it was from a gate adept, and that was bad news. As long as Will's group had access to gate magic we couldn't outrun them—they'd just gate ahead to cut us off. The only way to lose them would be to get away from their gater's known locations.

I dodged between chimneys and scrambled over roofs, trying to get to the end of the street. Anne can't see in the dark but she's quick and fit and she was keeping up well. Behind I felt the flicker of gate magic and knew Will and the rest were on the rooftops too. Sirens were starting to sound in the distance, but I knew that by the time they got here it would be too late, and Will's adepts were more than a match for the police anyway. Running barefoot on the bricks and tarmac I felt vulnerable. I was wearing only my T-shirt and trousers, and the only item I was carrying was the two discs of my forcewall, left forgotten in my pocket after my meeting with Cinder and Deleo. Maybe if I used them to block the roof behind us . . .

I felt the flicker of gate magic again and skidded to a halt. "Shit," I said into the darkness.

Anne dropped down behind me. "What's wrong?"

"They've split," I said. "Half in front, half behind." They were in two groups of three now. Looking into the futures in which we kept running, I saw all of them turn into a flurry of chaos and battle. If we kept going as we were we'd be caught in minutes.

Anne looked around. "The house below's empty—"

"We'd be fish in a barrel," I said. Going across the rooftops was out. To our left was the street, but that would just get us boxed in. The safest direction was through the back lots to the right, but then we'd run into the railway line . . .

. . . Oh.

That could work.

I turned and headed for the edge of the roof. "This way. Fire escape over the edge."

The fire escape was painted black and almost invisible in the darkness. I dropped and heard the metal *clang* beneath my feet, then kept going down until the fire escape levelled out. Ahead was a fenced area leading into the building's car park and to our left was the brick wall of the building itself. To the right was a sheer drop onto railway lines.

I led Anne across until the second set of lines were right beneath us. They emerged from a tunnel under the building and continued for about a hundred feet before disappearing beneath the next street over. "Jump over and hang on to the other side," I told Anne, pointing at the railings.

Anne hesitated for an instant then obeyed, swinging her legs over to stand on the walkway on the other side of the railings. "You know what you're doing, right?"

"There's a freight train coming in two minutes," I said. "We're going to hitch a lift. I'll time it for both of us but you're going to have to let go exactly when I tell you."

Anne looked down. It was more than a twenty-foot drop to the wood and steel of the railway tracks. She looked back up at me. "Just so you know, there are *really* few people whom I'd trust if they told me to jump onto railway lines."

"I know."

"Please make sure you get this right." There was a trace of nerves in Anne's voice.

"I will," I said. "Can you see Will's gang?"

Anne nodded up and over my right shoulder. "They're coming."

A rumbling sound echoed through the tunnel and I felt the walkway beginning to tremble beneath my feet. "I'll count you down," I said. "When you hit, drop and stay low."

Anne took a breath and then slid her hands down the railings, swinging down to a crouch. The rumbling grew louder, rising to a roar. "Get ready," I called over the noise of the train. I heard a clang from above and knew Will was close, but I didn't take my eyes off Anne. She looked back at me through the railings, silent and tense. "On zero," I called. "Three . . . two . . . one . . . *zero!*"

As I said *one*, the rails below us brightened and the engine roared past in a sudden rush of wind and metal and noise. Anne dropped exactly as I said *zero*, twisting as she fell. She landed catlike on hands and feet in the centre of the first freight carriage, and I vaulted the railing and dropped after her.

There was one sickening moment of free-fall where everything hung suspended, then I crashed into the metal of the carriage with a painful *thump*, bruising my feet and shoulder as I rolled. I came up just in time to see the roof of the next tunnel heading towards me and I went flat.

The train went into the tunnel and the world became pitch-darkness and deafening noise. The tops of the freight cars were flat metal and there was nothing to hold on to, so all I could do was lie flat and hope. I could feel the steady vibration of the wheels through the car, the carriage going *cha-chunk cha-chunk . . . cha-chunk cha-chunk* again and again. The time in the tunnel felt like an age, but looking back I don't think it could have been more than a minute. Finally with a *whoosh* we were out in the open and I rose to a crouch, looking around.

The train had come out onto a stretch of open track. To one side houses and gardens slid by, while behind us the tunnel mouth receded away, one freight car after another emerging into the fuzzy darkness of the summer night. Cables and girders slid by above as the train rolled along at a steady twenty-five miles per hour. The freight carriages were rectangular and dark-blue; the metal gave good footing but there was no cover unless you wanted to get down into the gap between the cars. Anne was at the front of the train on the first carriage, but behind us the cars were still appearing from the tunnel and I looked into the future, searching for movement. Nothing . . . nothing . . . crap.

I heard a clang from behind me and didn't look around. Anne stepped up next to me, peering back through the darkness. "Anything?"

"Do you want the good news or the bad news?"

Anne sighed. "Bad."

"We've got three of them still on our tail," I said, pointing down to where the end of the train faded into darkness. "Will, the Chinese kid, and Captain America."

"What's the good news?"

"The good news is I think we've lost the others."

Anne shook her head. "You've got a funny definition of good news." She touched my shoulder and I felt a soft warmth spread through me as the ache from the bruises I'd picked up went away.

"Thanks." I walked to the middle of the carriage, taking the gold discs out of my pocket.

"I guess this is a problem with trains as an escape plan," Anne said, looking around. The rush of wind was steady, but not loud enough to drown out voices. "Once you're on it's kind of hard to get off."

"Does tend to be." I placed the discs at either edge of the car, checking to make sure the vibration of the train wouldn't bump them off. The timing on this was going to be tight. Will's group was advancing up the train; we had no more than a minute.

"Is that another forcewall?"

"Yep." I squinted down the line of where the forcewall would activate, then looked around. We were on the train's fourth carriage: behind us were the third, second, and first carriages, followed by the engine. "Okay. When I tell you to go, I need you to get back off this carriage to the next one up."

Anne raised her eyebrows. "While you stay behind?"

"Oh, don't worry, I'll be right after you," I said. "I don't want to get any closer to this than I have to." Movement caught my eye from down the train, and I stepped back. "Here they come."

Will and the other two adepts came out of the darkness like flitting shadows, leaping from car to car as the train rumbled through the night. As they saw us waiting for them they slowed, Will letting the other two catch up, then they made the jump onto the fourth carriage where we were standing and stopped about twenty feet away. Will stood in the centre with Captain America backing him up; both wore what looked like light ballistic vests and Will was holding a shortsword in his left hand that I was pretty sure was the same one that he'd stabbed me with back in the casino. The Chinese kid hung a little farther back. Unlike the other two he didn't have any visible weapons or armour. The five of us stared at each other in the darkness.

"So," I said at last. "I'm guessing I should take this as a 'no' on the truce offer?"

Will's eyes stayed locked on me. "End of the line."

"You wish," I said. Will didn't look away, and neither did I. The seconds stretched out, violence hanging in the air.

"You know," Will said suddenly, "before we do this, there's something I want to know." He stood facing me in the darkness, easily keeping his balance on the rocking train. "Why us? You could have picked any adept in England. What was so important about my family that you had to destroy our lives?"

I looked at Will for a moment, then sighed. "I don't know."

"You don't know." Will's voice was flat.

"Richard told us to get Catherine. He never told us why."

Will studied me. "Just following orders, huh?"

"I'd like to say it was something better than that," I said. "But yeah. That pretty much sums it up. I tried to undo it, but by then it was too late."

"Wow. Guess you've had a tough life."

I looked at Will silently.

"Good thing it's over." In a blur of motion Will levelled a handgun at my chest and pulled the trigger.

Before the gun fired I said the command word. To normal eyes nothing happened. In my sight the two gold discs flared to life and a forcewall flicked into existence on top of the train, forming a vertical barrier separating the adepts from me and Anne. An instant later I saw the flash of the gun.

Forcewalls work by transferring momentum; any body impacting the wall from either side has its momentum transferred into the object the forcewall is anchored to. Force mages can anchor their walls as they choose but for one-shot items like this, which work on command and only for a limited time, the anchor target has to be built in. In the case of my gold-disc walls, the anchor is set to whatever the discs rest on—in this case, the freight car.

The bullet from Will's gun left the barrel at a little over twelve hundred feet per second and travelled the distance to the forcewall in much, much less time than it took me to flinch. As it struck the forcewall its momentum was transferred through the gold discs down into the body of the freight car. The bullet was fast, but momentum is a function of both velocity and mass, and the bullet had a mass of only about a quarter of an ounce. The freight car had a mass of somewhere north of sixty thousand pounds, not counting its cargo. The freight car didn't even quiver.

Will emptied his gun at me, the steady *bang bang bang* muffled through the forcewall. The rest of the shots accomplished about as much as the first. At last the gun clicked empty and he lowered it, staring.

The squashed bullets were lying at the foot of the wall on Will's side, vibrating slightly with the movement of the train. It was hard to tell in the darkness but it looked like Will had been using hollow-point ammunition, designed to expand upon hitting its target. It's not much good at getting through armour or shields but leaves very nasty wounds in a living body, making it the kind of bullet you use for shooting someone whom you don't expect to be well protected and whom you really aren't interested in taking alive. "Are you done?" I asked.

Will pulled out a clip and began reloading. As he did he spoke sideways to Captain America. "Got anything that'll blow through that?"

Captain America gave Will a disbelieving look. "On a train?"

"Wait," Anne said. "You're the one who set that bomb?"

"Uh . . ."

"How could you do that?" Anne demanded. "You could have killed everyone in the flat!"

"It wasn't aimed at the room you were in," Captain America said, but he sounded defensive.

"Not aimed—! You dropped the roof on my head! If Alex hadn't gotten me out of the way it would have crushed me!"

"Wait," the Chinese kid said uneasily. "You were in the living room."

"I *moved*!" Anne was nearly shouting, which was quite something from her. "Don't any of you realise what you're doing? You can't just play around with this! People are going to die!"

"That's the idea," Will said curtly. "Get out of the way and you won't be one of them."

"How can you still think you're the good guys when you do things like this?" Anne demanded. "You're going to—"

Will had put away his handgun and shortsword. Now he held his hand out to Captain America, who reached into what looked like thin air. I felt the flicker of space magic as Captain America pulled two full-sized submachine guns out of a portal so faint as to be almost invisible, handing one to Will and keeping the other for himself. *Dimensional storage,* I thought. *So that's where they keep getting those weapons from.*

Will cocked the gun and levelled it at Anne. "I'm not asking," he said in a flat voice. "Verus murdered my sister and I'm going to kill him for it. Get in the way and I'll do the same to you."

Anne hesitated, her eyes flicking between the guns, and I knew what she was thinking. Life magic is powerful, but it has two weaknesses: it's touch range only, and it doesn't have any defences against direct physical attack. Anne is very good at healing, but both she and her patient have to be *alive* for her to do any healing, and bullets do damage much faster than she can heal it. The last time she'd run up against men with guns it hadn't gone well for her. "Let me ask you something," I said to Will. "Say you actually manage to pull this off. What then?"

Will had moved up to the wall of force and now he kicked at it, keeping his gun trained on me. "Not your problem, is it?"

"Is that the only thing you care about?" I said. "Killing me?"

Will shook his head. "You don't get it, do you? This isn't about you. This is about every adept who's ever been fucked over by a mage who wanted something. You're not the only mage we're going after. You're just one more name on the list."

"And this is how you're planning to work your way down it? Killing everyone one by one?"

Will shrugged. "It's all you mages listen to, right? Anyway, it works."

"No, it doesn't! Using violence to solve all your problems just means you end up with *bigger* problems that'll multiply faster than you can deal with them. Let me put this in terms you'll understand. You will run out of bullets"—I pointed down at the spent ammo at Will's feet—"and out of *people*"—I pointed at Captain America and the Chinese kid—"before you run out of problems."

Will didn't even look at me. "I figured you'd say something like that."

"Rachel's the next one on your list, isn't she?"

Captain America glanced at Will. Will stepped back from the wall without answering. "You'll lose," I said.

"We beat you," Will said.

I pointed at the Chinese kid. "You. Your name's Lee, right?"

The Chinese kid—Lee—drew back a little. He'd been standing well back and looked like he'd been trying to avoid attention. "Uh . . ."

"You found me for Will, right?" I said. "So I guess he'll be using you to keep looking for me, and then for Rachel too. Well, Rachel is stronger than me. Much stronger, and that's not counting the guy she hangs out with. If you're having this much trouble with me, how the hell do you think you can beat her?"

Lee looked around. Captain America gave him a nod. "We'll be stronger by then," Lee said. "We'll have had more practice."

I threw up my hands. "Jesus Christ, you think you're playing a computer game! Killing someone does not make you level up! All it gets you is nightmares for the rest of your life and the never-ending hatred of everybody who ever cared about the person you murdered!"

My voice had risen to a shout, and both Lee and Captain America stood staring at me; without looking I knew Anne had turned to do the same. I stood balancing on the train, the wheels rumbling beneath my feet. The futures of Lee and Captain America flickered, shifting. Will's didn't, and his eyes stayed steady. "They said you were good at talking your way out of things," he said. "Not going to work this time."

I felt Lee and Captain America's futures waver and then fall into line to match Will's. I wanted to swear, wanted to keep shouting, but my precognition was starting to sound a warning and I knew we were out of time. "Anne," I said. "Go. Get down."

Anne turned and ran, crossing the gap from the fourth

to the third carriage with a running jump. I gave Will's group a last glance and followed, putting a little extra speed into the leap to make sure I cleared it. Up ahead I could see a dark wall with streetlights running along the top of it, and the tracks ran into a black circle. We'd had a long run in the open but London's a built-up place, and every railway line in the city goes underground sooner or later. In this case *sooner or later* meant *now*. As soon as I'd made it onto the third car I dropped and craned my neck back to look.

Will, Lee, and Captain America were staring at us through the forcewall, watching the tunnel entrance draw nearer. I wasn't close enough to see their expressions but I saw the jolt go through Captain America as he figured it out, and as the tunnel mouth swept over us he yelled a warning and turned to run. Lee followed; Will stayed a little too long and had only just started to sprint away as the fourth carriage passed into the tunnel, and through the shrinking window of the tunnel mouth I had one last glimpse of their backs before the forcewall hit the top of the tunnel and physics took over.

I didn't get much of a view of what happened next. It was all very fast and my attention was focused on hanging on. Looking back on it with the benefit of hindsight and having read the accident reports, what I think happened was this.

The forcewall hit the brickwork at the top of the tunnel and, just as it had with the bullets, the forcewall tried to transfer the momentum of the impact down into the freight car. The forcewalls I use are powerful by one-shot standards but there's a certain maximum amount of momentum they can transfer. This doesn't matter in normal situations because there's no way a normal human can break the wall's limits. The momentum in the sixty-thousand-pound freight car fell well outside the wall's limits. The wall resisted for a fraction of a second, then vanished as the energy stored in the discs ran out.

But in that fraction of a second the wall transferred

enough momentum to put a major dent in the freight car's velocity, and all of a sudden the fourth car was moving at a different speed from the rest of the train. The freight car wasn't harmed, at least not directly—the discs spread the momentum through a large enough volume that the car got away with only minor buckling. The coupling between the third and fourth cars didn't do so well. It had been designed to withstand gradual stress, not instant stress, and it snapped, separating the first three cars and the engine from the rest of the train and sending a massive jolt through the metal.

The coupling between the fourth and fifth cars had a different problem: instead of being stretched, it was suddenly and violently compressed. The buffers absorbed some of the impact but the rest was transferred into the cars. Something had to give, and the back wheels of the fourth carriage went off the track, followed by the front wheels of the fifth carriage as the two freight cars jack-knifed into the side and mouth of the tunnel.

The rest of the train ploughed into the now-derailed carriages at full speed.

From my point of view I just heard a massive grinding, booming crash, something like a gigantic set of dinner plates being thrown down a staircase, and I felt a shudder through the wheels and metal of the train. Dust and debris went flying, along with shattered bricks from the tunnel mouth. And then just that quickly it was over, and the carriages kept rolling, carrying us away down the tunnel. Anne and I were left in the darkness, riding the back end of the suddenly much shorter train.

With the roar of the train there was no way to talk, and the tunnel made it too risky to move, so I lay flat and waited for the train to stop. After only a couple of minutes I felt the pressure as the train engaged its brakes and began decelerating, slower and slower. It came to a halt with a final screech of metal and a moment later I heard the engine door open up ahead. I knew the driver would be coming down on the right and I reached up to touch Anne, signalling for her to descend on the left. We climbed down the carriage, slipped by the driver as he hurried past on the other side, and started walking towards the fuzzy grey patch that marked the end of the tunnel ahead.

By the time we came out into the open we could hear distant sirens, but the section of track we were on was empty. We walked along the lines until we found an exit and climbed up and out to street level. No one followed.

chapter 8

By the time Anne and I cleared the area the sirens had converged behind us. We took a looping course around, heading back towards Camden Town as more and more emergency vehicles arrived. My phone was under half a ton of rubble in my bedroom but Anne had managed to keep hold of hers, and as we walked back through the empty streets the first thing we did was check what had happened to Luna and Variam. Anne's first call didn't get an answer, nor her second, nor her fifth, but as we crossed Chalk Farm her phone beeped. Anne read the message and gave a sigh of relief. "They're okay."

"Both of them?"

"Both of them."

I relaxed a little. Putting Anne in danger had been bad enough. If Luna and Vari had been hurt . . . "Can you call them?"

Anne shook her head. "They're busy with the police. It . . . didn't sound like they were going to get away soon."

"Oh yeah," I said. "Bomb going off in Central London.

Right." Now I was going to have the antiterror divisions of the Metropolitan Police and MI5 crawling over my flat. This was going to be a major headache.

"Is it going to be a problem?"

"I can probably call in some favours and get it settled, but I'm going to have to stay away from the shop for a while. Getting dragged into a police station with Will's lot out there would be bad." I nodded at a side street. "This way."

We crossed the street. "Will Luna and Vari be okay?" Anne asked.

"Believe it or not, I've actually drilled Luna on this." My contingency plans had been for something more along the lines of a fireball than a high explosive, but still. "She knows what to do, and she and Vari haven't done anything illegal lately as far as I know. They should be fine."

"Okay. That's good." Anne looked around. "Ah, where are we going?"

"I've done enough running around in bare feet for one night," I said. "I'm going to get some shoes."

⁙⁙⁙⁙⁙⁙

The Morrisons supermarket in Camden Town is a huge white building sandwiched between railway lines, and it's so big it has its own roundabout and bus stops. By the time we got there the sky was lightening in the east, and I spent a few seconds checking for watchers before we slipped onto the grounds and to the outbuilding beyond the car park. The door to the outbuilding was locked; I took a key from a hidden location behind a ventilator and let us in.

The inside was dark and filled with the hum of machinery. I led Anne through the pipes and generators to a locker in the corner of the room labelled *HAZARDOUS WASTE DO NOT TOUCH*. It had a combination lock, which I opened and handed to Anne. "Hang on to this a sec."

Anne watched curiously as I pulled out a big gym bag. "You hide that here?"

"Nobody comes here except the maintenance guys," I said, unzipping the bag. I pulled out a pair of shoes and some socks and started putting them on.

"What's inside?"

"Shoes, a coat, two full changes of clothes, shaving kit, and a towel," I said, tying my laces. "Plus loose cash, a prepaid credit card, a knife, a multitool, spare keys, a first-aid kit, a phone, rope, cleaning supplies . . ."

"Why do you have all of this here and not at your flat?"

"In case I can't go to my flat." I grabbed the knife, phone, and cash, slung the bag back into the locker, and relocked it. "Let's go before this place starts waking up."

　　　　　ı ı ı ı ı ı ı ı ı

"An annuller?" Anne said in puzzlement, looking at the white arch.

We were in the old gym in Islington. It's Council property, and I'd managed to talk my way past the sleepy watchman on the door and up to the duelling hall. The azimuth focuses at either end of the duelling pistes were old, but the annuller was new; they'd installed it recently. "Yeah," I said, putting my fingers to the arch. This one was made out of what felt like carbon rather than stone; it must be one of the new models.

"You're worried about a spell?" Anne asked.

"Not exactly." The material was different but the design was familiar, and it took me only a few seconds to confirm that I knew how to work it. I focused my will into the item, letting it charge. "Something that's been bugging me for a while is how those guys keep finding me. It's been years since I've been to that casino, but they seemed to know exactly where I was."

Anne thought about it. "Do you think they followed you?"

I shook my head. "I think it's something to do with that Chinese kid, Lee. Remember what he said on the train? He knew you were in the living room."

"That's true." Anne frowned. "And he couldn't have seen me through the windows . . . Do you think that's the kind of magic he can use? Some sort of seeking?"

"That's my guess. He was the first one to show up back on Friday night. I think Will's using him to find me."

The annuller hummed briefly and then came to life, a pale silvery glow hanging in the archway. "You too," I told Anne.

Anne nodded and moved next to me. We stepped through the archway at the same time and there was a silvery flash, followed by a moment of vertigo that passed quickly. Looking around, I saw that the archway was dark again.

Anne shivered slightly. "That always feels weird. Like I'm in the wrong place."

"I know what you mean." There were some chairs along the wall, and I dropped into one with a sigh. "Well, if it was a standard tracer that should have broken it." All of a sudden I felt completely exhausted. I'd had only a few hours of sleep and I'd been running on adrenaline ever since the attack. Now the aftereffects had set in and I just wanted to collapse.

"I could wake you up," Anne offered.

"Thanks, but no. I'd just have to pay for it later." I looked at her. "Thanks for what you did tonight. I'm not sure I would have made it on my own."

Anne smiled and we sat for a little while in silence. The gym was quiet and empty, and from outside the morning sun was sending shafts of sunlight through the windows above, motes of dust hanging visible in the air. All around us the rumble of traffic and voices was starting to grow to a gentle swell, the steady rustle of London waking up for another summer's day. It felt peaceful and calm. "Can you talk to me about something?" I said. "Otherwise I'm going to fall asleep here."

"Well, I was going to ask," Anne said. "Are we safe here?"

"Right," I said with a sigh. "That." Nothing like the

prospect of violent death to keep you awake. "It depends on whether the annuller broke their tracking ability. If it did, they'll have to figure out a new way to pick us up."

"Actually, what I meant was whether you *know* we're safe here," Anne said. "With your magic."

"I've been looking nonstop since we left the train," I said. "I haven't seen any sign of them finding us here but that doesn't mean they *can't* find us, it just means they're not doing it right now. If some of them were hurt in that crash they've probably pulled back to regroup."

"Do you think they're okay?"

I shook my head. "Anne, I swear, only you would worry about something like that."

Anne was silent. "I'm not sure," I said. "I think they got off the carriage before it hit."

"What if they didn't?"

"I don't know."

"Alex?" Anne said. She was looking at me with those odd reddish eyes of hers. "What you said on the train, about killing someone? Did you mean it?"

I looked off into the corner of the gym. "Yes."

Anne sat quietly. I knew she was deciding what to ask next and the question I was afraid of was *how many*. Somehow I knew that no matter how I answered, it wouldn't lead to anything good.

"You feel like you're on the same side as people like Will, don't you?" Anne said.

I looked at Anne in surprise, then nodded. "Pretty much. You know what's really screwed up about all this? If Will's lot had just come into my shop asking for help defending themselves against Dark mages, I'd probably have said yes." I sighed. "And Will might be trying to kill me, but a lot of what he's saying is *right*. Mages *do* treat adepts badly. And if I were his age and in his position, I'm not a hundred percent sure I'd be doing anything different."

"What about now?"

I shrugged. "When you're twenty you're all about action. You want to change things. If you make it to thirty you learn about consequences. Will's lot haven't learnt that yet. But then the reason they're after me is because of the crap *I* did when *I* was twenty . . ." I raked my hand through my hair. "Damn it. I don't know what to do."

"There has to be some way," Anne said.

"Right now I don't know what it is," I said. "Will's lot might be stupid and they might not care about consequences, but that doesn't make them *less* dangerous; it makes them *more* dangerous. And as long as they're together I don't think I can beat them."

"You're not on your own, though," Anne said. "You've got me and Luna and Vari."

"So Vari should burn them to death?" I said. "Luna should curse them and have a bullet bounce into their head? Is that what you mean?"

Anne looked away. "No."

I looked at Anne curiously. "Other people really matter to you, don't they?"

Anne was silent. "You know, Will was willing to kill you back there," I said. "He would have tried to get around you, but if you'd made him choose between shooting you and letting me get away, he would have shot you."

"I know."

"But you still don't want to hurt him."

Anne stayed quiet for a little longer this time. "Do you know what I see when I look at someone?"

I shook my head.

"Everything," Anne said. "Their movements, their nerves, the play of their muscles and skin . . . It's like a tapestry of green light, layer on layer. Every part connects to every other part and everything works together. Even when it's hurt it works to repair itself." Anne's voice was quiet, and she was watching me as she spoke; I knew she was trying to make me understand. "That's all I do, when I use my magic. Your body *wants* to heal; I just give it a little help. Watching it rebuilding, growing . . . It's beautiful. I can't imagine ever wanting to hurt it. I know what Will and his friends were trying to do. But . . . even then, I don't want them hurt."

I was silent. "You don't want to hurt them either, do you?" Anne said. "That's why you're trying to talk to them."

"We don't always get what we want."

"But there are other ways," Anne said. "You might find something in Richard's mansion, or in Deleo's memories. You're not going to try to kill them. Are you?"

I hesitated. Anne was looking right at me, those odd reddish eyes searching mine, and I felt trapped. I wanted to say no, but somewhere inside me a darker, more cynical voice was warning me not to make promises I might not be able to keep . . . "No," I said.

I felt Anne relax. We sat quietly for a while, watching the sunlight move across the wall.

By the time I was sure Will's lot weren't pursuing, it was too late to go back to sleep, and I wouldn't have felt safe doing it anyway. A quick check confirmed that the police were still swarming over my shop, so I told Anne to meet up with Variam and Luna. "Do you want me to come with you?" Anne asked. We were a couple of streets away from my shop, near Camden Market.

I shook my head. "You've risked your life for me once today already. Besides, the more people we have, the more chance one of us is going to set something off."

Anne nodded, then to my surprise gave me a quick hug. I flinched slightly—it had been so long since anyone had done that, it took me a second to realise what she was doing. "Be careful," she told me, then turned and walked away.

I watched her go, then shook my head and went to get ready for my return to Richard's mansion.

' ' ' ' ' ' ' ' '

Preparation is important for a diviner, and if I have to go somewhere dangerous I always make sure I've got as much leverage as possible. With my flat occupied by the police I couldn't access my items there, so I had to go scrounging. By the time I'd begged, borrowed, and traded for enough magic items to make me feel reasonably safe, it was past noon.

The one item I hesitated over was my mist cloak. It's the most effective form of stealth I have, but it was also back in the safe room in my flat. I might be able to get it out without the police stopping me, but then again I might not. What decided me against it in the end was that I'd be with Caldera—for various reasons I'd much rather the Keepers didn't find out that I own that particular item. I picked up a last few bits and pieces and dialled Caldera's number.

Caldera didn't sound happy. "What kept you?"

"Sorry," I said. "Long night."

"I left you two messages, didn't you get them? Never mind, just get over here. We're on our way to the park near yours with the grounding circle. You know the place?"

"I'll be there."

' ' ' ' ' ' ' ' '

The park near my shop is about a ten-minute walk away. Even though it's in the middle of Camden it always seems to be deserted, maybe because of the construction vehicles parked around it. As a result of some geographical oddities it has an unusually low level of background magic, which is handy if you want to study something or use a tricky spell. It's not widely used, but I'm far from the only one who knows about it and this wasn't the first time I'd met another mage there.

Caldera was under the trees at the far end, and she wasn't alone. I crossed the park, ducked under the branches, then looked between her and the person she'd brought along. "This is a bad idea."

Sonder was standing next to Caldera, wearing the kind of get-up city dwellers buy from camping stores when they want to go hiking. "What?" he said.

"Why is he here?" I asked Caldera.

"Because he's a time mage," Caldera said, glancing between us. She was wearing old workman's clothes, patched and mended from long use, as well as a webbing belt with sealed pouches. "You've worked together before, right?"

"I thought this was supposed to be a quick in-and-out."

"We know the place is empty," Caldera said. "I need to know if anyone's been using it, and that means timesight."

"Timesight only shows you one location at one time," I said. "Scanning the whole mansion is going to take hours."

"Then we better get started, hadn't we?"

I looked around reluctantly. Sonder looked a little offended, but that wasn't why I was feeling uneasy. All my instincts told me that visiting Richard's mansion was dangerous. Trying to do a full search, like it was some sort of crime scene . . .

But I'd given my word and it wasn't enough to make me back out, at least not yet. "All right."

Caldera raised a hand, weaving a spell under the cover of the trees. A pale brown light sprang up next to the tree trunk, growing and widening until it steadied into a vertical oval. Shapes appeared in the oval, the colours changing from pale brown to green and grey and then sharpening and becoming clear, forming an image of earth and grass and trees. For a moment it was only an image, as if seen through a window, then the window was gone and we were looking through a gateway. A cool breeze blew through, ruffling my hair; the place we were going was a few degrees colder than the summer heat of the park.

I led the way. Sonder followed and Caldera came last, letting the gateway vanish behind her.

ı ı ı ı ı ı ı ı

You can tell a lot about a mage by where they live.

Apprentices usually live with their masters. Sometimes they'll have a flat or shared rooms, but it's still generally the master who arranges it. They're not really expected to be responsible for themselves; it's their master who provides for them, and in return they're expected to do as they're told.

Once an apprentice graduates to journeyman status, things change. Now they're free to do as they like, and usually one of the first things they do is get themselves a place of their own. Mages rarely have to worry about money and it's easy for them to buy themselves a house, as long as they don't go for anything extravagant. Of course, lots of them *do* want something extravagant, and it's common for established mages to own a mansion. Some of it is about status—my house is more ostentatious than yours—but there's a practical element too. Some of the things mages get up to require a fair amount of space, and if you're trying to perform a large-scale ritual then there are a lot of benefits to being able to stage it in your own home rather than an unsecured area.

The next thing to sort out is location. Light mages like to place their mansions in the hearts of big cities or in attractive and well-populated areas of the countryside near towns and main roads. It makes it easy for guests to get there, and it makes it easy to get hold of servants and catering staff to entertain the guests. A mage who chooses an easily accessible location is making a statement; he's saying that he's willing to entertain visitors (though probably only select visitors). Other mages go for a compromise, choosing to live in the suburbs or in slightly more removed areas of the country. You can still reach them easily enough but they've got a little more privacy.

And some mages don't want to live near anyone else at all.

Richard's mansion was the last type. It was in a remote

corner of Wales, hidden away amidst forest and rolling hills. The mansion itself was an oblong with two jutting wings but with no car park, no driveway, and no roads. Rail lines didn't go anywhere near the place and there wasn't so much as a gravel path leading to the front door.

It's very rare to build a house in a place so isolated, and there are only a few reasons anyone would want to do it. It can be because you don't want visitors. It can be because you don't want anyone getting in. And it can be because you don't want anyone getting out.

I stood in the shade at the edge of the tree cover, looking across at the mansion. When I'd last seen the grounds they'd been cleared, but now they were wild and overgrown; the old plots had been reclaimed by the forest around us, wild-flowers and bushes a tangled riot in what had once been an ordered garden. The lawn was now a meadow, and behind the mansion green hills rose up into the blue sky. It would have been beautiful if I hadn't known what the place had been used for.

"Anything?" Caldera said from behind me.

"I wasn't looking," I said. It's a weird feeling, seeing something that was once the centre of your life. For a moment the old memories flooded back; my last glimpse of the mansion, lit windows against the black night, snatched over my shoulder as I fled. I'd sworn never to come back—or if I did, it would have been to destroy the place. In the end I never did return . . . not physically, at least. For a long time I saw it every night in my dreams.

But emotions fade, and as I looked at the mansion I realised to my surprise that most of the old hate and fear was gone. For all that it represented, for all the danger that might still be inside, it was just a building—steeped in history, ancient and dangerous, but for now at least, deserted.

"When you're ready," Caldera said.

I shook off the memories. Time to focus. "The grounds are clear. Let's move up."

We picked our way through the overgrown trails, brushing through the grass. Birds sang from the nearby trees and the air smelt of pollen and of summer. Richard's mansion grew larger as we approached; despite its age the building didn't look weatherbeaten or damaged, and apart from a little roughening around the edges it looked just as it had when I'd lived here. The walls could have been mistaken for brickwork but weren't. Despite its sprawl, the mansion only had two storeys. "I thought it'd be bigger," Sonder said.

"Most of it's underground," I said absently, scanning ahead. "That's funny."

"What's funny?" Caldera said.

"There are wards."

Caldera looked at me in surprise. "After ten years?"

I shook my head. "No, the old gate and scrying wards are gone. But there's a trigger there." I pointed at the front door. "It's not locked, but if you walk through you'll set off a silent alarm."

Caldera frowned at it. "I can't see anything."

"It's not designed to be visible," I said. There are ways of shrouding or inverting wards that make them difficult to detect. This one was hard to spot, but the design was familiar. In fact it was *very* familiar . . . "Wait a minute," I said, my heart sinking. "Let me check something."

Sonder and Caldera waited for me. "Deleo," I said after a moment. "Great."

"She's here?" Sonder said in alarm.

I nodded at the door. "If we set that thing off she will be. It's designed to alert her."

"What's her response time?" Caldera asked.

"Fast. Minutes."

"I thought this place was deserted?" Sonder said.

"I think we might just have found out *why* it's deserted," I said. The futures of Deleo gating in were chaotic and unpredictable, but I was pretty sure I didn't want a closer look. I had the feeling that if she found us here she'd kill first and ask questions later.

"Can you disarm it?" Sonder asked.

I nodded. "It'll take a while, but yeah." I studied it with narrowed eyes. "Doing it safely is going to be slow but we can probably—"

"Yeah, let's speed this up," Caldera said. She pointed at a section of wall to the right. "Is *that* bit warded?"

"Uh," I said. "No."

Caldera walked up through the bushes and placed both hands flat against the stone wall. Brownish light flared and the stone melted and flowed. The section of wall in front of her thinned and vanished, becoming an archway, the stone that had occupied the empty space moving to buttress the gap. The stone stopped flowing, Caldera took her hands away, and the light faded. Where there had been a blank wall was a reinforced arch, leading into darkness. "There," Caldera said. "We clear?"

"I guess that's a faster way to do it," I said, walking up to the gap and taking a glance through. "Clear."

Caldera summoned up a light and the three of us walked in.

⁞⁞⁞⁞⁞⁞⁞⁞⁞⁞

The inside of the mansion hadn't aged as gracefully as the outside. Dust covered everything and bits of furniture had been overturned. "You two stick together," Caldera said. "I'm going to take a look around."

I gave her an exasperated look. "Do the words 'safety precautions' mean anything to you?"

"Yeah, people keep telling me something about that," Caldera said. "Be right back."

"Just don't go below the ground floor," I called after her as she left. Her footsteps faded away and I shook my head. "And people tell me *I* take risks."

Sonder didn't answer. He played the light of his torch around the hallway, the glow flicking over dusty paintings. "Well, this is your party," I told him. "Where do you want to start?"

"Is there any kind of meeting room?" Sonder asked. "Somewhere people would assemble?"

I nodded down the hall. "That way."

The rooms on the ground floor of the mansion were the kitchens, storerooms, dining room, and servants' quarters. The room we entered had once been a living room, but as I walked in I slowed and stopped. The light from our torches showed broken chairs, and drawers and shelves had been emptied, their contents strewn over the floor. The sofa in the centre had been cut in half, a huge section of the middle missing and the stuffing spilling out.

"Was it . . . always like this?" Sonder said, staring at the sofa.

I shook my head. "No." This was the room where Shireen, Rachel, Tobruk, and I had all gathered with Richard that first night, and where we'd kept meeting in the months afterward. "What happened here?"

"Wait a minute," Sonder said, frowning. His eyes became distant.

I stood in silence, looking around. While we'd been Richard's apprentices this had been a kind of briefing room; it was where he'd given us our assignments and where we'd gathered to talk in our free time. My eyes drifted to Richard's old armchair; unlike the rest of the furniture it hadn't been touched and I unconsciously stepped away from it. The fireplace was dark and cold.

Sonder stayed in his trance for a long time, fifteen minutes at least. When he finally looked up at me, he looked uneasy. "It was Deleo."

"She trashed the place?"

Sonder shook his head. "No. Three other men did. They

were here five months ago. I think they were looking for something."

"Looking for what?"

"I don't know," Sonder said, looking around. "I don't think they got the chance to find it. Deleo walked in that door and she . . . killed them. All of them."

I looked around the empty room. There was dust but no bones. "What happened to the bodies?"

Sonder pointed at the dust at my feet.

"Oh." I stepped aside. "Right." I'd thought there was something familiar about the way that sofa had been destroyed. Rachel had grown a lot more powerful in the years since I'd left, and she seemed to specialise in disintegration. "Did they have any kind of magic?"

"Not enough," Sonder said.

We stood in the empty, dead room, the beams of our torches the only light. "You don't think Deleo's still living here, do you?" Sonder asked.

I shook my head. "Nobody's living here. I shouldn't have to tell you that."

"Then why's Deleo still coming?"

"From the sound of it she only shows up if someone trips the burglar alarm," I said. "I think she's just guarding this place. All she cares about is making sure no one else touches it."

"But . . ." Sonder looked around. "It doesn't make sense."

"What doesn't?"

"Doing it like this!" Sonder said. "There wasn't a warning anywhere or anything like that. The front door wasn't even locked! We could have just walked in without knowing any better and she would have tried to kill us!"

"From the sound of it that's exactly what she's been doing."

"But why doesn't she do it the normal way?" Sonder said. "No one even knows that this is her house! She could have . . . I don't know, registered it with the Council or something."

"She *is* letting people know that this is her house."

"They can't spread the message if they're all dead!"

I shrugged. "She probably lets a few go. Or maybe she just assumes that if enough people go missing then sooner or later the others will take the hint."

Sonder shook his head. "That's insane."

I looked at Sonder for a moment. "If you want to be a scholar," I said at last, "you have to learn not to see things so simply."

"What do you mean?"

"Deleo and Dark mages seem insane to you because you're judging them by your standards," I said. "You're assuming they have the same goals you do. What makes you so sure Deleo *wants* to warn people off peacefully?"

Sonder looked at me, puzzled. "What are you saying?"

"I'm saying that if you're the kind of person who likes to take out your frustrations on other people, then occasionally having to murder some burglars is less of a drawback and more a perk of the job."

Sonder stared at me in revulsion. "Are you serious?"

I sighed. "I'm not saying that's why she does it, I'm saying it *might* be. The point is that Deleo doesn't live in your world. What you said about registering with the Council? To Dark mages that'd be a joke. They only respect authority if it's backed up by force. Registering might actually *attract* them—they'd figure that if she was trying to get the protection of Light mages, then she couldn't handle it herself. And it would mostly be other Dark mages she'd be worried about."

"You're telling me they'd listen to people being murdered, but they wouldn't read a sign on the door?"

"Yes! Dark mages are *different* from you, don't you get that? They don't follow rules and they don't do as they're told! If you set a boundary the first thing they'll do is push it to see if you'll do anything. What Deleo is doing is a normal way to send a message in Dark society, and if you don't understand that then you shouldn't be here."

Sonder and I stared at each other for a moment, then Sonder looked away. "I'm not here because of you." He sounded defensive. "I've been doing Council work for the Keepers since last year."

"I know."

"I know what I'm doing," Sonder said. "It's not like I'm an apprentice anymore. They keep saying—" He stopped and went on. "It's not like it's all new to me. I see things that most people never do. Crimes, secrets . . . They think it's hidden, but it's not."

"But they don't quite take you seriously, no matter how much you know, do they? Trust me, I know all about that."

Sonder stood in silence for a moment. "How could you ever join people like this?" he said at last.

I knew Sonder wasn't talking about Light mages anymore. "People change, Sonder," I said. "I know you see a lot, and I know you see things that others can't. But you've always been detached from it. Keepers like Caldera don't need you to be involved, they just need you to be good with your magic."

"I *do* get involved."

"Because of other people," I said. "The main way you use your timesight is to help everyone else out. You're not the one who causes the problem—you're the one who gets called in after someone *else* causes a problem." I looked at Sonder. "In a lot of ways you're an example of what's best about Light mages. But it makes it hard for you to understand people like me and Deleo. When you really and truly screw things up—when you look around and realise that your life's a disaster and it's nobody's fault but your own—then it makes you ask some hard questions. You look into the mirror and you realise you don't much like the person looking back at you. And you start figuring out how to change that." I shrugged. "Or you stop looking into mirrors . . . You've never had to do that. You've never had to really stop and question your beliefs, because they've worked. It's not a bad thing. Just . . . remember that it's not that way for everyone else."

Sonder didn't answer. "What else did you see?" I asked.

"What do you mean?"

"Come on, Sonder," I said. "Our magic types aren't *that* far apart. You were looking back for the last time I was here, weren't you?"

Sonder's not a good liar. He hesitated just long enough to make it very obvious what the answer was. "Don't worry about it," I said. "I was going to ask you to do it anyway. Did you see any trace of Catherine?"

"No," Sonder admitted.

"But the wards are down."

"They're down now," Sonder said. "They're not down *then*. Anything past about nine years just blanks out. And it's at the edge of my range anyway."

I nodded, hiding my disappointment. I hadn't really been expecting it to be that easy but it had been worth a try. "I guess we keep looking."

Caldera came back a few minutes later. "Anything?" I asked as she walked in.

"Waste of time," Caldera said. "This place hasn't been used in years."

"Deleo was here," Sonder said. "She killed three men who tried to loot this room five months ago."

"Dark-style home defence, huh?" Caldera glanced at the ruined sofa. "A couple of the other rooms have been trashed too."

"Should I check them?" Sonder asked.

Caldera shook her head. "No, it's Richard I want. Deleo's only important if she can lead us to him."

"So we're going?" I said.

Caldera raised an eyebrow. "In a hurry to leave?"

"I'm in a hurry not to run into Deleo."

"So watch for her."

"I've been watching for her nonstop since we gated in," I said. "You know the best way of making sure we don't run into her? Not sticking around any longer than we have to."

"I'm a Keeper, Verus," Caldera said. "If we ran scared every time we had to deal with a Dark mage, we wouldn't be much good at our jobs." She looked at Sonder. "Can you follow where Deleo went?"

"I don't think she came in the front door," Sonder said.

"She wouldn't have to," I said. "She knows the whole mansion and there are no gate wards. She can gate into any part she likes."

"Then let's check the basement," Caldera said.

I sighed and started towards the doorway. "I knew you were going to say that."

⁙⁙⁙⁙⁙

"It's warded," I said.

We were at the end of the main hallway on the ground floor. The entrance to the lower levels was a simple arch in the wall, and the glow from Caldera's light illuminated stone steps leading down into shadow. "It's another alarm ward, right?" Sonder said, concentrating on the archway. "It looks the same as the first."

"It is."

"Right," Caldera said, walking to the wall. "Same again, then."

"Don't!" I said sharply. "It's a trap."

Caldera frowned at me. "I can't see anything."

"The alarm ward is just a cover," I said. "It's meant to make you think that you can get past it the same way you did the first. The real defence is there." I pointed down into the darkness. "Anything that goes down there is going to summon a nocturne."

"What the hell is that?"

"Darkness elemental. They hunt by sound. You don't want to meet one."

"So what's the trigger?" Caldera said. "How do we get around it?"

"If there's a limit to the trigger area, I can't find it," I said. I'd been looking through potential futures and I couldn't find a single one where we went down there without fighting the thing. "And it's sensitive. It's not just set to living things, objects are going to trigger it too."

"There has to be some way to avoid it, right?" Sonder said. "Maybe a password?"

"I'm not sure there is."

"Really?"

"Look, I've seen a lot of magical defences and they usually have a pattern. They're designed to let the right people in and keep the wrong people out. This one isn't made that way. It's the kind of ward you set up if you don't want to let *anybody* in. Even Deleo would have trouble disarming this without setting it off first."

"Why would she do that?" Sonder asked.

"If she wasn't coming down here either," I said. "This trap is the equivalent of filling a room with poison gas and then sealing it from the outside. You don't do it if you're planning to use it." I looked at Caldera. "Deleo hasn't been using this mansion. The only reason she comes here is if someone trips the burglar alarm, so she can reset the wards."

"You mean that's what she's been doing until now," Caldera countered. "She could have set this ward up to last for ten years and be planning to disarm it when Richard came back."

"Which we've seen absolutely no evidence for."

Caldera looked down the steps with narrowed eyes. "If we took this thing on, could we beat it?"

I looked at Caldera in disbelief. "You've got to be kidding me."

"Well?"

"I have no idea! Combats are way too chaotic to see more than a few seconds ahead. I can tell the thing's going to go out of its way to try and kill you, isn't that enough?"

"Why her?" Sonder asked.

"Because she makes the most noise."

"So make an educated guess," Caldera said. She folded her arms and looked at me. "Can we get past this thing?"

It's times like this that remind me just how big a gap there is between elemental mages and diviners. For me, combat is dangerous. A bullet or a blade will kill me as fast as anyone else and the best way to avoid that is not to be in a fight in the first place. I have to be afraid of physical threats, or I wouldn't survive. For mages like Caldera it's different. The shields and defensive spells of elemental mages aren't invulnerable but they're damn close, and the kinds of weapons that would kill an unarmoured human—guns, knives, grenades—don't do much to an elemental mage except piss them off. Bringing them down in a straight fight takes the kind of firepower that the average person is simply not going to be carrying around, which means that when an elemental mage looks at an ordinary human being, they know that barring something unexpected they've got nothing to fear from them. It gives them a very different mindset from someone like me.

I looked at Caldera, sizing her up. Heavyset and overweight, she didn't look like most people's idea of an action heroine. But I'd been watching her on the way here and I'd noticed that she didn't move like someone who was unhealthy, and also that she hadn't gotten out of breath once. There might be a lot of fat on her but I had the feeling there was a lot of muscle too, and the way she acted gave me the impression that she knew how to take care of herself. A sparring match with her would be interesting.

"Well?" Caldera said.

"Probably," I said reluctantly. I really didn't want to encourage Caldera but I also didn't want to lie. "Nocturnes don't have the power of true elementals. But I can't guarantee that the fight won't tip Deleo off too. And I don't care how good you are, you couldn't take her *and* a nocturne at the same time."

Caldera looked away. "Look, don't you think it's time to get out of here?" I said. "Maybe you're right about Richard and maybe you're not, but this place has been empty for years. If there's anything to find, it's not here."

Caldera hesitated and, looking ahead, I could tell she was at last seriously thinking about it. I would have liked to know more, but I'd already spent too long focusing on the futures of us fighting the nocturne and I needed to get back to watching for danger. I sent my senses branching out ahead through the futures of us waiting where we were now, looking for any shift in the status quo.

And with a jolt I found it. We weren't alone in the mansion anymore. There were people here—familiar people, heading straight for us. "We have to go," I said. "Now!"

Sonder and Caldera looked at me in surprise. "Why?" Sonder asked.

"Because there's a bunch of people coming here to kill me, and they're going to do it unless we get out of here *right now!*"

Sonder's eyes widened. "Wait, it's—?"

"Yes!"

"How do—?" Caldera started to ask.

"Because I've seen them!" I was frantically mapping out escape routes and it didn't look good. They were directly between us and the front entrance—they must have come in the same way we did—and they were closing in fast. We'd have to get around them or go over.

Caldera frowned at me. "Why do they want to kill you?"

"Because of something I did ten years ago—I'll tell you the story, but not here!"

"Wait," Caldera said. "I'm not moving unless you tell me more than that."

I wanted to scream. "Are you *trying* to get us—"

I'd been searching as fast as I could through the futures and in that instant I realised two things. First, using the annuller hadn't worked. In all of the futures in which I shifted my position, the path of the incoming group adjusted to match me. They knew exactly where I was and trying to hide wasn't going to help. Second, they were moving faster than we were. Even if I could get Caldera and Sonder moving, they would be on us before we could get out of the mansion. "Too late," I said, looking down the corridor. A moment later Will appeared around the corner.

chapter 9

The Nightstalkers had come out in force this time, and they just kept coming around the corner one after another. Will was at the front with Lee and Dhruv flanking him, gold-hair girl and Captain America were right behind with Ja-Ja the life-drinker, and at the back, almost hidden by the others, was a girl I hadn't seen before who looked English. Seven in all. They advanced down the corridor towards us.

Caldera stepped between me and them. "Who are you and what are you doing here?"

Will came to a halt and the rest of them followed his lead. He didn't look at Caldera; just like each time before, his eyes stayed locked on me. "I'm not here for you."

"You're William Traviss, aren't you?" Caldera said. "Mind telling me what you're doing on a mage's property?"

"I don't care whose property this is." Will shifted his stare to Caldera. "The man behind you murdered my sister and I'm here for him. Get out of my way."

Caldera looked back at him, then turned her head just slightly towards me, not taking her eyes off Will. "Verus?"

she said, and there was a slight edge to her voice. "Anything you want to tell me?"

I let out a breath. The futures were shifting too much to make any useful predictions now. It was all going to depend on Caldera, and I couldn't tell which way she would jump. "When I was Richard's apprentice, I was part of a team that captured Will's sister," I said. I kept my voice level. "Will thinks she was killed. I don't know if it's true."

"Liar!" Will snarled, his eyes flaring. "You knew what was happening to her!"

I looked away, unwilling to meet Will's eyes. "You think I didn't know?" Will said, and I could hear the hate in his voice. "A year she was held in here. So you sick fucks could use her for fun!"

"And that was why I tried to break her out!" I snapped back. "Yes, I screwed it up, but at least I tried!"

"Right," Will said scornfully. "You were trying to save her."

"Whether you believe it or not, it's the truth. And how are you so damn sure she's dead? Even *I* don't know what happened to her!"

"She died here in this mansion," Will said. "And I'm going to make sure the same happens to you."

"We just did this! You were in a train crash twelve hours ago! How are you even here?"

"Enough!" Caldera shouted.

Will and I both stopped. "You," Caldera said, pointing at Lee. "How did you get in here?"

"Uh . . ."

"Through the door, or through the archway in the wall?"

"None of your business," Will said, just as Lee said, "The archway."

Will glared at Lee and Lee dropped his eyes. "At least you've got some sense," Caldera said. "Now let's see if I've got this straight. Are you telling me the reason you've come here is to murder the mage behind me?"

"*He's* the murderer!" Will said.

"And I'm Keeper Caldera of the Order of the Star," Caldera said calmly. "That means I police crimes involving mages. Are you about to commit one?"

"The only crimes you Keepers care about are the ones where it's mages that are the victims," Will said. He was focused on Caldera now, eyes narrowed, and he wasn't backing down. "Murdering an adept doesn't even count in your book, does it? We're nothing to you."

"The law is the law," Caldera said. "And it applies to adepts as well as mages. You might want to think about that."

The rest of Will's group had been silent until now, but at this point gold-hair girl spoke up. "So what are we supposed to do when some mage decides to enslave us?" She looked angry. "Just take it?"

"You can bring your case before the Council," Caldera said. "Your petition will be heard."

"Right," gold-hair girl said sarcastically. "And they're going to care."

"I don't make the laws," Caldera said. "But I do enforce them." Her voice sharpened. "Now let's get something clear: this is not up for debate. I'm here on Council business and you're trespassing. I'm going to have to ask you to leave."

"You're right," Will said, and his voice was soft. His eyes were fixed on Caldera. "It's not up for debate."

I felt the mood in the corridor shift, and the futures shifted with it. All of a sudden I could sense violence. "Walk away, William," Caldera said quietly.

"I walked away from Verus yesterday," Will said. "Not this time." He held out his hand to Captain America without looking. I saw Captain America's eyes flick between Caldera and me and he hesitated for just an instant, then he reached into thin air. Space magic flickered as he pulled out Will's shortsword and handed it to him then took out a submachine gun for himself. Gold-hair girl's eyes narrowed on Caldera and I felt the familiar trace of fire magic beginning to build.

"One more step forward," Caldera said, "and you'll be attacking a Council Keeper." Caldera was standing in the middle of the corridor facing all of them, her voice steady. "All of you listen to me very carefully. You might think you're fighting some sort of war against mages. You're not. The Council knows all about you and they've left you alone. Use those weapons in your hands and that will change. And you will not like the consequences."

"The Council isn't here," Will said. He was standing quite still and I knew he was holding his magic ready. When he moved, it would be very fast. "Just you."

"And me," I said, stepping forward and looking between the adepts. "If you keep following Will, it's going to get you killed. Don't you see that?"

"Stay out of this, Verus," Caldera said.

I didn't look away from Will. "In case you haven't noticed, I've kind of got a stake in this."

"Ignore the Keeper and the other one," Will said over his shoulder. "We're only here for Verus."

"That's not how it works," Caldera said sharply. "If you—"

"Look out!" I snapped and jumped back just as Will lunged for me.

I'd seen Will in action enough times now to figure out that in terms of straight-up combat ability, his magic was a close match for mine. I could predict his moves, but he was so quick that all my divination let me do was keep up with him. He closed the distance between us in a flash, and if I hadn't already jumped back he would have run me through.

But while Will might be faster, Caldera had a lot less distance to cover than he did. She stepped into his way and Will slammed straight into her centre of mass with a *thud*. Caldera didn't even budge; it was as if Will had run into a wall. She tried to grab him, but even though Will had to be hurting from the impact he was still fast enough to dodge aside and try to get past again.

But they'd forgotten about Sonder. Sonder had kept his mouth shut in the conversation and stayed behind Caldera, but now he put out his hand towards Will, his face set, and cast his own time spell, similar to Will's but inverted. The two spells met and cancelled each other out and all of a sudden Will was moving at normal speed. He stumbled and came to a stop, a look of surprise flashing across his face.

Caldera hit Will in the chest. It was an open-hand strike, and she drove up off the floor with all her weight behind it. The impact lifted Will into the air and threw him the best part of ten feet, and he hit Dhruv on the way down. The two of them went down in a tangle of arms and legs.

Caldera glared at the adepts, her hands low and spread. "Who's next?"

Will pulled himself up, gasping. He'd been winded and it took him a few seconds to catch his breath. "Shoot him!" he said, pointing at me. "He's right there, just kill him!"

Captain America and gold-hair girl had both been ready to fire when Will had rushed in, but the people in the way had made them hesitate. Now they both aimed at me, and as they did I sidestepped behind Caldera. Captain America tracked me with his gun, saw that Caldera was in the way, and checked his fire.

Gold-hair girl didn't. Red light flared around her hands and ground fire roared out. It was directed at me but hit Caldera instead, and Caldera disappeared in a flash of flame. An instant later the fire was gone. Caldera wasn't. Her clothes were scorched and smoking but she didn't even look scratched and I could see earth magic glowing about her, reinforcing and strengthening her body. "You," she said to the adepts, "are starting to piss me off."

Several of the adepts took a step back. Will didn't. "You cowards!" he snapped. "We've beaten mages before!"

Without looking back he charged straight for me. After a moment's hesitation the rest of them followed, and that was when things got really messy.

The corridor dissolved into a melee, weapons and fire and confusion. Will was trying to get past Caldera, bullets and ground fire flashing out past them, and the hallway was a press of bodies and blows. There was too much going on and it was all I could do just to keep myself alive. Again and again I saw myself fall dead or wounded, stabbed or shot or burnt, and again and again I slid aside just enough that the strike would miss. The air heated from the fire magic, and bullets struck chips of stone from the walls. Caldera stood alone against the tide but the corridor was narrow and they couldn't all reach her at once. They kept getting in each other's way, and whoever was at the front would be focused by Sonder's slowing magic and by Caldera's punishing blows. One hit was all it took to send them staggering back, but as soon as they did another would move in to take their place.

The Indian boy, Dhruv, threw a set of metal spheres into the air; an invisible field caught them and sent them spinning around him in an elliptical orbit, moving faster and faster before zipping towards me as though hurled from a sling. I ducked behind Caldera and they slammed into her instead, cracking off her hardened skin. "Stop doing that," Caldera said through clenched teeth, aiming another punch at Will.

"Some of us don't have stone skin," I said just as Captain America popped up around Will and fired at me point-blank. I was already dodging and the burst hit thin air; he fell back instantly, ejecting his magazine and reaching for a new one.

"Find us a way out," Caldera said over her shoulder, but I couldn't answer; Dhruv was sending another volley at me from over Will's head and this time he curved them in, attacking from the side. I had to dive sideways, stumbling for a second, and as I came to my feet another blast of flame engulfed Caldera.

Ja-Ja was on her instantly. The life-drinker had stayed at the edge of the fight, lurking and waiting to strike, and in the second that Caldera was still blinded from the blast he struck. Green-black light flashed at his palm as he touched Caldera's side, and even at a distance I felt a draining, tugging sensation, like being on the edge of a whirlpool.

Caldera gave a roar that was half rage and half pain, and struck at Ja-Ja with the ferocity of a wounded bear. I heard the crack as her blow landed and Ja-Ja went flying down the corridor, but Caldera stumbled and went to one knee. She was up again in an instant and I knew combat reflexes were keeping her moving—you *never* stay down in a fight, you always get up as fast as you can—but she was swaying and I could tell she was badly hurt.

Ja-Ja picked himself up. Caldera's punch should have broken his bones but my heart sank as I looked at him and I saw that he was smiling. Whatever he'd taken from Caldera, it had been enough to let him shrug off the hit. "Tastes nice," he said. "I could go for dessert."

"What the fuck are you doing?" Captain America snapped at Ja-Ja. He was still holding his gun, but he wasn't aiming it at me anymore.

"We said don't hurt her!" Dhruv shouted.

Ja-Ja gave Dhruv a contemptuous look. "Yeah, you were doing so great."

Will was hesitating, looking between Caldera and Ja-Ja. For the moment the adepts were distracted but I knew it wouldn't last. One of the metal spheres Dhruv had been firing at me was lying on the floor, and I scooped it up. "Caldera!" I said sharply with a note of command in my voice. "Watch!"

Caldera turned, hurt but angry, and Sonder did as well. Before Caldera could speak, I flicked the sphere back down the corridor. It glanced off the wall and through the archway down to the basement, and I heard the *clack-clack-clack* as it went bouncing down the steps. Caldera and Sonder stared for a second, then their eyes went wide at the same instant. I put my finger to my lips.

"Keeper," Will said, and all three of us turned to look at him. He was frowning at Caldera. "We're not here for you. You and the time mage can go. We just want Verus."

Caldera looked back at him, then gave him the finger.

Captain America raised his eyebrows; he actually looked impressed. Ja-Ja looked eager, and I knew he was hoping Caldera would say no. Will just looked pissed off. "You aren't going to win this," he said. "Get out of—"

The nocturne came out of the shadows, homing in on Will like iron filings to a magnet. Its body was black smoke and blended into the darkness behind it so perfectly that only its blue-white eyes were visible. Will leapt back, eyes going wide in shock, but even he wasn't quick enough and a tendril of darkness twined around his leg, yanking him off his feet.

The corridor erupted into chaos, the adepts scrambling to get away from the nocturne or rushing to fight it, but this time I wasn't watching. I grabbed Caldera's arm and yanked at her. Even wounded as she was, it was like trying to move a rock, but it got her attention. "Come on!"

We fled towards the stairs. Before we got out of sight I took a glance back and had one glimpse of Will on his back, slashing at the nocturne as it pulled him in. Captain America was kneeling and firing, gun flashing in staccato bursts, the nocturne reaching for him, and then we were racing up the stairs with the shouts and gunfire fading behind us.

By the time we made it up to the second floor Caldera was staggering and I knew we wouldn't make it out of the mansion in time. I made a snap decision and pulled a door open. "In!" Once they were inside I slammed it behind us.

Sonder looked around, dismayed. We were in a bedroom, old and neglected, the bed covered in dust and the light dim through the grimy windows, and I realised that it was my old room. I hadn't been intending to pick it but my feet had remembered the way. "There's no way out!"

"You'll have to gate us from here," I told Caldera.

Caldera looked around and I knew what she was thinking. Gating is one of the more general elemental spells, but also one of the most dangerous; it works by creating a similarity between two points in space and to do it reliably you have to be very familiar with both the place you're leaving and the place you're going to. Caldera had studied the copse of trees on her last visit here; that was why she'd gated us there and not directly inside. She hadn't studied this room. Gating from here would be risky.

On the other hand, trying to make the run out of the mansion with a bunch of homicidal adepts on our tail would be a lot *more* risky. I felt the futures fall into line as Caldera made her decision, and she began the spell. "Cover me," she ordered.

I could hear the battle going on downstairs, and I didn't know how much time we had. Nocturnes are semi-insubstantial and shooting them just draws their attention, but they can still be burnt and they're still alive. If Will's group could get organised—and unfortunately for me, they seemed to be pretty good at getting organised—then they'd be able to banish it. "I've got a forcewall," I told Sonder, nodding at the door.

"I can do better than that," Sonder said, and raised his hand towards the door. For a few seconds nothing happened, then the area around the door seemed to twist and warp before suddenly reflecting our images back at us. Where the door had been was a mirrored sphere, radiating from the wall. I could feel the time magic in the effect but it wasn't a spell I'd ever seen before. "What is it?" I said.

"Stasis," Sonder said, not taking his eyes off the sphere.

I raised my eyebrows. Even slowing someone down as Sonder had done a minute ago isn't easy, and a temporal stasis is supposed to be even tougher. Sonder had gotten a lot better over the past year. From below I felt a flare of life magic, the draining, tugging sensation of Ja-Ja's spell, and there was a whining, rasping sound just on the edge of hearing that made both me and Sonder flinch. The stasis flickered briefly, then strengthened. "I think the nocturne just lost," I said. "Caldera?"

"Working on it," Caldera said.

Sonder and I glanced at each other, then Sonder focused again on his stasis and I started calculating probabilities. I couldn't see any future in which the adepts got through the stasis . . . yet. I also wasn't sure how long it would take Caldera to pull off the gate, or whether she could manage it at all. From the stairs I heard running footsteps. They paused briefly in the corridor, then started towards us. "Caldera?" I said again.

"I'm working on it!"

The footsteps halted. The stasis was muffling the sounds, but I was pretty sure they were on the other side. I wondered what would happen if they opened the door into the spell. I couldn't see the answer from my angle; in all of the futures I could see, the stasis remained as it was, smooth and unbroken. I heard a distant banging sound.

Then from behind I felt the catch as the gate spell took, and the portal opened behind us. Looking around, I saw the brown-rimmed oval hanging in the air, and through it someone's living room. "Move!" Caldera shouted.

I didn't argue, jumping through and landing on carpet. Caldera followed and Sonder came last, backing through the gate, still holding his focus on the stasis spell. The instant he was through, Caldera let the gate collapse and I had one last glimpse of my old bedroom before the gate winked out and was gone.

We were in the living room of what looked like a flat, an old sofa and armchairs surrounding a messy coffee table piled with books and letters. Dirty glasses and tea mugs were scattered around the papers, and one shelf was filled with bottles of spirits. It was a comfortable sort of untidy, the kind of room where it's easy to fall asleep on the sofa. Through the window I could see London houses: we were on the second floor. I checked and rechecked the futures and confirmed that we were safe. No one was following us . . . at least not soon.

"What the hell was that?" Caldera said.

I turned to see that Caldera was glaring at me. "What?"

"How long have you known that Will and his Nightstalkers have been trying to kill you?"

"Since the last couple of times they tried."

"And you didn't tell me?"

"No."

Caldera grabbed at me, trying to shove me up against the wall. It caught me by surprise and Sonder jumped back wide-eyed, but Caldera wasn't fast enough to catch me, at least not wounded as she was. I knocked her hand away and she stumbled past. "What were you expecting?" I snapped. "I met you three days ago and you're a Keeper. You think I'm going to tell you everything?"

Caldera rounded on me. "You put us in danger! You nearly got us killed!"

"And *you* led us in there! Which part of 'going into Richard's mansion is fucking insane' did you not follow, Caldera? Was I not clear enough?"

"You should have told us!" Caldera still looked furious, but at least she didn't seem about to lunge for me again. "We could have—"

"You could have *what*? I told you going into Richard's mansion was suicidal. I told you Deleo had the place warded and there was nothing to find. I told you we were staying too long and it was time to get out, and you didn't listen! You didn't pay attention to anything I said that didn't relate to your bloody job!" I shook my head in disgust. "Mages like you treat diviners like we're some kind of information feed.

You ask us a question, we pull out the answer, and you forget about us. Well, we don't always have the answers you want, but what we *are* good at is telling when something's dangerous. So next time a diviner tells you that, try *listening*!"

Caldera and I faced each other, glaring, until a cough broke the silence. We both turned to see that Sonder was raising his hand nervously. "Um," he said. "Could we maybe talk about this quietly? Without the shouting and grabbing?"

All of a sudden the tension ebbed away. Caldera swayed on her feet and I caught her shoulder, staggering a little as I tried to hold her up. I'm pretty strong, but Caldera wasn't light. "I'm fine," Caldera muttered, trying to push me off.

"You're not fine," I said. "You need a healer."

"I could call Anne," Sonder said.

"That girl from the shop? Isn't she ex-Dark?" Caldera shook her head. "I'm not letting her touch me."

I sighed. "Caldera, you might be an asshole, but you just got hurt because you stepped in the way of a bunch of people trying to kill me. I'm not leaving until I know you're okay."

"Yeah, thanks for that." Caldera dropped into one of the armchairs. "I'll call one of the Keeper healers."

"Then do it."

Caldera gave me a look. "You aren't supposed to be around."

"Oh, you've got to be kidding me," I said. "What, you're not supposed to have non-Light mages around for medical care? What exactly are you afraid I'm going to see?"

"It's procedure, Verus," Caldera said. She looked very weary all of a sudden.

"I'll stay with her," Sonder volunteered.

I looked at him for a second. I would have liked to stay, and despite everything I had the feeling Caldera didn't really want to throw me out. But Caldera was probably right; if she was going to call in Keeper personnel they weren't going to have much use for a non-Light diviner of questionable background. I wouldn't be doing anyone any favours by staying. I turned to go.

"Verus," Caldera said.

I stopped and looked back. Slumped in the chair, Caldera looked weary but still alert. "Don't go after Will. Stay away from him."

"That's kind of easier said than done."

"They attacked a Keeper," Caldera said. "This isn't your problem anymore. Just keep your head down and we'll take it from here."

I looked at Caldera for a moment. "I'll give it a try," I said at last, and walked out into the hall. The door to the flat was warded. I let myself out.

. . . .

had a lot to think about on the journey back.

There's a feeling you get when you're under pressure: a kind of nonstop anxiety, where it seems as if you're spending all your time reacting to one crisis after another instead of doing anything yourself. I've had that feeling before, and one of the things I've learnt over the years is that when you get it, it means you're doing something wrong.

I'd just nearly been killed three times in four days. The first time I'd been saved by Luna, the second time by Anne, and the third time by Caldera. If I kept this up, then sooner or later Will's lot were going to catch me when I *didn't* have a super-powered woman around to help me out. When what you're doing isn't working, you stop and figure out what's wrong.

What was I doing wrong?

The first time, Will and the adepts had found me at the casino. The second time it had been at my house, and the third time it had been at Richard's mansion. But looking back on it, I had advance warning each time. Before the casino, I'd met Lee on the rooftops, and I'd gone out anyway. I'd spoken to Will in the shop, and even though it was obvious they knew where I lived, I'd gone to sleep in my flat. And then, even knowing that they had a way to track me, I'd gone to Richard's mansion. I'd used the annuller, which would have blocked most tracking spells . . . but I hadn't known for sure that it would block *their* tracking spell. What I should have done was find an empty, quiet place and then look into the future for however long it took to confirm that they weren't going to find me. Trying to make sure that something can't happen is slow and frustrating work, but I should have spent the hours to do it and I hadn't.

Arachne was right—I *had* been careless. And I'd put Caldera and Sonder at risk as a result.

It's an unpleasant feeling to realise that other people are paying for your mistakes. Worse, this was something I was supposed to be *good* at. I'd been careful about this kind of thing once. Back in Richard's mansion I never would have been so thoughtless—if I had, I wouldn't have survived. The only thing that had kept me alive through those two years had been a hair-trigger sense for danger. Every second and every thought had been utterly focused on survival. What had changed?

I'd changed. It was as simple as that. For most of the past year I'd been spending my time teaching Luna, helping Anne and Variam, dealing with customers, working, relaxing, socialising, and generally having something much closer to a normal life. Oh, there had been danger, but it had been the sudden kind of danger, usually solved by running away. I'd never been seriously and persistently hunted. Even when I'd realised that Will and the adepts were coming for me, I'd treated it as a problem to be investigated.

But right now I wasn't an investigator, I was prey. If the Nightstalkers caught me, they would kill me.

First they'd have to catch me.

Understanding that felt like opening a door to a part of my mind that had been closed for a long time. I felt the old animal wariness start to seep back, and I looked at the problem coldly and dispassionately. As long as the Nightstalkers had a reliable way to track me, they could keep forcing fights on their terms. If I allowed them to do that then sooner or later I'd be brought down and killed. The first priority had to be to break their tracking link.

The only thing so far that seemed to have blocked the link was Arachne's lair. I'd been there for a day and a half after the casino fight, recovering, and the Nightstalkers hadn't gone after me there. It had taken them much less time than that to track me down everywhere *else*, so evidence suggested that the wards on Arachne's lair were strong enough to hide me. Which meant that whatever their spell was, it wasn't unstoppable.

But I couldn't stay in Arachne's lair forever. I needed a way to hide while moving, and my best chance at doing that was my mist cloak. The first task was to retrieve it.

⁝ ⁝ ⁝ ⁝ ⁝ ⁝

Getting past the police was the easy part.

I could only guess at the number of detectives who must have been swarming over my flat throughout the morning, but London's a busy place and, no matter how spectacular the explosion, sooner or later the police have somewhere else to be. There was only one PC on duty, standing at the front of my shop and waving tourists away from the blue-and-white *POLICE DO NOT CROSS* tape.

Humans have a habit of thinking in two dimensions rather than three. We remember to guard the back door and the front door; we don't usually guard the roof. I got onto the rooftops via the nearby flats, passed the railway line where Anne and I had made our escape last night, then crouched in the shadow of a chimney stack and looked into the future of what would happen if I stayed here.

The Nightstalkers were on their way, which wasn't good news but by this point really wasn't much of a surprise. Not only had the nocturne not shaken them, they actually seemed to be homing in on me faster and faster each time. I followed up the routes to check and . . . yes, they were going to gate onto the roof ahead, probably at the same spot they'd used to try to cut me and Anne off last night. I had maybe five minutes before they arrived.

I could run, but that would just be making the same mistake all over again. They'd keep chasing, and I'd be burning energy running away, reacting to them instead of doing anything constructive myself. Instead I looked into the futures in which I got my mist cloak. There wasn't time to confirm that it'd hide me but it looked possible, and even if it didn't work I'd have a better chance behind my home defences than out in the open. I moved quickly across the rooftops to my flat, skirted the hole in the top, and climbed down to the balcony to let myself in. My flat was a mess. While Anne and I had been busy with Ja-Ja, Variam and Luna had been fighting off the rest of the Nightstalkers below. It looked like they'd made their stand on the top landing, and the walls and banisters were charred. I moved down the stairs, heading for my safe room.

There are three floors to the building I live in. The first floor is the shop, along with a small boxroom for storage. The third floor is the flat where I actually live, with my bedroom, living room, bathroom, and kitchen, as well as the way out to the balcony and the roof. The second floor has the main storage room, a spare room which I converted into a bedroom last year and which is currently being occupied by Anne, and another door which looks sealed off. It isn't—it's my safe room, and it's where I keep anything really valuable or dangerous.

I touched a spot on the door, said the command word, and felt the wards go down as I let myself in, shutting the door behind me. My safe room doesn't have any windows and with the door shut it was pitch-dark. I didn't turn on the light, relying on my diviner's senses to navigate. My mist cloak was hanging on a peg at the side of the room; I pulled it around my shoulders, feeling the magic in the item meld itself around me, then I stepped to the corner and waited.

It's easy to pick up magic items when you run a magic shop. I've been doing it for years and the size of my collection would surprise most mages . . . if I'd ever show it to them, which I wouldn't. Although the safe room was dark, I could feel the dozens of overlapping auras from the items, holding steady in an uneasy equilibrium. The contents of the room would have looked bizarre to anyone able to see them. There was a sword hanging on the wall, oddly curved and with a hilt sculpted into the shape of a crocodile. A pale green egg rested on a shelf, point up in apparent defiance of gravity. Three darts were clamped tightly into a metal holder with a lock on it, and a white-and-blue tube of lacquered wood carved with flowers sat on its own in the middle of the table, far away from everything else. Odd items with odd purposes, most of them useless except for the person or situation for which they were designed. But just a few were very useful indeed, and my mist cloak was one of them.

My mist cloak is an imbued item and actually alive, though not in a way most people would understand. It's weak by imbued-item standards, which makes it vastly more powerful than the one-shots I usually carry, and it does two things. The first is a type of adaptive camouflage, its colour changing to match its surroundings. It's not invisibility—you can be seen if you move, and in broad daylight you just look very unfashionably dressed—but in cover or shadows, it makes you pretty hard to find.

The second ability is more specialised and from my point of view much more valuable. A mist cloak hides its wearer from magical senses, turning them into a kind of black hole against magical detection. Very few other mages know that I have access to that particular trick and I work hard to keep it that way—I've done a few things which the Council would have nailed me to the wall for if I hadn't been wearing my mist cloak at the time. Now I was counting on it yet again.

Looking into the future, there was good news and bad news. The good news was that the mist cloak was definitely doing something—the lines of my futures and the Night-stalkers' didn't automatically converge into combat any-more. The bad news was that combat was still possible, it just wasn't certain. I looked to see what would happen if I left the room and went back the way I came, and saw that the Nightstalkers were already here and heading in my direction. There were only three this time: Lee, Dhruv, and Captain America. I held my position and waited. After only a couple of minutes I heard footsteps through the wall, try-ing to be quiet.

One of the simpler uses of divination magic is short-range spying; you can look ahead into the futures in which you move closer to a target in order to watch them. People are unpredictable, so they have to be only a few seconds away, but as long as the environment is static it works consistently enough. My house was silent and empty, and the futures in which I opened the door were easy to follow. All three of them were there, standing close to one another. None had visible weapons, which was interesting. I knew Captain America and Dhruv would only need a second to draw them, but I could do a lot in a second. It looked like I wasn't the only one making mistakes.

"I can't find him," Lee said at last. In the ambient light from the windows he looked nervous. He was right to be.

"You're sure he was here?" Dhruv asked.

"I think so," Lee said, glancing around.

"Was he moving when you lost him, or did he just vanish?"

"I'm not sure."

"Well, which spot did you lose him in?"

"I don't *know*," Lee said, sounding aggravated. "I keep telling you, I just know the direction. You didn't give me time to triangulate."

"He probably gated," Captain America said. He had an

American accent too, though I didn't recognise what kind. He didn't look as edgy as Lee but he did look alert.

"Diviners can't use gate magic," Dhruv said.

"Didn't stop him before."

"That was the Keeper," Dhruv said. "And Lee said she wasn't with him anymore. Right?"

"No . . ." Lee said reluctantly.

"So."

"Why were we fighting her?" Lee said. "I thought you just wanted Verus."

"Because she wouldn't get out of the way."

"We could have waited."

"That was Will's decision, not yours," Dhruv said. "You want to take it up with him?"

Lee was silent, but Captain America spoke up again. "He's got a point." As he spoke he kept looking from side to side, watching each door in turn as he faced Dhruv. "And what the *fuck* was Ja-Ja doing?"

"It was the middle of a fight," Dhruv said. But there had been a moment's hesitation, and I could tell he wasn't quite as sure of himself as he was acting.

"Yeah, and it was supposed to be against Verus," Captain America said. He didn't sound happy. "What, we're killing everyone in our way now?"

"Ja-Ja didn't obey orders," Dhruv said.

"Ja-Ja's a psycho."

"He's our big gun."

"Which doesn't *change* the fact that he's a fucking *psycho*." Captain America's voice was hard. "He shouldn't be on the team."

"As long as we can point him in the right direction, he's useful."

"I'm not seeing that," Captain America said. "Didn't he just nearly murder a Keeper? Isn't that a problem?"

"When did you get so picky?" Dhruv said in annoyance. "'No problem that can't be solved by high explosives,' wasn't that what you used to say? You didn't argue about that bomb. And *you*, Lee. You think the Keepers would have gotten you away from Locus? You're here because of Will. Don't forget that."

Both Lee and Captain America were silent. "Look, we'll talk about it back at base," Dhruv said. "Let's check this floor and get out of here. Have you tried all the rooms?"

"Those two," Captain America said. "This one's locked."

"Lee?" Dhruv said. "Anyone on the other side?"

There was a pause and I tensed. "No," Lee said at last.

"Can you get it open?" Dhruv asked Captain America.

Captain America hesitated and I held very still. I'd deliberately left the wards on the safe room down. They could have held the Nightstalkers out for a while, but they would have as good as told them that there was something in here to find. It would have taken them a while to break through, but I had no doubt they could do it eventually and once inside they couldn't fail to find me.

But right now they *weren't* expecting to find me, or they never would have had that conversation where I could hear them. For once I had the advantage of surprise, and I was done screwing around. My knife was hidden beneath the cloak, and if they forced their way through into this room I was going to kill them, simple as that. I'd promised Anne that I wouldn't, and back when I'd said that I'd meant it, but I'd rather break a promise than die and that was what it was going to come down to at this rate. I'd take Dhruv or Captain America from ambush, then I'd bring up the wards to split the remaining two, kill whoever was on the same side as me, then run. Will would be on my trail in seconds and the chase would be brutal and ugly, but I'd been pushed as far as I was willing to go. I watched the futures flicker before me, Captain America making the decision, and wondered if he had any idea how close he and his friends were to death right now.

"No," Captain America said at last. "Not without the cops hearing."

"Fine, it looks sealed anyway. Let's go." Their footsteps started up again, trailing down the hall and then up the stairs. And then they were gone.

I waited for a long time, listening and looking ahead, but in both present and future the building was silent. I'd shaken the Nightstalkers. Now I had to figure out what to do next.

· · · · · · · · · · ·

I stayed in that room for the rest of the day.

My mist cloak could hide me from Lee, but it's not the best fashion choice for walking outside in broad daylight and while I waited for the long summer evening to end I called Luna. The phone rang for a while before picking up. "Hello?" Luna asked.

"It's Alex. You guys okay?"

"Alex!" I could hear the relief in Luna's voice. "We're fine. Where are you?"

"You first. Did you sort things out with the police?"

"Uh, more or less," Luna said. "They kind of want to talk to you."

"Yeah, well, I don't want to talk to them." I could probably convince the police that the explosion hadn't been my fault—which was the truth, ironically enough—but I absolutely couldn't afford the distraction. "What did you tell them?"

"There wasn't much we *could* tell them. The house blew up and you and Anne were on the wrong side, then all of a sudden they came up the stairs and it was me and Vari holding the landing. I thought they were going to swarm us then all of a sudden they were gone, I guess they were chasing—" I heard a voice in the background and Luna's voice suddenly became muffled, as though she were talking to someone else. "Yeah, it's him . . . I don't know, how am I supposed—Fine, I'll ask, just shut up." Her voice became clear again. "Vari wants to know what happened at the mansion."

"Managed to avoid Deleo, didn't manage to avoid the

Nightstalkers. Sonder was there and Caldera got hurt but we made it out alive."

"Sonder was there? Why— Never mind. Are you okay? We didn't know what had happened until we got Anne's message."

"I'm fine. Is Anne there too?"

"Yeah, we're all at my flat. Where are you?"

"Hiding."

"Um . . ." Luna said. "Okay."

"There's been a change of plans," I said. "I'm not going to meet up with you."

There was a moment's silence. "Why not?"

"Right now I'm using my mist cloak to shake them. That won't work if I'm with you guys. And Will and Ja-Ja have attacked a Keeper now. The Council is going to have trouble ignoring this."

"Wait, so that's the plan?" Luna sounded very sceptical. "Hope the Council sorts it out?"

"I haven't given up on Elsewhere," I said. "I was interrupted last time and I'm going to go back tonight. For now there's not much you guys can do. Just stay together and stay safe."

Luna took a while to answer. "All right," she said at last. She didn't sound happy, but she didn't argue. "Be careful, okay?"

We spoke for a little longer, then I talked briefly with Anne and Variam. Even over the phone, speaking to them made me feel better, like warming my hands at a distant fire. At last I said my good-byes and hung up, then looked at the phone. I wasn't happy either, and I knew why. It was because I hadn't really been telling Luna the truth.

I hadn't been lying. Waiting for tonight and the next visit to Elsewhere *was* a good plan, and it made sense to at least give Caldera a chance to see if she could keep her promise, even if deep down I didn't really believe that the Keepers were going to bail me out. But there was a second reason I was staying away from Luna and Variam and especially Anne, and it was because of a quiet dark voice growing at the back of my mind telling me that there was only one way this was going to end. I wasn't yet willing to follow that line of thought all the way through, but I knew better than to ignore it.

I stayed in my flat as the sun dwindled in the western sky, haunting the empty building like a ghost. The police didn't return and neither did the Nightstalkers, and I spent my time digging through the ruins of my bedroom, salvaging what I could. There's something unpleasant about having your home attacked, a kind of violation. I've had my flat invaded by various intruders before, including an assassin construct, two or three different Dark mages, and a particularly unfriendly shapeshifter, but none of them had wrecked the place so badly. Despite the damage I would have liked to sleep in my own flat, but common sense advised against it and once the sun had set I left my shop. I wondered how long it would be before I'd come back again.

⌁⌁⌁⌁⌁⌁⌁⌁⌁

Being able to look into the future gives you a certain amount of protection against being killed in your sleep, but as last night had demonstrated it's not reliable. The basic problem is free will; once someone's made their plans to kill you it's easy to see them coming, but if they don't decide on the details of their assassination attempt until *after* you've gone to sleep then it gets iffy. Until this was over I wasn't going to be sleeping in any of the places I'd been attacked in. In fact, I wasn't going to be following any of my usual routines at all.

This is the reason being hunted sucks so much. If you know who's chasing you and how, it's not difficult to throw off pursuers. The problem is doing anything *else*. I couldn't run my shop, or live in my flat, or hang out with Luna or Anne or Variam or Sonder, or follow any of my usual patterns, because if I did I could be traced. Most people can get away from hunters in the short term—it's the long term that trips them up. Even if you're being hunted, life goes on: you have a job to do, places to go, and a home to live in. All those things make you predictable, and sooner or later some-one will use them to find you. I couldn't keep hiding forever. Right now, though, I just needed somewhere to sleep.

The Royal National Hotel is next to Russell Square, a gigantic concrete-and-brick building that sprawls over an entire city block. It's the largest hotel in London and feels like a small airport, right down to the people sitting on the carpets in the lounge with luggage piled around them. My mist cloak drew stares but I was too tired to care. The reception staff didn't even blink; either they were too well trained or they'd seen so many weird guests that nothing fazed them anymore. Probably both.

My room was on the second floor with a view out over the flagpoles of the inner courtyard. I didn't undress or even empty my pockets; I just dropped on the bed and closed my eyes. I was asleep inside two minutes.

chapter 10

The plaza was filled with white light, doves pecking on the stones and roosting in the branches of the line of trees in the distance. I was sitting on the same bench, looking up at the glowing sky, and in the distance I could hear the rustle of wind. "You know," I said, "each time I go back to Elsewhere it feels like I get here faster."

"You do," Shireen said from next to me. She was sitting on the bench; I didn't know if she'd been there before I spoke, but I'd known she'd be there after.

"What's changed?"

"Finding your way in Elsewhere is just like anything else," Shireen said. "The more you do it, the easier it gets. Are you ready to go back?"

"One thing," I said. "I'm seeing Rachel's memories when I do this, aren't I? What's it like for her? Can she feel anything?"

"Maybe," Shireen said. "I think to her it just feels like another dream."

"Could she tell the difference? Find me while I'm there?"

Shireen hesitated. "I'm not sure."

"You're not very good at being reassuring, you know that?"

"Sorry."

I wanted to ask more, but I knew this would only get harder the longer I waited. "All right," I said. "Let's do it."

Shireen nodded and extended her hand. I took it, feeling the touch of her skin—

ιιιιιιιι

I was back in the girls' room in Richard's mansion, but something was different. I couldn't put my finger on what it was, but somehow I knew that this memory was from the end of my time in Richard's mansion, after I'd tried to rescue Catherine but before I'd escaped.

The mission to America had changed things for the four of us. In our first year we'd competed, but there had always been a vague sense that even if we might not like each other we were still on the same team. After the fight in the canyon things were different. Tobruk had always been dangerous, but killing Matthew had made him worse; it was as if there wasn't anything holding him back anymore. Shireen was on edge, angrier. I hadn't realised it at the time, but the same things that had gotten to me must have been bothering her too. Only Rachel had stayed the same. Right now she was sitting on the bed with her back against the wall, reading. It was daytime and light was streaming in through the open windows.

Shireen was in an armchair, her elbow on one of the armrests and her head propped up on her hand. She was studying an old clothbound book and frowning, and as I watched the frown kept getting deeper. "This is really messed up," she said at last.

Rachel didn't answer. "Rach?" Shireen said. "Have you read this?"

"Hmm?" Rachel said without looking up.

"Listen to this," Shireen said. "It's a study about mages who Harvested someone. Are you listening?"

"Uh-huh."

"'Mages in Category A appeared to complete the ritual successfully with no significant side effects. Mages in Category B displayed symptoms of mild psychological consequences. Mages in Category C displayed symptoms of moderate to severe psychological consequences. Mages in Category D were unavailable for study for reasons including: (a) subject location unknown, (b) subject unwilling to participate in study, (c) subject deceased in subsequent altercation before sufficient data could be obtained. It has been suggested that a significant fraction of mages who should have been assigned to Categories B and C may have been incorrectly assigned to Category A due to lack of relevant data . . .'" Shireen looked up. "Rach? Are you listening?"

"*Yes.*" Rachel looked up. "What?"

"This is important."

"No, it's not," Rachel said. "We're supposed to be learning *how* to do this, not what's happened to other people."

"Isn't some of this stuff worrying you?" Shireen said. "'Psychological consequences'?"

"That's only if you do it wrong."

"Look, this is starting to sound really freaky. Pulling someone else's magic out and taking it for yourself? What does that do to them?"

Rachel shrugged. "I guess they can't use magic anymore."

"Then how is it none of these books say anything about what happens to them afterwards?"

"How should I know?" Rachel said in annoyance. "Are you going to help me with this or not?"

Shireen looked at Rachel, frowning. "Why is Richard getting us to learn this stuff?"

"Look," Rachel said. "What's the one thing we've learnt that mages care about? Power, right? Well, this is a way of getting it. Besides, if we don't use it, everyone else is going to."

Shireen frowned again but didn't argue. Rachel went back to her reading and the two girls sat for a little while in silence. "Rach?" Shireen asked.

"Mm."

"Have you ever thought about leaving?"

Rachel looked up in surprise. "You mean here?"

"Yeah."

"Why would we want to?"

"Look, think about it," Shireen said. "Do we actually *like* anyone in this mansion?"

Rachel shrugged. "Not really."

"Then why are we living here?"

"We get training from Richard and we've got servants to do whatever we want," Rachel said. "Anyway, it's not like you expect to like the people you live with." Rachel narrowed her eyes slightly. "Is this about Alex?"

"No," Shireen said.

Rachel looked at her.

"Okay, maybe."

Rachel shook her head. "I told you not to talk to him."

"It's not just Alex, okay?" Shireen said. "I just . . . Look, I don't feel like this mansion is such a safe place anymore. And Tobruk is seriously starting to freak me out."

"You're the one who was screwing him."

"*Was,*" Shireen said, glaring at Rachel. "Have you seen what he's doing to that girl?"

"I told you about him, didn't I?" Rachel said. "You didn't listen."

"Yeah, well, I'm listening now. How about we do something about it?"

"I'm not getting near Tobruk," Rachel said with a shiver.

"So what?" Shireen said with an edge to her voice. "We sit around while he goes down to visit every night? This is fucked up."

"Better her than me," Rachel snapped. "She's going to die anyway, what difference does it make?"

Shireen drew back, startled. "She's not . . ."

"Oh, come on," Rachel said impatiently. "You think Richard's just going to let her go?"

Shireen looked away, and there was an awkward silence. "Rach, I'm serious," Shireen said. "I feel like something bad is going to happen."

"It is, just not to *us*." Rachel put the book aside and turned to Shireen. "Look, we need to stick together. Tobruk's just waiting for us to slip up. If we break Richard's rules like Alex did, he can get us. But as long as we do what Richard says, Tobruk can't do anything. Promise me you won't do anything. I don't want anything to happen to you too."

Shireen didn't meet Rachel's eyes. "Promise," Rachel insisted.

"All right," Shireen said.

"Okay?"

"Okay," Shireen said. But she still wasn't looking at Rachel.

Rachel didn't seem to notice. "Come on," she said. "It'll be just like that time with Mrs. Ellis. You remember that?"

Shireen gave a half-smile. "I was the one who came up with that."

"I did all the work though. Anyway, it's not for much longer."

"What isn't?"

"This," Rachel said. "Being Richard's apprentices."

Shireen frowned. "How do you know?"

Rachel glanced at the door, then leant closer to Shireen, lowering her voice. "I don't think Richard's going to be around much longer."

"Why not?"

"Last week, when I went into his study," Rachel said, "he left some papers out on the desk, and there was a letter. I couldn't see who he was sending it to but it was Richard's writing and he was saying something about not being back in England for years. Maybe more."

"But where's he going?"

"Who cares?" Rachel said impatiently. "Don't you see, this is why he picked us. Remember how everyone keeps saying how he's never taken any apprentices before? This is why he did it *now*. He wants someone to leave in charge while he's gone."

"And that'd be us?"

"Why not? We've earned it. Once we're Richard's Chosen, this place is going to be ours. The other mages are going to have to respect us. We'll be the ones in charge, not Richard."

"And once he gets back?" Shireen said.

"It won't matter."

"I don't know, Rach. I'm not sure we're doing the right thing anymore."

"We can't back out now," Rachel said. "Come on, just a little longer. Then it's all going to be ours."

Shireen looked back at Rachel and gave a halfhearted smile. The scene blurred and shifted, and—

⁚⁚⁚⁚⁚⁚⁚⁚⁚

I was in Richard's study, thick carpet covering the floor and shelves lining the walls. The room was shadowed, the only light a low fire burning in the fireplace. Three people were inside, one behind the desk and two in front of it.

The first was Rachel, and she looked different from how I remembered her. For all the nine months I'd been imprisoned Rachel had avoided me, and I'd barely seen her. Now that I got a good look at her I was surprised at how drawn and harried she looked, as if she'd been on edge for far too long.

Next to Rachel was Tobruk, and unlike her he looked exactly as I remembered him, steady and confident. Becoming a Dark apprentice hadn't changed Tobruk; it had just brought out what was already there. He stood with his arms folded, ignoring Rachel, all his attention on the man behind the desk.

That man was Richard, and even in the dream, seeing him again made me flinch. There was nothing intimidating about his appearance; he was average height with an average build, and looked completely ordinary in every way. He could blend right into a crowd without ever being noticed, at least until you heard him speak. But just seeing him terrified me and I was suddenly sure that dream or no dream, he knew I was there. If he'd turned to look at me I think I would have run.

But he didn't; instead, he was speaking to Tobruk and Rachel. Even in the memory Richard's voice was captivating, deep and commanding and utterly assured. No matter what he said, he always sounded natural and reasonable, and anyone who disagreed with him foolish and out of their depth. Arguing with Richard felt like swimming against the tide: no matter what you did you would be carried away, not because the water bore you any malice but because it was so much vaster and stronger. ". . . that we discussed," he was saying. "Have they been resolved?"

"I found Bennet," Tobruk said. He sounded confident. "He's not going to give us any trouble."

"I set up the wreaths," Rachel said at the same time. Neither she nor Tobruk were looking at each other; both were acting as though the other wasn't even in the room. "They'll be ready."

"Excellent," Richard said. "I believe you are ready for your final tasks."

Rachel and Tobruk did look at each other then: a quick glance with no friendship in it. "I have been strict these past weeks," Richard said. "Our schedule has been tight and there have been threats you have not been aware of. Despite this, both of you have fulfilled your roles admirably and without complaint. It is time you learnt what you have been working towards."

Richard looked towards the two apprentices expectantly, as if waiting for questions. I'd thought it would be Tobruk who'd speak first, but to my surprise Rachel beat him to it. "It's to do with gate magic, isn't it?"

Richard inclined his head. "Go on."

"That book you had us read," Rachel said. She was frowning, looking thoughtful. "It said that gate magic used to be able to do more. That the old gate spells couldn't just move us between places on Earth, they could move between worlds."

"Which is done today, after a fashion," Richard said. "Modern gate magic can be used to access shadow and bubble realms—but both are very limited things. What if it were possible to open a gate not just to a small pocket reality, but to an entirely new world?"

"Can you do that?"

Richard raised his eyebrows. "What do you think?"

"I . . . guess," Rachel said slowly. "I mean, gates just work on a similarity, it doesn't matter how far apart they are . . ." She shook her head. "But wait. You need to know where you're going."

"Unless you have a gate stone."

"Oh yeah." Rachel frowned again. "Those work even if you don't know where you're going."

"Because gate stones share a sympathetic link with the location they are keyed to."

Tobruk was starting to look restless. "Who cares about this?"

"Soon I will be departing this reality through a world-gate," Richard said. "When I do, your time as my apprentices will be at an end."

The room was silent but for the crackle of the fire. Both Tobruk and Rachel were visibly taken aback; whatever they'd been expecting, it hadn't been this. "You needn't be surprised," Richard said. "Your studies have progressed far. Both of you are strong enough now to stand without my protection."

Rachel and Tobruk stood staring at Richard. "What are we supposed to do?" Rachel said at last, and for the first time she sounded unsure.

"Whatever you like," Richard said with a smile. "Isn't that the point?"

"Who gets to be your Chosen?" Tobruk said.

Richard nodded, as if he'd been expecting the question. "I will need someone to watch over this mansion while I am away and to be ready for my return. Should either of you become my Chosen, this will be your responsibility, along with managing the rest of my property and affairs. It is of course a voluntary position."

Both Tobruk and Rachel waited, and there was a tension in the air. "Who—?" Rachel began.

"Come now," Richard said, and he sounded almost kindly. "Did you really think that was how it was going to work? I'd pick one of you and dismiss the others? Once I am gone, I will have no further influence over this world for a significant time. To pretend I could simply *appoint* someone would be sheer hypocrisy. The only qualification that matters for the position of my Chosen is the strength to keep it. That is how it works—how it has always worked. The position cannot be given, only taken. If you are unable to hold it, it was never truly yours."

Rachel started to turn to Tobruk, then stopped. Tobruk looked . . . pleased, and there was a kind of anticipation in his face that sent a chill down my spine: I remembered that look.

"There is, however, a more immediate issue," Richard said. "It seems our last deception has thrown most of the Light mages off the trail, but not Lesandra. She wants the secrets of the worldgate, and she will be coming for it. Soon."

"Here?" Rachel asked.

"Lesandra may be overconfident, but only to a point," Richard said. "I do not expect her to assault me within my own mansion. However, while I am dealing with her, the two of you must watch Catherine Traviss."

Tobruk frowned. "Why her?"

"Did you ever wonder why I sent you to America to bring her here?"

Tobruk shrugged.

"The Traviss family share some unique traits," Richard said. "At some point in the past, one of their ancestors acquired an unusual type of interdimensional connection. It has manifested throughout the family line as an affinity for time and space magic but has the potential for much more. Her parents unfortunately proved unsuitable, but she has the ideal combination of attributes. Just as a gate stone can be used as a focus to travel to another location, she can be used as a key to travel to another world. Her nature will provide the link, her life energy the fuel." Richard glanced between Rachel and Tobruk. "She is the key to this ritual. Without her, we have nothing. It is absolutely essential that she be kept under guard. On a more positive note, it appears that Lesandra has kept her findings a secret from the rest of the Council. I do not anticipate any other Light mages but her to become involved. Regardless, there are time factors outside her control and she will be forced to confront me within twenty-four hours. Until then, Catherine Traviss is your responsibility."

"Lesandra had some apprentices, right?" Tobruk said. "Why don't we take them out?"

"Securing Traviss is more important," Richard said. "I will deal with Lesandra."

"What about Shireen?" Rachel said.

"The same applies to her, of course," Richard said. "Please pass on the message when you see her."

Rachel hesitated. "And Alex?" Tobruk said with a glint in his eye.

"Your dealings with Alex are and have always been your own concern," Richard said. "Until your time as my apprentices ends, all four of you are still candidates for the position of Chosen. However, let me make one thing very clear." Richard looked from Rachel to Tobruk. "Your priority is to guard Catherine Traviss. Should your personal issues with Alex come in the way of that, I expect you to put them aside. Your dealings with each other are your own affair; your dealings with my property are not. Is that understood?"

"Yes," Rachel said after a moment. Tobruk didn't answer.

"Excellent." Richard rose to his feet. "I will be out of contact for some time. The two of you are in charge of the mansion until I return." He walked out of the room without looking back. Tobruk and Rachel were left alone in the study.

There was a long silence. At last Rachel stirred and turned to face Tobruk. "So who's on first?"

"Huh?"

"We're on guard duty, right?" Rachel didn't try to hide the dislike in her voice. "You going first or second?"

Tobruk laughed. "Yeah, that's not how this is going to work."

Rachel frowned. "Richard said—"

"Richard said, Richard said," Tobruk mimicked. "You're going to stay here and be a good girl. I'm going to find Alex."

"Shireen's—"

"Shireen's lost it."

"I don't have to do what you tell me."

Tobruk had started to turn away, but as Rachel said that he stopped and looked at her. "What did you say?" His voice was suddenly soft and dangerous.

Rachel flinched but stood her ground. "I'm not—"

Tobruk moved very fast. All of a sudden Rachel was pressed back against the mantelpiece, eyes wide, with Tobruk looming over her. Rachel's hand came up, light starting to glow around it, and Tobruk caught her wrist. "I fucking hate little rich girls like you," Tobruk breathed into Rachel's face. "You think you're better than me? Well, guess what? Richard's not going to be around to protect you anymore. And the second—the *second*—he's out that door, you'd better be too. Because if you even think of staying . . ."

Rachel struggled, trying to break free, but Tobruk held her effortlessly with one hand, reaching in with the other. Then Rachel summoned her magic, a shield of water pressure flashing out from around her in the same instant that Tobruk called up his dark flame. Fire met water in a flash and a roar, and the room vanished in a cloud of steam.

The mist cleared in only seconds. Tobruk was standing in the middle of the room, shrouded in shadow, black flames licking at his arms and legs. Rachel was on the floor in the corner; her eyes were wide and I could feel the fear seeping from her. "You stupid bitch," Tobruk said contemptuously. "You're nothing. You hear me?" He took something from his pocket and held it out; it was black and crystalline, and it gleamed in the firelight. "Know what this is?"

Rachel stared back at him, frozen. "Harvesting crystal," Tobruk said. "I'm going to find Alex and I'm going to Harvest him so I have his power too. You?" He grinned suddenly; it was wide and genuine and quite terrifying. "You I'll keep around. I'm going to need a new slut when Richard knocks off the last one."

"You can't do that," Rachel said, her voice high. "Richard won't let you."

"Richard doesn't give a fuck," Tobruk said. "I can do whatever I want to you. Richard told you all what it meant to be a Dark mage. None of you listened. I'm going to be Richard's Chosen and if you *ever* talk back to me again"—Tobruk's grin faded—"I'm going to fuck you up so bad you'll be begging me to stop. You know what I did to Catherine? That was just fun. You . . ." Tobruk waved a finger. "You, it's personal." He looked at Rachel for a moment longer, his eyes burning into her, and then, like a mask snapping back, his grin returned. "Don't go anywhere!" Tobruk turned and walked out.

Rachel was left alone in the room, staring after Tobruk. As the door swung closed behind him she curled up and hugged herself, shivering. She stayed like that for a long time before slowly picking herself up and starting towards the door.

_____

The shift was faster this time, only a flicker, and when it steadied I was standing in a long, dimly lit stone room, with an archway at either end leading into darkness. Murals were carved into the stone: scenes of battles and quests, mages and their servants fighting strange and inhuman creatures, with lettering in odd runic script. To the side was something that looked like an altar, and four statues of armoured men stood in the corners, each carrying tall spears and wide round shields. I remembered this place; it had been the entryway to the lower basements. Rachel had once asked Richard what the murals meant and he'd told her it had been built by the mansion's creators. We'd taken to calling it the chapel, but we'd avoided spending any time there. There was something eerie about the place, and the longer you stayed the more uncomfortable you got. The archway at one end led up to the ground floor, where I'd set off the trap to summon the nocturne. The archway on the other side led to the deeper basements and to the cells.

Rachel was sitting in the middle of the room. She was wearing the same clothes she'd had on for the confrontation with Tobruk and she was still shivering; the stone was unheated and cold. Apart from her the room was empty, and as I looked at her I felt an unexpected flash of pity. She looked lost and alone.

Footsteps echoed from the stairs, and Rachel was on her feet in an instant. Blue light flashed up around her hands as she summoned her shield and faced the archway, back slightly hunched. There was a flicker in the darkness, the glow of a fire spell. I saw Rachel's muscles go tense and knew she was ready to fight or flee.

Then Shireen walked in, her spell winking out as she came into the dim light of the chapel, and the tension went out of Rachel in a slump. "It's you," she said, and closed her eyes, her shield vanishing. "Thank God."

"Hi, Rach," Shireen said. She sounded tired and her clothes were rumpled and worn, but there was something different about her; she looked alert, more focused, as if she'd finally made a decision. Something about it looked familiar, and as I watched her my memory clicked; this was after I'd met her at the old flats, when we'd spoken for the last time. I'd been readying myself to face Tobruk. Shireen had gone back to the mansion. Now at last I was seeing what had happened after.

"Where have you *been*?" Rachel said, hurrying towards her. "There's been so much happening, Richard and Tobruk and . . . Where *were* you?"

"I'm sorry," Shireen said. "I had some things to think about." She paused. "I found Alex."

Rachel had been about to say something else but stopped. "You did?"

Shireen nodded.

"What did you do?"

"We talked." Shireen looked away. "About a lot of things."

"Why didn't you bring him back? We could have—" Rachel shook her head. "Never mind, it doesn't matter anymore. Listen. Richard's going away. I don't know where, some kind of other world, but he's going to be gone soon. Really soon. And he's going to pick his Chosen. It's just like we guessed, he wants someone to take over after he's gone, but he's not going to pick anyone, he's going to leave it all to us. And Tobruk . . . Tobruk's gone crazy. You didn't meet him, did you? No, you would have said."

"Rach," Shireen said.

"We have to do something. I'm serious, he's finally gone off the deep end. I was talking to him and . . ." Rachel shivered. "It's just the two of us now. Richard's not going to step in anymore. We can get rid of Tobruk, but—"

"Rach," Shireen said.

Rachel paused. "What?"

"I'm not going to be Richard's Chosen."

Rachel looked at Shireen in confusion. "What do you mean?"

"I'm not doing it anymore," Shireen said. "I'm not staying on as Richard's apprentice. I'm not living in this mansion and I'm not watching anyone else get killed. I'm out."

There was a long silence. Rachel stared at Shireen. "Why?" she said at last.

Shireen nodded towards the archway behind Rachel. "Who's in the dungeons right now?"

"Just that girl."

"Her *name's* Catherine," Shireen said, and her eyes didn't leave Rachel's. "What's going to happen to her when Richard leaves?"

Rachel looked away.

"Come on, Rach."

"The ritual needs her as a component," Rachel said defensively. "It might not kill her."

"Oh, come on," Shireen said wearily. " 'She's just going to die anyway'—remember? You said it, not me. Well, you were right. It took me a long time to figure that out, but you knew all along."

"Fine," Rachel said. "So what?"

"You wanted to know why?" Shireen said. *"That's* why. I'm sick of this, Rach. I'm sick of getting sent on these missions and I'm sick of knowing that people are getting raped and tortured in the same building where I'm sleeping at night! And now I get sent out to bring Alex back so they can do it all over again?" Shireen shook her head. "Not anymore. I'm done."

"Richard never told you to go after Alex."

"No," Shireen said. "But it was pretty obvious whose side we were supposed to be on, wasn't it? We should never have signed up with him."

"*You* were the one who wanted to sign up with him! This was your idea! You talked me into it!"

"And I was *wrong*!" Shireen shouted. "Okay? I was wrong to sign up with Richard, *you* were wrong to go along with it, *Alex* was wrong to join up after *us*, and Tobruk was—" Shireen paused, then shrugged. "Actually, come to think of it, this place fits Tobruk just fine. Guess he really did know what he was doing."

"But why *now*?" Rachel said. "It's— We're nearly finished. It's been two years and it's almost over. Richard's about to go away." Her voice was pleading. "It's only a week or two then it'll all be done. It's—it's like you want to quit school just before the final exam. It's just a little longer."

Shireen looked back at Rachel steadily. "Rach," she said. "The final exam is going to kill the girl in the cell behind you."

"Can't you just stay?" Rachel said. "You don't have to do anything. We can be Richard's Chosen. Once he's gone we can do whatever we like."

"There's no 'we.' There never was."

"What?"

"Think about it," Shireen said. "How many Dark mages have we seen? Hundreds, right? How many of them had more than one Chosen?"

Rachel looked taken aback. "I don't know."

"Think. Think hard."

"I don't *know*. Some of them."

"Like who?"

"That guy in Edinburgh. And there was that Traysia woman."

"Okay, that's two out of how many?" Shireen asked. "Two hundred? More? Now think about it. Did Richard ever say he wanted more than one Chosen? Did he *say* there was room for more than one of us? Or did we just assume that was what he must have meant?"

Rachel frowned. "What are you saying?"

"Ever since we've been here, what's the one thing Richard's kept telling us Dark mages are supposed to have?" Shireen said. "Strength. The strong rule, the weak serve. Can you really see anyone who believes that *sharing*?"

"We've been working together," Rachel protested. "I know there's been trouble, but we're supposed to be on the same side."

"Uh-huh," Shireen said. "And that's why Tobruk went psycho? More psycho than usual, anyway. Tell me something. Did Richard say anything before Tobruk went off the deep end? Like about his protection getting taken away?"

Rachel hesitated.

"This is how it was always going to end up, Rach," Shireen said. "Richard doesn't want four Chosen. He wants *one* Chosen. But he's not going to pick for us. He wants us to fight it out until just one of us is left, because that's the Dark way. The meanest and strongest and smartest one gets to be top of the heap. And you know what? We've been helping him do it." Shireen shook her head. "Not anymore. You want me to stay? I've got a better idea. We leave."

Rachel looked confused. "Leave?"

"Leave. Both of us, tonight." Shireen tried to take Rachel's hands but Rachel pulled back. "Out of this mansion. No more missions, no more deaths, no more prisoners. We don't need Richard or Tobruk or any of them. It'll be just you and me again."

"And we leave all this to Tobruk?" Rachel demanded. "Just let him be Chosen?"

"Who *cares* who's Chosen? It's just a name! We don't need anything Richard can give us."

"And where would we go?"

"Anywhere! Some other mage, some other place, I don't care. Anywhere but here."

Rachel stared at Shireen for a second. "You really don't get it, do you?"

Shireen frowned. "What?"

"How did you find Alex?" Rachel asked. "How's Tobruk going to find Alex?"

"You know how," Shireen said. "Tracers."

"And?"

"And we asked the mages he'd spoken to—"

"And they told you where he'd gone."

"Yeah . . ."

"So they helped you and not him," Rachel said. "If we run away, that's going to be *us*! The only thing keeping every other Dark mage from selling us out is Richard. As long as we're with him, we're safe. But as soon as we leave, that's it! You think anyone cares about a Dark runaway? You think we haven't made enough enemies? Everyone who hates us, everyone who wants us, they're all going to be chasing us down!"

"So what's your plan?" Shireen demanded. "Stay here and hope for the best?"

"Yes! It's just a week! Why can't you wait that long?"

"Because it'll mean that Catherine dies."

"So what?"

Shireen drew back a little, startled. Rachel was glaring at her. "Have you talked to them?" Shireen asked.

"Who?"

"Catherine," Shireen said. "Alex. Everyone who's passed through those cells. Have you ever looked at them and talked to them?"

"Why does that matter?"

"You haven't, have you?"

"So?" Rachel snapped. "What, you think talking to them means you've learnt something special?"

"YES!" Shireen shouted. "When you actually *meet* someone who's going to die because of what you've done, when you look into their eyes and listen to their voice, it makes you *think* about what you're doing! And that's why you haven't done it! Deep down you *know* what you're doing is fucked up, but as long as you don't talk to her you can pretend it's not real. But it is, and if you keep doing this you'll be murdering her the same way Tobruk murdered her boyfriend."

Rachel flinched but didn't look away. "Why are you doing this?" She sounded hurt, betrayed. "I thought I could trust you."

"You *can* trust me," Shireen said. "But as long as we're in this mansion we're always going to belong to Richard." She glanced around. "Where is he?"

"He's gone after Lesandra," Rachel said unwillingly. "But he'll be . . ."

"Whatever," Shireen said. "I'm not sticking around to see who wins." She started walking towards the far end of the chapel.

"Wait! What are you doing?"

"What I should have done a long time ago. I'm getting out and I'm breaking Catherine out too."

Rachel's eyes went wide. "Are you crazy?" She ran around, blocking Shireen. "You can't!"

"Can you think of a better time?" Shireen demanded. "Richard's busy with Lesandra. We're not going to get a better chance than this. We'll be out of the country by the time he even figures out she's gone."

"He'll come after us!"

"When's he ever done anything like that himself?" Shireen asked. "Even when Alex tried to break Catherine out he didn't lift a finger. He just let Tobruk handle it all for him."

Rachel stared at Shireen for a long moment, then shook

her head. "Wow. You really don't understand him at all, do you?"

"What?"

"Richard's let us do whatever we like because we've never threatened anything he really cares about," Rachel said. "He doesn't care if we mess up the mansion or fight each other. But he cares about this. I don't know where he's going or what he's going to do once he gets there, but it's really, *really* important to him. If he loses that girl you think he's going to say, 'Oh well, too bad, let's go home'? He's going to come after her with everything he's got."

"So we go to someone who'll help."

"No one's going to help! They didn't help Alex and they won't help us!"

"Maybe they won't," Shireen said quietly. "But at least we'll be doing something decent for once."

"What are you talking about?"

"Rach, think about it," Shireen said. "Remember how we always talked about how we'd be the heroes? How we'd change the world? Look at what you're doing right now. We're not the heroes. We're the *bad guys*."

"No, we're not."

"You're keeping a girl in prison so Tobruk can use her for his fucked-up games until Richard gets around to sacrificing her for a ritual," Shireen said. "Wake up, Rach! What does that sound like to you?"

"Everyone always tells us what we're supposed to do," Rachel snapped. "Maybe we're allowed to be selfish for once."

"We've never *not* been selfish! When have we *ever* used our magic for anyone else?"

"Well, why should we? What's wrong with using it for what we want?"

"We said we were going to help girls with magic, remember?"

"Yes!" Rachel shouted. "Girls like *us*! The two of *us*! Not someone else!"

Shireen drew back in shock, staring at Rachel. "Everyone tries to use us," Rachel said. "We always have to be afraid of people like Tobruk and I'm sick of it. *I* want to be the one everyone else is afraid of. I want to be Richard's Chosen and own this mansion and have people be scared of *me*."

"Rach, listen to yourself," Shireen said in disbelief. "This isn't you. Richard's made you like this. If you just—"

"How would *you* know what's really me?" Rachel snapped. "You decide stuff and you expect me to do it too. You never ask me what *I* want."

Shireen looked taken aback. "I thought—"

"You always talk the most, you act like you're in charge, you get all the attention." Rachel looked like she couldn't stop if she wanted to; all the years of frustration were pouring out. "Your magic's stronger, you get everything first, it's you, you, you, but the one thing I could count on was that you were always on my side. Now for once I want something and you don't care! It's still all about you. You change your mind and you just expect me to follow you. Well, I'm not doing it! Not this time! I want this and for once this is going to be about what *I* want!"

Shireen was staring at Rachel. "You always felt like that?" she said. "Why didn't you tell me?"

"Because you never *asked*!" Rachel shouted. "You just assumed I was going to do whatever you decided! I followed you to sign up with Richard but I'm not following you now."

"How many times are you going to throw that at me?" Shireen shouted. "I know I was the one who talked you into coming here. I *know* it was a mistake. Now's our chance to fix it."

Rachel opened her mouth to give another angry reply, then something seemed to break. All of a sudden she just looked tired and miserable. "It's too late." Rachel sounded desperately unhappy, and just for an instant I wondered if this had been how she'd always felt. "Everything we've done . . . Who's going to want an *ex*–Dark apprentice? We have to stick it through. It's the only way we're going to be safe."

"We're *never* going to be safe, Rach," Shireen said gently. Her anger was gone too; she only looked sad. "And that's our fault. I know you want me to stay and help you with Tobruk. But after Tobruk there'd be someone else and someone else. As long as we live as Dark mages there'll always be another Tobruk. The only way to get away from them is to leave."

Rachel hesitated, and for the first time I had the feeling she was really wavering. Shireen put her hands on Rachel's shoulders, and this time Rachel didn't push her away. "Listen to me," Shireen said, looking straight into Rachel's eyes. "We might have made bad choices, but we don't have to keep making them. We *can* turn back, if we admit we were wrong and start fixing our mistakes. I can't undo what we've done but I can help Catherine right now. And that's what I'm going to do." Shireen moved Rachel to the side and started walking towards the archway leading to the cells.

Rachel stared after her for a second, then fright leapt into her eyes. "No! Don't!"

"It's the only way, Rach."

"You can't do this!" Rachel's voice rose, broke. "He'll kill me! *You're supposed to be on my side!*"

Shireen didn't stop or turn; she was passing the altar. "Stop!" Rachel shouted. Her hand began to lift, blue-green light flickering around it. Shireen didn't react. "Stop!" Shireen kept walking. *"Stop!"* And a thin blue-green ray flashed from Rachel's hand, striking Shireen's lower back and passing through into the archway beyond.

Shireen stumbled and stopped. She turned and looked at Rachel in complete surprise, then her legs gave out from underneath her and she crumpled to the stone.

Rachel stood frozen, her hand still raised. "I didn't—" she began. "I didn't mean to—"

Shireen stared at Rachel for a long moment, then a kind of realisation crept into her eyes and she leant her head back against the stone. "Oh," she said quietly.

"Oh God, you're bleeding." Rachel looked around wildly. "Just stay there. I'll get you something, I'll—"

"Don't worry about it," Shireen said softly. She took a breath. "I guess . . . you get what you want after all." Her eyes drifted closed.

"Shireen?" Rachel rushed to her side, then fell to her knees. "Wake up! Shireen! *Shireen!*"

chapter 11

When Richard walked in through the archway, Rachel was kneeling next to Shireen. Blood was pooled on the floor and smeared over Rachel's arms and clothes; she'd taken off her top and wrapped it around Shireen's middle. Rachel looked up at Richard with haunted eyes and he stopped and took in the scene. "Well," he said at last. "It seems I've missed a few things."

"Please . . ." Rachel's voice was shaky. "I can't stop the bleeding. She won't . . ."

"Yes, yes. Let me have a look at her." Richard walked forward and crouched by Shireen's body. His suit was crumpled and covered in dust but his eyes were bright and his movements full of energy. He looked like he'd just come through a desperate battle and won. "Hmm, nasty wound. Disintegration?"

Rachel didn't answer. "Well, it shouldn't be much trouble," Richard said, standing and dusting himself off. "There's internal bleeding, but that's easy enough to stop."

Rachel stared at him. "You're going to help her? But she—" She stopped.

"Tried to break into the cells. I know."

"She won't— I didn't—"

Richard raised a hand. "Please don't apologise, Rachel. Your show of loyalty is admirable. I appreciate how difficult this must have been for you."

Rachel looked down at the floor. "So given the course of events, I think we can safely assume that Shireen has resigned her position," Richard said. "Normally I would leave her to her fate, but I think in this case the decision should be yours. If you'd prefer her to be treated I will of course respect your wishes." He paused. "Assuming that's what you want."

Rachel's head came up. "What?"

"Your aim was quite precise," Richard said in a conversational tone. "Exactly enough damage to incapacitate Shireen, but not enough to kill her. Some would call it accident. Personally, I believe you have more skill than that." Richard reached into his pocket. "I could heal her, of course. But perhaps you'd prefer the use of this." He opened his hand and I caught my breath. On Richard's palm was a black crystal, a twin to the one Tobruk had shown Rachel.

Rachel stared at the crystal, a sort of dawning horror creeping across her face, then she shook her head violently. "No."

"Are you sure?" Richard asked. "On some level, wasn't this what you were considering? Why else would you have used the spell you did?"

"No." Rachel kept shaking her head. "I can't."

Richard watched her for a moment, tilting his head, then closed his hand back over the crystal, hiding it from view. "As you wish," he said, beginning to walk away. "I've never attempted to force you into anything, Rachel. Remember that. Threats and bullying may suffice for lesser men but a true mage must be willing and aware. I can offer suggestions, but the final decision is always yours. So it was for Alex and Shireen; so it is for you."

Something was happening near the altar: the shadows seemed to be deepening, growing. Richard was walking in a slow circuit about the room, passing the ancient murals, while Rachel sat frozen, staring. "Perhaps we should consider the options," Richard said. "I always find it helpful to talk these things through. We could stabilise Shireen, take her to Maria or some other life mage to have her healed. Of course, I doubt reviving Shireen would persuade her to respect your earlier decision. I suspect she would simply try to retrieve the Traviss girl again once she was recovered and, if she again chose a time when I was otherwise occupied, she might actually succeed." Richard glanced back at Rachel. "If she did, I would hunt her down and kill her, along with any accomplices. My tolerance goes only so far."

The darkness around the altar was taking shape. In the shadows I could make out something tall and thin, but neither Richard nor Rachel seemed to notice. "Of course, this leaves Tobruk out of the equation," Richard said. "I believe his intention was to use his own crystal upon Alex. Should he succeed—and he seems quite confident that he will— then when he returns he will have Alex's power in addition to his own. I imagine his first action will be to go looking for you and Shireen to settle some old scores. And given Shireen's condition, it's hard to imagine her offering much assistance."

"You're just going to let him?" Rachel said. She looked shocked. "You said—"

"Rachel," Richard said, and his voice was almost gentle. "I appreciate the loyalty you have demonstrated. But I cannot be here to protect you forever. Sooner or later you must learn to stand alone. And to do so you'll need strength of your own."

"Shireen could help me." Rachel's voice was pleading. "We could do it together."

"In terms of raw magical ability, perhaps," Richard said. "But do you think she would want to? After tonight, when she looks at you, what do you think she'll see?"

Rachel hesitated. "You've depended on Shireen too much, Rachel," Richard said. "It's weakened you. You could be so much more, but your reliance on her is holding you back. Now, you could heal Shireen. She might forgive you—or pretend to." Richard turned to face Rachel, holding her with his gaze. "And it will all be back to how it used to be. You'll be back in Shireen's shadow, less noticed, less powerful, less appreciated, always second place in everything you do because no matter how hard you try there is someone at your side who can do it more easily. And perhaps she'll let you have your way from time to time, but in the end she'll always be more important than you are because that's simply the way things are." Richard began to walk towards Rachel, while she stared at him as though hypnotised. "Or you could take Shireen's power for yourself. She'll live on, in a way. But then . . . ah, things will be different. Instead of being the weaker one, you'll be the stronger. Strong enough to stand on your own. You won't have to be afraid of other mages—they will be the ones who fear *you*. You'll be powerful enough to defeat Tobruk and anyone else who tries to take this mansion from you." Richard stopped in front of Rachel, looking down at her. "This is your choice, Rachel. Everything you have done since becoming my apprentice has led you to this. Go back to your old life, the way it used to be—if you can. Or take what you want, and your place as my Chosen. The decision is yours."

Richard held out his hand to Rachel, the black crystal in his palm. Rachel stared at it, frozen. Behind them, the shadow thing had taken form; the darkness around it made it hard to see but I could make out a shape that was humanoid yet distorted, unnaturally thin and stretched. As I watched the darkness started to drift towards Shireen's body, and towards Rachel and Richard. I backed away.

Slowly, Rachel took the crystal from Richard's hand. Richard took a step back and stood watching, hands behind his back. The darkness seeping from the altar reached his feet but shied away from touching him, flowing around him like water towards Rachel and Shireen. Rachel stared down at Shireen; she was pale from blood loss and quite still. Lying on the stone floor, she looked very small.

Then Rachel closed her fingers over the crystal and started the ritual.

I've never seen a Harvesting ritual, not in the flesh. In mage society it's kind of the equivalent of murder; a lot of people talk about it, but not many have witnessed one. I don't know how to perform it, and I don't want to. Rachel was speaking lines in another language, the sounds harsh and guttural, and as she did the darkness seeping from the altar began to swirl around her. The shadow thing was there too and it was behind her now, leaning over her and Shireen, and for one fleeting moment I wondered whether it hadn't really been there and this was all some trick of Elsewhere, or whether it *had* been there all along and it was because of Elsewhere that I was able to see it. The shadows around Rachel began to swirl faster, becoming a vortex, and her voice rose to a chant. I had one fleeting glimpse of her as she stood there, and there was something terrible in her face, desire and fear and horror all mingled together. As Rachel cried out the last words there was a thundering *crack* and Shireen's back arched, her body spasming as something flickered from Shireen and into Rachel, too fast to see. And as it did the shadow thing behind Rachel plunged its hands and head down into her back, slipping inside her. Rachel threw back her head and screamed, and everything went black.

When the lights returned the shadows were gone. There was no trace of the seeping darkness or the nameless thing looming over Rachel. The room was empty except for Richard, Rachel, and Shireen. Shireen was lying with her head to one side, and somehow as I looked at her I knew she was gone.

Rachel was lying next to her, looking groggy. She opened her eyes to see Shireen's body and jerked, scrabbling back on the stone.

"You are my apprentice no longer," Richard said. He hadn't moved throughout the ritual and still stood with his hands clasped behind his back. "What is your name?"

Rachel stared at Shireen's body for a moment longer, then looked away. She came to her feet to face Richard, not letting her eyes rest on the body. "Deleo." Her voice was shaky. "My name's Deleo."

I heard a noise from behind me and turned.

Rachel was standing there. Not the younger Rachel but the present one, the one I'd fought with and against last year, the one I'd met last night in the old brewery and who'd screamed at me to get out. She was looking straight at me and she could see me. She raised her hands and in a flash of pure terror I pulled myself away, trying to copy what Shireen had done, desperately trying to get out of Elsewhere because Rachel had seen me and she was coming—

ı ı ı ı ı ı ı ı ı

I came awake with a gasp, sitting up in the bed, heart hammering. I was in the room in the Royal National Hotel. The lights were off and the only light in the room was the ambient glow from the window looking out onto the courtyard. I should be safe, but my precognition was screaming at me and I could feel the aura of a spell, familiar and very close. I looked right.

Rachel was standing ten feet away, in the doorway to my hotel room. Sea-green light glowed about her and there was a look of death on her face.

I rolled off the bed as a green ray stabbed from Rachel's hand, striking the bed and disintegrating it into flaring particles. I landed awkwardly, coming to my feet, Rachel shifted her aim, I dodged back the other way, and her second ray hit the window, causing it to disappear in a cloud of dust. Rachel was between me and the door but there was empty air behind me and before I could think about what I was doing I dived through the window as a third ray cut the air above me. There was a flagpole below and I slammed into it, got a grip with my hands just before I would have slid off, let go on the backswing to come down with both feet on a tiny ledge in the wall above the main doors, then bounced to fall the last ten feet to the concrete below. I hit with a jolt and rolled—pain flashed through my shoulder and knee but I could still run and I came to my feet in a dead sprint.

From above I heard a scream of fury and felt another spell; I followed my precognition and dodged right just as a green ray flashed over my shoulder and opened a hemisphere in the concrete ten feet wide with a hollow *whuff*. A second ray fell short behind me, and a third struck the hotel building as I put the concrete pillars of the main entrance between me and Rachel. She screamed in fury again, the sound fainter now, and I knew she wouldn't stop coming. I'd seen the madness in Rachel's eyes; I'd found her deepest, darkest secret and she was going to kill me for it.

I raced out into the main road, bending right. My heart was pounding, every bit of my body surging with adrenaline. A blue van was passing just ahead and I moved without thinking, bounding onto the hood of a parked car, bouncing up onto the roof, and leaping into the air. I hit the roof of the van with a thump and nearly slid off, my precognition giving me just enough warning to drop and cling to the smooth metal as the van accelerated southeast towards Russell Square. I'd been awake for less than thirty seconds.

Twisting my head to look back I could see the facing of the Royal National shrinking behind me. One or two people were staring in my direction but it was the early hours of the morning and the streets were nearly deserted. I couldn't see Rachel but my precognition was still screaming *danger*

danger danger, and as I looked ahead I felt the surge of another gate spell.

Gate magic isn't meant to be used in combat. It's too slow; the minute or so it takes to form a gate is just too long to be practical. You can speed it up, but almost no one does; the chance of something going wrong is so much higher that you'd have to be insane to take the risk.

Trouble was, Rachel *was* insane. And she didn't care about risks.

I saw the green flash as Rachel appeared in a second-floor window ahead and to my left. With a flick of her fingers she vapourised the glass and then looked down, her eyes locking on to me as the van carried me towards her. Her hand came up, sea-green light intensifying, and I could feel the spell charging.

The van was going at maybe thirty miles an hour, but I didn't even stop to think. I jumped off and for one terrifying moment I was free-falling at what felt like fatal speed. The ray hit while I was in midair, and I had a fleeting glimpse of the whole side of the van evaporating into dust, looking like some crazy sort of engineering diagram as the cross-section of the vehicle opened to the night. It slewed sideways and began to crash, and then I hit the road.

It hurt. Rolling, bumping, tumbling, feeling pain in every part of my body before fetching up against a parked car with a final *thud*. I was half dazed but I knew that I was still in Rachel's line of sight and I managed to stagger to my feet and start running again just as the front half of the car dis-integrated in a dust cloud behind me. A second later I was under an awning and out of Rachel's vision; there was an alley to the right and before she could get in sight of me again I sprinted down it.

I ran and kept on running. I didn't even think about turning to fight—it would be like trying to fight a tidal wave. If Rachel got a straight shot at me for even a second, she would snuff my life out like a candle in a storm. But no matter how powerful her disintegration magic was, it still needed a direct line of sight. As long as there was something between us she couldn't hit me, and as long as I kept running fast enough it would stay that way. I kept turning corners, angling south towards Holborn, cutting across roads and through parks, always feeling Rachel behind me in my future sight. The sounds of the city were muted in the early morning, and the few people I passed turned to stare as I raced by. I hope none of them tried to stop Rachel; I didn't have time to look and see.

I don't know how long that chase went on; it felt like hours but was probably only minutes. I could so easily have died that night and in my mind I did, seeing future after future where Rachel's rays struck me, my world vanishing in a green flash and a moment of terrible agony and darkness. But I survived, and looking back on it now, I think what saved me wasn't my magic but my legs. Rachel's water magic is very, very good at destroying things, but one thing it doesn't give is mobility. She can gate, but trying to gate on top of a sprinting man is like trying to swat a housefly with a hammer. Rachel had to catch me before she could kill me and I could run harder and longer than she could. I kept weaving through the streets, switching directions randomly, always looking ahead.

I finally stopped running somewhere around Covent Garden. A theatre's back door made a black gap in the wall, and I ducked inside it, my breath coming in ragged gasps. My mist cloak blended with the shadows, hiding my trembling. I was invisible . . . but that hadn't stopped Rachel so far. I couldn't see any trace of her in the futures ahead, but that didn't reassure me; she'd found me in Elsewhere and jumped to me in the flesh. How had that even been possible? I couldn't see any danger, but I didn't want to stop. The rules that I'd thought would protect me hadn't worked and even hiding didn't feel safe anymore. The only thing I could think to do was to keep moving and I set off into the darkness.

I walked all through the night. I had a destination in mind to begin with but somewhere along the way I got lost and my sleep-fogged brain couldn't think clearly enough to come up with a new one. I kept moving and searching, looking for danger, finding nothing but afraid to stop and rest. The stars wheeled overhead, the summer constellations dipping below the horizon, and the people I passed in the night became faceless blurs, threats to be avoided.

By the time the sky started to lighten in the east I was too tired to keep going. I was afraid to stop moving and afraid to sleep, but my limbs felt like lead and I was starting to get the weird light-headed feeling that comes with sleep deprivation. Going to Elsewhere doesn't refresh you in the way that true sleep does; your body rests, but your mind doesn't. The constant stress was draining my energy reserves and I was reaching my limits.

I didn't know where in London I was anymore; I had the vague feeling I was south of the river but I'd gotten lost after crossing Waterloo Bridge. I'd passed hotels, but I didn't want to use them; hotels had people, and people were dangerous. Instead I searched the short-term futures as I walked, looking for somewhere empty.

There was an old building down a narrow back street in the shadow of a red-and-brown tower block. It had been a pub once, but the sign was faded and the windows boarded up. Someone had smashed one of the boards around the back, and I used it to climb in. The ground floor was covered in bottles and plastic bags and old needles and rotting food, and it stank of piss and decay. I found a way up to the second-floor rooms; they were bare planks but at least they didn't stink as badly. There were signs someone else had used the place—a lice-ridden mattress and some food wrappers—but it was empty now and that was all I cared about. I curled up in a corner and tried to rest.

It took me a long time. Even though I was exhausted, I couldn't fall asleep; every time I was beginning to drift a noise would jerk me back to wakefulness, searching the future for danger. As long as I stayed awake I could keep watch, but as soon as I fell asleep again I wouldn't be able to protect myself. Fear isn't new to me, but I couldn't remember the last time I'd felt this kind of paranoia. Rachel shouldn't have been able to find me. I'd been in a random room in a random hotel wearing my mist cloak, and everything I knew told me that I should have been safe. But I hadn't been, and now I didn't feel as though I was safe anywhere. The mist cloak felt warm and comfortable around me, softening the bare planks, but I couldn't stop my mind worrying over what could happen next. The last two times I'd gone to sleep I'd woken up to near-death. I didn't want to do it again.

But I'm not Anne and I can't switch off feeling tired. In the end, exhaustion won out.

⋅⋅⋅⋅⋅⋅⋅⋅⋅⋅⋅

I didn't sleep well.

I used to have nightmares about my time in Richard's mansion. Over the last year they've been getting better but sometimes they come back, and this was one of those times. I had dreams of being chased, running with leaden limbs but never being able to get away. I knew the people after me wanted revenge for what I'd done and the worst part was that I knew I deserved it. From time to time I'd drift half awake, vaguely aware that I should be watching for something, but I was too tired to remember what.

And then the nightmares passed and I was in a peaceful dream. I was in my shop, minding the counter. Luna was upstairs and there were customers passing through, and for the first time in days I felt safe.

Then I looked to one side and saw Shireen standing there, and suddenly I didn't feel safe anymore. I threw up my hands. "No! Not again!"

"It's okay," Shireen said.

"I'm through with this! You hear me? Variam told me,

right at the start. He asked what someone as crazy as Rachel would do if she found me sneaking around in her head. I shouldn't have tried to spy on Rachel in the first place. It was fucking insane and I nearly died for it. I'm not doing it again, Shireen, you hear me? I'm done!"

Shireen didn't look upset. She stepped over the rope to the magic items section and picked up a wand, turning it over in her hands. "I was shielding you while you were in her memories," she said without looking. "I've had a lot of time to practice with Elsewhere. I was trying to hide your presence so she wouldn't see you. Rachel must have become suspicious. I'm sorry."

"You don't think you could have warned me about that BEFORE?"

"I know."

"Jesus." I looked away. The customers were still in the shop, their conversation a gentle background murmur. Outside was the strange white glow of Elsewhere; at some point we'd left my dreams. I knew that I could go back if I wanted—Shireen couldn't actually keep me in Elsewhere against my will—but I didn't. There were things I wanted to know, and this time I knew the right questions to ask. "I know what you are now," I said. "You told me when we first met, didn't you? You told me you were a shadow. I didn't know what you meant, but I should have figured it out from the start. Harvesting steals someone's magic, but your magic's part of you, isn't it? You can't take one without the other. When Rachel Harvested you, she wasn't just taking your magic, she was taking *you*. And you've been living inside her head."

Shireen was silent for a while. "At first I didn't know what had happened," she said at last. "I thought I'd died and gone to . . . I don't know. The next life, maybe. I felt wrong, like there were bits of me missing. And there were new memories. I could remember things I'd done with Rachel, except when I remembered them I was looking at *me*, from the outside. And then I started to see other things. The present as well as the past. I could see what Rachel saw." Shireen looked up at me. "And finally I found I could talk to her."

I stared at Shireen. "She can see you, can't she?"

Shireen nodded.

I covered my eyes. "Jesus." I remembered my reunion with Rachel last year. She'd been talking to thin air, speaking to someone who didn't answer. Now I knew who she'd been talking to. "So all these years she's had you looking over her shoulder?" I shook my head. "She murdered her best friend and now she's got her ghost following her around. No wonder she's crazy . . ."

"It's . . . worse than that," Shireen said.

I stared at her. *"How?"*

"You saw something in Rachel's memories, didn't you?" Shireen said. "Something they couldn't see."

"That thing . . ." I remembered the spindly, inhuman form and had to hold back a shiver. "It's real?"

"It's real."

"What is it?"

"Do you know what it feels like, being Harvested?" Shireen asked.

I shook my head.

"It feels like your soul's being ripped away." Shireen's eyes were distant. "You can't move and you can't scream, but you can feel every bit of it. It takes minutes but it feels like years. I knew what was happening to me, and I knew it was Rachel who was doing it. And I hated her for it. She was my oldest friend and she was killing me, and I wanted her to suffer, hurt her as much as she was hurting me . . ." Shireen fell silent for a moment, staring past me. "There's a vulnerability to Harvesting. When you open yourself to take in the person whose magic you're absorbing, you open yourself to . . . other things. I called out, and something came. It passed into Rachel. I don't know what it is and I don't think it has a name. I know it doesn't talk. I don't think it can do anything to me. But it can do things to her."

We stood in silence for a little while. "Are you really Shireen?" I said at last. "Or are you some sort of copy?"

"I don't know," Shireen said simply, and somehow she sounded very sad. "I can remember my life, but it's patchy. Like old plaster flaking off a wall. Sometimes Rachel's memories feel more real than mine. Maybe the real Shireen died and she's gone away and I'm just an echo. Or maybe I am still Shireen, and I won't die until Rachel does . . ." She looked up at me. "How would I know?"

I sighed, my anger draining away. "I guess you wouldn't, would you?" I thought for a minute. "What happened after Rachel killed you?"

"At first Rachel was preparing for Tobruk to come back," Shireen said. "She wanted to be Richard's Chosen and she was going to fight him for it, kill him if she had to."

"But Tobruk never came."

"And in the end she figured out why. She didn't believe it at first, but after they found the body even she couldn't pretend. In a way the two of you were on the same side back then, though she didn't see it like that . . . And then it was time for Richard to leave. And they brought out Catherine."

I felt a sick sensation in the pit of my stomach. "Did Richard kill her?"

Shireen shook her head.

"Then is she—?"

"Rachel did," Shireen said, looking at me steadily. "You remember the room that was being built at the end of the catacombs? That was what it was designed for. Catherine begged and pleaded but Rachel didn't listen. She did the ritual and it worked just like Richard said. It drained the life from Catherine's body and opened a gate, just for a few seconds.

Richard went through it. The last thing he told her was to watch for his return."

I stared down at the floor, feeling numb and hollow. So this was how it all ended. A part of me wanted to argue, tell Shireen that she must have made a mistake—but hadn't I always known deep down that this was what must have happened? How likely was it that Catherine could have gotten away and survived for all these years without me or her brother or anyone else ever knowing? Will had been right after all. I *had* killed Catherine by capturing her—it had just taken a while for her to die. "Why did Rachel do it?" I said.

"Because she didn't have any choice," Shireen said with a sigh. "That was how she saw it. She'd wanted to be Richard's Chosen, and she wanted it so badly she killed me for it. Once she'd done that . . . If she stopped being his apprentice and walked away, it would all have been for nothing. She would have killed me for nothing. It was like . . . as long as he was giving the orders, she could pretend it wasn't really her fault. He gave her an excuse."

"That's bullshit! She always had a choice; she could have stopped!"

Shireen looked past me. When she spoke, her voice sounded different, as though she were reciting.

> *For mine own good,*
> *All causes shall give way: I am in blood*
> *Stepp'd in so far that, should I wade no more,*
> *Returning were as tedious as go o'er . . .*

I stared at her. "Where's that from?"

"A play I once saw," Shireen said. She looked at me. "Do you know why Rachel hates you so much?"

I shook my head.

"Because you *did* go back. You stopped being Richard's

apprentice and started a new life. Every time Rachel looks at you she knows that she could have done it all differently, that she *did* have a choice. And she hates you for it because deep down there's a bit of her that wishes she'd done the same thing. You're a living reminder of the one thing in her past that she's most ashamed of and that no one could ever forgive, and the worst part is that she knows she didn't have to do it and that it was all her own fault."

"And then there's you," I said quietly. "She thought once she killed you it'd all be over, but she has to see you every day and be reminded of what she's done. And on top of *that* she's got this horror from God-knows-where in her head as well." I shook my head. "Jesus."

Shireen nodded and we stood for a while in silence. "All right," I said at last. "What do you want, Shireen? You said that after I'd seen all of this, there was something you were going to ask from me. What is it?"

"I want you to help Rachel," Shireen said. "Redeem her."

I stared at Shireen. "You have got to be kidding me."

Shireen shook her head.

"You want me to do what? Save her soul?"

"Something like that."

"I thought you didn't believe in that stuff?"

"When you've been a disembodied soul in someone else's body for ten years it changes your attitudes a bit."

"She killed you!"

"I still love her," Shireen said simply. "She was my best friend and I never stopped caring about her, even after everything. I know what she did but you haven't seen how much she's suffered for it. Besides, if anyone's got the right to decide whether she deserves to be forgiven, don't you think it should be me?"

I couldn't think of anything to say to that. "Will you help me?" Shireen asked.

"Shireen . . ." I dropped into my chair and covered my eyes, resting my head in one hand. "What do you expect me to do? You said it yourself, she hates me. And that was *before* she saw me spying on her. Now she's moved me up to 'kill on sight.'"

"I don't think she'll try to kill you," Shireen said. "Not again."

I stared at Shireen. "Are you serious?"

"She's never actually tried to kill you before," Shireen said. "Not really. The only reason she did this time was . . . well, she lost control a bit."

"A *bit*?"

Shireen clasped her hands and gave me a hopeful look. "I'm pretty sure I can talk her around for next time."

"Have you considered," I said carefully, "that hanging around in Rachel's head for ten years might have messed up your standards a little?"

"Maybe," Shireen said. "But this is what I want. I'm not changing my mind on this one, Alex. If you want me to keep helping you, this is the price."

I looked at Shireen for a long time. "You know there's no guarantee she's going to listen to me," I said at last. "Or anyone. If she makes a decision I can't stop her."

"I know."

I stayed silent for a little while then shook my head. "I can't promise anything," I said at last. "Not yet. I understand why you want this, but . . . Look, tell me something. How the *hell* did Rachel find me?"

"She's always been able to," Shireen said. "Didn't you notice?"

I started to answer, then stopped. When I'd seen Rachel last year at the British Museum I'd been in the shadows wearing my mist cloak. Rachel's two companions, Cinder and Khazad, hadn't noticed a thing . . . but Rachel had. She hadn't found me but it had been close, and every time since then that I'd spied on her the same thing had happened. "Why?" I said.

"Do you remember the first time you went to Elsewhere?" Shireen said. "The very first time?"

"Yeah." It had been Richard who'd shown us how to do it. The four of us had travelled there together—me, Shireen, Tobruk, and Rachel. It had been a memorable trip.

"When you go to Elsewhere with another person, it leaves a connection," Shireen said. "I think when Rachel Harvested me something happened that strengthened that somehow. She can sense you and you can sense her."

"I'm not sure I can."

"Last autumn, when you were working for Belthas," Shireen said. "You found Rachel and Cinder just by walking around London. Didn't you ever wonder why that worked?"

I hadn't, not until Shireen mentioned it. "So she can find me through my mist cloak?"

"The cloak makes it harder," Shireen said. "I think the reason she could do it was that you were actually in her memories. It intensified the connection, at least for a little while. She must have traced the link."

"Then don't take this personally," I said, "but I'm never doing anything like that again."

"I understand."

We stood in silence for a while, listening to the buzz of conversation, then I shook my head, pulling my thoughts back to the present. "So all of this was for nothing. Catherine was dead all along and there's nothing that'll stop Will from coming after me."

"You know the truth now."

"And you couldn't have just told me?" I looked at Shireen. "You knew what had happened to Catherine. You could have told me I was wasting my time."

"You think learning how I died is a waste of time?" Shireen said quietly. She didn't raise her voice, but her eyes sparked and something in them made me want to draw back. "You don't think what happens to me and Rachel is important? I've helped you every time you've needed it. You think that's all I'm here for, doing you favours and then disappearing when you don't need me? I might be just a shadow but

I'm not your slave. You don't have the right to tell me what to do."

I looked away, feeling a flash of shame. "I'm sorry," I said at last. "That wasn't what I meant. But Will and the Nightstalkers are still out there and they're still after me. I know that for you this is the most important thing in the world, but you don't have to worry about getting killed in your sleep."

"This is more important than Will and the Nightstalkers," Shireen said, and her voice was utterly certain. "They're a short term problem."

"Short-term?"

"You've faced worse," Shireen said. "So has Rachel. They're not going to be around in the long term but she will be. You needed to know this, you needed to see it, so that you understood. And yes, it was dangerous, but I'm not sorry for doing it. It was worth the risk."

Easy for you to say, I thought, but didn't say it out loud. For the first time since meeting Shireen's shade, I felt I was starting to understand her. She had her own priorities and to me they might seem crazy, but from her point of view they made sense and now that I had some idea of what they were I could deal with her. It wasn't like it was the first time I'd had to work with someone with a skewed point of view . . . and somewhere at the back of my mind I couldn't help but wonder if our points of view might not be so different after all. "Anything you can do to help?"

"I can't fight for you," Shireen said. "Not in your world. But there's a place I can show you. You won't enjoy it but it might help you find something you've been looking for for a long time."

chapter 12

I came awake to realise someone was talking. Just the knowledge that I wasn't alone sent a spike of fear and adrenaline through my system, and in an instant I was fully alert. I could smell stale air and unwashed clothes, and from the shuffling of footsteps I could tell there was another person near me. Without moving any other part of my body, I opened my eyes.

There was a man standing a few feet away. He wore an ancient stained greatcoat over dirty torn clothes, and from his smell neither he nor his clothes had had a wash in a long time. Straggly grey hair framed bleary eyes and a face prematurely aged. "—you doing here?" he was saying. "Huh? What you doing here?"

I stared back at him, motionless. "This is mine," he said. "You don't get to sleep here, see? It's mine. What you doing here?" When I didn't answer he took a step forward, his voice gaining a little confidence. "My mates are coming back. They're going to be angry. This is mine, see? You shouldn't be here." His manner was halfway between pleading and threatening, and when I still didn't answer it began to edge towards threatening. "You know who I am? I know people, I do. No one messes with me." He took another step, moving to poke me with his foot. "You—"

I caught his ankle with my left hand as my right came out from under my cloak in a flash of steel. Before the man could react I had my knife pressed against his leg, the point digging through his trousers towards the upper thigh, where the femoral artery runs close to the skin. He tried to jerk away but I clung on and he nearly fell backwards. "Hey man!" he said, his voice squeaking suddenly. "Why—"

I hissed at him, showing my teeth, and his eyes went wide in fear. He tried to pull away, but I dug the knife in deeper and he froze. I held his eyes for a slow count of five then let him go suddenly. He scrambled back to the door. "You shouldn't have done that," he said, trying to hold up his dignity. "This is mine, see? You shouldn't . . ."

I stared at the man without blinking and he trailed off, then backed away into the shadows. I lay still, following his movement through the futures as he clattered his way down the stairs. Once I was satisfied he was gone I got up.

I'd slept through the day, and yellow-gold light was shining through the newspaper covering the grimy windows. For some reason the afternoon felt shadowed and dark, even through the sunlight; I tried peeling back the newspaper to get a better idea of the time, but the light stung my eyes. I drew back into the shadows, waiting for darkness.

I'd been out of contact and I knew I ought to be checking in, but I felt a strange reluctance to talk to anyone; it felt as though it could be dangerous. Miserable as it was, the abandoned pub was safe, and in the end I stayed there for hours, while the sun set and the sky turned from blue to purple to grey. Only after night had fallen did I leave, and even then it was only hunger that forced me from the building. There was a cluster of shops at the end of the road but I didn't want to draw the attention of shopkeepers; the summer night was too busy and it made me nervous. Clusters of men and women passed by in the darkness, and it felt as though all of them were looking at me. It was too much and I turned down a small residential street, used my divination magic to find an empty house, and broke in through the back door.

Once I'd stolen a makeshift meal from the kitchen, I finally took out my phone. As soon as I placed it on the kitchen table and thumbed the button the screen lit up with a dozen messages. My mist cloak really messes up incoming signals—usually I don't wear it long enough for it to matter, but by now I'd been wearing it for more than a day straight. Most of the messages were from Luna and Anne and at a glance they sounded worried, but I didn't want to answer them. The last message was from Caldera and it asked me to call her back as soon as possible. I touched the screen to return the call and sat in one of the kitchen chairs, waiting. Caldera answered on the fourth ring.

One of the dubious privileges of being a diviner is never having to wait for bad news. Usually conversation is unpredictable—there's too much randomness and free will to see more than a few seconds ahead. But when someone's already decided what they're going to tell you, then every possible conversation goes the same way. The only question is how long it'll take to get to the point. "Verus," Caldera said.

There was a new note in Caldera's voice, one I hadn't heard before. She sounded . . . subdued. "Feeling better?" I said.

"What? Oh." Caldera brushed it off. "I'm fine. You?"

"I'm alive," I said. I didn't really want to talk. "So?"

Caldera didn't answer. "You said you were taking this to the Council," I said. "You said to stay out of it and keep my head down."

"Yeah," Caldera said after a pause. She didn't sound happy, and in a sudden flash of insight I wondered how often she had to do this in her job. Give bad news and then walk away . . .

"So?"

"I filed my report yesterday. It had a full account of our encounter with Will and the Nightstalkers and their attack. I recommended the Nightstalkers be brought in for violation of the Concord." She paused again. "I got the reply back this evening."

I listened silently. "It's been kicked upstairs," Caldera said. "There's a Council committee scheduled to look into it."

"Did they give you a reason?"

"I had some questions about the decision," Caldera said. From her tone of voice it sounded like it had been more than that. "They said . . ." She hesitated. "They've decided the Nightstalkers aren't an immediate threat to the Council or to Light or independent mages."

I was silent. "I see," I said at last.

"I put in a request for a task force. I haven't had an answer."

"Weren't you in the middle of investigating Richard when the Nightstalkers tried to kill you?" I said. "You know, the ones who 'aren't an immediate threat'?"

Caldera was silent for a moment. "I've been taken off the Richard Drakh case," she said. "I'm on medical leave."

"Medical leave."

"I didn't request it."

"Thought you said you were fine."

Caldera didn't answer.

"Don't suppose you know where these orders of yours come from, do you?" I said.

"I'm not authorised—"

"Don't worry, I can guess. From the Council, right?"

"What makes you so sure?"

"Does it matter? It's not like you were going to do anything about it."

Caldera was silent again. I'd expected her to snap at me, but she didn't. In a way it actually made it worse; I wanted her to get angry so I could yell at her. "There's a mage on the Council called Levistus," I said. "I don't have any proof, but this is his style. No risk, no involvement. He never gets his hands dirty, he just gives the orders and stays at a distance."

"I'm sorry," Caldera said.

A part of me wanted to shout at Caldera, blame her for all the Council's hypocrisies. Whoever had given Caldera those orders must have known that the Nightstalkers were out for blood. The Council had a thousand times the resources of Will's group—they could crush them without even trying. But they weren't going to, even after the Nightstalkers had blatantly violated the Concord, because the Council only enforced the Concord when it suited them.

But an older, wiser part of me knew that it wasn't Caldera's fault. And deep down, had I ever really expected anything different? The Council has never helped me before and I'd never really believed that they'd start now. If I was going to live through this it would be because of myself and my friends, and nobody else. "Forget it," I said. "You have to follow your orders."

"What are you going to do?" Caldera asked.

I thought about it for a second. "I don't know," I said at last. "Good-bye, Caldera." I hung up before she could reply.

· · · · · · · · · ·

That night seemed to last a long time.

I didn't have any appointments to keep and for now at least I'd lost my pursuers. I was free to go wherever I wanted—except that I couldn't think of anywhere to go. For the first time in years, I didn't know what to do.

Ever since Will had attacked me in the casino I'd been trying to figure out a way to end this. I'd tried talking to the Nightstalkers and I'd tried fighting them and I'd tried running from them. I'd tried searching Rachel's memories for the truth, and I'd tried relying on Caldera to fix things for me. And every single one had been a failure. Things weren't any better than they had been at the start—if anything they were worse. I'd nearly been killed half a dozen times, and the only reason I was still alive was that my friends had put themselves at risk to save me. Anne and Variam and Luna and Sonder had been in danger and were still in danger, and it was because of me.

I know I come off as arrogant sometimes. When you can see the future it's easy to pretend you know everything, and to other people it probably looks like I do. But being able to see the future doesn't make you any smarter or wiser than anyone else, and it doesn't stop you making stupid mistakes. It lets you know what a problem is and how big the problem is, but it doesn't give you the power to do anything about it. When it comes down to it, the reason I act all-knowing isn't because I think I know everything. It's because I know I *don't*, and I'm desperately trying to stop my enemies from figuring that out. And if you keep up an act to fool other people, sometimes you end up fooling yourself as well.

But now I couldn't pretend anymore. Everything I'd tried had been a failure, and I'd lost my confidence. If I tried to do something else, I felt like I'd just screw that up too. Worst of all, there was a nagging voice at the back of my head wondering whether this was what I deserved. Will had been right all along: I *had* killed his sister, it had just been Rachel who'd delivered the final blow. I knew I was leaving Anne and Luna and Variam in the dark, but I couldn't face talking to them, not now. Instead I just walked, flitting from shadow to shadow through the London night. Eventually I realised where my feet were taking me.

⁙⁙⁙

The cemetery was in Camberwell, tucked away behind an old church with a faded sign. Black iron spike railings surrounded it from the outside, and trees were planted around the edges, giving it a sheltered, shut-in feel. The gates were locked and I had to climb them to get in.

The inside of the cemetery was quiet and empty. The nearest main road was two streets away and the trees had a muffling effect, silencing the area so that the loudest sounds were the echoes of my footsteps around the tombstones. I suppose most people would have found it creepy, but I've never really been scared of cemeteries. It's living people I'm afraid of, not dead ones.

The headstone was small, and it took me a long time to find it amongst all the others. It had once been white, but wind and rain had darkened it to grey. Flicking on my flashlight, I crouched down in front of it. The inscription read:

CATHERINE HELENA TRAVISS
1984–2002
BLESSED ARE THE PURE IN HEART,
FOR THEY SHALL SEE GOD

Two larger headstones were set a little way behind it. I didn't read them: I knew who they were for. I sat cross-legged on the grass and stared at the small headstone. The cemetery was dark and silent, and any wind was kept out by the trees. I was alone with the dead.

Catherine's body wasn't here. Shireen had told me that. Rachel had been the one who'd killed her, and Rachel hadn't been concerned about funeral rites . . . or maybe she just didn't want anything left to remind her of what she'd done. She'd disintegrated the bodies and left the dust to blow away. But at some point someone had found out what had happened, learnt that Catherine was dead, and cared enough to leave a headstone, and I wondered who it had been. Will, maybe? But he would have been in America. Maybe some other relation—a cousin, an aunt or uncle. Everybody has someone who'll miss them, even if it's just to notice they're gone.

"So this is where it ends," I said. My voice sounded very loud in the quiet of the cemetery. "All this time, you were just waiting here . . . I wonder how many people still remember this grave? You must have had people who cared about you, but it's been ten years. They'll have gone on with their lives." I was silent for a little while. "Maybe I'll end up in a place like this someday. Just a little headstone, and a few people who'll forget . . ."

A train passed by along the railway lines one street over, the rumble of its wheels echoing over the rooftops. "I'm sorry I screwed things up," I said. "I wanted to save you, but the only person I saved was myself. I just ran and I didn't go back. All this time I've been trying to forget what I did, but now your brother's here and he's trying to kill me for it. What do *you* want? If you were here, would you tell Will to go away and live his own life? Or would you tell him that he was right, and I deserve it . . . ?"

There was no sound but the wind in the trees. Shireen might have stayed on after her death—or at least some part of her had—but Catherine wasn't Shireen. Wherever she'd gone, either she couldn't hear me or she wasn't answering.

I sat by the grave for a long time, then got to my feet and left, leaving the cemetery empty behind me.

ı ı ı ı ı ı ı ı ı

My memories of the rest of that night are fuzzy. I know I kept moving, but I don't remember where I went or how. Most of the other people in the city were asleep and the few I met on the streets seemed to blur past without seeing me. I didn't know where I was going and wandered aimlessly through the London night. The streetlights hurt my eyes, and I found myself sticking to parks and back streets where I could merge with the shadows. I felt strange: hyped and on edge, yet thin and stretched. I felt tired but my movements were quick and I could sense the presence of the people nearby. It seemed to be getting easier and easier to hide from them.

By the time the sky started to brighten in the east, I was

on Hampstead Heath. I don't know how I ended up there but I guess it's like they say: home is the place where when you have to go there, they have to take you in. I didn't want to go down to talk to Arachne but the grey light of dawn was spreading across the sky and the thought of being caught in the morning sunlight made me flinch. I found the ravine that hid the entrance to Arachne's lair and touched the spot on the root that signalled her. I don't remember what I said, but she opened the door.

I was stumbling by the time I made it down into Arachne's cave, weaving from side to side. Arachne was working on something blue and white, but as she saw me she stopped, turning her head towards me. "Alex?" she said, the clicking rustle of her mandibles an undertone to her words. "What's happened to you?"

"Nothing," I said, shielding my eyes. "Can you turn the lights down?" I didn't remember Arachne's lair being so bright, but the glare was making me squint.

Arachne stayed still. It was hard to tell but I had the feeling she was staring at me. "How long have you been wearing that?"

"What?"

"Alex." Arachne's voice was sharp and clear. "How long have you been wearing your cloak?"

"I don't know?" The light was making it hard to concentrate. "I just need to rest until the sun goes down. I'll be—"

"Take it off," Arachne said.

"What?" I squinted at her. "Why?"

"Take off your cloak," Arachne said, pronouncing each word carefully. "Now."

It was a simple enough request but I felt reluctant. The cloak was the only thing keeping me hidden; without it I wasn't safe. "Look, just—"

It's easy to forget how fast Arachne can move. She's the size of a station wagon and by all rights she should be slow, but she's much, *much* faster than she looks and she can go from a standing start to full speed in the time it takes you to blink. I should have seen it coming but my precognition's tuned to sense danger, not movement, and by the time I realised it wasn't registering, Arachne was on top of me. Her two front legs caught the mist cloak and yanked it off me in a single precise movement.

Light stabbed into my eyes, burning through my brain, erasing everything in white fire. My skin seemed to ignite, flaring in sudden agony, and I couldn't see or hear or feel. All I could feel was light burning into me, too bright, too—

ııııııı

When I came to my senses I was lying on one of Arachne's sofas. I tried to open my eyes, and the light sent a flash of pain bouncing around inside my head. I winced and screwed my eyes shut again.

"Why were you still wearing your cloak?" Arachne asked. I could smell her herbal scent, and from the sound of it she was right next to me.

"Why shouldn't I be?" I muttered. I felt groggy, but also more awake; it was as though something that had been making my thoughts fuzzy was gone.

"I warned you," Arachne said, and her voice was sharp. "When I gave you that cloak, I told you to be sparing about when you used it. Did you forget?"

"It was ten years ago, okay?"

Arachne sighed. "I suppose for you that *is* a long time, isn't it? I keep forgetting how short human memories are."

I pulled myself upright and forced my eyes open. I had to shade them with my hand; everything was much too bright. "What happened?"

"Hold your hand up to the light," Arachne said.

I had to squint but I did as Arachne said, and as my eyes cleared I frowned. My hand looked . . . weird. Too much of the light was getting through around my fingers; it was like my skin was almost translucent. It was eerie and I looked away. "What happened to me?"

"Mist cloaks aren't meant for extended use," Arachne said. "You were starting to fade."

"But . . ." I felt confused. My mist cloak's always been the one magic item I've completely trusted. "It's trying to help me." Somehow I was sure of that. "It keeps me safe."

"Imbued items don't have a sense of proportion," Arachne said. "They're alive, but they're not human." She lifted a foreleg and I looked to see the mist cloak neatly folded on the next sofa over. "The cloak *does* try to help you. Its purpose is to hide its bearer, and that's what it does. And it does it so well that if you wear it long enough, then *nobody* will be able to find you. Not even you."

I looked at the folded cloth, fading into the sofa, and couldn't help but shiver. "What happens then?"

"No one knows," Arachne said simply. "I imagine the cloak still keeps them safe. Somewhere."

I put a hand to my head. "I can't do anything right, can I?"

"Focus," Arachne said. "You can feel sorry for yourself later. There's someone here to see you."

I looked up in surprise. "Who?"

A flicker in the futures made me turn my head. Standing in one of the tunnel mouths, hand resting on the rocky wall, was Variam.

· · · · · · · · ·

"You don't look so good," Variam told me.

"That's about how I feel." Variam and I were sitting opposite each other while Arachne sewed quietly in the corner. The orb lights set into the walls of Arachne's cave were soft and muted, but they were still enough to hurt my eyes if I looked directly at them, and I still had that weird disconnected feeling. I could feel the mist cloak's presence, resting quietly on one of the sofas, and even now I had the urge to put it on and hide. I pushed it away with a shudder; I wasn't going to feel comfortable touching that cloak for a long time. "What's been happening while I've been gone?"

"Those adepts showed up while we were at Luna's," Variam said. "One of them can track people, right?"

"Is everyone okay?"

"There wasn't a fight," Variam said. "They just hid outside. Think they were trying to spy on us."

"Anne spotted them?"

Variam nodded.

"The Chinese kid's called Lee," I said. "He can find people—anyone he's met, probably. Did they show up the night before last, or yesterday?"

"Night before last."

That would have been just after I'd started wearing my cloak. I'd lost the Nightstalkers at my shop and they hadn't picked me up again. "They couldn't track me, so they tracked you. I guess they were hoping I'd show up and they could ambush me . . . But they don't know what Anne can do, or they wouldn't have tried to hide like that. Are they still there?"

"Not since yesterday. We've been waiting in case they come back, but they haven't shown up."

"They're waiting for Lee to find me again," I said, half to myself. No reason for them not to—it had worked every time before. As long as I was in Arachne's lair her wards would hide me but as soon as I stepped outside . . .

"So what's the plan?" Variam asked.

"I don't have one."

"Seriously."

Variam was looking at me expectantly. He'd changed into a black shirt and turban and looked ready and alert. "Vari, you know all the times in the past I've told you guys what to do?" I said. "Most of the time I'm making it up as I go along. I'm not as tough as you think I am. Right now I don't know what to do."

Variam frowned. "You haven't got any ideas?"

"I've got lots," I said. "The problem is that all of them are *bad*. You know what? You listen to them and tell me what you think." I held up a finger. "Plan number one. I keep running and hiding. Will and the Nightstalkers keep chasing. I hope they give up or get themselves hurt and go away."

Variam gave me a look.

"I told you it was a bad plan." I held up a second finger. "Plan number two. I keep trying to talk some sense into Will. Settle this peacefully."

"Won't work," Variam said.

"You said that before."

"Because I saw him," Variam said, and shrugged. "If I knew someone had done that to my brother, I wouldn't listen either."

"Anne thought there was a chance."

"You destroyed his *life*," Variam said. "That's how he sees it, right? What are you possibly going to say to make it all better?"

I looked back at Vari for a second, then shrugged. "I wish you were wrong, but . . . yeah. That's how it seems, isn't it?"

"So?" Vari said.

"So plan number three," I said. "The one you're thinking of. I get you and Luna and Anne, we gear up and pick our ground, and we have a fight."

Variam nodded.

"Say we do," I said. "On our side we'd have me, you, Anne, and Luna. They'd have Will with his time magic, the American guy with his guns, Dhruv the life-drinker, and ground-fire girl. They've got at least two others, so figure they'll fight too. Four against seven. You think we'd win?"

"Yeah, I do," Variam said. "We've been talking it over and we've done the math. Luna's good with that whip, and

Anne and I have gone up against a lot worse. And you're a frigging mage. They're just adepts."

"Okay," I said. "So we kill them all, is that the plan? I shoot some, you burn some, Anne stops the heart of a couple more, and we throw the bodies in a pit somewhere?"

Variam looked taken aback. "Uh . . ."

"Your magic creates supernatural heat, Vari," I said. "It doesn't have a stun setting. If you hit someone full strength, it's not going to knock them out, it's going to kill them. Same with Luna. The more of her curse she puts into someone, the less likely they're going to be walking out alive."

"You think I don't know that?" Variam said. "I've done this before. I can scale my spells back."

"I know," I said. "You can go for glancing hits, try to just scorch them. But now it's not four against seven, it's the four of us *at half strength* against their seven, and they *won't* be holding back, not against me anyway. They'll be trying to kill me. Would you be willing to do the same to them? Even knowing they're not that different from you?"

Variam was silent. "You remember I told you how Anne got kidnapped by Sagash?" he said at last. "And I went to look for her?"

I nodded.

"It took a long time," Variam said. "I had to look in a lot of places." He looked at me. "Sometimes things get messy, you know? Someone starts something and there's a guy in your way. And maybe you might have been friends if you'd had the chance, but you don't have time to talk it over, do you?"

"But this is different," I said. "I know you're no coward, and neither is Luna. But you're not murderers either. And Anne . . . you think *she's* going to go along with a plan that involves killing anyone?" I leant forward. "I've thought about this a lot over the last few days. I've run the scenarios in my head and if it comes down to a fight between us and them, here's what I think's going to happen. Most of us and most of them will start out nonlethal. We won't be fighting to kill. But Will will be, and so will Ja-Ja. And sooner or later something'll go wrong. Someone'll step in front of a bullet, or they'll take a fire blast head-on, or Luna's curse'll hit someone the wrong way. Once that happens it won't be just about me anymore, it'll be about revenge. They'll want blood for blood, and there won't be any way to stop it." I looked steadily at Variam. "Best case? Four or five of them end up dead and you and Luna have their blood on your hands. Worst case, they wipe us out. But the most likely way I see this ending is that they lose but they don't go down alone. You three are good and so am I, but these guys aren't pushovers either. They're fast and they're strong and they know how to work together. They haven't been trying to kill the three of you so far, but as soon as the first one of them dies that's all going to change. Would you want to win the fight if it meant Anne's life? Or Luna's, or yours? Maybe two out of three? Does that sound like a good deal to you?"

Variam didn't answer. "We aren't strong enough to be able to beat these guys without a good chance of them taking us with them," I said. "And we *definitely* aren't strong enough to take them down without hurting them. Your magic's lethal, Luna's magic is lethal, and the only weapons I've got that can take these guys down fast are lethal too. I've been trying to think of some way of finishing this that doesn't end up with people dying and I can't see it."

"So what are you going to do?" Variam demanded. "Sit around? Okay, so the odds aren't great. We've fought worse."

"Because you didn't have a choice," I said. "But this time *I'm* making the choice. And if I lead you guys into this then one of two things will happen. Either you get killed, or you'll be responsible for *them* getting killed. You'll have their blood on your hands for the rest of your lives, and someday in the future someone else will wind up coming after *you* the way they've come after *me*." I looked steadily at Variam.

"I won't do that, Vari. I'm not letting the three of you pay for my mistakes and I'm not letting you do the same things I did. Not for my sake."

Variam stared back at me. I held his gaze, and in the end it was Variam who looked away. "Fine," he said. He was trying to act annoyed but I knew I'd gotten through. "Great. So what, keep on hiding?"

I sat in silence. For all that I knew that Variam's plan would end badly, he was right about one thing: I couldn't hide forever. Sooner or later I'd have to face Will again.

For what felt like a long time now I'd had a quiet dark voice whispering at the back of my mind, telling me that running wasn't going to work, that talking wasn't going to work, that there was only one way this could end. Now at last I stopped resisting and listened.

What do you want?

I wanted to survive. For Will and the Nightstalkers to be gone. For Anne and Variam and Luna to be safe and not to have any sins on their conscience.

So, then.

I wasn't strong enough to defeat them on my own.

Is it the first time?

It wasn't the first time I'd gone up against enemies able to beat me in a straight fight. Belthas, Vitus, Onyx . . .

How did you survive?

Each time, I'd survived by making sure it *hadn't* been a straight fight. Mostly, I'd done the same thing . . .

And suddenly the plan was laid out before me, as if it had been written down in a book and hidden away until it could just now be opened. It was simple and brutal and I'd had all the pieces I needed for days. But until now, I wouldn't have been willing to do it. Maybe this was what I'd really been waiting for, the reason I'd been running from Will all this time. My old instincts hadn't been gone; they'd just been buried, covered over with the habits and memories of happier times. Will and the Nightstalkers had cut through those, worn me down to the point where I was willing to do whatever it took to survive.

I looked up at Variam. "Will you help me?"

Variam nodded.

"I know you've been practising with gate magic," I said. "Can you bring someone with you?"

Variam hesitated for a second. ". . . Yeah, I can do it. How fast?"

"Speed's not an issue," I said. "I'm going to need to get somewhere and I won't be able to take a car or a train. Lee'll be tracking me and if I'm out in the open they'll home in on me before I get there."

"Okay. Where to?"

I took out a notebook and wrote down the location, sketching out a map before tearing out the paper and handing it to Variam. "Here," I said. "You'll need to go there to study it so you can make a gate safely. Choose a staging point. More than one would be better." I tapped my pen on the map, picking out two areas. "These probably have the most cover, but farther away is fine as long as you're not too far from the building. Just don't go inside."

Variam frowned as he looked at the map. "I can do it but how's this going to help?"

"If we're lucky it won't have to," I said. "I'm going to have one last try at talking this out. Come back tomorrow. One way or another, it'll be settled by then."

⁛⁛⁛⁛⁛

When I want to find something out, I usually use my divination magic. On the other hand, I've been around long enough to learn that even though divination can *theoretically* find out anything, sometimes doing things the mundane way is more efficient. In this case I wanted to find out someone's phone number. I don't have the contacts or the resources to get that kind of information but I know people who do. I had to call in a favour, but it didn't take long.

At the same time, I was watching the futures for danger. I wasn't wearing my mist cloak anymore, and as soon as I stepped outside Arachne's cave Lee would be able to pick me up again. I needed to know how fast he could do it and so I spent several hours path-walking, trying out one future after another.

As usual, there was good news and bad news. The good news was that Lee couldn't instantly home in on me. It would take time, and the more I kept moving the slower it would be. I'd been paying close attention to that conversation I'd overheard between him and Dhruv and Captain America, and I was fairly sure his magic only gave him a direction, not a location. To narrow down the distance he'd have to triangulate from multiple points.

The bad news was that while it would take time, once the process started it was also more or less inevitable. As soon as he picked me up he could just keep on closing in, getting a more and more accurate fix with each attempt. I could delay it as long as I kept moving, but sooner or later he'd catch up. Worse, the Nightstalkers weren't stupid. If they noticed I was moving in the direction of a place they'd been to before, they could take a guess and jump straight to it. That was how they'd tracked me down to my shop so quickly after the fight at Richard's mansion.

And the last problem was that it wasn't predictable. The trouble with divination magic is that it's only one hundred percent reliable if you're dealing with systems that are one hundred percent deterministic, which human beings aren't. At any point Lee might change his mind and start searching for me in a different way, or have a sudden flash of brilliance and guess exactly where I was, and unless I was watching closely I'd have no way of knowing. On top of that I was about to do something guaranteed to get their attention.

Well, it wasn't like this was more dangerous than anything else I'd done lately.

I waited until after dark, resting in Arachne's cave as the hours dragged by. Arachne didn't disturb me, leaving me to my thoughts; she didn't ask what I was going to do but I think she had a good idea. Once the sun had set I went outside.

The Heath was quiet and peaceful in the summer night. Distant chatter and laughter drifted through the darkness, the last picnickers and dog walkers lingering in the warm weather. The air smelt of grass and pollen, and the stars of the Summer Triangle hung overhead, bright enough to shine through the orange glow of the city. The traffic from the main roads around the Heath was a steady rustle, not close enough to be loud but a constant noise in the background. I stood in the ravine next to the entrance to Arachne's cave and dialled the number on my phone.

It rang for a while before picking up. "Hello?"

"Hi, Will," I said.

It took only those two words for Will to recognise my voice. He was silent for a second, and when he spoke again he sounded sharp and alert. "What do you want?"

"I just want to talk."

"Okay. Come by and we'll have a chat."

"I said *talk*," I said. "If I wanted another fight I'd just wait for you guys to show up for another of your assassination attempts."

The phone went briefly silent as I was speaking: Will had pressed the Mute button and I knew he was giving orders to find me. I started scanning the futures for danger, searching for the ones in which the Nightstalkers gated in. "Fine," Will said. "Talk."

Will was buying time, probably hoping to keep me on the line while Lee tracked me down. "I'm sorry for what happened to your sister," I said. "I know what I did back then was wrong, and if I could take it back I would. But I can't. And killing me isn't going to bring her back."

"This isn't about bringing her back," Will said. "You think I don't know that? This is about making sure you don't get to do it again."

"I haven't been doing it again!" I snapped. "I'm not a Dark mage anymore! You're trying to kill me for something I don't want to do!"

"Right, you're a good guy now." Will's voice was sarcastic. "You think you get to walk away? You've had enough and now everyone should leave you alone?"

"Yes! I walked out of that life! I'm not asking for anything from anyone, I just want to be left alone! It's been ten years, isn't that long enough? Isn't there some point where you stop being the person you used to be and it stops being right to blame them for what they've done?"

"No," Will said. "I don't care if you've been Mother Teresa. It doesn't matter how long it's been, you deserve to die."

"Then how long *does* it take? Twenty years? Thirty? Fifty? You can't keep blaming someone forever!"

"Bullshit," Will said without sympathy. "You're just trying to weasel out of it."

I could feel the futures shifting and flickering and I knew Lee was searching for me. I couldn't see him and the Nightstalkers arriving at my location . . . at least not yet. "This isn't just about you and me," I said. "Dhruv and the rest of the Nightstalkers—they're your friends, right?"

"Like you even know what that means."

"They follow your lead," I said. "That makes you responsible for them. And if you keep leading them the way you've been going, then sooner or later you're going to take them into a battle you can't win. They're going to die and it'll be your fault."

"You mages think you're so much better than us," Will

said. "We always get told we're not good enough and you know what? It's bullshit. There's nothing we can't do if we work together. You aren't the first Dark mage we've taken down and you won't be the last."

"And when you lose?" I demanded. "When you see your friends dying in front of you?"

"*If* they get hurt it'll be the fault of whoever hurts them," Will said. "You know what, Verus? I'll make you a deal. Come here on your own. You're so worried about people getting hurt? Stop hiding behind them. Come here and stand in front of me and take responsibility for what you've done."

"So you can try and kill me again? No thanks."

"That's what I thought," Will said contemptuously. "You're a rat. Keep running. We'll catch you."

The futures shifted abruptly as something changed. I looked ahead and now I could see strands of danger. I couldn't yet see a clear future in which the Nightstalkers homed in on me, but it was drawing closer. Whatever Lee had just done to track me down, it was working. "Listen to me, Will," I said. "I've done a lot of things wrong in my life. But it's *my* life and I'm not going to let you take it. If you come after me again I'm not going to hold back."

"It doesn't matter if you hold back or not," Will said calmly. "We know what you can do. You can't beat us, Verus. We're better than you."

I knew I was running out of time. I didn't have the time to figure out exactly when Lee would get a fix on me, but I knew it had to be soon and I couldn't risk talking any longer. "You called me a rat," I said. "There's a saying about what happens when you corner one. Don't come after me again, Will. If you do you'll pay in blood." I hit the End button on the phone and moved back into the blackness of Arachne's cave, hearing the rumble as it closed behind me. I stood there in the dark for a long time, searching the futures for any trace of pursuit, but nothing came.

‖‖‖‖‖‖‖‖‖

didn't sleep well that night. Even though I was still tired from the days on the run I couldn't relax, and whenever I tried to clear my mind and rest I'd find myself thinking of what I'd seen in Elsewhere: Shireen's body on the stone, Rachel's face as she stood over her, the black shadow hanging behind. At last I gave up and rose from my bed. I'd still been using the small side cave that Arachne had prepared for me and I went down the tunnel to the main chamber, listening to my footsteps echo off the rock walls.

Arachne was there, working at one of her tables. It didn't really surprise me that she was still up; Arachne doesn't follow human sleep patterns and I never know when she'll be around. Sometimes she'll seem to be in her cave for weeks on end, and other times she'll just disappear. I've never asked her where she goes—for all her hospitality, Arachne's quite private—but I think it's got something to do with the tunnels beneath her lair. "Hey," I said as I walked in.

"Hello, Alex," Arachne said without looking up. She was concentrating on something, working with all four front legs at once. I could feel magic radiating from it, complex and layered. "Can't sleep?"

I shook my head, dropping onto one of the sofas. "Did that cache have the items you needed?" Arachne asked.

"Yeah. Thanks for holding on to them."

"When will you be using them?"

"Tomorrow."

"I see."

"Will and the Nightstalkers aren't going to stop," I said. "I've checked."

Arachne kept working. "Do you think I'm making a mistake?" I asked.

"You've always been good at surviving, Alex," Arachne said. "I think the reason you've been so good at it is that you focused on it completely. You didn't have any doubt or hesitation; you just did what you needed to stay alive. Now for the first time you're wondering whether you *deserve* to stay alive. Before you can face your hunters again, you'll have to decide how much your life is worth."

I was silent. "Here," Arachne said, shaking out what she was working on. "Come and take a look."

I rose and walked over, looking curiously at the outfit on Arachne's table. It looked like some kind of black-and-grey uniform with mesh layers. "What is it?"

"Armour."

"Who's it for?"

Arachne gave me a look. It's hard to read a giant spider's body language, but I had the feeling she was exasperated. "For someone able to see the future, you can be remarkably slow on the uptake."

I blinked. "It's for me?"

"The outer layer is a reactive mesh," Arachne said, tapping the jacket with her left front leg. "It responds to impacts by stiffening to spread the force over a wider area, and it can adjust its angle to change a direct blow into a glancing one. Enough to turn a knife or a blade. It should resist most other low-velocity impacts, but once an attack gets fast enough it does become difficult for the mesh to react in time, and of course anything with enough penetration can still punch a hole. It doesn't stop momentum either, so—"

"Whoa, whoa," I said, raising my hands. "Look, I appreciate this, but I don't want you to do all this work for nothing. You know how I feel about armour—if you wear anything that's not really heavy, an elemental mage will just blast straight through it, and if you *do* wear something that heavy it slows you all the way down. For someone like me the best way not to get hurt is not to be there in the first place."

"And how well did that work in the casino?"

I scowled.

"Your life is changing, Alex," Arachne said. "I know

you've always preferred to rely on evasion but things are different now. More and more you're going to find yourself facing dangers that you can't run from or hide from." She tapped the jacket again. "You're going to have to take risks. This will help you survive them."

Dubiously I lifted the material a few inches, feeling its texture. "Well, it's light enough," I admitted. "Is this going to do anything against a battle-mage?"

"A direct hit?" Arachne said. "No. But against area-of-effect spells or glancing blows it'll keep you alive against something that would kill an unarmoured human."

"Bullets?"

"Lower-powered ones should be manageable. For higher-power shots it depends on the angle of impact. The mesh will try to reshape itself to curve projectiles but there's only so much it can do."

"This is an imbued item, isn't it?" I asked. Now that I was close I could sense the presence from the suit. It felt incomplete, as if it wasn't fully grown yet, but there was definitely something there.

"Yes, and on that subject, do make sure not to wear this at the same time as your mist cloak," Arachne said. "They both have a protective purpose, but they do so in very different ways and the variation in mindset will cause problems. Also, I don't know if you've noticed, but imbued items can be . . . possessive about their bearers."

"It's okay," I said, suppressing a shiver. "I'm not going to be using my mist cloak for a while." I could still remember the weird stretched feeling, and it frightened me. The scariest part was that I hadn't even really noticed what was happening. If Arachne hadn't made me take it off, I didn't know where I would have ended up, and I absolutely did not want to look into the future to find out. "Thanks for doing this for me."

"Don't you remember what I told you last year?" Spiders can't really smile, but I had the feeling that was what

Arachne was doing. "After what happened with Belthas? You have my help whenever you want it, Alex." She tilted her head. "You don't ask for enough, you know."

"Old habits," I said, and yawned. "You know, I'm feeling better. I think I'll go to bed."

"Good night."

chapter 13

When I woke the next morning I felt alert and refreshed. Although a few parts of me ached, none of it was enough to slow me down, and I knew I was in good shape. I was as ready as I was going to be. It took me a minute to remember what I needed to be ready for, and once I did that killed my enthusiasm. I lay on the rocky floor with my eyes open, staring up at the ceiling.

There's something weird about waking up the day of a battle. I knew that as soon as I left Arachne's cave, I was going to walk into a confrontation that would end in blood. Death and violence were in my future . . . but as long as I stayed in bed or mooched around the tunnels, I'd be perfectly safe. I've run into this situation a few times as a diviner, and it's always a bizarre feeling, violence and chaos alongside comfortable routine. It's like having someone tell you that as soon as you step out of your front door he's going to shoot you, but he's not in any rush and he'd be happy to give you time to finish your breakfast and would it be more convenient if he came back tomorrow?

I couldn't sense Arachne's presence, and searching through the short-term futures I couldn't find her in the tunnels. I found a different presence, though, something close, and I raised my head to see the armour Arachne had been making for me. It was finished, and it hung from the wall, waiting. I rose and walked to the suit, studying it.

When a mage takes up an imbued item for the first time, it's a big thing. It's not exactly an introduction, or an offer of partnership, or a challenge, although it's got something in common with all of those. What it's most like is a mutual test. The mage gets a sense of the item's purpose, as well as its power and its sentience. In turn, the item sees the mage for who he truly is, maybe more clearly than any human could. If the item likes what it sees, it accepts you as its bearer, at least on a provisional basis. If it's unimpressed, it'll stay inert. If it *really* doesn't like you . . . well, the less said about that the better.

I reached out and placed a hand on the black mesh of the chest armour, and as I did I felt the item's presence strengthen. I could feel it, and I knew it could feel me, too. It was different from my mist cloak; the cloak was subtle, difficult to detect even if you were looking for it. This was forceful and active, and I could feel it probing at my mind. In reflex I shoved it back; I've had a few too many bad experiences with mental control over the last year or two. The presence receded but didn't go away. There was a pause, as though both of us were waiting for the other to make the next move.

"I'm about to go into battle," I said to the suit. "I don't know how it'll end, but I know how it'll begin. I'm going to be outnumbered and probably outmatched as well." I looked at the suit. "I don't have any right to demand anything from you, but I'm asking for your help. If you decide to go with me it'll be dangerous. Not just now, but in the future. Even if I survive this battle there'll be others, and the odds aren't likely to get better. I'm never really going to be safe . . . but it's *because* I'm never going to be safe that I need the kind of defence you can give. I don't know if there's anything I could offer in return that you'd care about, but if there is, I will. Will you protect me?"

The suit rested silently on the wall, watching me.

⁙⁙⁙⁙⁙

Variam was sitting on one of the sofas in the central chamber. He looked up and did a double take. "What are you getting ready for, a war?"

"Something like that," I said. The armour was lighter than I'd expected but it still felt strange. I'm not used to wearing anything with any real weight to it—most of my clothes are light and designed to let me move quickly—and in the new outfit my movements felt awkward. With each step I took, though, it got easier. I could feel the armour adapting itself to my movements, adjusting to my steps. Most of all, I could feel the item's presence, like a passenger at the back of my mind. It takes time for an imbued item to decide whether to accept a bearer: throughout the battle to come, the suit would be watching me.

"I've never seen you carry a sword."

"I don't usually carry weapons, full stop."

Variam looked at me curiously. "Why not?"

"Attitude, mostly," I said. "If you carry a weapon it means that at some level you're planning to use it. Leaving them behind reminds you that you're supposed to be running first and fighting afterwards."

Variam pointed at the sword at my belt. "So what's with that?"

"Because right now I'm through with running," I said. I nodded towards the entrance. "Ready?"

Variam rose and we began walking up the tunnel towards the surface. "Luna and Anne were asking about you," Variam said.

"Are they okay?"

"It's whether *you're* okay that they're worried about."

I sighed. "Yeah. I guess I haven't been doing that good a job of taking care of myself lately, have I?"

We left Arachne's cave and sealed it behind us. It was midmorning and the sunlight was filtering down through a bank of grey-white cloud. The air was humid and a little oppressive but I could still hear the chatter and calls of people around us. "We clear?" Variam asked.

I scanned ahead. The futures of the nearby people on the park weren't intersecting ours, at least not yet. "Clear."

Variam got to work on his gate. It was messy and although he tried to hide it I could tell that having an audience was making him nervous. I waited patiently; nothing's more annoying than having someone distracting you when you're doing a difficult spell. On the third try the orange flame solidified into an oval of light and an image of trees and grass appeared through it. I stepped through quickly and Variam followed, letting it vanish behind him.

Richard's mansion looked the same as it had when I'd arrived here three days ago. In fact it looked *exactly* the same, which was wrong; there should have been a big hole in the wall where Caldera had done her improvised building works. Looking down the grassy slope, I saw that the wall was smooth and unbroken again. Somebody fixed it, and I was pretty sure I knew who: Deleo. Although we could see down through the trees to the mansion, we were under tree cover and the branches would hide us from any viewers. Variam had chosen his spot well. "Well, we're here," Variam said, walking out behind me. "You going to tell me what the plan is?"

I told him.

"That's it?" Variam asked.

"Pretty much."

"That's . . ." Variam was silent for a moment.

"What?"

"I don't know. Efficient. Cold."

"It's what I do, Vari," I said. "I can't take things on head-to-head the way you can. I have to stack the odds in my favour first."

"I know what you're trying to do," Variam said, and he was watching me. "You want to set this up so none of this is our fault, don't you?"

"Have you ever killed anyone?"

Variam looked away. "I don't think so," he said after a pause.

"Heat of battle is one thing. Premeditated is worse."

"We'd fight for you. Me and Anne and Luna."

"I know. And that's why I can't let you do it. This is my responsibility and I'm the one who should pay for it."

Variam didn't answer. We stood under the trees, looking down over the grass towards the mansion. Birds were singing in the warm summer day, though the air was still muggy and close. "So what do we do now?" Variam said at last. "Wait for them to show up to kill us?"

"Me, not us. But yeah, that pretty much sums it up."

"Are they on their way?"

"Not yet," I said. I hadn't stopped scanning the futures and I couldn't see the Nightstalkers coming yet. "They're probably having breakfast."

Variam gave me a look. "Having breakfast."

"I can't make them go any faster," I pointed out. "Right now Lee isn't looking for me or he'd spot me. As soon as he does, the next thing he'll do is check the direction and see that it's pointing straight to this mansion. They've been here before so their gater will know the location. They'll assemble and gear up, and as soon as they're ready they'll gate in." I shrugged. "Figure ten to forty minutes, depending how good their prep time is."

"This is so weird," Variam said, shaking his head. "We're just sitting here waiting for them to notice?"

"Welcome to being a diviner," I said. "It's a lot more passive than what you're used to." I cocked my head. "Ah."

"Ah?" Variam said. "Ah, what?"

"Looks like Lee just spotted me. They're coming." The futures were shifting now, narrowing fast. Decisions make a distinctive pattern in divination magic; if someone genuinely hasn't made up their mind about what they're going to do, it's obvious. This was nothing like that. Will and the Nightstalkers must have already worked out a plan for this situation, and they were acting on it. "Looks like twenty-five minutes," I said. "Figure twenty to be safe." I leant against an ash tree. "You going to meet that Keeper?"

Variam gave me a disbelieving look. "Is this really the time?"

"Can't go inside yet," I said. "So?"

Variam looked down at the grass. "I don't know. Maybe."

"I think you should," I said.

"What about Anne?"

"You can't protect her forever, Vari."

"That's not what I'm worried about," Variam muttered.

I frowned. "What?"

"Never mind," Variam said. "I still don't like the Keepers."

"You're not going to get any argument from me. But look at it this way. If decent people never join the Keepers, they're never going to get any better, are they?"

"So what, I'm supposed to reform them?"

I grinned. "Maybe not. But . . . there's a practical side to it, too. You've been worried about the Council causing trouble for you or Anne some day, right? Well, think about it. If you want to protect yourself from the Council, having a position in the Keepers would be a pretty good way to do it."

Variam started to answer and then stopped. It was obvious that he hadn't thought of that. "You think that'd work?"

"It's worth a try." I took another glance into the futures and straightened. "Time to go."

"I'm staying," Variam said.

"Vari—"

"You don't want us killing anyone because of you," Variam said. "I get it. But you're still going to need a way out. So just in case things *don't* go so smooth, I'll be waiting out here. Okay?"

I looked back at Variam, then gave him a nod. "I'll see you soon."

⸻

As I walked down the hillside towards Richard's mansion, I put Variam out of my mind. The timing of this was going to be tricky; too late and the Nightstalkers would overwhelm me, too early and I wouldn't have them as a buffer. The futures were narrowing quickly, and I knew Will and the Nightstalkers would make their gate in minutes. The alarm ward on the front door waited quietly, at rest. I opened the front door, feeling the faint tingle as the ward triggered, and walked in.

As soon as I was inside I broke into a run. I'd already checked that the nocturne trap hadn't been reset but I checked again as I ran down the corridor, just to be safe. It was gone, and I ran down the dark stairs, my diviner's senses guiding me. The chapel was cold and pitch-black, and my footsteps echoed on the stone. I made what few preparations I had time for, then stood in the archway and waited.

As I stood in the darkness I checked my weapons. My 1911 rested in its holster, its weight an unfamiliar presence at my hip. I didn't honestly expect it to do me any good, but with any luck the Nightstalkers wouldn't know that. My combat knife sat next to it and my one-shots were distributed in pockets around the belt. I'd already laid out one of my force-walls at the chapel exit at my feet, the gold discs placed so their wall would block the path between the chapel and the deeper basements. It was the same exit that Shireen had been trying to reach when Rachel had killed her.

On my left side was the weapon I'd brought in anticipation

of Will. I'd deliberated a long time deciding what to use. Will's speed made most ranged weapons useless; he was practically fast enough to dodge bullets and by the time I'd fired enough rounds to have any chance of a hit he'd have closed the range and gutted me. From my experience in the casino I knew Will liked to get up close, where he could use his gun and shortsword to deadly effect. The best counter to that would have been the battle-magic of an elemental mage—something powerful enough to blast a whole room, force him to hold range or be burnt to death. But I didn't have that kind of power, and the one-shots I'd brought wouldn't do more than slow him down. I'd toyed with the idea of some kind of staff or spear, something to hold him at arm's length, but the tunnels below Richard's mansion were too cramped for such a long weapon and I had the feeling Will was quick enough to just grab the haft and stab me.

In the end I'd settled on a jian: a Chinese one-handed sword, a little over two feet long. It had enough reach to give an advantage over Will's shortsword but not so much that he could easily get inside my swing, and it was light enough to be useful at close quarters. I didn't want to fight Will hand-to-hand if I could avoid it, but if there was one thing I'd learnt about him over the past few days it was that he was really hard to shake off. I wasn't going to be caught unprepared this time.

And beneath the weapons was Arachne's armour, its weight a constant reminder of why I was here. I could feel its presence, ready and eager. From above a distant sound echoed through the mansion and I knew the Nightstalkers had arrived. I folded my arms and waited.

I heard them first, cautious footsteps echoing through the darkness, then the first flickers of light appeared at the foot of the stairs. There was a murmur of voices and I knew they were hesitating; they didn't want another nocturne set on them. A minute ticked by as I stood, tense, trying to stay calm. At last the futures shifted; someone had made a decision. The footsteps started up again and the flickers became the shifting beams of torches as the Nightstalkers descended into the dark. They reached the foot of the stairs and formed a defensive semicircle, and yellow-green light flared up as chemical lights were broken. I shielded my eyes as the lights were thrown outwards, illuminating the chapel in an eerie glow and throwing the murals and the altar into sharp relief.

In the yellow-green glow I saw the Nightstalkers. Gold-hair girl and Captain America were watching the flanks, with Ja-Ja behind in the shadows and Dhruv at the centre. Lee was at the back, along with the girl I'd seen once before; I didn't know her name but I was sure she was their gater. At the front was Will. He'd been already looking across the chapel and he saw me almost instantly, standing in the shadows of the far archway. He began to stalk across the stone floor.

"Will, wait," Dhruv said sharply, looking from side to side. "It might be a trap."

"Then check it," Will said, not taking his eyes off me.

The Nightstalkers advanced slowly, crossing the floor of the chapel. They didn't bunch up but didn't space out as much as they should have either. Their movements looked nervous, and in a sudden flash of insight I realised how I must appear in their eyes. They didn't see me as an ordinary man with a few tricks who'd survived the last few encounters only through help and luck. They saw me as a *mage*, mysterious and powerful, someone who derailed trains and summoned monsters. I knew that together the seven of them could defeat me . . . but *they* didn't know that. To them I was an unknown, standing alone against the seven of them and not running away, and they were afraid. So I stood still, held Will's gaze, and waited.

The Nightstalkers came to a ragged halt thirty feet away, leaving Will out on his own in front of them. Sensing that he was alone he stopped and half-turned his head back towards them. "What are you waiting for?"

"This doesn't feel right," Dhruv said uneasily. "Why's he just standing there?"

Will let out a breath in frustration, then drew a gun from under his jacket with lightning speed, aiming and firing in a fraction of a second. As he pulled the trigger I spoke the command word for the forcewall and the gold discs flared with energy. The roar of the gun was loud in the enclosed space, echoing and rolling around the stone walls, and several of the Nightstalkers flinched at the din, but to my ears the forcewall muffled the sound, sending the bullet tumbling harmlessly to the floor. The barrier blocked off the archway completely, separating me from the Nightstalkers. Now the chapel didn't have two ways out, but only one.

"There," Will said curtly as the echoes faded. He lowered the gun. "If he's so tough, why'd he seal himself in?"

Captain America and Ja-Ja moved forward. Captain America had what looked like a submachine gun levelled at me; Ja-Ja had no weapon but for his lethal touch. Both watched me warily; forcewall or no forcewall, they'd obviously learnt to respect me. "How do we get through?" gold-hair girl asked from behind them.

"We can't," Dhruv said. "Not without bringing the roof down."

"We could gate," gold-hair girl said, nodding towards the English girl.

"No," Will said. "We're not taking the chance. Those walls don't last long; we just have to wait." He stared at me. "No train this time."

From above, in the mansion, I sensed gate magic. The Nightstalkers didn't notice. "Why isn't he talking?" gold-hair girl asked.

"I don't know," Will said. "What's up, Verus? Not going to tell us to go away?"

I shook my head.

"No more threats?"

"No," I said simply.

Lee had turned and had been looking towards the stairs up to the mansion. "Uh," he said. "Will?"

"Later," Will said.

"Will." Lee sounded nervous.

Will didn't take his eyes off me. I could sense how badly he wanted to kill me, and I knew only the forcewall was stopping him from trying. "Whatever it is, it can wait."

"Will, *someone's coming.*"

A ripple went through the Nightstalkers and they traded nervous looks. I saw something flicker on Captain America's face and on Dhruv's, and I knew they'd just figured out the problem with their position. I had only one way out . . . but so did they.

"I warned you," I told Will quietly.

Just for a moment I thought I saw something in Will's eyes, then footsteps echoed from the stairs and he turned just as Cinder and Rachel stepped out into the chapel behind him.

The plan had always been very simple: get the two people who most wanted to kill me and put them next to each other. The layout of the chapel meant there was only one way into the deeper basement, and my forcewall was blocking it. Will needed to get past the wall to reach me, and Rachel needed to get past Will to reach the rest of the basement. As long as the wall held Rachel and Will would be forced to stay there.

I'd followed many different paths to this meeting, but I hadn't been able to see beyond it. I didn't know what would happen next or how this would play out. All I could do was wait for Will to act like Will, and for Rachel to act like Deleo.

Cinder and Rachel had come prepared. Cinder was wearing some kind of black-plated body armour I hadn't seen him in before, and red light licked at his hands. His eyes roved, passing over each member of the Nightstalkers in turn, ready to strike. While Cinder was dressed for war,

Rachel looked as though she'd stepped out of a masquerade. She wore opera gloves, a black feathered cape and dress, and an elongated mask in the shape of a beak that left only the lower half of her face bare, her skin pale against the black cloth. It should have looked silly but to me it only looked frightening. As she twitched her head left to right, she made me think of a human bird of prey, and I felt a tingle as her eyes locked onto me. "Alex," she said, and her voice was cold.

I saw Will stiffen as he heard her voice. "You," he breathed. "It's you."

Rachel ignored him and the beak of her mask turned as she surveyed the Nightstalkers. Her movements carried an aura of menace so strong it was almost tangible, and I saw some of the adepts flinch. "Is the Council sending children now?" Rachel asked softly.

"We're not with the Council!" Will snapped.

"Will!" Dhruv whispered. He was looking between me, Rachel, and Cinder. "Really bad idea. *Really bad idea!*"

"Why should I?" Rachel said suddenly. Her head was turned and she was talking as if to thin air. Once I wouldn't have understood what she was doing; now I did. *Shireen? What are you saying . . . ?*

"Will?" Captain America said quietly. His hand was by his side and I knew he was poised to pull a weapon. "Who is she?"

"No, I haven't," Rachel said.

"Kid," Cinder said. He was watching Will steadily. "You get one warning. Get out."

"I've never seen him before!" Rachel snapped.

"You've seen my sister!" Will shouted. "Catherine! Remember her?"

Rachel turned to Will in surprise; it was as though she'd forgotten he was there. "Who are you?"

"You killed my sister," Will snarled. "Remember me now?"

Rachel looked at him curiously for a moment. "Not really."

Will's eyes flashed with insane rage. "You. Killed. My. Sister."

"Who?"

"Catherine," Will said slowly. I knew he had to be seething with fury but he kept his words clear. "She used to live here in this country. You wanted her magic so you hunted her down and killed her for it."

Rachel thought about it, then shrugged. "Not ringing any bells, sorry."

"You killed her right here in this mansion!"

"Doesn't narrow it down much."

Cinder gave Rachel a glance. "You killed more than one Catherine in this mansion?"

"Well, I might have done," Rachel said in annoyance. "It's not like I stop to ask their names."

"No!" Will shouted. "I won't let you forget who she even was! Her name was Catherine Traviss! Remember it!"

Rachel had been looking at Cinder, but as she heard the full name she froze. She stared at Will for a moment before turning to me. "Catherine Traviss," she said slowly. "You wanted to know about her." She shifted her gaze back to Will. "But then you'd have to be . . ." Her eyes went wide suddenly. "No. I don't believe it."

"Yeah," Will snarled. "You remember now, don't you?"

"It *is* you," Rachel said softly. Suddenly she threw back her head and laughed. The noise was loud in the enclosed space, startling, and I flinched as Rachel looked back down, eyes shining. "Now I remember! The little brother. We thought we'd got all of you, but we didn't, did we? You were the one that got away!"

"Del," Cinder said, a note of warning in his voice. He hadn't taken his eyes off the Nightstalkers and red light hovered at his hands.

Rachel laughed again. "I know, you don't know. But don't

you see how perfect this is?" She extended her arms, looking between me and Will. "It's like our own little reunion! We just need Tobruk and we'd have everyone!"

The Nightstalkers shifted uneasily. I knew what they were thinking—that Rachel was crazy. Except the scary thing was that Rachel *didn't* sound crazy anymore, not to me. "For me?" Rachel asked the air curiously, then turned to Will. "Is that true?"

Will stared at Rachel. "What the hell is wrong with you?"

Rachel's laughter cut off as if with a knife, her smile vanishing. "You're after me, aren't you? That's why you came."

"No," Dhruv said quickly.

"Shut up, Dhruv," Will said, not taking his eyes off Rachel. "You thought you wouldn't have to pay for what you did?"

"You don't even know what that means, you stupid child." Rachel's voice was ice; she stalked towards Will, her eyes glittering in the darkness. The Nightstalkers stepped into a defensive stance, and I saw Cinder ready himself to cover her. "Yes, I killed your sister. I drained her life and turned her body to dust and she was too weak to stop me." Rachel spread her hands and light flickered around them, sea-green energy seeping out of the darkness. "So what are you going to do about it, *boy*?"

"Will, this is a really bad idea," Dhruv began.

"I said *shut up*," Will said.

"Dhruv's right," Captain America said with a warning note in his voice. He glanced towards the English girl. "Get us out of here."

"No!" Will snapped. "We can end this!"

The English girl hesitated, looking nervously between Will and Rachel. "This is the one you were telling us about? Rachel?"

Rachel's right hand flicked up and a greenish ray stabbed from her hand. Will dodged in a blur of motion but it hadn't been aimed at him. The ray struck the English girl and for one instant she was backlit in an eerie, lethal light, spine arching, face twisting in agony, mouth opening to scream. Then there was a flash and her body and clothes disintegrated into dust, a cloud of fine powder puffing out to swirl downwards towards the stone. The other six Nightstalkers stood frozen, and I stared at the dust that a moment ago had been the girl's body. I hadn't known her name, and now I never would.

Only Rachel didn't turn to look. She hadn't taken her eyes off Will, and now she spoke slowly and clearly. "Don't call me Rachel."

For a long moment everything was still.

Then everything happened at once. Will charged Rachel, his shortsword flickering into his hand, and Ja-Ja darted in by his side. Fire flashed from Cinder, forming a barrier and driving them back. Rachel shifted targets to gold-hair girl, light strengthening at her hand as she aimed another disintegration ray, but before she could get her spell off Captain America had pulled an assault rifle from nowhere and opened fire. The bullets glanced off Rachel's green-blue shield, but Dhruv threw something into the air that looked like a metal fan. It twisted, opened out to form a disc, and slammed into Rachel's shield like a saw blade; the shield bent and held but the impact made the ray go wide.

Everything was so fast it was hard to follow, like eight cats all fighting at once. Images caught in my mind, brief moments in the chaos: Captain America pulling a transparent riot shield and throwing it to Lee; Will sliding back to dodge a disintegration ray by inches; gold-hair girl's ground fire meeting Cinder's dark flame. The Nightstalkers were fighting with a berserk fury at the loss of their friend and for a moment Rachel and Cinder were on the defensive, two bears surrounded by a wolf pack.

Captain America pulled a grenade, hurled it. Dhruv's magnetic field caught it in midair and sent it arrowing in, driving into Rachel's water shield. Will and Ja-Ja jumped clear; Lee crouched behind his shield, and the others dived behind Lee just as the grenade went off. Rachel's shield took the blast but not the momentum; the explosion lifted her off the floor and she hit the stone hard. Will and Ja-Ja charged but Cinder was ready, and a glowing dark-red sphere exploded in a roar and a flash of flame right in the middle of them. Cinder, Rachel, Will, and Ja-Ja were all caught in the blast, but Cinder and Rachel had shields. Will and Ja-Ja didn't. Ja-Ja was thrown backwards, screaming in pain, one arm alight; Will's speed left him only smouldering. Cinder sent another fireball streaking towards the rest of the Night-stalkers; Lee hunched his shoulders and crouched into his shield as the flash of searing heat rolled past them. "Will!" Dhruv shouted.

Will snatched one look back at the others, then at me. As Rachel came to her feet again he glanced back and forth, judging distances, then moved in a blur of motion. I saw the futures flash and change and knew it was time to leave. I turned and started to run down the corridor just as Rachel's gaze locked onto Will and another green ray flashed out.

Will's course had taken him between Rachel and me and as Rachel fired he slid aside. The ray missed him and the rest of the Nightstalkers and hit the forcewall separating us. The forcewall resisted for an instant but its energy was low; the ray overwhelmed the wall, the discs shorting out as it was wiped into nothingness. I was already gone, running through the darkness, only my diviner's senses guiding me.

The tunnels under Richard's mansion spread a long way, dark and cold and smelling of ancient stone. None had lamps; they'd been made for people who could conjure their own light. The rooms and corridors were like a maze but my feet knew the way and I took the turnings without breaking stride. Tobruk had hunted me through these tunnels over and over again all those years ago, playing with me like a cat with a mouse, and I'd memorised every twist and turn.

Now his cruelty was keeping me alive. From behind I could hear shouts and knew the Nightstalkers were close on my heels. I didn't know whether they were chasing me or fleeing Rachel; as long as Will was with them it made little difference.

As I reached the laboratory I heard running feet and knew Will was at my back. For all my preparations I'd still under-estimated just how impossibly fast he could move. My next forcewall was at the entrance to the cell block on the other side of the lab—too far. I should have laid out a third one between them but it was too late now. As I ran the laboratory lit up in a yellow glow from a chemical light behind me, revealing long benches, dusty ironwork, and a ritual circle. From behind I heard Will's footsteps stutter and I ducked left as the crash of a handgun echoed around the stone walls, bullets zipping overhead.

As long as they could see me, the Nightstalkers could use their numbers to bring me down. I caught up a condenser from a pocket and crushed it. For one instant I glimpsed Will, standing in the entrance aiming his gun one-handed, then mist rushed out and I was blind. I was already dropping behind the benches and as Will opened fire again his shots passed through the empty air where he'd last seen me. The crash of gunfire and the whine of ricocheting bullets faded into the sounds of reloading and running footsteps. "Will!" someone shouted. I recognised Dhruv.

"He's there!" Will shouted. "Take him out first!"

The natural thing for me to do would have been to keep running and put the mist between me and my pursuers. Instead I held still, mist swirling around me, all my attention on the futures ahead. "Do you see him?" Will called, and from the sound of his voice I knew he was circling.

"We don't have time!" Dhruv shouted. From behind I heard the muffled *whump* of a fire blast. "Find us a way out!"

"No!" Will snarled. "Ja-Ja, with me!" Running footsteps converged on me.

I paused for two seconds, watching the futures narrow. Will would come around the bench to my left, Ja-Ja to my right. If I struck from ambush I could take one . . . but not the other, and I'd give away my position. I ducked under the bench and saw dark shadows slip by as Will and Ja-Ja passed, missing me.

Shouts and curses echoed around the laboratory. Will and Ja-Ja blundered in the mist, their powers useless without sight. Looking through the futures, I saw what I'd been searching for. Will was shouting something, trying to rally the Nightstalkers to flush me out. I waited, counting off the seconds, then moved towards Ja-Ja, deliberately making enough noise to be heard.

Ja-Ja heard me and spun, his hand flashing out with the speed of a striking snake. I leant back and let the strike breeze past, then stepped away. "He's here!" Ja-Ja shouted, but amidst the yells no one heard. Ja-Ja kept coming after me, the lethal magic of his touch hovering ready, and I let him push me to the edge of the cloud and out of it. As soon as I emerged from the mist I ducked left.

Ja-Ja followed me out half a second later and stopped. I'd led Ja-Ja in a circle back towards the entrance by which I'd arrived—and face to face with Rachel and Cinder, who'd just finished fighting their way in. Cinder's attention was turned towards the rest of the Nightstalkers, trading fire with Dhruv and Captain America, but Rachel had been looking straight towards me as I'd stepped out and she faced Ja-Ja from less than thirty feet away. Ja-Ja saw Rachel just an instant too late and I saw a brief expression of terrified realisation flash across his face before the green ray of Rachel's disintegration magic hit him in the chest.

The effect was faster this time. Ja-Ja's body seemed to flicker for a second and then simply puffed into dust, life converted to death in an instant. Without missing a beat Rachel sent a matching beam at me but I was already moving, stepping back into the blanket of mist as the ray went wide. From beginning to end I'd been out of the mist cloud for less than three seconds. *Two down.*

I backed off through the mist as screams and gunfire echoed around me. The Nightstalkers were still trying to fight, but the tide had turned; by leading Ja-Ja into the mist, Will had split the Nightstalkers' focus between the Dark mages and me. If the Nightstalkers had fallen back and fought defensively they might have been able to hold Rachel and Cinder off, but they hadn't. Will's aggression might have worked against me, but against Cinder and Rachel it was the worst possible thing he could have done.

Fire and disintegration beams slashed into the Nightstalkers, scattering their formation. Ancient beakers and bottles exploded into shards of glass, and clouds of smoke and steam covered the laboratory. A blast from Cinder sent Lee stumbling aside, beating at the flames licking up his arm. Dhruv stepped up to fill the gap, face pale, his metal disc rotating vertically to block a gout of flame from Cinder as gold-hair girl sent ground fire back. Cinder kept up the stream of flame for a second then changed the spell; the fire narrowed, intensified, as if being focused through a lens, becoming a white-hot beam only an inch or two wide. The beam cut through Dhruv's disc, the metal flashing red-yellow-white as it liquefied, molten drops splashing to the floor before the beam sawed through Dhruv's arm and into his side. Dhruv had time for one scream, then his body caught fire from the inside out and he became a flaming torch, thrashing and falling.

The Nightstalkers broke and ran. Will was still shouting, but no one was listening anymore. I caught a glimpse of Captain America and Lee sprinting for the exit leading to the duelling hall; gold-hair girl was running for the tunnel mouth in which I'd placed my forcewall. Will saw that he was the only one still fighting, jumped out of the way of another disintegration ray, and sprinted after gold-hair girl, rapidly outpacing her.

I'd had a couple of seconds' head start and was already

running for the exit that Will and the girl had chosen. In the smoke and chaos they didn't realise it was me and for one bizarre moment we were running together. I made it through the archway first, with Will right behind. Before gold-hair girl could follow I shouted the command word. The force-wall snapped up and gold-hair girl slammed into the invisible barrier, staggering back with a bloody nose. Will whirled, looking to see where she'd gone.

Gold-hair girl was left alone in the laboratory, cut off by the forcewall. The heavy tread of booted feet sounded from behind her, and she turned.

Cinder came out of the smoke, a hulking silhouette outlined in red flame, eyes shadowed in the darkness. He looked like a demon of the underworld and gold-hair girl shied away, sending a blast of ground fire at him. The flame raced towards Cinder, engulfed him in a roaring blaze. For an instant he was hidden, then he strode out with fire licking at his legs and clothes. He hadn't even slowed down. Gold-hair girl threw up her hands. "Wait, don't! Please!"

Cinder kept advancing. Gold-hair girl backed away until her back came up against the forcewall. "No, please! I don't want to fight you! I'm not with them!" Her voice was high and terrified. Cinder kept coming. "I can tell you things! About the others, why they were looking—" Cinder came to a stop fifteen feet away; red light sprang up at his hand and he lifted it to point at the girl, a dull red orb forming at his palm. Her voice rose to a scream. "Wait! Don't you want to know why we're here?"

The orb sprang from Cinder's hand and exploded against her, the force of the blast slamming her torn and burning body against the forcewall before letting it drop. "No," Cinder said to the corpse, then turned and vanished into the smoke.

"Bev!" Will shouted.

Will had his back to me, silhouetted against the lights and fire of the laboratory. Without hesitating I drew my gun and fired. Some sound or sixth sense warned him just in time and he threw himself sideways, moving in a blur of motion faster than I could adjust my aim. Will fired back and I stepped down a side passage as the deafening crash echoed down the narrow corridors. Yellow light flared as Will cracked another light and charged after me.

I fired and moved, leading Will deeper into the tunnels, away from help. The sounds of battle from behind faded away, drowned in the roar of gunfire. I watched the futures, counting off the shots in Will's gun.

Will's gun clicked empty and I stepped out into the corridor, trying to line up a shot, but Will flicked out his shortsword and charged. I fired, missed, and had to drop the gun and draw my own sword as Will came in low. Blades clashed and Will was driven back.

"Just you and me," I said.

"You bastard," Will said. He was breathing fast and his eyes were wild in the yellow light. "I'll kill you!"

"So far the only ones you've managed to kill are your friends."

Will screamed in fury and lunged, stabbing for my throat. His blade was only a flicker in the darkness, but my jian outranged his shortsword and again he was forced back. "You did this!" he shouted. "They're dead because of you!"

"Because you led them here," I said coldly. "Was it worth it? All of them dead for your revenge?"

"This was your fault! You set this up!"

"Of course I set this up," I said, putting as much contempt into my voice as I could. "What did you think I'd do, wait for you to kill me? Were you really that arrogant? I thought I'd have to work to lure you here, but you walked right in. Though I guess you had some cannon fodder in case it went wrong—"

Will went berserk, going for me with everything he had. I'd been trying to make him angry, and it had worked too well. I put a gash on his arm on the way in, then he slammed into me and we both went down, rolling and stabbing with lethal intent. My longer blade was a disadvantage now and I dropped it to catch Will's wrist, twisting his sword aside. He managed to get on top of me and rained down blows with his free hand, bruising my face. On the fifth or sixth punch I managed to kick him off and rolled away, snatching up my sword as I came to my feet. Will got me in the back before I could turn and I staggered, but I could still move and my own blade slashed him as I spun, forcing him away yet again.

We stared at each other in the yellow light, just outside strike range, probing for a weakness. My lower back was aching where Will had stabbed me but I couldn't feel any blood and I didn't let anything show. Will attacked again and I gave ground, backing down the corridor.

Will had pushed me all the way into the cell block, the featureless stone rooms on either side of the corridor standing silent and empty. I knew this place like the back of my hand and didn't need to look around—and it was just as well, because I couldn't spare a second to do it. I was a better swordsman than Will but his impossible speed made it hard for me to press the advantage; every time I tried to exploit an opening he'd dodge aside. But for all his speed I could see his attacks coming, and whenever he tried to close the range he found my blade waiting for him. The stone walls echoed with the clash of metal on metal and the scuff of footsteps.

Back and forth the battle went, and neither of us could gain an edge. We were too closely matched, his speed and my precognition cancelling each other out. Twice Will tried grabbing for my sword but got only a cut hand for his trouble. I'd opened up half a dozen cuts and slashes on Will but he didn't slow down; he was running on high-octane hatred and the pain was just spurring him on. Again and again I manoeuvred into position for a killing blow, and every time he would slide back just out of range, making me over-extend. I didn't talk and neither did he; we couldn't spare the breath.

This couldn't go on forever. I was getting tired, feeling the first traces of real fear. If I kept fighting I might win . . . but I might lose, too. You don't live long if you keep staking your life on coin flips. I needed an edge.

I felt in better shape than Will looked. He'd landed two or three glancing hits, but I didn't feel any wounds, not even on my back. But Will had stabbed me; I ought to have been—

My armour. As soon as I thought of it I remembered its presence again, watchful and protective. It had blended with my movements so completely that I'd forgotten I was wear-ing it. I'm not used to being protected in a fight—usually I can't afford to get hit. But now I could.

But Will didn't know that. In the darkness and confusion he couldn't be sure I was protected, or how well. And he hated me so badly that he didn't care; he'd do anything to hurt me, no matter the risk . . .

The plan flashed through my mind in an instant, and I turned and ran. Will was after me in an instant but I was already dodging left into my old cell, the one place in this mansion that I knew better than anywhere else. As Will caught up I turned, my sword deliberately out of position, leaving my lower body vulnerable. Will didn't hesitate, going in for another low lunge, and this time I didn't block. Instead I struck, matching his all-out attack with my own.

Will's sword rammed into my stomach in the same move he'd used to cripple me in the casino. It felt like being kicked by a horse, but as the point of the sword drove into my gut the armour hardened into a rigid plate, spreading the impact over my lower body. Pain flashed through me and I stum-bled, but the spell-woven cloth held.

At the same instant my jian hit Will, and he didn't have any armour. The blade sank into his abdomen with a sensation exactly like cutting into meat with a kitchen knife. Will staggered, tried to back up, and I twisted the blade as he pulled off it, tearing the wound open.

Will righted himself. He didn't look in pain or angry; he just looked surprised, as though he hadn't quite caught up to what was happening. Still he attacked, but he wasn't as fast now. I parried the first two strikes, then knocked his sword aside and skewered his thigh, tearing through the big muscle and leaving him nearly unable to move. Still Will fought on, blood dripping on the stone. A little voice told me to stop; I didn't listen to it. One more pass, then I closed and rammed my sword through Will's gut, and this time I put it all the way through. Only then did Will fall.

Will lay in his own blood, gasping, his face a hideous colour in the yellow light. "Are you happy?" I snarled down at him. "Is this what you wanted?"

Will tried to bring his sword around and I kicked it out of his hand, then pointed my sword down at him. Blood dripped from the tip, the blade trembling slightly. "Was it worth it? Your friends, dead. You, dead. All for your stupid revenge! Was it worth it?"

"You—" Will gasped. "You think you've won?"

"Won?" My voice rose to a shout. I'd been keeping this bottled up for so very long and I was close to snapping. "I never wanted this! Ten years I've had Catherine's death weighing me down! *Ten years!* I was starting to forget, I was almost happy, then you brought it all back! Why couldn't you just let me be?"

"You don't—" Will struggled for breath. "You don't deserve it. You're a murderer."

That was where I finally lost it. "Shut up!" I screamed. I kicked Will, making him double over. "This is *your* fault! Not mine! *You* made me do this! I never wanted to hurt any of you! All I wanted was to be left alone!"

Will was on his side but I couldn't stop screaming at him,

all the pain and hatred and anguish boiling to the surface. I spend so much time keeping my self-control but I couldn't keep it now. "None of this had to happen! I kept trying to talk to you, all you had to do was stop trying to kill me and listen! That was it! Just listen! Now I'm a murderer again; I got Catherine killed and now I've killed her brother too! I promised I'd never be this person again, but you made me do it and I hate you for it!"

Will's eyes were hazy with pain and dark blood was pooling around his body. I knew he was dying but somehow he found the strength to laugh. "You'll never change. Never get away—"

"*Why not?* Why can't I start a new life? Haven't I've paid enough?"

"Never enough—" Will drew a gasping breath. "Isn't over."

"It *is* over! The Nightstalkers are *dead*! They followed you here and they died for it!"

"There'll be more." Will's voice was trailing off, but he managed to get the words out. "After today . . . they'll come for you . . ."

"No!" I screamed at Will. "I don't believe this! How many times are you going to keep coming? How many of you am I going to have to kill before you leave me alone?"

Will didn't answer, and as I looked at him I realised he never would. His eyes had glazed and as I watched, the slow rise and fall of his chest stopped.

I stared down at his body for a long time, then turned and began, very slowly, to retrace my steps.

⁌ ⁌ ⁌ ⁌ ⁌ ⁌ ⁌ ⁌ ⁌ ⁌ ⁌

By the time I made it back to the laboratory the battle was over. Smoke hung in the air, but the fires had been starved to nothing and only smouldering patches marked where the flames had raged. The nauseating stench of burnt flesh filled the air, thick and sweet and horrible.

Captain America was propped up against one of the benches, his face pale from blood loss. His leg was gone at the knee; an open first-aid kit lay next to him and he'd managed to put a tourniquet on. It didn't look like he was going any further.

I could have finished him but just the thought of killing anyone else made me want to throw up. The adrenaline rush from my battle with Will had worn off and I was bone-tired and sick, drained of emotion. I tapped the point of the jian against the stone, the noise echoing in the silence.

Captain America's head snapped up and he peered through the smoke at me. His eyes were hazy and his movements sluggish and I knew he had to be in shock, but even so, looking through the futures I saw him pull out a gun and level it at me. "Please don't," I said wearily.

Captain America hesitated and we stared at each other for a long moment, then I saw the futures of violence thin and slip away. "Where's Will?"

I didn't answer but looked at him steadily. Captain America's eyes flickered from me down to the jian. Will's blood was still on the blade.

"Lee?" I said.

"Gone," Captain America said. His voice was weak, but he held his head up. "You're not catching him."

"I never wanted to catch any of you."

The tread of heavy feet echoed from one of the side corridors. I thought about dodging back and hiding but I was too tired. I stood my ground and waited.

Cinder came out of the darkness, massive and steady. A red glow hovered at his shoulder but he didn't have any attack magic active, not yet. His eyes registered me, then turned to settle on Captain America. Cinder came to a stop, looking at the adept, and the message was clear. *Take your shot.*

Captain America stared back at him. He didn't draw a weapon and he didn't look away. After a few seconds Cinder glanced at me. "Verus."

"Where's Deleo?"

Cinder tilted his head, as if deciding whether to answer. "Gate chamber." He studied me. "But they weren't here for that, were they?"

I was silent.

"They wanted you," Cinder said. "You led them here. Got us to handle them. Sneaky." He studied me, then shrugged and nodded towards the exit. "You better go."

I glanced at Captain America. "What are you going to do with him?"

Cinder looked at me steadily. "Not your business."

I hesitated.

"Don't try anything, Verus," Cinder said. "Been a long day and fighting you is just a pain in the balls. I'm not in the mood."

I looked Cinder up and down, then turned back to the boy I'd thought of as Captain America. "Your name's Kyle, right?"

Captain America—Kyle—looked at me. "Yeah."

"For what it's worth," I said, "I never had anything against you." I turned and crossed the laboratory, my steps heavy. I skirted Kyle just in case he tried a last desperate attack, but nothing came. He and Cinder watched me go.

I walked down the tunnel in the darkness and through the chapel. The pile of dust had been scattered in the battle and there was no trace that anyone had been left there. I didn't hear any sound from behind. I could have stopped to spy on Kyle and Cinder, see what Cinder was going to do, but the thought of staying here any longer filled me with nausea. As I trudged up the steps to the mansion's ground floor I pulled out my phone and dialled. Variam picked up almost instantly. "Alex?"

"It's over," I said. I felt utterly drained, so much that it was all I could do to put one foot in front of the other. "I'm coming up."

"Gate's ready when you are," Variam said.

I hung up and started the long walk back to where Variam was waiting to take me home.

chapter 14

I t was a few days later.

I stood under the trees of the South London cemetery. The sky was overcast, low clouds forming a thick blanket that held in the heat, and the weather was close and humid and tiring. I held still, the tree obscuring my silhouette enough to make me easy to miss, and watched the people gathered around the new grave in the far corner. It wasn't a large crowd—less than a dozen—and the priest was reading from a small leather-bound book. I couldn't make out what he was saying and I didn't want to get close enough to hear. Up ahead, through the legs of the crowd, I could see Catherine's grave, her parents' tombstones just behind. A new grave marker had been added next to hers, of the same size and shape.

I've never been to many funerals, though God knows I've been involved often enough in what causes them. When someone bites it in my line of work it tends not to get advertised, either because no one wants the publicity, because there isn't enough left to bury, or both. It had been a long time since I'd been to one, and I hadn't really known what to expect. Few had shown up. Either Will's lifestyle had left him without many friends, or they just hadn't wanted to come. Those who had were either young—his age—or sixty or more.

You'd think there'd be something more dramatic about the passing of someone from this world to the next, but I guess by the time the funeral comes it's all done. All that's left is to go through with the ritual. So I stood alone and watched, and the priest read through the ceremony and the guests listened in silence, until eventually it was done and the small crowd began to disperse, people splitting up in twos and threes. Maybe it was my imagination but they seemed to move a little more briskly as they walked away, as if they were returning to the world of the living and leaving their brush with death behind. None came in my direction, for which I was glad. I stayed in the shadows and let them pass by in the sun, going back to their lives.

There was one person, though, whom I couldn't hide from. I'd seen him in the crowd, standing next to a girl I didn't recognise, and I knew he'd seen me. It was what he did, after all. I didn't make a move towards him and as the crowd broke up I expected him to disappear, but instead he said something to the girl and walked towards me. He stopped just outside the shade of the tree, as if afraid to come out of the light.

Lee looked very different from when I'd first seen him. It had been less than ten days since we'd first met on the roof of my flat and he'd aged harshly in that brief time. There was a haunted look in his eyes now, and in his funeral clothes he looked less youthful, more careworn. It's one thing to see someone forced to grow up; it's something else to make it happen. Lee didn't speak at first and neither did I. We looked at each other for a while. "Why are you here?" Lee said at last.

"Not for you, if that's what you're wondering."

"You killed them," Lee said. I expected him to be angry but he just sounded bitter and tired. "Those two might have done it but you were the one who set it up."

"You shouldn't have tried to kill me first."

"It was Will who wanted you dead. Not us."

"Then why'd you follow him?"

Lee was silent. "You know, everyone's been talking as though this was just between me and Will," I said. "You know what I think? The one who really made all this happen was you."

Lee stared at me. "What? I just—"

"You just find people. Like I just found Will's sister." I looked at Lee. "I saw how Dhruv and Will treated you. Your magic isn't for combat so they acted like you were less important. But you were the one who was really driving everything. Everywhere the Nightstalkers went, they went because you pointed them there."

"I just did what he told me to."

"Why? Because it's not your place to question orders?" I shook my head. "You could have stopped this anytime. All you had to do was say no."

"And you didn't have to get them all killed," Lee said bitterly.

"Maybe you're right," I said wearily. "So what are you going to do, Lee? The same thing as Will? Go away and nurse your hatred until you can gather more people and do it all over again? Is that how it works? Revenge for revenge, over and over until everyone's dead? When does it stop?"

I held Lee's gaze and we matched stares. For a moment I saw anger flickering behind his eyes and then it faded, becoming something sadder, harder to recognise. "If I were Deleo, I'd just kill you," I said. "But I want to believe that it doesn't have to end that way. That something better can come out of all this." I shrugged. "I guess it's up to you whether I'm right."

I turned and walked away, heading for the cemetery gates. Lee watched me go.

। । । । । । । ।

The police tape around my shop was gone but the sign on the door said *CLOSED*. I'd had the talk with the police, and it had been exactly as unpleasant as I'd been expecting. They couldn't really charge me with anything—it's not illegal under U.K. law to get your house blown up, at least not yet—but you didn't exactly have to be a genius to know something was going on. They questioned me for a long time, and only after it became clear that I wasn't going to tell them anything did they finally give up in disgust. From the Council I'd heard only silence.

Inside, my shop and flat were quiet. Variam had moved out; the room he'd been living in had been one of the ones hit by the bomb and in any case he'd had a new offer. While I was being interrogated by the police Variam had gone to meet Dr. Shirland's Keeper, and things must have gone well because Variam had sent me a message saying he'd been accepted on probation. As part of the deal he'd moved into apprentice accommodation. I hadn't met the Keeper in question but I was curious as to what he'd said at their meeting. Either he'd been *very* persuasive, or Vari was just getting less suspicious.

Luna had gone back to her classes. She'd probably been the least affected out of all of us, and when I'd spoken to her yesterday she'd told me that none of the other apprentices seemed to have heard what had happened. It wouldn't last—sooner or later, word would get around. The only one whom I hadn't seen was Anne. I'd met Luna and Variam at Arachne's cave and told them the story, but Anne hadn't been there and I hadn't seen her since. But looking through the futures, I saw that Anne was upstairs in the guest room and her door was open. I climbed the stairs to the landing, knowing that she'd have seen me coming. As I reached the doorway I slowed and stopped.

Anne doesn't have many possessions but in the months

she's stayed with me she's managed to take the little guest room and leave a definite impression of her personality. There had been potted plants by the window and clothes neatly folded on the chair, and a smell of leaves and flowers. Now the plants were gone, the ornaments were gone, and the last of the clothes were packed in a suitcase lying open on the bed. "You're leaving?" I said in surprise. It wasn't the most brilliant comment but I couldn't think of anything else to say.

Anne was silent for a moment. She was standing with a pullover in her arms; as I watched she tucked it carefully into the suitcase. "I didn't think you'd be back this soon."

I looked at Anne. She didn't meet my eyes but kept packing her clothes. "Where are you going?"

"Sonder's found me somewhere," Anne said. "I can stay there a little while."

I noticed that she didn't tell me where. "Why?"

Anne paused, not looking at me. "Vari told me what happened."

I had a hollow, sinking feeling. Somewhere at the back of my mind I'd known this was coming. "You killed them," Anne said, her voice flat.

"Technically I only killed one of them."

Anne looked up at me, anger flashing in her eyes. "Setting them up to be murdered by Dark mages isn't any better! You promised you weren't going to kill them!"

"I tried," I snapped. "Okay? I tried talking and I tried running and I tried calling the Council. You think I wanted it to end like this?"

"You could have found another way."

"*What* other way? What was I supposed to do that would stop seven magically gifted assassins? I don't have that kind of power, Anne! I can't walk through bullets and knock people out with a touch. The only way I could beat Will and his friends was to call in help."

"*We* would have helped you! But not to do something like this!"

"And that was why I called in Cinder and Rachel. Because they're killers and you aren't. Because Will wanted revenge on Rachel as well. This was always going to happen—I just made sure it happened *first*."

"How can you talk about them like that?" Anne looked like she was about to cry. "They're *people*, not things! How could you just let them die?"

"Because they were trying to kill me!" I snarled. "Because I survive and that's what I do! I don't want to fight but if it has to be me or them I'm going to make damn sure I'm the one still alive on the other side. That's why I'm still here! Why are you so surprised? It's not like it's the first time!"

Anne stared at me. "What?"

"Remember last year?" I said. "When those gunmen came after you? When you were dying in that flat and I went to deal with them, what did you *think* I was doing? I didn't hear you complaining when you got away alive!"

"That was different!"

"Why? Because they were after you, not me?"

Anne jerked back at that. "How can you be like this?"

"What kind of person did you think I was?" I demanded. "I told you the truth about what I used to be. How the hell could you listen to that and still have any illusions about the kind of man I am?"

"Because I thought you were different now!" Anne shouted. "I thought you were better than me!"

I stared at Anne in disbelief. "Where the hell did you get *that* idea?"

Anne looked away, her hair hiding her face. "Anne, I've never thought I was better than *any* of you," I said. "Why do you think I tried to keep the three of you out of it? If someone had to take the weight, better it should be me . . ."

"You shouldn't have," Anne said. Her voice was muffled and I knew she was crying. She shut the suitcase and picked it up, then walked towards the door, head down, aiming to pass me.

"You're just going to walk out?" I demanded. "That's it?" Anne didn't lift her head or stop, and as she moved to go by me I felt a sudden surge of fury. I slammed my hand into the wall, blocking her path. "No!" I snapped at her. "At least tell me! You owe me that much!"

Anne flinched back, an instinctive, frightened move. She looked up at me with a tear-streaked face, so close I could smell her. There was something in her eyes I didn't understand, a complex mix of emotions, but one thing I was sure of was that she was afraid, and my anger disappeared in a sick, miserable feeling. Anne shouldn't be afraid of me. Standing close like this, *she* was the one who was threatening. Her life magic was far more dangerous than mine . . . but she wouldn't use it as a weapon, not like this. That was why I'd always felt safe around her; I'd known I could trust her.

But she didn't trust me. Not anymore.

I let my arm drop and stepped away. Anne walked past me onto the landing. For a moment she hesitated and I saw the futures flicker as if she wanted to say something, and then she bowed her head and started down the stairs. I watched her go until she disappeared below the landing. The sound of her footsteps crossing the floor drifted up from below, then the shop door closed and I was alone.

। । । । । । । ।

With everyone gone my flat felt empty, and I wandered aimlessly through the rooms. My bedroom was still missing a roof; the rubble had been cleared but I hadn't arranged for repairs. I needed to start the work of rebuilding my flat but I couldn't muster the energy. The living room had been emptied of furniture and I couldn't help but remember it as it had been, full of games and talk and laughter. It felt like a long time ago, and now the room seemed gloomy and bare.

I fixed myself a meal in the kitchen. It seemed to take a long time and when I was done it tasted bland. I couldn't help comparing it to Anne's cooking. I washed up and went back to the living room. I had work I should be doing, but I couldn't make myself care. The conversations with Lee and with Anne kept going round and round in my head and my flat felt lonely and depressing. At last I gave up and headed to Hampstead Heath.

⹂⹂⹂⹂⹂⹂

I found Arachne in her cave, sitting at rest. For once she wasn't working on any clothes and she greeted me as if it were just another day. Walking into her cavern didn't exactly make me feel happy, but at least the empty feeling didn't get any worse.

"Well, the armour worked perfectly," I said after we'd finished with the small talk. I felt listless but didn't want to show it. "I think it's accepted me, too." I looked at Arachne. "Did you know it was going to . . . ?"

"Imbued items make their own choice," Arachne said. "But I knew what it was looking for. You aren't wearing it?"

"I've gotten a bit edgy about these things lately."

"The armour will be safe," Arachne said. "I designed it with that in mind. It'll grow with you too, as long as you spend enough time with it." She tilted her head at me. "But that isn't what's bothering you."

I was silent. "Anne's gone," I said finally. "I'm not sure she's ever coming back." I told Arachne the story, not leaving anything out.

Arachne sat thoughtfully for a little while once I was finished. "With regard to the adepts," she said at last, "how do you feel about what you've done?"

"How do I feel?" I sighed. "Right now . . . Mostly, just

empty. I feel like to do what I did to Will and the Nightstalkers, I had to kill a bit of myself. All these years I've tried to prove to myself that I'm not the same person as I was back then, and it's like it was all for nothing. I wish it had ended some other way but it's not like I've got anyone else to blame, is it? And . . . I don't want to admit it, but there's a part of me that doesn't regret it one bit. That thinks that they hurt me, they tried to kill me, they deserved everything they got. And then there's a bit of me that's afraid feeling that way means that I really *am* a monster. That I can kill a bunch of kids and be glad they're dead." I was silent for a moment. "I've driven Anne away and probably Sonder too. They're probably the two most good mages I know, and they're both gone. What does that say about me?"

"You're afraid of becoming like Richard," Arachne said. "That you're following his path, just as Tobruk and Rachel were."

I smiled slightly. "You always get right to the heart of it, don't you?"

"I *am* a little older than you, you know." Arachne's opaque eyes studied me. "Would you like some advice?"

I nodded.

"Well then." Arachne settled back into a more comfortable position, rearranging her eight legs. "First, though it may be little consolation at this moment, I don't believe there was very much else you could have done. As soon as these adepts made the decision to pursue you, someone's death was inevitable; the only question was whose. I don't think there were any truly *good* solutions to this problem. Only bad and less bad."

"I keep thinking about what Anne said, whether there was some other way. Knockout magic, some sort of trick . . ."

"Perhaps. But perhaps not. And even if you could have disarmed them, what would you have done afterwards? It's not as though you could have kept them prisoner. You aren't invincible, Alex. They nearly killed you once, and the longer you hesitated the better the chance they would have finished the job. And personally, I prefer having you alive."

"Thanks."

"Second." Arachne lifted a leg. "Because you did genuinely try to resolve this peacefully, and because you resorted to lethal force only at the last extreme of defending your own life, I think you will eventually be able to live with what you've done. You'll never be happy about it and you will feel the weight of it for a long, long time but you will survive, as you have survived before."

I was silent. "Third," Arachne said. "It seems to me that much of the reason for your unhappiness is not just because of how *you* see your actions, but how you believe they are seen by others. Particularly by your friends."

I nodded.

"In which case you can take some consolation in knowing that the worst is over. You've shown Anne and Variam and Luna and Sonder the darkest side of your nature and what you are most ashamed of in your past. No matter how painful it may have been they know the worst of you now, and they can come to terms with it themselves. If they choose to accept you, knowing what they do, then your friendship will be stronger for it, and nothing else you do is likely to test it for a long time."

"If."

"If," Arachne agreed. "But that decision is theirs, not yours."

I nodded again. "Fourth," Arachne said. "As I'm sure you know, the news of how you dealt with the Nightstalkers will spread. It may seem to you as though your sins are being paraded but, once the excitement has died away, you may find that the effect on your reputation has been helpful."

"Helpful?"

"You know how magical society works, Alex," Arachne said soberly. "Being known as a ruthless, dangerous man willing to kill those who threaten him has its benefits. After seeing what happened to the Nightstalkers, anyone else thinking of coming after you is going to hesitate."

"Or they'll just bring more firepower."

"Perhaps—but this should at least scare away the little fish, and I don't think you'll be similarly challenged for some time. And it might work to Luna's benefit too. You've told me before about your worries that the further she goes with her training, the more problems she'll face for being an adept. Well, after this story spreads, I think it's considerably less likely that anyone will choose to make an issue of it."

"So—what? If I'm a killer, I might as well enjoy the perks of the job?"

"Fifth," Arachne said, "and most important. You're afraid of becoming like Richard."

I sat up and nodded.

"In which case I would suggest that the very fact that you *are* afraid of that is good evidence that you are *not* like Richard. As long as you are afraid of becoming like him, as long as you consciously choose not to be likc him, then you never truly will. It is our choices that define us. Richard understood that. He could suggest and he could tempt, but he knew the final decision was always yours."

"And the things I've done?"

"Not everything you've done has been dark, Alex." Arachne lifted her legs, as though ticking points off. "You chose to help Luna in the hunt for the fateweaver, when you could have hidden yourself away and been safe. You saved me at the risk of your own life when confronting Belthas. You protected Anne and Variam when they were in danger at Fountain Reach. Even in dealing with the Nightstalkers you were acting in your friends' interests. You took the risks and the responsibility upon yourself. If you've done things to be ashamed of, you've done things to be proud of as well."

"Do you think it balances out?"

"Would I have stayed with you all this time if I didn't?"

Spiders can't really smile, but Arachne sounded as if that was what she was doing. "Although . . . if it concerns you so much, why not do something about it?"

I looked at Arachne curiously. "Like what?"

"If you're worried that your good deeds are outweighed by your bad ones, why not do more of them? You've spent a long time trying *not* to be like Richard. Perhaps it's time you started considering what sort of person you *do* want to be." Arachne rose. "Think it over."

·········

That evening found me back home, sketching the first notes and plans for what would eventually be a new set of blueprints for my flat. I wasn't going to simply rebuild it—the Nightstalkers' little demolition exercise had done a good job of exposing the weaknesses in my home defences and I had several upgrades in mind. A flicker in the futures caught my attention, and a moment later I heard the sound of the shop door being unlocked below. I looked up, then went downstairs.

Luna and Variam were just switching on the lights in the shop. "Vari?" I said in surprise. He was dressed in a hand-me-down set of formal robes that almost fit him but not quite. In a weird sort of way he looked like the mage equivalent of someone who'd just come home from the office. "I thought you were in Scotland?"

"I was," Variam said cheerfully. "Knocked off early. I can gate now, remember?"

"Haven't you moved out?"

"Well, yeah, but I can still visit, right?"

"We figured you could use some company," Luna said. "Unless you want to be left alone?"

I looked between the two of them and smiled. "Come on up."

They came up, and the three of us spent the evening together. We all had stories to tell: Variam of his first few days as a Light apprentice, and Luna of what had happened while I was gone. We cooked dinner together, and after Luna and Variam had caused the expected culinary disaster we spent another half hour deciding where to order takeaway. It wasn't the same, but it wasn't so bad.

ı ı ı ı ı ı ı ı ı

I dreamed that night.

I saw Rachel—or perhaps I *was* Rachel. She was walking across a grassy ridge in the starlight, and in some strange way I both watched her from outside and at the same time felt and moved as she did. The sky was clear with no moon and the only light was from the stars, yet I recognised the silhouette of Richard's mansion, a black shadow in the darkness. The sight filled me with a strange mix of emotions, familiar and alien: fear, anticipation, a distant sadness. As Rachel neared the front door she spoke a word and the door swung open, for she'd crafted these wards and they obeyed her commands.

Through the corridor, down the stairs, and into the darkness, a sphere of sea-green light forming to light the way. The glow backlit Rachel's face strangely; she wore no mask this time, and in the greenish light her features were beautiful but cold, with little trace of feeling or warmth. Through the chapel, and now Rachel's path curved to skirt a patch of floor. To me it looked the same as any other but to Rachel's eyes it was the place in which Shireen had died, and a trace of her blood still stained the stone. Just for a moment I felt another presence in the ancient shrine, and I thought I heard an echo of footsteps behind us.

Through the corridors and the laboratory, past the cells and through the labyrinth. The signs of the battle still scarred the benches but the bodies were gone. Maybe the dust and ashes in the corners might have been a part of them once but no one would be able to tell, not anymore. Still Rachel walked on, her feet picking out the paths as though she'd walked them a hundred times before, until at last she came to the room at the very end of the labyrinth, the final one to have been completed all those years ago.

The room was smooth and circular, pillars supporting the ceiling, all illuminated in the green light of Rachel's spell. At the centre of the room was a wide dais. Three black hemispheres protruded from the stone, forming a triangle. Rachel stopped a little way from the dais and waited.

Time passed. Rachel waited, paced. Twice she looked towards the exit, as though on the verge of leaving, but each time she stayed. Suddenly she snapped her head around and an instant later I felt what she did: a slow surge of magical power, growing stronger.

With a faint hiss black energy erupted from the dais, dark lightning crackling to join the three hemispheres in a triangle. At the centre of the triangle the air darkened, a black oval appearing in midair. Rachel stood stiff, as though paralysed. The black oval grew, stretched. For a moment it was almost transparent and there was the hint of something visible on the other side, then a man was stepping through, alighting on the dais. His feet touched the stone and the black lightning snapped off, the portal vanishing into nothingness. The man was ordinary-looking in every way; but for his entrance no one would have looked at him twice.

Rachel moved first, bowing her head. A complex mixture of emotions flickered across her face and were gone. "Master."

"Deleo," Richard said with a smile. "It's good to be back."

And I woke with a gasp, heart pounding in my chest.

From
BENEDICT JACKA

cursed
An Alex Verus Novel

Since his second sight made him infamous for defeating powerful Dark mages, Alex has been keeping his head down. But now he's discovered the resurgence of a forbidden ritual. Someone is harvesting the life force of magical creatures—destroying them in the process. And draining humans is next on the agenda. Hired to investigate, Alex realizes that not everyone on the Council wants him delving any deeper. Struggling to distinguish ally from enemy, he finds himself the target of those who would risk their own sanity for power . . .

Praise for the Alex Verus novels

"Harry Dresden would like Alex Verus tremendously—and be a little nervous around him. I just added Benedict Jacka to my must-read list."
　　—Jim Butcher, #1 *New York Times* bestselling author

"Benedict Jacka writes a deft thrill ride of an urban fantasy—a stay-up-all-night read. Alex Verus is a very smart man surviving in a very dangerous world."
　　—Patricia Briggs, #1 *New York Times* bestselling author

penguin.com
facebook.com/AceRocBooks
benedictjacka.co.uk

From

BENEDICT JACKA

ɪɪɪɪɪɪɪɪ

f a t e d

An Alex Verus Novel

ɪɪɪɪɪɪɪɪ

Alex Verus is part of a world hidden in plain sight. He runs a magic shop in London, and while Alex's own powers aren't showy, he does have the advantage of foreseeing the possible future—allowing him to pull off operations that have a million-to-one chance of success.

But when Alex is approached by multiple factions to crack open a relic from a long-ago mage war, he knows that whatever's inside must be beyond powerful—and Alex predicts that by taking the job, his odds of survival are about to go from slim to none . . .

"Harry Dresden would like Alex Verus tremendously—
and be a little nervous around him.
I just added Benedict Jacka to my must-read list."
—JIM BUTCHER

facebook.com/AceRocBooks
penguin.com

M1037T0112